I0731533

WOODEN NICKELS

WHITE LIGHTNING SERIES, BOOK 1

DEBRA DUNBAR

J.P. SLOAN

debra dunbar
FIENDISHLY FUN FICTION

Copyright © 2018 by Debra Dunbar

All rights reserved.

No part of this book may be reproduced in any form or by any electronic or mechanical means, including information storage and retrieval systems, without written permission from the author, except for the use of brief quotations in a book review.

❀ Created with Vellum

BALTIMORE, MAY 1926

Hattie held her breath, tightening the illusion on the bottles of brandy rattling in the back of the old Model T Runabout. A few more blocks and she'd leave the city behind as well as the worry that someone might see, or hear, the very illegal booze in the rear of the truck.

Alcoholic beverages weren't technically banned in Maryland due to the governor declining to enforce prohibition, but getting caught hauling hooch across state lines would land her in jail. And there were plenty of people looking to spot someone heading out of town for the dry states with a shipment, and turn them in for a reward.

With a sigh of relief, she rounded the last bend in the road leaving Baltimore. The overgrown grass on either side of the Middle Branch was high enough to conceal the truck from anyone's view except a few stray geese, so she released the illusion and shifted gears.

Illusion. Pinching light as it was called. This was her magical specialty, her gift and her curse. Casting an illusion was never what she would've called "easy". There was a physical strain the magic inflicted on her, a cost. And there were dangers if she got caught—dangers far greater than feeling as if her insides were being twisted into a knot.

The truck transmission made a horrible grinding noise. "Aye...quiet, you!" she grumbled, a hint of her Irish parents' accents still haunting Hattie's words as she wrestled the vehicle into gear. The Runabout jumped forward, bouncing over a tree branch jutting out onto the dirt road. Hattie yelped, the bottles in the bed of the truck clanking together in a frenzied rattle. Swearing under her breath, she peered over her shoulder to check the six neatly stacked cases of brandy. When Jake was alive, he'd stuff the crates with straw —as much to dull the jolts from the tailbone-torturing back roads leading to the Bay as to offer the clients a convenient means to hide the booze on their end. Sometimes he'd cut the bottoms out of olive oil bottles and sleeve them around the gin and brandy, stamping Medina Oil of Greece on the sides of the crates, just for added protection in case the G-men came around.

That was back in the early years of Prohibition, when the Feds were more concerned with spilling the inventories of whole breweries into rivers and muscling down the traffic coming in from Canada. Back when little operations like theirs on the Chesapeake Bay remained unnoticed. Back before the mobs took over.

Back before Jake took a slug to the head.

Now it was just Hattie, Lizzie, and Raymond.

She pulled up to a row of wood-and-tin shacks lined up along the south bank of Curtis Creek, and wrestled the truck into park, waving at the handful of dark-skinned children who lingered by the side of the creek. One boy had a fishing pole angled over the water, kicking his feet as his friends waved back at Hattie from their perch. Hattie killed the motor and stepped out of the car, sucking in a lungful of clean springtime air. Clean, in a relative manner of speaking

—the aroma along Curtis Creek swam with notes of dead fish and tobacco smoke.

She looked toward Baltimore, pulling up her trousers a little as she leaned against the truck door. A plume of dark fog rose from the city, hanging like a ghost, swallowing up the coal dust from the mills and factories to the east. Dead fish and cigar smoke were a bouquet by comparison. Smiling, she turned her back on the dread pall of coal dust. Soon she'd be out on the water, where the air was cooler, cleaner, and filled with freedom.

A deep voice boomed from the row of shanties, "You're early!"

Hattie peered over her shoulder to find a tall, thick man in overalls, approaching with a grin. His dark skin glistened with sweat despite the mild, late springtime temperatures, but Raymond always sported a fine sheen of perspiration, even in the winter. That was his furnace, he'd say, chugging away deep inside his broad chest and barrel-wide belly.

"Wanted to put some road behind us before the sun was high," she replied, moving for the driver's side door.

"Uh huh. Anyone sniffin' around Lizzie's?"

"No." She shrugged. "I've nothing better to do and might as well move the merchandise. It's doing no one any good gathering dust."

He nodded. "You, uh…want me to drive?"

She got the subtext. A white woman driving a black man would raise eyebrows. But Raymond was her friend, the closest thing she'd ever had to a brother. Hattie wasn't about to bow to what others expected in terms of who should be driving who. Or anything else, for that matter.

"I'll be providin' a full-service treatment today. You just sit back and contemplate your lot in life while I do the driving." She shot Raymond a wry smirk. "If you play your cards right, I'll even let you pilot your own boat," she added as they climbed into the truck.

Raymond released a thunderous laugh that shook Hattie's chest. "Thank you, kindly!"

She coerced the engine of the Runabout into doing its job after about three tries, then hammered the gears into a forward motion as Raymond winced.

"How's the little one?" Hattie asked once they were about a quarter-mile down the riverside road.

"A pint-sized terror. How can a little bean like that make so much noise?"

"Keeping you awake, is he?"

Raymond pursed his lips, then answered, "More the missus than myself."

"Hardly seems fair, now."

"That's what she tells me. Naw, the baby's a little ball of miracles. Just wish he'd stop that damn cryin' for a hot second."

Hattie turned onto the crossroad. "Sounds like the colic. Maybe you should try some chamomile and basil."

"The what, now?"

"Make a tea of it. Soak it in a rag and let the little one suckle on't. Calms the stomach and gets the fluids moving in the right direction."

Raymond pivoted in his seat. "Didn't think you had any brothers or sisters."

The mirth on her face faded. "I don't. It's…just something I picked up."

Raymond continued his pivot and spied out the back of the truck at the crates of bottled brandy.

"How many you got back there?" he asked.

"Six crates."

He shook his head and released a sound, something

between a tsk and a grunt that Hattie had learned was his way of communicating polite disappointment.

"The truck can handle more than twice that," he grumbled.

"Then they'd overtop the sides of the bed."

"So, tie them down."

Hattie sighed. "That's not the point, and you know it."

"Old Jake could fit twenty cases. One good run to the Bay. He just took it easy on the clutch, is all."

"Aye, and how'd that brilliant scheme work out for him?" she snapped.

Raymond lifted his enormous brow, sending trickles of sweat down the sides of his face. "That's how it's gonna be?" he grumbled.

"Sorry. It's just…" She could say that it was harder for her to pinch light inside the city, thanks to all the eyes, all the sounds and smells, all the attention. That it was easier for her to cast an illusion over the back of the truck when all a passerby could see was the top two inches of the crates. That pushing herself too hard in a full-bore light pinch was a fine way to end up passed out and throwing up blood.

But none of those reasons passed her lips. Although Raymond was the best friend she had, he didn't know what she was, or what she could do. And she wanted to keep it that way.

Raymond cleared his throat and turned fully forward. "Don't mind, no how. Money's in the incomin' shipment, not the outgoin'. Any word from down the coast?"

"Lizzie's waiting to hear from the Baltimore Crew. Her man on the inside's got a full dance card, from what she tells me, but he'll have something for us soon. As long as the good folk from the Carolinas to New York City are thirsty for liquor, and Governor Ritchie keeps our fair state thumbing its nose at Congress, we'll have business on the Bay. So, don't you worry about't."

Driving the truck around the last inlet of Curtis Creek, she headed toward the well-sequestered Winnow's Slip, a ramshackle wharf running parallel to several boat houses and warehouses, the existence of which never landed on the ledgers of upright, law-abiding citizens. Raymond kept his boat in one of these boat houses, purchased for a handful of coin and barely running. He'd spent months re-decking the craft, rebuilding its engine until it made five knots and better. The boat was an eyesore, an outright shambles, and no one spent more than half a blink considering it.

Which was perfect for running hooch up and down the Chesapeake.

As the line of tin roofs slipped into view around the bend, Hattie swerved hard right to keep from colliding with a car tear-assing up the lane. Swearing out loud, she laid on the brakes, Raymond reaching a meaty arm across her chest and holding her fast against her seat.

Catching her breath Hattie peered out the driver's side window, ready to release a string of vulgarities fit to curl the bonnet of any Baptist mother, when she spotted the pale, hawk-nosed face of Little Teague.

"Watch out," Raymond warned.

Hattie sucked in a breath and gripped the wheel. "Aye, Teague Bannon! You're ready to put one or both of us permanently out of business."

The man ran a sleeve over his forehead as he eyed the two of them. "Sorry," he muttered. "Launching farther up the Bay today. And you should, too."

One of his associates leaned forward in the passenger seat, the soot on his face pooling away from the eyes, giving the man a ghoulish cast. He was one of Little Teague's lackeys.

Teague had inherited the family business from his father, Big Teague, who'd founded the Solomons Island Boys shortly after Prohibition took hold. They ran barrels into Baltimore from Richmond and the Carolinas—up to three hauls a week. Which made them the most successful rum-runners on the Bay.

Which also made them the competition.

"What's got your trousers in a lather, now?" Hattie smirked.

Teague leaned out the window, peering over his shoulder toward Winnow's Slip. "I'm tellin' you this out of good faith, 'cause there's more than enough traffic down the coast for the pair of us, and we don't need no bad blood between our organizations."

"What is it, then?" she pressed. "Spit it out."

Another look over his shoulder. "G-men are all up and down the Slip. Plainclothes, but you can smell them out easy enough."

Hattie's stomach dropped a few feet. "What, Treasury men?"

He nodded. "If you have business today..." he pointed to the bed of her truck, "...I'd take it elsewhere."

Though the governor of Maryland had decided to ignore the Volstead Act, the Feds still clamped down on anything leaving its borders with zeal. Hattie bit her lip, wondering what had made the law take notice of this tiny wharf in the middle of nowhere. Someone must have tipped them off. And here she'd been about to drive right on in with a truck full of brandy.

"Where are you off to, then?" she asked.

"North, to Lord Baltimore's."

She nodded. Lord Baltimore's Landing was the nearest friendly launch for people in their profession. One could find a boat there for hire, if one had to touch-and-go on account of the Feds. The only other suitable spot within a half day's drive would be McComb's well to the south.

Hattie forced one of her well-practiced smiles across her lips, and said, "Well, I thank you for your courtesy."

Little Teague waved off her comment. "Just get that ticker turned around and back on the main roads. Winnow's ain't safe today."

"I'll buy you a drink for this later," Hattie offered as he pulled his torso back into his cab. "Long as I sell these, first."

He gazed at her, his face filled with a mix of interest and conflict. Hattie was never any good at this sort of charm. Feather-smoothing wit was more her strength, especially when words and fists were about to be exchanged. But she knew Little Teague had seen past her trousers and farming shirt and had judged her an attractive woman. It wasn't any sort of notice she'd wanted, but if she had it, she'd use it.

He nodded twice. "Good luck, Malloy."

Teague gunned his engine, spinning the skinny tires against the loose gravel of the lane.

Hattie lingered over her wheel, staring into space.

Raymond asked, "You trust that little river rat?"

"I don't see any Feds," she whispered. "Which means they're probably there."

"Why today, I wonder?"

"Better we find out now than when we're inbound with a half-dozen barrels from Jamaica."

Raymond chuckled. "True enough. So, if they're beating feet to Lord's..."

"McComb's is our only real choice," she said.

"Suits me. I got a friend at McComb's. Won't cost Lizzie but maybe a couple fins and a bottle of something older than four months."

She nodded. "McComb's it is, then."

The ride down the waterside roads was teeth-jarring and

slow, and they made terrible time reaching the harbor just north of Annapolis.

"Busy day," Raymond grunted as Hattie eased the truck onto the patch of short grass nearest the boat houses, sidling alongside two of the half-dozen automobiles already gathered.

"Looks that way."

They stepped out of the truck and wound their way toward the bed.

"Your friend easy to find?" she asked.

Raymond didn't answer.

Nor did Hattie ask again.

They both stood rigid as two men in long coats and dull gray fedoras approached. One of the two had a pen pad in his hand. The other, a ledger. They both were packing heat, holsters slipping into view as their coats flipped wide with their strides.

"You steady?" Raymond whispered.

"As a boulder. You?"

"Pissin' myself."

The G-men lifted hands in unison to flag them down, though they had little more to do than simply stand there as they approached. The taller of the two Treasury men, a lean man with dark hair, sniffled and cleared his throat.

With a cough, he said, "What's your business here?"

Raymond pulled his hands in front of him, crossing them at the wrists, and tucked his head. It was a maneuver Hattie'd seen him execute several times before when face-to-face with any sort of person who might take offense to a colored man with an opinion.

"Delivery to the Eastern Shore," she answered.

The shorter of the two, a ruddy faced brute with a double-chin, spat, "Delivering what?"

"Oil," Hattie replied.

The tall man peered over the bed of the truck, and with the subtlest of gestures, Hattie pinched the light around the brandy cases. She wasn't as close to the cases as she'd like to be. Every inch of distance between her and her illusions meant more effort. Which meant more sickness once it was over. It was too late to close in now. Any motion toward those bottles could be construed as ill intent, and might even draw a gun from the G-men's holsters.

The man's eyes swept along the bed of the truck. She could feel his gaze on her illusion, rolling like a ball up and down the fabric of the pinched light. Just as the nausea began to swell inside her belly, the tall man scribbled something on his pad and turned away.

"Looks in order," he declared as he took a step back.

Hattie released a breath and waited for the right moment to drop the illusion.

"Hang on," the double-chin blurted. "What kind of oil?"

The tall man shook his head a couple times, then turned with a lifted brow.

"Olive oil. You know. For cooking?" Hattie told him.

Short and ruddy took a step toward the truck, reaching for the crates. Hattie redoubled her light pinch, hoping he didn't pull the bottle fully out of the crate.

He did.

Her stomach twisted into a fiery knot as she put the full weight of her powers onto the illusion, now manifesting it into two dimensions…sight and touch.

The short man held the bottle up to the sunlight. His gaze pressed hard into her illusion, sending shocks of pain into her chest. But she maintained focus, ensuring the man saw green glass with golden oil, not an amber bottle of embarrassingly young brandy.

He lifted the bottle to his face, giving it a sniff.

Three dimensions.

Hattie whimpered as the illusion flooded the man's nostrils with the aroma of olive oil.

Don't taste it. Don't taste it. That fourth dimension would be too much for her to handle at this distance. She'd pass out. And probably wake up in the hoosegow.

The man drew in a second sniff, then a third.

Hattie's heartbeat pounded in her neck, all the way down to her feet. Her guts lurched in waves as he breathed in the illusion, then breathed it back out. The ground softened, and she gripped the side of the truck to keep from falling over.

Finally, slipping the bottle back into the crate with a chuckle, the short man turned to his compatriot.

"Guess those Guineas gotta eat something besides crab!"

The tall man sneered at the coarse words, but simply made more notes on his pad before giving Hattie and Raymond a tip of his hat.

Hattie held tight to the side of the truck for what felt like an eternity, until the two men stepped out of sight. Then, with a low, husky moan, she dropped the illusion and pitched forward onto the grass.

Raymond dove to catch her, easing her onto her knees.

"You okay, baby girl?" he whispered.

Hattie swallowed hard against the tides of nausea threatening to send breakfast out onto the grass. After several long minutes of cold sweat, the nausea subsided. She opened her eyes, the field of parked cars still swimming in her vision.

Raymond gave her shoulders a brisk rub. "Hey. You with me?"

"Close call," she whispered.

He nodded. "Yeah. Thought we was pinched, for sure."

"Pinched," she said as she ran a sleeve underneath her nose and pulled it back to reveal a long smear of blood. "Not today."

"Come on," he urged as he guided her to her feet. "We're gettin' you home. You look like death warmed over."

"No. We have a job."

Raymond cocked his head. "You're a stubborn mule of a child. You comin' down with the fever or something?"

"I'm fine." She shot him a look filled with significance. "The Feds are *here*. That means Winnow's is clear."

Raymond scowled. "Little Teague set us up. You know that, huh?"

"Aye," she snarled. "Pieced that together on my own."

"It'll be dark before we let in. You sure you want to run these out today, with the goons sniffin' around?"

She gripped the side of the truck and sucked in a long breath. The headache began its inexorable slide into the space behind her eyes. Hattie lifted fingers to her temples to give them a quick massage. "I'm sure. Let's go. I want to get out on the water."

He shrugged. "Suit yourself. But I'm drivin'." He held the passenger door open for Hattie. "I don't think you or the truck will survive in your condition."

She took a seat, and as he closed the door, she shot him a weary smirk.

"Bully."

He smiled in return. "Brat."

CHAPTER 2

The cramped closet had barely enough room for Vincent to change into his costume. He called it a costume. In reality it was his usual black suit, with the addition of a fez and lots of stage makeup. Gripping a horse-hair brush in one hand he drew his left cheek away from his brow, spreading the eye shadow across his top eyelid, and giving his already olive complexion a dark Valentino quality. Then he set aside the brush and double-checked his face, pulling the single lit candle closer to the mirror.

Perfect.

He stood up, leaning away from the wood shelves loaded with dry goods for the downstairs grocer, and snatched the fez to settle it onto his thick, black hair, which had been slicked into a neat part down the middle.

Clearing his throat, he spoke out loud, "Mysterious." Not good enough. "Mys…teerious." The accent was everything. Without the accent, he was just Vincent Calendo. But with the right lilt and tone, a hiss of consonance here, an exaggerated gesture there…he was The Great Mustafa Damir.

"Showtime," he whispered, before gathering himself and

blowing out the candle. Stepping out of the closet, he ducked beneath two red satin curtains he'd nailed to the door frame and stood with fingers neatly tented up near his necktie.

Three elderly women watched with blanched interest from a tiny card table draped in black velvet, their jaws slack and eyes wide.

"Good...ev-en-ing," he declared. "I am the Great Damir."

One of the women started to clap, but the others glared her down.

Vincent took long, dramatic strides as he paced around the table. The old ladies sat stiff, their heads on swivels as he rounded them like a panther.

"I am the purveyor of the Secret Knowledge," he announced with his finely practiced if utterly manufactured Arabic inflections. "The keeper of the Hidden Flame. I see beyond the veil between the living..." he leaned in close to the third woman, "...and the dead."

One of them released a low gasp.

He straightened and continued his circle back to his seat.

"I understand you are seekers, each of you. You have loved ones who have passed...beyond." He lifted his hand out in front of him, palm down, sliding it out to the side as if to reach into the afterlife itself.

They all nodded.

"Now," he said with sudden volume, taking a seat at the tiny table. "I trust you've each brought what I've requested. The names of your dearly departed, and a personal item you feel they have clung to."

Each nodded, the first lady going as far as to pull her purse up to the table. She unsnapped it and reached inside.

Vincent held up a hand. "Please, please. I do not wish to see them. I only require that they be present. Here, in the room with us. For it is this item which beckons your loved ones. They call to them." He closed his eyes and lifted his chin a little. "A song of life, echoing only a little into the great beyond. With luck, these songs will be heard."

He opened his eyes once again. Each of these women sat in that same familiar posture. Stiff, rigid, upright. Face pale. Eyes so wide the irises were surrounded by white. This was the mix of blasphemous fear and desperate need he'd learned to cultivate in his audiences.

Vincent cracked his knuckles and laid his palms flat on the table.

"And so, first I must find my center…before reaching out across the Veil."

He closed his eyes and released a low hum. That hum lifted into a major third…and back again. This continued for several seconds until he put words to the chant.

"Al…leppo. Al…manna. Al…Jeddah. Khartoum."

In the dim, candle-flickered space, with a bowl full of fresh pipe tobacco smoldering in the far corner, this chant sounded perfectly foreign. Perfectly spiritual. In truth, Vincent got the words off a world globe he spotted at the Old Moravia Hotel sitting room, and felt they sounded sufficiently Arabic. But his clients weren't world travelers. They were widows, by and large, most barely literate and desperate for some sort of closure.

Vincent ramped up his chant, opening his eyes into a maniac's leer, shivering his arms in the air. He had to watch it at this point…sometimes the old ladies were so frightened by the theater of the moment, they'd either bolt out the door or pass out.

When he felt he had their nerves stretched to a proper tension, Vincent balled fists and hammered them onto the table top.

And with a blink, he pinched time.

The smoke rising from the bowl in the corner froze midair. The street sounds from the open window dropped into stony silence. The women all sat in mid-cringe, their eyes clamped shut out of reflex from the sudden slap on the table.

This was Vincent's method. Make them flinch, then pinch time when they couldn't tell the difference. It helped when he released his grip on the flow of time, just in case he didn't return to his seat at just the proper and exact position. If any of the women had kept their eyes on him, the effect from their point of view would be like a moving picture, when the jump from reel to reel isn't quite perfect.

He'd done this enough times, however, to iron out such wrinkles. Now he had them all frozen. Now he could do his reconnoiter.

Vincent eased out of his chair, pushing through the stiffened air as he reached for the first old lady's purse. He snapped it open and removed the tiny slip of paper within. He found the name scrawled in impeccable script. Harold. Within the purse, alongside two five dollar notes which he assumed was his donation, was a thick silver ring. He recognized the emblem on the sides as it rose to a fake ruby. Knights of Columbus.

He pressed on, swimming through the time-frozen space to the second woman, searching her belongings for the name of her dearly departed. It seemed she was looking for Horace. He shook his head. The H-names had a bad year. Tucked in the pocket of her coat, Vincent found a monogrammed statesmetal flask, a florid "HTM" etched onto the side. He shoved the flask back into her pocket, making sure it reached bottom before moving on. When he pinched time, he found that gravity by-and-large kept its grip on things, but it wasn't as sure as it was without his assistance.

Finally, he moved on to the third woman. She carried a purse as well, and Vincent was glad for it. He had to extend his powers to encapsulate the entire room. Life out on the street was progressing as normal. He didn't have the constitution to freeze an entire street. As it was, this dimension of space was enough to tug at his guts. That familiar wave of nausea was creeping into his throat, and he knew that the second dimension of duration would prove detrimental to his health.

Vincent slipped his fingers into her purse, pulling away a tiny scrap of paper. When he lifted it to the light in order to read the final name of the dearly departed, he winced. This was a name...of sorts. He assumed it was. Problem was, it wasn't written in any language he recognized. Certainly not English, and he only knew just enough Italian to get by with his coworkers.

But this? This was some sort of Slavic scribble. Letters just familiar enough to be strange greeted his eyes. A back-facing R. A lowercase A. Something strange, and a loopy-loop.

Vincent clamped his eyes shut, then shook his head. What now?

He searched the rest of her purse as the pressure began to build inside his stomach. His fingers hooked around a ring of steel, and he pulled it up. It was heavy, and completely filled the woman's purse. This wasn't any trinket. It was massive. When the nose of a 6.35 millimeter revolver emerged from the mouth of the purse, he bit down on his tongue. This was a vest gun, the sort with which Vincent was far too familiar.

A spasm rocked his midsection, and he shoved the gun back into place alongside the slip of paper, and eased the purse back into the woman's lap. Vincent pumped his legs, shoving himself through the time-frozen molasses-like air back into his seat, settling his fists onto the black velvet.

And with another blink, he released his pinch.

The smoke wafted up to the ceiling. Cars outside chugged

alongside outspoken pedestrians. The women all released a sudden gasp.

And Vincent swallowed back a throb of bile.

The effect of the time pinches suited the task. To these ladies, he was wracked with pallor and a cold sweat due to his contact with the spirit realm...whatever that was supposed to be.

They watched as he collected himself.

Turning to the first woman, he cleared his throat and declared, "Madame." He winced immediately, unsure why he decided to go French on her. Oh well, they probably wouldn't notice, or care. "I sense a presence."

She leaned forward, lower lip trembling.

Vincent reached for his brow, rubbing it as if nursing a phantasmic migraine. "The Great Damir speaks to you who approaches! Stop now, and speak your name." He closed his eyes and made listening motions. "Ah...Har...Harold?"

The woman sucked in a sharp breath, and tears immediately flowed from her eyes.

Vincent stared at her. "Your husband?"

She nodded.

"His name is Harold."

She nodded again.

"The Great Damir sense that his faith...in the Church... was strong."

She clasped her hands in front of her face, and whispered, "He was a lay minister."

Vincent reached for her hands and gripped them with firm assurance.

"Your husband, I am happy to say, is in the glorious embrace of the Christian God."

Her mouth lifted into a laugh-grimace, and she sucked in several breaths.

Vincent added, "And though he urges you never to treat

with…this is embarrassing for me, but I am only the messenger…a Moslim such as myself, he wishes you to know that you are welcome at the Gates of Peter. And he awaits you there. Be at peace."

She clamped her eyes shut, sobbing so thoroughly that it produced high-pitched moans. He nodded, and the other two offered a meager applause.

He waved them off, then stared at the second woman.

"My dear…" Yes, that was better than French. What was he thinking? "I sense the presence of…Horace?"

More tears, more nodding. This would be simple, but his thoughts were already planning for the tough nut of the group.

"Was he your husband?"

"He was," she whispered.

"Did he have a love for…the fermentation of the grape?"

She sighed. "The man was a drunk."

"I see," he cooed. "And this was the cause of his death, I feel?"

She nodded sadly.

"Well, I can tell you by his posture, such as it is. He is contrite. He blames himself, and he feels grief that he has caused you great suffering during his time in the light."

The old woman wiped tears from her eyes.

"However," Vincent declared with a lift of his expression, "your Horace sees things now unclouded by the fume of liquor. He sees farther than any of us still living. And what he sees…is a bright place."

The woman smiled and clutched her purse to her bosom.

Vincent nodded. "Yes. His guilt is assuaged by the Universal Mind. The great kings of the ancient world have granted him mercy. And he is prepared to move on to the next life."

Vincent waved his hands in what he assumed was a mysterious fashion.

She asked, "Next life?"

"My dear, his soul sees beyond the ultimate mystery. I am not permitted to inquire further, lest my own life become forfeit. So please, simply know that he is at peace, and that you are free to seek your own destiny."

She released a held breath and shook her hands in thanks.

This was the best line of lemon juice to pour for the widows of drunkards. Too often they resented their husbands, and often with the bruises to drive that home. Time to time, they were looking for confirmation they were roasting in Hell. But this one, Vincent could tell, was simply sad. She needed the memory to die, as well as the man. With luck, that's what he gave her. In truth, if the man had lived in any other state in this great Union, he'd probably be alive today. But Maryland chose to sit out this Prohibition. The clubs were open and pouring spirits when the rest of the country had to get their gin in basements and back alleys.

All this musing amounted to so much stalling. Vincent had to rely on a cold read for this last woman. It'd been a while since he'd had to feel out a goose like this the hard way. He didn't like it. Less control. And control was everything when he was performing for little old ladies in his free time.

Control. That's what this was all about, really. He didn't keep the cash. Vincent earned enough from his stipend from the Baltimore Crew. This was about his powers, and using them on his own terms for a damn change.

Still, though, he had a woman staring at him with increasing agitation. He had to come up with something.

"I feel as if," he began, searching for the words in long pauses both for effect and in genuine, "someone is not eager to answer your call."

She tucked her head.

Vincent nudged, "However, he...is here. This shyness proves difficult, but if I may be so bold... I sense violence." He kept a firm gaze on her as she lifted her frail eyes to meet his.

Bullseye.

"Violence," Vincent repeated, "that has haunted his life for quite some time."

She nodded once.

"Violence...that has brought you great suffering. I fear this may have been the strong wind that has snuffed out his flame?"

The old woman closed her eyes, and through trembling lips she whispered, "Yasha."

Vincent's stomach dropped.

That name…

"This was not your husband, I think," he prodded.

She shook her head. "He was my son."

The word escaped Vincent's mouth before he could check it for the faux-Arab accent. "Dmitrivich?"

The woman straightened in her seat, then nodded vigorously.

Vincent closed his eyes and shook his head, the knot in his stomach not due to his powers, but from genuine misery. This wouldn't be a cold read, after all.

With a clearing of his throat, Vincent checked back into character and said, "Yakov Dmitrivich, I call to you."

At last, tears flowed from the third woman's eyes.

"Yakov Dmitrivich, I compel you. Face your mother now. Tell her of your guilt. Of your deep regret. I...sense his presence now. Yes. He was a, what is the word? A gangster?"

She covered her face with her fingers.

Vincent surged on, "He worked for the mob. This...Baltimore Crew. He was not...family, as they would say. But they hired him all the same."

She whimpered, "We are Russian. They only take in their own kind."

He hid a wince. "Indeed, but they make use of the rest. No?"

She lowered her hands and nodded with a scowl.

"And this use," Vincent continued, "put your son, Yakov, into great danger unto his own death." He reached out a hand, and after a long moment, she took it. "You should know that he is filled with regret. Both for what he has done in the name of these...Italians. And for what you have suffered. He has much to pay for in the hereafter. The Universal Mind weighs his soul. But here..." Vincent cleared his throat to force down the frog threatening to croak its way through his stage act. "Here is where I leave you with some hope. Men are neither good nor evil in total. They respond to what life gives them. And your son made his choice. This choice, I think, was not as complete as he would have wished. The Universe understands this. And so, he is given time. Time to make amends. To earn his destiny. And in this pursuit, your son has found new purpose."

She leaned forward a little, and Vincent responded in kind.

"He wishes you to know that he finds hope in the light. His last burden before he may commence his journey of redemption...is the guilt he feels for leaving you with his memory."

"What must I do?" she whispered.

"Tell him. Tell him that you love him. That you have always loved him. Tell Yasha that he may move on, and that you will remember the innocence of the boy you raised. Tell him this...and he will find peace."

"Yasha!" she shouted. "*Ya tebya lublu!*"

Vincent released her hand as she poured heart-wrenching emotion into the air in husky tones. When she was finished, doubled over in sobbing, the other two women stood up and reached for her, throwing arms around her.

Vincent watched the scene, misery simmering in his chest.

Once the pageantry was complete, he made his usual demonstrative exit, encouraging each of the old ladies to leave any manner of "gratuity or honorarium" in the bronze bowl near the door. He withdrew back into the closet behind the red satin drapes and sat in front of his mirror. Then he lit the candle with a match and stared at his reflection, listening for the scuffles and footfalls to subside. Usually this was an agony, waiting for the clients to file out until he could collect the donations and go about his merry.

But tonight, he needed a moment.

Yakov Dmitrivich.

Vincent knew him. He knew him all too well. More specifically, he knew precisely how the man died. He'd pilfered payments to Capo Vito and the Baltimore Crew over the years. They were small sums, only a dollar here and there. Usually from the cat houses up near the Jones Falls. But it was enough to be noticed, and since he wasn't family, Yakov's life was forfeit. However, since he'd holed up in the Russian blocks with a half-dozen armed men waiting to plug anyone with an Italian accent who came knocking, Vito had sent his time pincher to ease the process.

It wasn't hard. Only about ten seconds and ten square yards. He'd cleared the guns out of the room, then stepped aside long enough for Vito's boys to spray lead.

Vincent wiped the makeup from his face then jerked the fez off his head and tossed it onto the bench. It'd been a while since he heard any noise from the other room, so he figured it was safe to emerge. Returning to the rented second-story room over the grocer, he sprinkled some water over the tobacco bowl, closed the window, and scooped up the evening's take to stuff into his pocket.

The night air still held just a little chill, still early in May. A fog settled in over the city from the waterfront, filled with the stench of mud and death. Vincent took the short way home, less eager to enjoy the evening now that his mind dwelled on Yakov Dmitrivich's mother.

A soup kitchen was in the process of closing up shop just a few doors away, and more than a few men in threadbare jackets stumbled out onto the street. Vincent lingered by the soup kitchen stoop, watching as a bald-headed fellow swept the floor's debris out onto the street. The bald man paused and gave Vincent a nod.

"Oh! Heya, there, Vinnie."

"Vincent," he corrected as he reached a hand into his pocket.

"Another donation?"

Vincent pulled his take of the evening from his pocket…a handful of coins and bills. He thumbed through the money, counting it all before handing the entire lot over.

The bald man pulled the tails of his shirt out of his trousers to make a basket. He received the donation, winking up at Vincent.

"You had a good night, tonight."

"No, but you're welcome."

Vincent turned to continue his march home. His room sat atop a two-story brick row house on Fremont—a concession from Vito. Vincent never paid rent, and never dealt with the landlords. Vito didn't want his one and only pincher hung out to dry.

As he trotted across the street, he spotted a familiar figure leaning against the stoop of the row house—a middle-aged man with shiny silver-streaked black hair drawn back against a widow's peak. His light beige trench coat drooped unbuttoned, its most remarkable feature being the right sleeve, which was sewn shut high up at the shoulder. It was a nice piece of tailoring that made anyone who wasn't staring assume he was just wearing the coat over his shoulders.

Vincent released a sigh, balled a fist in his trousers pocket, then lifted his chin.

"Hiya, Lefty. Kinda late for you to be kicking heels this part of town, ain't it?"

Lefty Mancuso pulled himself from the shabby wood door to the row house and stepped down the stoop to street level, his eyes sharp like ice picks.

"You're late."

"What, we had a date?" Vincent jibed. "I woulda bought you flowers or something."

Lefty stood resolute in his typical monolithic dignity. "You're usually home by nine."

"What can I tell you? Old ladies got no kinda schedule." He sized up Lefty's clothes. Black suit. Thin tie. Working hat. "What's the beef? We got a job?"

Lefty nodded once. "We have a job."

"What, tonight?"

"What do you think?" Lefty replied with an impatient lift of his chin. "Get dressed. We're driving to Cumberland."

Vincent shook his head. "Is this from Vito?"

"Yes, it's from Vito."

That settled it. There was no escaping this late-night errand. When Vito called in Vincent, that meant the Capo needed his powers. That was what Vincent was there for.

That was his purpose.

"Alright, alright," he waved. "Give me five minutes."

CHAPTER 3

$\mathcal{H}$attie sat cross-legged on the bow of Raymond's boat. This was her place. Out on the Bay, in the dark of the night, everything in the world seemed right.

The engine house at the center of the vessel chugged away, sending diesel smoke into the air and vibrations through the wood planks below. The boat didn't make any kind of appreciable headway along the wide, semi-choppy water of the Chesapeake Bay, so the breeze that rushed over her face was all Mother Nature. Her bangs flipped along her cheekbones, rushing along her eyelashes in the wind, and she shook her head to settle them back in place.

The moon had nearly set to the west, meaning it was about an hour past midnight. They still had an hour's travel ahead of them before they could deliver the crates of illegal brandy into the hands of the Upright Citizens, an upstart mob out of Richmond who'd developed a regular working relationship with the Baltimore Crew. This new relationship had generated plenty of work up and down the Bay. And that work was enough to keep both Hattie and her partners as well as Little Teague's group flush with business.

Now, it seemed, Teague had seen fit to remove the competition. Hattie fumed on it, watching as the bow split the waves along the surface of the water.

"What'd you think?" Raymond called from behind her. "'Bout the Solomons Island Boys?"

"I think," she replied with a composed tone, "that they've kicked a hornet's nest."

"Are we the hornets?"

"When I'm done with them," Hattie replied, turning to Raymond with a smirk, "they'll be stung plenty."

"Thoughts on that? What ya planning?" he asked as he settled himself on the engine house behind her.

"Oh, I'm thinking 'bout smacking Teague with a leather strap. Maybe a bat, if I'm not feeling charitable."

He chuckled. "Serious, though. He's got twenty men working with him. What're you gonna do about it?"

Probably nothing. Hattie scowled, then stretched her arms high over her head with a yawn. "Can't do much until I talk to Lizzie, can I? It's her show."

Raymond nodded. "She's gonna drop bricks."

"Count on it."

He crouched down a little, his face easing into a soft mound of concern. "Are you feeling better? You looked pale as hell back there."

She nodded. "Fresh air does a person good."

"Wouldn't say it's all that fresh."

"It is, if you're used to city air."

Raymond released another thunder-laugh. "True 'nough. I'm happy far away from that city. You should move if you're fancyin' a rural life more."

If only it were that easy. How many times had she begged her parents to move out of Baltimore? To flee somewhere safe and sequestered? But there was no money, and the only jobs were in the city. Her mother spent long hours in the

Magnus Fields Textile Plant, working a mechanized loom. And her father…well, he was one of several hundred who slaved away most of their lives at Bethlehem Steel. The new buildings…the taller buildings…they all had skeletons of steel, and Bethlehem was the provider of choice for the city of Baltimore. Because of this, they remained in Hampden, alongside so many other Irish families, working and sleeping and digging themselves deeper and deeper with each passing year. Worse, they had to worry about her.

No one with her abilities remained free for long. The mafia snapped up pinchers like toads eating flies, using threats and violence to keep them in what amounted to slavery for the gang's own purposes. That was the destiny her parents had sacrificed so much to protect her from. So, she kept her head low, her bangs over her eyes, and she kept her illusions close to the truck.

And she stayed out on the safety of the water as much as possible.

They continued south toward Newport News, letting in at some unnamed inlet on the Bay side of the peninsula. So many of these fingers dug into the mainland, draped in thick canopies and cattails. They were a wonderland of secrecy that the Treasury men could never manage to fully cover. Good thing too, since they were now under the auspices of the Commonwealth of Virginia, where Prohibition wasn't just the law of the land, it was the spirit of the land.

A line of orange light flickered along the water's edge as Raymond piloted the boat along the muddy banks. Six men stood in a line, one waving them in with his torch. Raymond killed the engine with a kick of his boot and tossed a mooring line to one of the gentlemen gathered on the shore. They tied up the boat to a tall stump, the remains of some bizarre execution mid-trunk which the former tree had suffered.

"Evening," one of the Richmond boys bellowed. "Or, morning. Whatever."

Hattie rushed up the side of the boat to pull back the canvas tarp covering the crates of brandy.

The lead man stepped onto Raymond's boat, steadying himself for a half-second as he waved the torch over the crates.

"Six cases, huh?"

"That's all we were given," Hattie replied.

He shrugged and made a bit of theatrical agony over the disappointing numbers. In truth, they knew precisely how many bottles they were taking delivery of. Therefore, they had precisely the correct dollar amount to pay upon delivery. This was just him being an ass, and Hattie knew it.

The man released a whistle from between two fingers rammed between his teeth, and the others hopped on board to lug the crates onto dry land.

Hattie stood by to supervise. Her special skills were rarely needed on this sort of run. The hooch was delivered, and she took payment. If there was any talking to be done, she did it since the Virginians were even less patient with someone of Raymond's complexion than those up north were.

"You're up awful late," the lead man muttered as the last crate left the boat. "For a girl."

"A girl?" she asked with as much playful lilt as she could muster.

"Don't you have someone waiting for you at home?"

Here it was…the obligatory gesture of manly dominance. Hattie rarely saw these river rats without there being some sort of display of braggadocio, or some other assertion that she ought not to be wearing pants and running booze after hours. This was the terrain upon which she plied her trade. She didn't like it, but she accepted it.

With a sharp grin, she turned to the lead man, bangs

shading her eyes, and said, "Several someones are waiting at home for me, but I won't tell if you don't."

The man turned toward her, taking the bait perhaps too well. "And how many of these someones are willing to make you honest?"

"Honest?" she repeated, not liking where this was going.

"An honest woman. Or are you one of *those* girls? A loose dame?"

She strapped her grin against gritted teeth like a steel vice. "You going to talk living arrangements all night, or am I getting paid?"

He shook his head and released a low snicker. Turning to his compatriots, he gestured for a tiny package of brown paper wrapped in twine. He extended his hand to shove it into her chest, the backs of his knuckles grazing the curve of her breast as he did so.

Hattie sucked in a breath, then snatched the package. The twine was tight, and she sighed.

"You can count it now, if you like," he declared with a lift of his brow. "I won't take offense."

She tried to hook her finger into the twine, but found it was pulled far too taut.

"I'll give the Upright Citizens the benefit of the doubt," she replied, pocketing the stack of paper-wrapped bills into her trousers' pocket.

He shook his head. "A young woman like yourself ought to be wearing a dress, don't you think?"

She guffawed. "You want me to wear a dress? Out here?" She extended her arms toward the Bay.

He didn't miss a beat. "Dames in pants...you're just asking for trouble."

Raymond shifted in his position. So practiced was he that even Hattie had ceased to notice him looming behind her.

But the increased provocation on the part of this Virginian jerk-weed had stirred his protective instincts.

Instincts which could get him killed.

One of the land-bound Richmond boys pulled a pistol from his holster and cocked it before Hattie realized what was even happening. She lifted a hand to Raymond, and out to the rest.

"Boys," she shouted. "Let's be civil."

The pistol-bearer snarled. "You keep your darkie on a leash, little girl!"

The hand she'd spread against Raymond's overalls balled into a fist. A dozen illusions filled her mind. How best to teach this turnip-brain a lesson? Fill his brains with a living nightmare? Some horror? Or should she simply conjure up a bevy of G-men for them to piss themselves over?

Even as she thought of drawing on her light-pinching powers, her stomach flipped. She wasn't quite recovered just yet. Trying another large-scale light pinch might send her unconscious.

And her being unconscious wouldn't be wise in the company of these mule-heads.

Hattie cleared her throat and looked up at Raymond. His nostrils were flaring. This needed a smooth hand.

"Oh, come on now," she declared with a hint of swagger. "We've had ourselves a proper exchange. Let's not sully the moment with unkindness." She stepped up to the lead man, tossing her bangs aside with a flick of her neck so that he could see her eyes. "You've got six cases of Baltimore's finest, there. I'm sure there's thirsty folk who could use a drop. Let's not keep them waiting, shall we?"

She pressed a finger onto his chest, flipping it up to his collarbone as she drilled the slightest, most miniscule pinches of light into his eyeballs.

In an instant she was as sultry and alluring as Clara Bow.

Close quarters, one-on-one…this magic was cheap as they came. And it better work, because this was about all she could manage right now.

His eyes swallowed her illusion with great gulps, and his knees buckled just a bit. With a clearing of his throat, he barked, "Okay, load it up. Let's get moving."

She turned her back to him, ready to shoot Raymond an assuring wink, when a hand slapped down onto her arm.

Hattie sucked in a breath as the lead man leaned close to her ear to whisper, "A word?"

She forced her muscles to relax. Best not to betray her terror. The man eased her away from Raymond, and off the boat onto the water's edge. The others hauled away the crates one by one, leaving them alone.

"How many words do you think you'll need?" she quipped. "I have a long pull back up the Bay, and I'd like to get started."

He released her arm and folded his hands in front of him. His face had eased. This wasn't intimidation. If anything, it looked like a confession.

"Look…miss."

"Malloy," she offered.

"Miss Malloy, I've seen you on the water before. Maybe we've done business, I can't be sure. But I want to keep you on the right side of this business, if you take my meaning."

She squinted. "I'm not sure where to take that."

"Your boy," he pressed, nodding toward Raymond.

"What, Raymond?"

"Whatever. Time's coming, his kind won't be welcome on the water. Now, you're a smart girl. A go-getter. I respect that. So, I want you start thinking about the future. Get clear of his kind. Do you hear what I'm saying?"

She pulled in several breaths, releasing them in guarded volume. "I think I've got you figured right."

"That's good."

"I'll be leaving, then."

She moved away from him, keeping her face forward until she eased up against the side of the boat. Hattie stepped high and boarded.

"Let's go, Raymond," she whispered.

He rushed for the engine house to give the crank a good spin, and as the engine turned over to release several plumes of black smoke into the air, he reached for the bank to push off.

Hattie watched the lead man as they swiveled back out to open water. He stood there with his torch held at face level. Jesus, that illusion had worked far too well. That was closer to these brigands than she ever wanted to get.

After a few minutes, Raymond finally spoke. "Did he hurt you?"

She shook her head. "Raymond?"

"Mm-hmm?"

"You still carry a pistol with you?"

He squinted. "Not for a while. Ain't seen no snakes for a bit. Figured it wasn't worth it."

She folded her arms across her chest. "Well, we seen some snakes tonight. Best you keep yourself prepared, no?"

He nodded slowly and steered the tiller with a thoughtful cast.

At last, as they rounded the neck of Cherrystone Inlet, Raymond declared, "I don't know about you, baby girl…but I need a drink."

She shook her head. "What?"

He nodded up the bank to a ramshackle building hanging over the water, tucked between two marsh flats. Several figures stepped in and out of the pool of light sifting the smoky windows. As the boat eased closer, the plinking of a jazz piano filled the air along with low-murmured conversation.

"What's this, then?" she asked.

"Maudite's," Raymond answered. "Best little gin joint on the water. Come on. We stared down Feds and ignorant-ass fools today. We earned ourselves a little cheer."

Hattie smiled and didn't protest.

Maudite's could barely be described as a building. Several hand-hewn timbers ran in uneven lines along a series of pilings, bolstering a siding of corrugated tin and dimensional lumber that was weathered with age. A series of hurricane lamps flickered inside the half-opened space. A dozen or so dark-skinned patrons sat at planks strewn across barrels or milled about the pier with drinks in hand.

At the near end of the bar stood a warped upright piano, its strings clearly distressed from weathering. Their tones were sour, dulled…moist and damp as were the surroundings. Aside from the cacophony of the piss-poor tuning, the sound suited the music. This wasn't the usual radio tunes, the up-tempo swing of big bands from Radio City or the West Coast. Nor was this the old-timey twang of the mountain stretches, with their mandolins and yodel-like refrains. No, this was the new music.

Jazz.

The discordant tones washed over Hattie as Raymond steered her toward the bar with a large but gentle hand on her shoulder. It wasn't so much the melody, or lack thereof, that hooked her in. It was the rhythm. No simple down-beat, up-beat. This was pitter-patter. Syncopation. It matched her heartbeat, the chaos of her thoughts, the random collision of smells from the Bay and the sweating bodies and the hooch they were swilling.

Raymond ordered two cups of something, and Hattie lifted her pewter mug to Raymond's.

"Aye, may the bastards never grind us down."

He clinked her cup and took a hard pound of the liquor.

Hattie sniffed hers, regretting it instantly. She took a tiny sip, fluttering it past her lips. Her sinuses filled with thick fumes, and she coughed immediately, spraying a fine mist of whatever poison was in that cup.

"Just shoot it…damn," he admonished.

"Not sure that's wise," she said. "But…hell. Here it goes."

She shot the liquor, then stood stiff, waiting for the paroxysm of coughing to overtake her.

When it came, the effect was utterly humiliating.

Once she'd calmed down and taken a seat, and Raymond had ordered some fruit wine for the both of them, he gestured at the dark faces gathered around them.

"Man says my kind got no place on the Bay. What's he know?"

Hattie nodded in sympathy. "There will always be people cut from his cloth. Best to just ride them out."

"Maybe I don't wanna ride them out," he grumbled.

"And maybe that sort of thinking will get you killed," she warned.

He shook his head and they sipped his wine in silence, finishing all too soon and heading back to the boat.

The sun rose in three hours, and they coasted into Winnow's Slip in time to watch the eastern clouds catch fire. Hattie had finally mustered the twine free of the brown paper on their return trip, checking that the Upright Citizens hadn't joined Little Teague in some conspiracy to screw them out of their business. Thankfully, the contracted amount was there in small bills. She'd bring the payout back to Lizzie tomorrow, after some well-earned sleep. Giving Raymond a quick hug as he shut down the engine, she hopped onto dry land. The smokestacks to the north were already belching their soot into the sky. Back to the city air.

Hattie's home was a two-bedroom apartment in the Irish quarter of Hampden. She trotted up the three flights of stairs until she reached her front door. Stepping inside, she was greeted by the aroma of fresh-brewed tea. Releasing a tired sigh, she wove her way toward the kitchen where her mother stood at the stove, stirring what smelled like a pot of porridge.

"Long night, was it?" Her mother smiled as Hattie kissed her on the cheek then went to sit at the table.

"Aye, Ma. Too long."

Her mother brought her a cup of tea, which Hattie gripped for dear life.

"I haven't changed my mind about this business of yours," she chided.

"Where's Da?" Hattie deflected.

Her mother pointed to the main room. Her father, Alton, sat slumped in his chair, his head cocked at an awkward angle. His lips quivered as he released a light snore.

Hattie frowned. "When'd he come home?"

"Just past midnight."

"Da's working nights, now? Even with his lungs?"

"Just for this week. Least, that's what they tell him."

Hattie sipped her tea and managed her way through half a bowl of the porridge before fatigue overtook her. She surrendered the remains to her mother, who dropped it back into the pot. Finishing the tea, she set the mug onto the table, then stepped lightly into the main room to plant a kiss on her father's brow.

"Good night, Da," she whispered, before trudging to her bedroom and collapsing.

CHAPTER 4

Vincent peered out the windshield of Lefty's Alfa Romeo to gaze at the moon, shining brilliant white high in the sky. As the road eased to the left, he jerked his attention back to the driving.

"Eyes on the road, you mook," Lefty chided.

"You wanna drive?"

"Sure," Lefty grumbled. "You think I can't drive? I can steer and shift just fine." He waved his arm in the air. "I never let this get in my way, so you want to pull over? I can take the tiller."

Vincent shook his head. "Didn't mean anything by it, Lefty."

Lefty glowered in his seat. "Then just keep us on the road."

The road weaved in and out of a couple forested bends before heading up the side of a hill. The long, wavy curtains of the Appalachians swung into view, and Vincent kept driving west.

"So, who're we meeting this far out?" Vincent asked.

"Tony and Cooper."

"Hell's bells. We're gunning for them? What'd they do to Vito?"

Lefty shook his head. "They aren't the job."

"Then what is the job?"

"Dryfork Brothers," Lefty said. "They're moonshiners from West By God. Like to tend their still up in the mountains and run barrels into Maryland on account of the governor giving the Feds the shine-off. Easy on them, since they don't got to sweat the Gee. Harder on them, since Vito takes his cut. It's an arrangement that's suited everyone well enough."

"I suppose that's changed?"

"We got a man on the inside, sent word the Brothers have been bootlegging their hooch straight north, cutting across Cumberland to sell direct to Pittsburgh. Cutting Vito out completely."

Vincent scowled. "How violent is this likely to be?"

"How am I supposed to know?" He gave Vincent a sharp leer. "You're the one with the crystal ball and the fez." Once he realized Vincent didn't find the comment even remotely humorous, he continued, "It's just a conversation. A Come-to-Jesus meeting. We'll set 'em straight, then bring whatever they're hauling back with us as a tax for revenue lost, or some monkeyshine along those lines."

The engine whined as the grade up the hill increased. Once they rounded the bend, a narrow valley opened up below. A spattering of lights greeted their eyes in the distance.

Cumberland.

"Where's Tony and Cooper?" Vincent asked. "In town, or outside?"

"Just east. Our man on the inside says they found a back lane they like, keeps them out of plain sight."

Lefty directed Vincent along the narrow roads between

cow pastures until they reached a copse of white oaks, dark shadows rising above the moonlit fields. A Triumph two-seater sat parked beneath the trees, its former occupants leaning against its hood.

Vincent parked Lefty's car alongside the Triumph and remained behind the wheel as Lefty stepped out. This sort of company time was typically meant for the *famiglia*...not Vincent, so Lefty convened with the others while Vincent kept an ear peeled.

"What're we lookin' at?" Lefty asked.

The taller of the two, Tony, replied, "Oughta be blowing through here in about a half hour. You guys took your sweet time."

Lefty gestured at the car. "Blame the pincher. Got all moonstruck."

Tony crouched down and gave Vincent a nod. When he straightened, he said in volume not that much quieter than before, "He gonna sit in there all night, or what?"

Lefty pounded on the passenger door. "Vincent. Stop putting these gents off their feed."

Vincent sucked in a breath, released it in a slow hiss between his teeth, then stepped out of the Alfa Romeo. When he rounded the front of the car, Tony gave him a second nod.

"Heya, Vinnie. How's tricks?"

"It's Vincent," he replied in a tone that was sharper it should have been.

The shorter of the two, Cooper, shook his head. "Freak's getting insulted, now. That's just cherry."

Vincent stuffed his hands into his pockets before balling fists.

Tony snickered. "Well, keep your shirt on...*Vincent*. We got some backward-ass hillbillies about to blow through here with six barrels of white lightning. We're here to teach them the error of their ways, bring them back into the fold, and keep the peace." He added with careful enunciation, "You know your part in this?"

Vincent replied, "Yeah. I'm here in case they don't want to keep no peace."

"Right. So, keep your eyes open. We got a mole riding with them, so we want this to stay nice and civil."

Lefty regarded Vincent, then turned to Tony. "He knows what to do."

Cooper spat onto the road. "Don't need none of his mumbo jumbo, anyways."

"You have a problem with my pincher?" Lefty asked, taking a step past Tony.

Cooper squared up on Lefty. "Maybe I do, maybe I don't. Maybe I think Vito's got enough muscle without this spook."

"It's Vito's call," Lefty stated. "Unless you've been promoted to Capo and no one told me."

Tony offered, "Coop's just a little religious, is all. Don't let him get you lathered up."

Lefty squinted and took another step into Cooper. "Right. Religious. I never see you at Mass."

The other man paled a little, then set his jaw. "I'm Protestant. Jeez. Get outta my face with this."

Lefty remained in his face. "Protestant?"

"Methodist, not that it's any of your business."

Lefty nodded. "A Methodist named Lou Cooper. That sounds unremarkably American. Now, a good Catholic by the name of…Luigi Capucci?"

Cooper took a step away.

"That," Lefty concluded, "sounds like *famiglia*. What's the matter with you, Luigi? You're too good for your heritage now? Too good for the Church?"

Cooper huffed through his nose as Lefty leveled onto his face the intractable glare Vincent knew so well.

Tony tapped Lefty on his good shoulder. "Alright, tuck it in. Car's coming."

A lone clunker with tall wooden rails straddling its bed rattled around a farmhouse in the distance, slapping against some of the high grass on the side of the road.

Tony and Cooper reached into the Triumph to produce two Tommy guns, housing a magazine in each.

As they strode out onto the lane, Tony urged, "Keep your chopper friendly, Coop. We're here to talk."

Cooper angled his gun toward the dirt to mirror Tony, though his shoulders were considerably more drawn.

Lefty brushed Vincent toward the trees.

"Just hang back. We're not here to do any lifting. We're just here in case it all goes sideways."

"Like usual?"

Lefty nodded. "Like usual."

The two gangsters remained in the road, adopting an almost casual posture. The clunker swung around the last bend before the lane straightened to reveal the two. The old truck was a Ford, but it had been through so much hell and rebuilding, Vincent couldn't recognize the model. And he wondered if the driver would see Tony and Cooper at all, since they were running with their lights dark.

The wheels locked up and slid along the dirt and gravel on the lane, and the truck managed its way to a stop underneath the weight of the six barrels slung in the back.

Tony held his ground and turned. Cooper withdrew six or so steps.

No one in the cab made a move. They just sat there, staring.

Finally, Tony snapped his fingers in the air. "Why don't you boys step on out?"

They remained frozen.

Cooper took those six steps forward, the nose of his gun lifting inch-by-inch.

Both doors opened, and three men stepped out into the moonlight. Their faces were drawn, eyes wide. Beads of sweat lined their foreheads.

Tony grinned. "There, fresh air. That's better, right?"

No one responded.

"So," Tony barked. "That's a lotta liquor! I can't help but notice you got that liquor pointed north. Not east."

One of the Dryfork Brothers, the driver, took a shuffle-step forward as he pulled his hat off his head.

"We, uh…we're not goin' North."

"That a fact?" Tony asked. He turned behind him, and made a slow, histrionic turn. "See, thing is this road noses straight north all the way up to Pittsburgh. You missed the Pike headed east by at least ten minutes."

"Oh?" the driver asked. "I, uh…must've missed the turn."

"I appreciate your humility, I really do. But I want to have a real grown-up conversation with you boys. So, maybe we dispense with the bushwa?"

The back two flinched and seemed ready to jump back into the cab…but the driver spun on his heel and held a palm out to halt them.

"Er, Mister…"

"You can call me Tony," he said. He nodded at Cooper. "And this one? Don't call him anything at all, because he's about ready to ventilate you mooks right now. So, keep your eyes up here." He whistled and pointed at his face.

The driver nodded.

"We happen to know you've been cutting the Crew out for the better part of a month, now. Which baffles me, because you people have a sweet deal riding east into Baltimore. No Feds. No cops. No grief. And a guaranteed buyer on our end."

One of the back two shouted, "Your prices are shit!"

The other…—Vincent figured they must be the actual brothers…—added, "Yeah, and you tax us whenever we sell to anyone else! Ain't fair."

Tony nodded and stared at the ground in deep contemplation.

Cooper sneered. "Let's just shoot 'em and be done with this. Teach them all a lesson."

Tony ignored him, still focusing on the Dryfork men. "I hear you. And I understand what you're saying. But the fact is, this is a volatile climate to do business in, gents. Supply and demand are not the only considerations for our industry, vis-à-vis the Volstead Act."

Vincent grinned, and looked over at Lefty. There were times Tony spoke like a college professor, a carryover from his honest-to-God college education.

Lefty just shook his head.

"Now look," the driver said with outstretched hands. "We don't want no trouble from the Crew. We just want a fair price."

Cooper rolled his eyes and lifted his weapon a few inches. "Well, trouble is what you've got."

Tony waved him down. "A fair price as compared to what? What you get from the boys up in Pittsburgh? Well, let me tell you this. What the Crew pays for your hooch accounts for protection. Surety, if you will. Man-hours devoted to keeping the streets clear."

One of the brothers in the back said, "It's less'n half what we get in Pennsylvania."

Tony's eyes lost their mirth. "Yeah? And you know who runs Pittsburgh? The *famiglia*. You know who owns the Crew? *Famiglia*. You think you're being so clever, but you're just robbing Peter to pay Peter. You think this goes unnoticed? You think we don't make one phone call and shut this down hard?"

Tony was shouting, now. Cooper had taken two steps forward, lifting his gun a few more inches, his eyes hard on the men by the truck. The elder Dryfork held his ground, but the brothers had nearly retreated all the way back into the cab.

Vincent watched them closely. They didn't have the poise of the man who Vincent assumed was the patriarch of the Dryfork moonshiners. They were angry and afraid. A rotten cocktail for any business transaction that involved moonshine and guns.

The driver nodded furiously. "You're right, and I see that now. We just got a whole buncha Treasury men nosin' around the woods these days. We need shorter rides and bigger paydays."

Tony sniffed. "That's a supply-side issue, my friend."

"Let's get this over with," Cooper muttered. "Teach these hillbillies a lesson."

One of the brothers swiveled his head toward the cab, and his lips moved in short, discreet motions. Someone else was in the car.

Vincent leaned in to call Lefty's attention to the fact, but paused as the dull sheen of gunmetal emerged from the cab.

The brother lifted what appeared to be a simple hunting rifle out of the cab, keeping it tucked behind the door.

Cooper cleared his throat, pointing his Tommy gun at the brother. "Hey, keep your mitts where we can see 'em!"

Tony jerked his head toward the gunman who pulled the rifle up to the door window and cranked the bolt with a shout. The barrel was trained directly at Tony, whose gun was still aimed at the dirt.

The gunman's finger clamped down on the trigger.

With a blink, Vincent pinched time.

The boom of the rifle shot shuffled into a muddy whisper, like a stone thrown into water with a deep *kerplunk.*

Vincent took a half-second to size up the postures of everyone gathered, and realized he was too far away—over twenty yards. The area of halted time had extended at least that far, plus a few more to capture the truck. He hadn't made a conscious calculation of his time pinch…he never did. He only knew what he needed, and his powers reached out and made it happen. It was often a bill that was tallied after the fact to Vincent's chagrin.

This bill was going to be painfully high.

Vincent reached for the tree trunk beside him and used it to push himself out into the time-frozen air. His legs hammered against the ground, swimming through the mire, trying to close the distance before the time pinch began to shred his guts. He could already feel it tugging at his chest.

It felt like an eternity, and from the inside of this bubble it might as well have been. Step after step, he strode forward through the thickness of air until he reached the truck.

The rifle was in mid-lift from the kick, the gunman's eyes squinted hard. A brilliant plume of hot black powder exhaust hovered in the middle of the truck door window, shedding its light in a dull shine like an overweight firefly. The slug itself hung in the air several feet away, almost halfway to Tony's chest.

Bile filled Vincent's throat as his abdomen twisted. It usually didn't set in quite this quick, but he was extending a larger area of effect than usual…and it was wearing him down. He wasn't sure how much longer he could hold it.

He had to make quick decisions.

First, he reached for the stock of the rifle, careful not to touch the fire-heated metal, and jerked it clear of the brother's hands. When time restored its flow, it would continue up in its recoil, probably flying into or over the gunman's face. There would be no second shot.

Vincent then gripped the open truck door and pulled himself into motion in a direct line alongside the flight of the bullet. He knew better than to touch the slug. His powers never actually fully halted time. The best he did was to slow the flow of time to such a speed that it appeared to stop. But some things that had enough speed, such as light itself, or even a bullet midflight, still packed enough punch to cause severe injury. He'd learned that the hard way, to be sure.

Keeping clear of the slug, he reached for Tony, pulling him by the arm until his body canted at an angle, like a diver going sideways through frozen water. When time returned, he'd fall to his side, gun clear of his legs…and most importantly clear of the bullet.

Vincent's throat lurched, and he dry-heaved. A burning heat filled his torso, and a trickle of blood slipped from his nostrils. He didn't have time to return to the trees. No, that would kill him. Best he could do was to step clear of the bullets.

He pushed hard against the ground, reaching his arms out, and dove. His body remained suspended for a half-second in the thickness of the space.

And with a blink, he released his time pinch.

Gravity grabbed hold of his body, sending him into freefall just as the rest of the rifle shot pounded in his ears. He landed in the grass beside the road and turned on his hip.

Tony lay sprawled out on the dirt road, turning his head slowly back and forth.

Cooper stood rigid, his gun half-raised, blinking. "What the—?" he bellowed.

A clack behind the truck caught their attention. The hunting rifle had swung up and over the gunman's head. He stood, hands still held in a pantomime of a rifle, eyes wide.

Cooper released a blood-curdling shout and pulled the Tommy gun to his shoulder.

Gunfire filled Vincent's ears.

Sparks flew off the angles and edges of the truck.

Shouts.

Blood.

Tony remained on his side, lifting his gun to join in the barrage. Bullets clinked along the undercarriage, pounding the tires flat. The Dryfork patriarch spun several times under the impact of Cooper's bullets, bouncing against the front fender of the truck, then onto his back. Tony angled his gun at the open truck door. The brothers turned on their heels to run, but the bullets from both gangsters perforated the door…and the brothers.

Both of the gangsters held their triggers down until their magazines had emptied, then remained in place, sucking in ragged breaths.

Lefty trotted out of the copse of trees, eyes scanning the scene back and forth.

Vincent pulled himself to his feet and waved him down. "Over here, Lefty."

Lefty trotted over to him, sizing him up.

"You hurt?" he grumbled.

"Pulled too hard," Vincent wheezed.

A gurgle in his throat announced a fresh wave of bile. Vincent spun around and vomited into the grass.

Tony stood up and eased Cooper's gun down. The two approached the driver, whose lifeless body didn't respond to repeated nudging from their wingtips. Then Tony rounded the door to check on the brothers. He lifted a hand and gave them a thumbs-up.

Cooper hustled around the opposite side of the truck, pausing only a moment to shake his head at Vincent. He proceeded toward the rear of the truck, then released a whistle. Six barrels sat on the bed of the truck, each branded with a stylized DF-WV emblem. Several streams of clear liquid sprang from the barrels closest to the cab.

"How's it look?" Tony asked.

"Looks like we still got ourselves four good barrels! Front two's spitting out, but there's four left."

Tony laughed. "Well, I suppose negotiations broke down. Huh?" He slapped Cooper on the shoulder with a chuckle.

Vincent spat his mouth clear and shook his head. It spun, and would continue to do so until he got some rest. His powers did real damage this time. Tomorrow would not be kind.

Lefty inched toward the truck. "Where's our man?"

Tony stepped back into view from behind the truck. "What, now?"

"You said we had a man on the inside. That he was with them. Either you two just laid him out, or he stayed behind."

Cooper said, "Maybe he knew this would hit the skids?"

Lefty approached the cab, then turned away sharply.

Vincent gasped, "What? What is it?"

Lefty's face, usually stone-cold and unaffected, fell several shades paler. He shook his head and moved away.

"No," he whispered. "He was here."

Cooper approached the driver's side door. He released a string of vulgarities and turned away, as well.

Vincent pulled in several breaths, straightened up...and regretted it. A migraine pounded inside his skull. Cold sweat erupted across his brow and the small of his back. He forced his feet forward, heel to toe, until he could see inside the cab.

The body of a young boy no older than ten years lay twisted and bloodied.

Vincent clamped his eyes shut and held himself up against the side of the truck, his face pulling into a grimace.

Tony said, "Hell's bells. Someone could've told us it was just a kid. What a damn mess."

The ground shifted beneath Vincent's feet, and he pitched to the side. He felt Lefty's hand guiding him to the ground, and though he opened his eyes…he could see nothing but darkness. Nothing but sickness and pain.

And grief for that little boy.

CHAPTER 5

*H*attie regarded herself in her mirror and pressed her palms against the yellow gingham dress her mother had given her. No matter how hard she pressed, the array of permanent wrinkles continued bunching up along the sides. Thin straps dug into her shoulders, and years of her mother's wear had created stretched-out swaths where curves had once filled what Hattie's figure couldn't. She was used to hand-me-down garments, but every time she received something "new," she ran through the ritual of identifying what was wrong with it.

One day, God willing, she'd have a dress that only she had worn. Or at least one her mother hadn't worn.

Reaching for her purple straw hat, Hattie settled it onto her head, making sure her bangs drifted across the front of her brow. The band of the hat was faded, and it had lost most of its ornaments long ago. The purple wasn't exactly a match for the yellow gingham, but it was her only hat, also inherited from her mother. She searched the room for some sort of purple accessory to at least make an attempt, but came up empty.

Not that it mattered. Hattie wasn't trying to impress anyone. She was only going to see Lizzie.

"Tin Lizzie" Sadler, the widow of the late Jake Sadler, kept long hours at the warehouse of corrugated tin panels at Locust Point, whence she'd earned her moniker. The warehouse was utterly unremarkable, save for Jake's Runabout parked at the front. It was a new car when Jake had bought it. That was almost one month exactly before he got himself shot. In the years since, Lizzie'd stepped into his shoes. In many ways, she'd improved the affairs of their tidy little booze-running business. Money still came in…not as many large payouts, but it was more regular. She'd even forgiven the loan Raymond took out from Jake in order to buy the boat they used to this day. And despite her sour puss and vinegared ways, the woman never played games with their money. No short dealing. She paid on time and in full.

What hadn't improved was their relationship with the Baltimore Crew. Jake had kept the mob at arm's length, choosing to do business with representatives of representatives. Those connections died with Jake—literally. The death toll on the day the Charleston deal went south was steep for both sides. So, Lizzie had little choice but to come to Capo Vito personally, in order to assert their place on the Bay.

It worked, to an extent. Lizzie'd drummed up a regular discourse with a man by the name of Tony Esposito. He was little more than a gunman, but he had a silvered tongue and some education. The man was all business, and Lizzie always defended him when deals were scratched, or shipments were delayed. "Professional courtesy" was what Lizzie called it.

Hattie figured otherwise, but she'd let it be. Whatever Lizzie did on her own time was her business, even if it was with some petty gangster.

The air inside the warehouse was a good bit cooler than outside, a welcome reprieve from the long road out of town.

On foot, the journey was enough to break a sweat, even in May. Hattie shoved the front door closed with a loud squeal, blinking at the darkness to allow her eyes a moment of adjustment.

"That you, Malloy?" Lizzie shouted from the rear of the space.

"Aye," Hattie replied, stepping over the even concrete with muffled thuds of her dirt-caked Spectators.

The entire warehouse was nearly empty, feeling more like a tomb than a place of business. The thought put a hook in Hattie's guts as she approached Lizzie's office. Two walls cut an office space from the far corner of the warehouse, up a tiny flight of stairs. An old oak desk sat at a meaningless angle to the corner of the office, strewn with newspapers and ledgers. Lizzie peered up through thick spectacles, her brown-and-gray hair pulled back into a long braid. The woman removed her spectacles and wiped them on her denim shirt, gesturing for Hattie to take a seat.

"Heard you had a long night," she grumbled, leaning back in her seat with a squeak of springs.

Hattie sat down across from the desk and pulled her clutch up to her lap. She snapped it open and removed the remainder of the payout from the Upright Citizens.

"It was, at that. No thanks to Little Teague."

Lizzie took the cash, then paused, leveling a glare at Hattie.

"What, now?"

"Raymond and I drove on up to Winnow's, like usual. We found Little Teague tearing out of there like his arse was on fire. According to Teague, Winnow's was crawling with Treasury men."

Lizzie pulled the wad of bills from the remains of the brown paper wrapping. "And they weren't?"

"No. He said he was heading north, so we shuffled down

to McComb's. Where the actual Treasury men were shaking down everyone with a skiff and a stick."

Lizzie's mouth drew tight, then curled downward.

She flipped through the bills and huffed.

"You're short Raymond's pay?"

Hattie nodded. "Didn't expect you'd mind, since we were out to dawn."

"It's fine." Lizzie doled out several bills, then slid them across the top of one of the ledger books toward Hattie. "Your math adds up."

Hattie took her pay and slipped it into the clutch. Lizzie flipped open a ledger book with verve, sending a couple papers flying in its breeze. She pressed into the ledger with sharp motions as she entered the payment.

"What're we going to do about the Solomons?" Hattie asked. "I don't expect we'll let this lie."

Lizzie answered with slow, deliberate syllables as she continued her accounting, "No. We will not let this lie."

She finally closed the book and dropped the remainder of the cash into a file drawer. Lizzie's eyes were narrow and hard. Hattie hadn't seen her this incensed in a long, long while.

"I'll tell you what we'll do," Lizzie declared. "We'll have a word with the Baltimore Crew. At this point, they've strangled all other traffic out of Maryland, and back in again. They only use us freelancers because it saves them money and a headache should the G-men get us. If I put a word in with Tony that the Solomons Island Boys are trying to run a racket on the Bay, squeezing out competition, I'm confident he'll understand the implications."

"Which are?"

"It's business, Malloy. You got two boat runners vying for business, they're going to quote you low so they make sure they get the job. The moment that number of boat runners drops to one, the quotes go up. Vito's going to have to pay more if he wants to keep from using his own men." Lizzie knitted her fingers together. "Though I doubt they'll be eager to stick their noses into the rank-and-file of a squabble between two freelancers."

Hattie shrugged. "Fine. We'll take care of it ourselves."

Lizzie shot her a sharp grin. "That's the best attitude. They'll want us to do the housekeeping for them. Best we offer that up front."

"What'll they give us?" Hattie asked.

"No way to tell until they do. But, and this is important, whatever we do, we'll have to keep the peace on the Bay. We have to give Teague nothing more than a bloody nose. Do him too much damage, and suddenly we're the ones asking too much money."

Hattie smirked. "Is that such a bad thing, now?"

"It's a bad thing when the Baltimore Crew decides they have some nephews or uncles who need work and are willing to cut us loose and keep all the business in-house."

Hattie winced. "Aye, I see your point." She regarded the warehouse behind them. "Lots of air in this place."

"You notice that, too?"

"What's our next job?"

Lizzie shook her head. "Not a lot's come in. I hear from the inside that there's some new artery shunting booze from West Virginia straight into Pennsylvania. With any luck, the Crew will shut that down, and we'll get the mountainside moonshine contracts flowing again. In the meantime, Teague's got the gin-juice locked down. And every boat coming in from the Carolinas is just asking for trouble." Lizzie's face darkened at that. Trouble from the Carolinas. That's what had made her a widow.

Hattie nodded. "So, what do you want from me?"

"Right now? Nothing. Raymond's got the little one to tend to, so he's happy for the time off."

"If you haven't noticed, I don't have any little ones screaming for my attention. I'd rather have a payday."

Lizzie sighed. "I know, I know. But things're tight. Been heading that direction for a while, now. Look…just give me a couple days to talk with Tony. I'll see what we can do about Little Teague."

Hattie lingered for a bit, helping to tidy up the warehouse for a few extra coins, before Lizzie gave her a lift back into the city.

The market had just opened, and Hattie had a clutch full of walking-around money. Why not pick up some produce for Ma and Da? She waved to Lizzie as the woman drove off, and stepped carefully past the ruts of the trolley line into the wide street in front of the Light Street Market.

A line of awnings stretched out over shop fronts and brick-paved archways, blocking out the late morning sun. Short shadows fell over barrels of lettuce and chard. A crate of radishes here, a box of spinach there. The row of produce was mostly green, devoid of the peaches and plums that came in late summer. Hattie hoped the business would take a turn for the better by then.

She nosed around the produce stand, walking away with a package of fresh spinach, a bag of pea greens, and some fiddleheads. A barker from the fish market called out some fresh-caught shad, and Hattie paused to consider it. Fresh fish. How often could they afford that? And with her father's health suffering the way it'd been for these past few months, some clean meat would do him good.

After a half hour and a lungful of fish fumes, Hattie had the shad fillets packaged under her arm. The exhilaration of shopping filled her chest with a light feeling. Paydays were the best days. Too often, Hattie'd resorted to passing slugs with tiny pinches of light to make them appear as nickels. She wasn't proud of it, but during the winter that was often the only way they got bread. And even though Hattie kept a strong tally of the money in her clutch, knowing that most of it would go toward her parents' rent, she managed to while away all her concerns for just an hour. It was enough to walk in public, among the regular people, and not worry about undue notice.

But as the day wore on, Hattie began to feel conscious of her dress again—her dress and her hat. She noticed as the occasional glance from passersby, usually women, tugged at her. The Light Street Market sat across from a dress shop, just down the street from the mill her ma worked at on the Jones Falls. Maybe it was vanity, maybe the urge to think about simpler things, but Hattie was filled with the need for something new to wear.

She trotted across Light Street, winding around a row of Model Ts parked in a neat herringbone, and stepped up to the dress shop window.

Satin.

Silk.

Beads.

Bold swaths of diagonal lines separated materials, dropping barely to the knees to allow a fringe to fill in the rest of the way.

Black and purple, tan and orange.

Her eyes drank in the colors and patterns, halting only when she found a price tag.

And the exhilaration was gone in a flash.

Hattie stepped away from the window, her chin low, bangs covering her eyes. This was stupid. That money was needed for a roof and food. Not bangles and baubles. Come the next day, she'd be back in trousers, and on the water anyway. She glanced up at the two-story brick buildings boxing her in. A car rushed past her, sending her staggering a step away from the street. She had to get home and away from all these things she couldn't have.

As she turned back for the trolley line, she spotted the last awning along the market lane. Bunches of flowers sat arranged in tiny paper cones, cocked at angles to face the street. Bold red blossoms. Yellow. White.

And purple.

A man rummaged through the cones of flowers, picking here and there. He was young, in his early or mid-twenties, and was sporting a light tan suit and straw hat. He had an amiable country quality to his face that belied his outfit. As Hattie paused near a bunch of purple hyacinths, she spotted him glancing at her from across the crocuses.

She looked away immediately.

Footsteps approached, and panic flooded her chest. Inside her head, she kept repeating "go away, go away," but his footsteps halted directly beside her.

"Hyacinths," he declared, reaching for the flowers.

Hattie cocked her head enough to watch him from underneath her bangs.

He cupped a hand behind the blooms and took a long sniff.

Hattie nodded once, then stepped away.

"Excuse me, miss?"

She froze.

He plucked a few hyacinth stalks, and reached over for two yellow crocus blossoms, and arranged them quickly in his fingers. Holding the bouquet up to forehead level, he nodded.

"This would look striking on your hat band, if I may be so bold."

She shivered, arms stiff around her groceries.

The young man lowered the flowers, his face filling with embarrassment.

"I...I do apologize. I was too bold. Please, excuse me."

He turned away briskly.

Hattie called out, "They're nice." Her voice came out more like a whisper than she'd intended, but it was the best she could do.

The young man paused and turned back to her with a sheepish grin.

"Would you allow me to buy these for you, miss?"

She gripped the groceries yet tighter, unsure what to say. When was the last time a young man had even looked at her, let alone offered to buy her flowers? Her whole life had been spent in the shadows, hiding, trying not to be noticed. Just once it would be nice to be a normal woman, accepting a gift from an admirer. Just once.

After a span of awkward silence, she simply nodded.

He released a sort of victory yelp, bounding over to the florist leaning half-asleep in the corner.

Hattie followed with tiny steps, unsure what would happen next. Would he try to tie these flowers to her hat himself? Would she have to do it for him? What would she do with the groceries? The moment was entirely too complicated all of a sudden, but beneath it all was still a rush of excitement. This is what young women did—this is what *normal* young women did.

The young man handed over a nickel, and the florist held it up to the sunlight.

"Everything okay?" he asked the florist.

The old man nodded and pocketed the nickel. "Someone was passing wooden nickels over at the bakery. Gotta be careful."

The young man sneered. "How unbelievably crude...false

coin. It's an outrage. What sort of guttersnipe would do such a thing?"

Hattie's face flushed, the excitement turning to mortification. *She'd* been the one passing the slugs. This young man would hate her for that if he knew. He'd hate her for what she was. What was she thinking letting him buy her flowers like this? Believing that someone like her could ever allow the interest of someone normal like him?

She balled a quick fist over the spinach bag and pinched light over her face. It was a cheap magic…just her face. Just for a moment.

Hattie lifted her chin and looked him full in the eye, allowing her bangs to fall aside.

The young man turned to her with the flowers in-hand, his face beaming with a cordial smile.

That smile snapped into a tight bow, and he released a quick, "Oh."

Hattie smiled at him, and through her illusion that smile revealed several crooked, unkempt teeth. Her nose would appear bulbous to him. Her skin would seem pitted and blotched.

The young man stood paralyzed for a second, flowers held at arm's length.

She reached for the flowers and offered a husky, "Thank you."

The young man pulled away his hand, flattening them against his jacket.

"Yes, well…uh. Yes. Lovely flowers for a…lovely…" He seemed to choke on the word. "Ah, well. Good day to you."

He bustled around her with a tip of his hat and strode away as fast as he could without seeming overtly rude.

Hattie released the light pinch, barely feeling its effects on her insides. With a sad smile, she took a long whiff of the flowers, then turned for home.

Her mother greeted her in the kitchen. As Hattie laid the groceries out on the table, she received a tiny verbal reproof for spending too much money, and then a peck on the cheek for spending so much money.

"Is that ma girl?" Alton called from the front room.

Hattie pulled off her hat and draped it over the leg of a kitchen chair before sweeping in to give her father a hug.

"Where ya been, girl?"

"Shopping." She lifted the bunch of flowers. "It's spring, you know. It ought to smell like't."

He nodded, smiled, and then doubled over in a fit of coughing. These were getting far too regular, and Hattie frowned.

He lifted a hand. "I'm alright. I'm alright. You go an' help your mother in the kitchen. I'm working tonight and would like some of that fish I smell before I leave."

She kissed his cheek and stepped back into the kitchen.

Her mother gestured with a knife at the shad. "You can de-bone that when you've changed out of that dress."

"Aye, Ma."

Hattie snatched her hat and retired to her room. Shimmying out of her yellow gingham dress, she draped it carefully onto her bed. The flowers lay in a heap on the bed beside the dress. She considered them for a second, then reached for her hat. One by one, she wove the crocuses and hyacinths into the hat band.

Maybe she wouldn't wear that hat again before they wilted. Maybe she would. But it was good to know, at least just then, that she had something nice.

A filmy wash of sunlight spilled through the white drapes of Vincent's bedroom window, framing the graceful curves of a woman's face as she looked down at him. Vincent blinked several times, trying to sort out dream from reality. This vision was one he wasn't eager to shake off, but if it was morning, he'd have to get on with his day. The more he blinked, the more his eyes cleared.

And the woman was still there. He groaned, then coughed, wondering what saint had so favored him to place this angelic figure at his bedside.

The woman shushed him, then turned to the side to reach for something on his nightstand. A single lock of brunette hair slid in front of her face. The rest of her hair hugged her head in a Marcel wave, well-manicured and minding its manners. Pulling her hand back, she produced a moist cloth, which she dabbed over the sides of his cheek and his bottom lip. He saw that the cloth came away with a pink smear.

With tremendous effort, he managed to form a coherent sentence. "Who are you?"

She smiled at him, her perfect bow of a mouth curling slightly at the edges, her soft brown eyes regarding him.

With another wipe of the cloth to his forehead, she replied, "I'm Fern."

"Hmm. Vincent."

"I know that, silly."

He lifted his arms and ran his hands up and down his midsection. At some point during the night, he'd changed into nightclothes. Or at least, someone had changed him. The excruciating headache had passed, leaving only the dull thumps of a brain that had slept too long. His stomach felt leaden and inert, but as he pushed his elbow against his bed to sit upright, it stirred to life in a swirl of hunger and nausea.

He released another groan and pushed himself against his bed board to remain upright. "So," he cleared his throat. "Who are you, Fern, and why are you here? Not that I'm complaining or anything."

"They called me last night. Said you were in a bad way, and that I was to come over to keep you cleaned up and breathing."

He peered at the stained cloth. "Am I bleeding?"

"You were, but it's stopped. Had to change the bedding once, too, you were bleeding so much."

"Sorry about that." He grimaced. So much for appearing suave and debonair. "Don't remember much."

Surveying the room, his gaze fell back onto her. She wore a pink dress with white lace sleeves running down to her wrists. Three strings of pearls drooped from her neck in lazy dangles. Her dark eyebrows lifted at elegant angles, drawn in so they slanted back to Earth at the very ends. The graceful beauty, the refined elegance of this woman stirred Vincent's pulse.

"Who called you to come take care of me?" he asked.

A voice sounded from the hallway, "I did."

Vincent craned his neck to find Lefty looming in the door frame. The man had changed shirts at some point, but otherwise bore the look of someone who hadn't slept.

"Everyone okay?" Vincent asked.

"Everyone 'cept for you and the Dryfork boys."

The image of the young boy filled Vincent's thoughts, splayed out sideways on the truck bench, chest and throat riddled with bullet holes.

As Vincent closed his eyes to will away that horrific sight, Fern laid a hand on his forehead.

"His fever broke about two hours ago," she said. "He's keeping water down."

Vincent opened his eyes. "I've been awake?"

Her smile tensed. "In fever dreams. Haven't said much, which is probably for the best."

Lefty stepped into his bedroom. "This is worse than it's been in a horse's age. What gives?"

Vincent shook his head. "I was too far away. You know, when he pulled his rifle."

"Didn't feel like it was that far," Lefty grunted.

"It wouldn't, from where you were. For me it was too long a stretch, too far."

Lefty shook his head. "This isn't good, Vincent."

"That boy…"

Lefty lifted a finger at him. "You broom that out of your mind. Can't let that sit in your noodle, festering so that you can't focus on your job."

"He trusted us. And we—"

"I said forget it."

Vincent sighed, leaning his head back against the bed board.

Fern glanced nervously between the two men, keeping

her mouth tightly shut as she folded the cloth into a neat square.

"Is he good to walk?" Lefty asked her.

"He should rest some more." Her voice was soft, hesitant, almost as though she didn't dare voice the opinion.

"Should's one thing," Lefty stated. "Can is another. Can he walk? Is it physically possible?"

"He can walk," she said, her eyes downcast.

"Good." Lefty called to Vincent over his shoulder as he filed out of the room, "Get dressed. We're expected at the hotel."

After Lefty had stepped out the room and down the stairs, Fern looked at Vincent and winced. "He was worried about you."

Vincent tried to chuckle, but it came out more like a cough. "Right. Sure he was. So, what are you, a nurse or something?"

"My mother was. Served in France during the War."

Vincent nodded. "Why didn't Lefty call her, then?"

Her lips tightened and she ducked her chin. "She's gone."

Vincent winced. "Ah, hell. Shoe-polished my tonsils, again. Sorry."

Fern shook her head. "How would you have known? No, I picked up enough from my mother. Lefty knew that, so he called me. For all his grousing, he seemed awful twisted up about you."

"Well, I'm his responsibility. He's just doing his job."

"Come on," she urged as she stood up from the side of his bed. "Let's get you on your feet."

She reached both hands to him. Vincent swung his legs over the side of the bed and took her hands. With a quick tug, she pulled him to his feet.

He wavered a step, nearly toppling into her. Vincent pulled one of her hands forward as he regained his balance and a row of three bruises slipped into view from her white lace sleeve.

She jerked her arm away with a quick snap, turning aside.

Vincent squinted at her, then straightened up. "Whoa, gonna have to find my land legs over here." He snickered a little, trying to lighten the mood.

It worked. Fern peered at him over her shoulder. "We'll put you on a boat, and you can paddle your way up Light Street."

Vincent wandered to his closet, his feet gaining traction with each step.

"I want to thank you," he said as he opened the closet door. "No man should put a lady out like this."

"I'm glad to do it." She stepped behind Vincent to a chair near the door to gather her purse. "I'll see ya around."

"Will you?" he asked, regretting the eager tone he'd taken.

She hesitated in the doorway as her eyes raised to his, soft and warm. A man could lose himself in eyes like that. They lingered on him for a moment, then she broke the contact and nodded. "Yes. I'm sure."

He watched as Fern closed the door behind her, then turned to rustle through his suits hanging on the closet rod, wondering where Lefty had been hiding a jewel like her.

It took a good while for Vincent to get dressed, more from fatigue and a bone-deep aching in his arms and legs than from any of the pinch sickness. It seemed he'd pulled through. That was the way of it. All he had to do was survive, and his insides would find their way back to their appointed places. It was the sort of sickness that ran so deep, he felt it in his very soul. The sort of sickness that made him wish he were dead as he suffered through it and offered a liquor-brained manner of euphoria once it passed.

When Vincent had himself put back together and had

taken the steps to the first floor one at a time, he found Lefty reading a paper by the front door.

"You got us a car?" Vincent asked.

Lefty folded the paper and dropped it onto the front table with a nod. He sized up Vincent with dispassionate eyes. "You look like a shaved cat, but better than last night."

"You smell like a pig."

"You smell like what the pig ate."

Vincent grinned at him.

"Come on," Lefty grumbled. "Can't keep Vito waiting."

"Vito?" Vincent asked, frozen in place.

"Yeah, who'd you think? He wants the skinny from last night, especially since we showed up with four barrels of hooch and a bunch of dead bootleggers."

Vincent nodded and stepped with vigor. Capo Vito would be there! It may have been one of the most painful pinches he'd ever pulled off in the service of the Crew, but if Vito took notice, recognized the fact that Vincent had saved the lives of both Tony and Coop…? That ought to get some kind of response. A public display of gratitude. A private thank you. Just one word, really, that's all Vincent would need.

This would be a good day.

The car rattled up to the curb, and Vincent pulled himself into the back seat with a hale tug. Lefty slapped the side of the car from inside the window, and the driver steered them out onto the street.

"That dame," Vincent said as they slipped into a line of autos heading north. "Fern?"

Lefty squinted as he kept staring forward. "What about her?"

"She do this sorta thing for all us mooks? Patch us up?"

Lefty's head swiveled toward Vincent. "Why?"

"You know her, or something?"

"I knew her mother," he replied, turning his attention back to the street.

"Fern said she was a nurse in the War."

Lefty nodded.

Vincent glanced down at Lefty's right sleeve, tailored to fold right at the shoulder. "You met her mother over there, didn't you?"

"She's Cooper's girl," Lefty stated with volume. "Fern. She's Cooper's."

Vincent blinked at the comment. "Huh?"

"Don't get your eyes too shined-up over her, is what I'm saying."

"My eyes weren't—"

"Good."

Vincent nodded, then looked out his own window. Cooper's girl. That stubby man was five feet of worthless shoved into a suit. Most everyone knew that. It was his temper that sparked off the firefight outside of Cumberland. Probably his bullets that killed that little boy.

The sight of those bruises on Fern's arm slipped into Vincent's mind. A righteous sort of anger burned up inside him at the thought, but he dampened it down. She was Cooper's girl. Cooper was family. Vincent was most definitely *not* family. Lefty was right. He needed to forget about her and mind his own business, because the alternative could quite possibly lead to a bullet in the back of his head.

Cooper. What kind of Italian changes his name to Cooper?

"You were hard on him," Vincent said. "Cooper."

"Yeah?"

"About his name? How he changed it?"

Lefty turned to face Vincent. "He's a monkey banging for bananas. Playing the part of Mister Jones, wing-tipped

American. Probably would wear a blond wig, if he could get away with it."

"Are you really that upset about him giving up the Church? You really that religious?" Vincent asked.

"I'm Italian."

"So am I," Vincent countered. "Not a big church man, though."

Lefty turned away. "Yeah, I suspect something like you wouldn't be."

Vincent winced.

Some*thing* like him.

The car pulled up to the Old Moravia Hotel. Lefty was out of the car and nearly to the oversized bronze-and-glass hotel doors by the time Vincent's feet landed onto the street. Lefty held the door for him and pointed for the lobby bar. Vincent stepped into the lounge, nodding to a face or two he recognized.

No one nodded back.

That was normal. At least, for now. Once Vito heard about the time pinch, and how Tony was standing at the end of the bar with an early morning cocktail in his hand instead of bleeding out on a dirt road in Western Maryland because of Vincent, they'd start nodding back. He might never truly be family, but maybe then they'd at least treat him as if he were human and not some disgusting aberration.

Lefty disappeared into a back room tucked behind the lobby desk. Vincent leaned against the front wall, eyes on the door Lefty had disappeared into. A figure stepped into his line of sight, and he sucked in a breath to prepare for the usual "you're a freak and an abomination" pleasantries he'd grown accustomed to.

He turned to find Tony staring at him.

Tony took a sip of his drink...gin, by the smell of it.

"You're still alive," he said, sizing Vincent up foot to fedora.

With a smirk, Vincent responded, "Yeah. So are you."

Tony sucked in a breath and cradled his glass. His lips parted once or twice, but no words came.

He simply nodded once, then walked off.

Vincent shook his head. That was probably as close to a "Thank you" as he was likely to receive from Tony. As far as things usually went, it wasn't bad.

Lefty stepped into the room, and the conversation of the gathering immediately dropped to a whisper. Footsteps clacked against the marble walls of the front lobby, and the whispers fell into silence. Vito Corbi entered the lounge. The man was broad-chested, with a square head. His eyes drooped beneath boxcar eyebrows, giving the misleading impression of a perpetually sleepy man. This man had his hands on the reins of the Baltimore Crew for five years, now. It hadn't taken him long to earn the respect of every man in that room, as well as the neighboring states.

Vito marched past the bar, waving away a flute of sparkling wine the bartender offered. His languid eyes scanned the room, settling finally onto Vincent.

Vincent pulled himself off the wall and straightened his jacket.

Vito turned to approach. The men between them hustled to make a lane.

Vincent cleared his throat and firmed up his posture.

When Vito was only about three steps away, he gave Vincent a long examination.

With a voice full of gravel, he asked, "You're still sick?"

"No, sir," Vincent replied with as much strength as he could muster.

"That's good," Vito replied with measured cheer. "Because

a *stregone* that kills himself with his own magic is useless to me."

Vincent's heart fell a few inches.

Vito turned toward Tony, who likewise stiffened his posture, and asked, "Are they all dead?"

"The ones that showed up, yes."

"Our man on the inside?" Vito pushed.

Tony blanched, then answered, "Dead, too. He was…just a little kid."

Vito shook his head. Addressing the crowd, the Capo declared, "This is what we get for dealing with animals."

A spattering of dry laughter echoed off the walls.

Vito continued, "They send *bambini* to do a man's work. They take the charity of civilized men such as ourselves, and they piss on it. Squeeze a few nickels out of our associates, all because they feel emboldened." He smacked a fist into an open palm. "If these *dogs* do not respect us, then how are we seen by proper men? They see us as weak. Weak, because we have it easy here."

Vito plodded around the room, never really looking anyone in the eye.

"These goat-men from the mountains…they pull hunting rifles on our own, like they were shooting quail. No fear. No respect. Only disregard."

Vincent squinted one eye. There had most certainly been fear in the eyes of the Dryfork Brothers. But this was the story Vito had chosen to tell.

A story that didn't involve Vincent.

Vito turned and laid a hand on Lefty's shoulder. "If Alonzo had not been there, they might have shed blood. And we would be at war."

Vincent pursed his lips.

Lefty stared down at the floor as Vito shook his frame in congratulations.

"This is why we must take great care when we deal with animals. Respect their brutality, but not their minds. Caution, yes. But not fear. We have power they do not."

Vincent lifted his head a little, waiting for a look...just one look...from the Capo.

He received none.

Vito released Lefty and returned to the bar. "Our dealings with West Virginia will tax our resources for a while. Just a while. Our business on the coast must continue in the hands of outsiders." He nodded to Tony. "Are affairs in order on the water?"

Tony replied, "We have several options, and fair prices in place."

"And they are discreet?"

"Highly. Our success is their success."

Vito nodded. "*Bene.*"

The meet concluded without ceremony, certain key individuals gathering around the Capo for specific marching orders...including Lefty. Tony turned away from the gathering, sucking back on his gin as he stared out the hotel window.

Vincent gave him a nudge. "You did good last night. With the Dryforks. Almost had them eating outta your hands."

Tony shook his head and just stared.

Vincent added, "Vito should've heard you. He'd have been proud."

"I'm lucky he doesn't blame me for the whole thing coming up turnips."

"That wasn't your fault," Vincent whispered, leaning a little closer. "That was Coop, and we both know it."

"Ahh..."

"Where is Coop, anyhow? Thought he'd be here."

Tony finished his drink and set the glass down onto the marble sill. "Probably flippin' cards uptown."

"Poker hall?"

"He heads a basement operation up by St. Eustace. I told him to keep his mug underground until Vito cooled off."

Vincent nodded. "Probably a good idea."

"Whatever." Tony turned away without another word, leaving Vincent alone.

The cloud of hangers-on began to disperse as Vito retired to his back room. Vincent caught a glimpse of Lefty as he eased away from the bar.

Lefty's eyes fell onto Vincent. And he looked away. A knot tugged at Vincent's chest as he balled a fist in his pockets. That was a fine trick, taking credit for Vincent's pinch. A pinch that nearly killed him.

Lefty approached, his lips stiff. "You need a nap, or something?"

"I don't need nothing."

"You need a shave, is what you need."

Vincent sighed, then ran a hand over his cheek. Lefty... wasn't wrong.

"Come on," Lefty chimed. "We'll get us both to a barber. We look like a coupla apes over here."

CHAPTER 7

It had been a long and lean week for Hattie and her parents. Despite her spree at the market, the fish lasted for two meals, and the vegetables for three. It wasn't four days until they were back on bread and watery chicken bone soup. Hattie was sure her father could kick his cough if they could only feed him properly. He'd always been hale and strong, and possessed the frame of a capable steel worker. But when something goes sideways inside the body, no muscles could help that.

Lizzie hadn't snared a shipment all week with the Crew. The one time Hattie'd ventured back to Locust Point, she found Lizzie nipping at the bottle of whisky from her desk drawer which the woman thought was a secret. *"Everything's going to the Solomons Boys,"* she'd told Hattie.

And so, when a knock came the following Tuesday morning, Hattie nearly leapt out of her skin. She opened the door to the apartment to find a tiny boy standing with his cap in one hand and a folded note in the other.

"Miss?" he asked, holding the note out.

Hattie looked down at the adorable child and took the

note. He cupped his hand out to her, eyes round and soft, brimming with some fairly convincing tears.

"A nickel, miss?"

She grinned. "Lizzie paid you a nickel already, didn't she?"

His lip trembled.

"Save it, kid," Hattie snickered. "Go spend your nickel before someone lifts it off you."

The boy's face shifted into an expression of disappointment. "Aw, nuts."

Hattie read the note as the boy bounded down the hallway to the front stairs.

COME TO THE WAREHOUSE. WE'VE GOT A BUSINESS. L.

Rushing into her working clothes, Hattie checked on her father who was sleeping off the night's labor and gave her mother a quick kiss on the cheek. She made excellent time to Locust Point, pulling the warehouse door aside with a clatter. Hattie was expecting to find a few barrels or a skid of bottles waiting inside.

Instead, she found the all-too-familiar emptiness.

"Malloy!" Lizzie shouted from the back. Her tone was less dreary than usual. Almost bright.

Hattie trotted to the end of the warehouse and up the stairs for the office. Lizzie ushered her in with a wave of the hand, adding, "Close the door."

Hattie cocked her head. There was literally no one in the warehouse to eavesdrop on the two of them, but she obliged anyway. "You said we have some business?"

"Yes, we do. Business with Little Teague."

Hattie's brow lifted, and she took a seat. "Do we, now?"

"So, I finally grabbed Tony by the ear and sat him down to talk cheese. He confirmed the Crew's sending all their business to the Solomons Island Boys right now."

"Why?"

"Prices," Lizzie replied with a roll of her eyes. "Teague's undercutting us."

"When'd that start?"

"About the same day you and Raymond failed to get snatched by the Feds. I get the feeling he's sore about that."

"*He's* sore?" Hattie blurted out.

"So, he's trying to wait us out. Scoop up all the Crew business while they're policing the west."

"Was this gangster of yours any use to us, then?"

Lizzie leaned forward, dropping her voice to a conspiratorial volume. "Tony says Vito's hot under the collar about these West Virginians, and Tony's been playing it safe. He can't get involved with the water side of the business right now, but he's eager to keep two boats on the Bay. Little Teague may be a bargain right now, but when we pack it up his prices go straight through the roof. Tony knows that. Man's got education. And so, he's thrown us a bone."

"What sort of bone?" Hattie prodded.

"The location of the Solomons Boys' next drop."

Hattie nodded. "And what're we supposed to do with't?"

"That's up to us. With your special skills, I'm sure we'll make good use of it."

"Fine. Where's the drop?"

Lizzie consulted a note beside her elbow. "They're running some moonshine down to the Upright Citizens. Drop's at night at a tiny inlet north of Richmond by the name of Deltaville."

Hattie nodded. "I know it. What night are they planning?"

Lizzie shook her head. "What do you think?"

"Tonight?" Hattie barked.

"Which gives you more than enough time to get down there, and…improvise."

Hattie leaned back in her chair. "I could take a car."

"Cheaper just to take the boat."

"If I'm using my *special skills*, then I don't want Raymond there."

Lizzie's shot her a weary grin. "You're still keeping him in the cold?"

"It's my choice."

"I suppose so, but it might make things a little easier on you if you just told him."

Hattie shook her head. She had one person in her life who treated her like a regular human being. No awkward distance, no undue concern, no fear or disapproval in his eyes when he looked at her. The last thing she wanted was for that one person to turn into yet another pair of eyes she'd have to worry about. Someone who might have to make even more sacrifices to keep her free.

Or worse yet, let something accidently slip to someone who'd be happy to take a payday and turn her in to the mob.

"I'll hire a boat," Hattie declared.

Lizzie waved her fingers. "Suit yourself. I'll toss in extra for the transportation. This is a business expense, way I see it."

They drove to McComb's, giving Raymond a wide berth per Hattie's request. The pier was clear of Treasury men, and even if it wasn't, she was doing nothing illegal on this side of the trip. Lizzie gave her a wave as Hattie stepped down onto the wide wood planks stretching over the Magothy River, connecting several warehouses and boat slips in a tenuous ribbon. She noted that roughly half had been boarded closed. Probably the working of the Feds. The Solomons Island Boys used McComb's more extensively than did Lizzie. That was the beauty of Winnow's Slip. It was too far inland to really be considered a proper pier.

Hattie found two dark-skinned gentlemen loitering on a menhaden trawler. She inquired whether they were outbound that day, and they informed her that the waters off

Hatteras had warmed up early, sending the hot currents right up the mouth of the Chesapeake. This was good news. These men were eager for a payday, just like she was. Plus, they'd be willing to pick her up on the return once their business was done.

To their credit, the men let her be on the run down the Bay to Virginia. Sitting at the bow, as usual, Hattie tried to cook up a plan as they chugged along. She hated it when she didn't have a course of action ready to execute. Everything in its place, step by step. This was what her father had taught her. That was what kept her a free pincher. But this? This would be sheer improvisation, and the more Hattie tried to create scenarios in her mind, the more she realized she really just had to wait and see what was waiting for her in Deltaville.

The menhaden trawler dropped her off just north of her destination, and she wove her way along the wooded water-side until she reached the finger of land stretching out into the Bay. The sun had just begun to set, the eastern sky rolling into a lush cobalt blue as the clouds overhead took a pink tone. If the drop took place at midnight, she'd still have hours to wait them out. At least it was safe. There was no way either the Solomons Island Boys or the Upright Citizens would bother standing ankle-deep in mud for hours on end, feeding the mosquitoes.

Hattie followed the sliver of land farther out. A tiny ribbon of pine forest split the peninsula wider, and as the last rays of daylight began to slip up the conifer trunks, Hattie spotted a gravel dust road leading to a handful of buildings at the water's edge. She counted maybe six shanties, most likely fishing shacks and ice houses meant to capture hauls and ready them for transport inland. Nothing in Deltaville looked permanent or lived-in. This was a working site.

Stepping out into the space between buildings, Hattie

looked around. The odor of fish hung heavy in the air. The road was in poor condition, the mud reclaiming much of the gravel, but the buildings were in good repair. This site wasn't abandoned. And it was perfect for the Upright Citizens. Hattie felt a twang of jealously. Even Jake had never invested in such reliably discreet drop-off points.

But then again, he never needed to. Maryland was still a "wet" state. They could load and unload barrels at proper piers. The Treasury men were always sniffing around for actionable offenses, such as transporting liquor out of state. But they were normally easy enough to sidestep, particularly when Hattie pinched light. It was a great job to have—while there was work. This past week had brought home to Hattie just how precarious their business future was. At any moment, the mobsters could decide to divert all their distribution to someone else, or decide they needed to do it themselves.

The notion that the Baltimore Crew would pull all their trafficking off the water was a constant threat to their livelihood. Lizzie kept hearing rumors from her contact in the mob that Vito was dissatisfied with outsiders moving his hooch. Should the day come that he chose to bring the work in-house, they'd all be out of a job. Luckily, the Baltimore Crew had never really expanded their numbers sufficient to take over the distribution.

Making her way around the cluster of shanties, Hattie tugged open one door. A slate floor greeted her eyes, with thick walls lined in cork. Ice house. If it weren't for the pervasive fish stench, this could provide good cover for when the mobsters arrived. On the other hand, she mused, what if they used these buildings to store the barrels?

That was unlikely. This being a nighttime drop, the Upright Citizens were more likely just to bring a truck and carry the hooch straight back to Richmond.

Shutting the door, Hattie continued exploring the rest of the fishing camp. One by one, she scoped out the structures and the slapdash gravel paving between them. One shack sat closer to the water, apart from the rest. It was larger by footprint, if not by height. The wood planks running vertically between metal panels looked particularly weathered and mouldered. Darkened. Perhaps even scorched. It could have been some original building at this site. Maybe a fire cleared out the rest, and the current structures were hammered together a little closer to the road?

She took a couple steps toward the shack, when her eye caught some movement.

She froze.

The shadows had grown long, and the cobalt sky was high overhead with the first stars popping into life above. If she didn't move, she might not be easily seen. And so, Hattie stood stiff as a statue, her eyes glued to the shack.

More movement, and a scurry near the eaves.

Hattie released a breath and swore to herself as a fat raccoon bustled along the edge of the tin roof, clambering down the side of the front posts without any sense of hurry. Just as her heartbeat settled in her ears, she heard a new sound. She cocked her head to the water. The chug of a diesel engine inched into her hearing.

The Solomons Island Boys had arrived early, after all.

Turning, Hattie bustled back up to the fishing village, slipping inside the ice house. The cork lining in the walls proved to be a problem, as she couldn't easily spy through gaps in the exterior siding. Stepping back out, she moved for the shack adjacent. Once inside, she breathed easier…literally. The fish odor was much milder here. As the darkness of night spilled into the clearing, she found she could see just fine through the wide gaps in the wood planking.

Voices called from the waterside. Shouts of names, expletives, and grunts of exertion. At last, she spotted four young men doubled over, rolling barrels up the center of the gravel path. Most of the barrels had picked up enough mud to put any discerning customer off. But as they rolled them into a neat line not far from Hattie's hiding spot, she spotted the heads of each barrel unsullied. All four bore a wood-burned brand. DF-WV.

The brand was ornate in a folksy way, with swirls at the ends of each letter. Whoever had wrought the iron that made those brands was either very proud or incredibly bored.

A fifth figure marched up the gravel path, a wide-brimmed leather hat still covering his face.

"Someone wipe that shit off! These are city folk."

Hattie balled a fist as the face of Little Teague turned in her direction with a disapproving wince. So, Little Teague had come to this drop himself.

The Solomons Island Boys busied themselves trying to clean off the barrels, serving only to spread the mud more evenly along them, as well as their clothes. One of the Boys stepped up to Little Teague, his head moving left and right.

"Boss?"

"What?" Little Teague spat.

"Want me to clear the camp?"

Hattie's stomach flipped.

Teague snickered. "What do you want to clear? It's just a fishing camp. No one uses this site after hours."

"Word's out that the Fed's are—"

"The Feds are chasing their tails down at the Outer Banks. Got word two days ago from Charleston. All kinds of headache down their way."

"You sure?"

Teague cast an eye in a slow circle, taking in the buildings all around.

Hattie eased away from the crack in the wall.

"I'm sure," Teague announced. "Bounce on up the drive. Keep an eye out for the Richmond boys."

Teague watched him leave then fished a cigarette from a tin in his shirt pocket and lit it. He smoked with a hand on his hip, turning his back to Hattie. The barrels stood in a neat line not far from an abandoned cart that was missing a wheel. The cart looked old, probably from the original site just like the flame-licked shack down by the water.

Teague's eye fell on the cart at the same time. He snapped his fingers and pointed to it.

"Horace! Go check that buggy. Save us a heap of trouble if we can get these damn barrels outta the mud."

One of his men abandoned mud duty and inspected the old cart. He returned with a shake of his head.

"Wheel's busted. Wood looks dry rotted. No use to us."

No use to them, Hattie thought. But maybe some use to her.

The gang lost their fervor for cleaning, and by the time Teague had finished his cigarette, they had all taken seats atop the barrels.

"Get your asses off that hooch!" Teague bellowed.

None of them budged.

"Useless little beet-eaters, all of you!"

One or two chuckled, and even Teague shook his head in silent mirth. This was so different from what Hattie was used to. They acted less like desperate businessmen, and more like…brothers.

After a long space of waiting, Hattie crouched down and massaged her calves. There were no chairs or benches in this shack, and she didn't want to drop her seat into week-old fish guts. Before long, a whistle called from up the road, and Teague snapped to life. He made a cranking motion with his finger, and they all got to their feet.

In minutes, the thrum of a truck engine filtered through

the wood planks. She could feel the ground vibrate. The thrum became a crunching of gravel. A wash of light swept across the space between shacks, and a truck eased into view. It made a half-circle, turning its tailgate to the barrels.

The engine killed, and four men stepped out of the truck. Hattie recognized two of them from her business with the Upright Citizens the previous week.

"Four?" the Richmond driver shouted. "Thought we were set for six."

Little Teague stepped up and offered a hand to shake.

The driver shook it briskly, then nodded at the barrels. "So?"

Teague answered, "Two barrels were busted in some sorta hanky-panky with Vito's boys. They're a loss."

The driver eyed Teague hard, then shrugged. "Fine, but we contracted for six."

Teague held up a hand. "The Crew says you contracted for four barrels, so don't go shorting me."

The Upright Citizens turned toward Teague, postures stiff.

Teague's boys stepped around the truck, half-surrounding them.

The driver coughed, then shrugged. "That'd better be some smooth as silk moonshine for what we're paying."

"I don't care what it tastes like, as long as you pay me," Teague replied.

The tension eased a little, and the Upright Citizens reached for the barrels to load onto the truck, swearing as their hands came away smeared in mud. A quick exchange of words ensued, but Hattie's eyes were on the busted cart just beyond the barrels.

They were expecting six barrels, not four.

Hattie lifted her fingers up to the wood panels, testing out

the distance to that cart. She pinched the light just a little…
just enough to feel out the distance.

She could barely make it.

Had to get closer.

Pushing lightly onto the shack door, Hattie eased it open.
The loud conversation helped hide the noise, and she
stepped into the darkness of night on cat's feet. Foot by foot,
she slipped in a wide arc down toward the water, and into
the trees behind the fishing village.

She had to hurry. There were only four barrels. If she
didn't get the pinch off before the Richmond boys got in
their trucks, the opportunity would be lost. And they might
not be in business long enough to see another.

Hattie pressed her back against the shack nearest the
busted cart. She sucked in several breaths, then reached into
the air with her fingers.

Pinching the light surrounding the shack and the wagon,
she extended the illusion as far as she felt was safe. Often
times she didn't choose the specifics of her powers' effects.
But she'd learned how to test the cost of her power.
Depending on how long these gangsters took to see the illusion she had spun, it could be very costly indeed.

Hattie gripped the illusion with her fingers, sucking in
breath after breath as the power tore her insides. Pain lanced
up and down her midsection. A trickle of blood fell from
her nose.

And she listened for some sign that they'd even noticed
that what had been an old broken cart just moments ago now
contained a tarp that almost, but not quite, covered two
barrels bearing a DF-WV brand.

Nausea filled her throat. Her head spun in tiny starts.

She bit down on her bottom lip and closed her eyes, just
listening.

"Alright," Teague shouted as a tailgate slapped shut and bolted, "that's that."

"Here," the Richmond voice replied. "Do me the courtesy of counting it after we leave."

"I suppose I will."

A door to the truck clanked.

Damn. They were leaving.

Hattie whimpered as her fingers gnarled from the pain.

"Hold on," a voice said. It sounded close. Too close.

Had she been spotted?

Footsteps slipped through the mud nearby, and she nearly dropped her illusion to give herself at least two seconds' time to flee.

"What the hell are these?" the Richmond driver shouted.

Hattie released a tight breath and sucked in another.

Teague grumbled behind the corner of the shack, but she couldn't hear what he'd said.

The driver pressed, "Are...are those the two barrels, you side-dealing sonuvabitch?"

A grin fluttered onto Hattie's lips.

They'd taken the bait!

Teague coughed his way through several fits and starts before saying, "That cart was empty!"

"Don't look empty now, dammit!"

"I swear to Christ God, there are only four barrels!"

A grunt sounded, with some shuffling.

Car doors clattered.

And then, a noise that broke Hattie directly out of her light pinch.

Gunfire.

She released the illusion and dropped to her knees, covering her ears. War cries and pop-pops of gunfire filled the night air. A figure stepped past the corner of the shanty... one of Teague's men. He held a revolver in an outstretched hand, squeezing off two shots before a whizz sounded, and he staggered backward into a pine trunk.

His throat burst into a plume of blood, and he slid down the tree. His eyes swiveled toward Hattie, and he lifted a brow before his eyes lost all focus.

Hattie slapped hands over her mouth, trying not to gasp audibly. She'd just watched a man die in front of her. The illusion was only supposed to complicate Teague's drop, and best case scenario, his business. She knew the Richmond gangsters would be angry, but never expected it to escalate this far and this fast. She'd never wanted *this* to happen. People were dying!

Pressing her back against the shack, Hattie blinked at the gunfire on the other side of the fragile structure. The wood near her face popped into splinters as a bullet flew directly through both of the shack's walls. This was no safe hiding place. She needed to get out of the range of these bullets. Leaning forward into a crouch, she crawled on all fours into a tuft of tall grass between the clearing and the woods. Even as visions of the man's dying gaze lingered in her mind, her instincts drove her to crawl on toward safety. She had to get the hell out of there.

Hattie pulled herself upright with the aid of a tree trunk, then bustled toward the water's edge. The woods remained thick as she made alarming speed through the darkened forest. The trees cleared abruptly at the shore, and Hattie took a quick look left and right to gain her bearings. She'd popped out of the forest just east of the near-burned shack. The gunfire had faded somewhat in her retreat, but the noise grew more sporadic...and closer.

Hattie gambled on making a break across the clear space behind the old building, but jammed her feet into the mud to stop herself as three of the Solomons Island Boys appeared from the clearing at break-neck pace. Teague, himself, brought up the rear, gun blazing back toward the Upright Citizens.

"Inside!" he bellowed, and the first of his two surviving companions rushed for the scorched oak door, gripping it and tugging hard. It flew open without resistance, and he waved the second man inside.

Teague was peering over his shoulder to check on his men, then he spun to the left, lifting his arm in a painful shrug. A line of red sliced across his shirt sleeve where a bullet had just grazed him. He released a string of profanities, then fired back until his gun was empty. Tossing it aside, he turned for the shack.

Hattie watched as he strode forward. The ground beneath her feet bubbled, and she pulled her boots out of the mire, hopping back toward the pine needles. But even the forest carpet seemed to shift. A low rumble met her ears, rising like a train approaching from the distance. But there were no train tracks here.

She reached for the nearest pine, which shivered under her palm.

Screams and gunfire erupted inside the shack.

Hattie turned back to find Teague's face bathed in a dull red glow. What was going on? What the hell was happening in there? She followed his shocked expression to the old fire-licked building. That red light seeped from between the cracks of the shack's clapboards and the corners by the corrugated roofing. The rumble continued in earnest, making it hard to stand. A fire? Had someone been hiding in the shack this whole time?

She moved out of the forest just a little, feet splashing back into the mud. The rumble faded rapidly, offering a brief second of absolute silence.

Someone from the clearing shouted, "What the hell?"

The silence melted in an instance as an earth-shattering

roar thundered from inside the shack. A plume of flame mushroomed out the front door. Teague dropped to the ground just before the fire could catch his head. Hattie's eyes shot wide. A bomb? What in the hell was going on in there?

The two Solomons Island Boys tumbled out of the front door, their bodies aflame. They each shrieked and flailed, staggering away from the shack like flaming windmills. Their cries subsided as they succumbed, both dropping to the gravel dust lane leading back to the clearing. Teague pivoted on the ground, his eyes filled with terror. Footsteps pounded as the red glow advanced toward the door. Hattie sucked in a breath and watched from behind her pine trunk as a being—that was the only word that could describe it— emerged from the shack. It looked like an old man. He wore a wide-brimmed fisherman's hat and a pair of overalls tucked into waders. He had a short white beard and wild salt-and-pepper hair that hadn't been trimmed in ages.

But his eyes... What should have been eyes were a pair of flaming pits. Yellow fire licked up from the sockets like under-trimmed candles. His hands were long and gnarled, and they too sported bright flames slipping from underneath the fingernails.

Teague paddled away from the creature as it marched forward.

The flaming being cocked its head at Teague, then threw back its head to release another roar. The sound echoed through Hattie's mind, shaking her to the bone. It was loud enough for God to hear, even if he wasn't listening.

Loud pops rang out from the clearing, and the creature blinked and lifted its claws defensively. The Upright Citizens had gathered at the top of the path, their faces illuminated by the burning bodies of Teague's men. They'd aimed their guns now at the creature instead of Teague.

The bullets sprayed into the shack and against the creature's skin. Tiny splashes of bright red dotted its face and torso, as if the bullets had melted in the air before they even made contact.

The creature dropped to a bit of a crouch, its claws low to its knees, then swung them in wide arcs. As the claws sliced through the air, heat rippled and ignited within its clutches, producing balls of flame which flew up the path.

The balls of fire tumbled into a long splash of flame, rolling across the mud and up one of the men's legs. The others scrambled to the sides as the being hurled more fire through the night in their direction.

Teague crab-walked backward to give more distance. Edging out from the trees, Hattie peered at Teague with the creature's back to her. She gave Teague a wave, but he didn't seem to notice her for the flaming monster standing over him. Hattie floundered. She couldn't make a noise and risk capturing the creature's attention. But with its focus on the gangsters up the lane, all Teague had to do was move to the woods, and the two of them could escape together.

She crouched down, reaching to the high tide line to snatch a rounded stone. With a quick flick of her elbow, she slipped the stone toward Teague with the same angle one would skip a stone on a pond.

The stone slapped against a bit of gravel, tumbling into Teague's lap.

He gazed over, eyes growing yet wider as he stared at Hattie.

The noise subsided. Teague's face turned to look at the creature. It loomed over him, breathing hot jets of air from its nostrils. The creature balled a fist, and in a single furious motion, set the entire space before the shack aflame.

Teague screamed in godless pain, rolling out of the ring of fire.

The Richmond gang renewed their gunfire, and the creature pounded up the lane in a slow lope, sending balls of fire in their direction.

Teague tumbled toward the water's edge as his clothes smoldered. Hattie rushed toward him but stopped short of touching him. The water hissed and sizzled against his skin and what was left of his clothes.

Teague gasped a wheezing breath. Splashing alongside him, Hattie reached for his head to keep it above the surface. The man's face was charred, all his hair and eyebrows gone. The tip of his nose had smoldered flat, the skin crisping away. He coughed, and his lungs struggled to take in new breaths.

Hattie's tears fell onto his face like rain. "T—Teague?"

He opened his eyes to her, shocking white and blue in contrast to his scorched flesh.

"Malloy?" he whispered. "What…are you…?"

"I'm sorry. I'm so sorry."

The gunfire subsided, replaced instead by screams up the lane.

Hattie whispered, "I'll get you to a hospital. I'll…I'll carry you. Get you fixed up."

He shook his head.

"Yes," she chided. "This is my fault. I'll get you put straight. Just—"

Teague lifted a shaking hand. His sleeve had burned away, leaving a red length of cooked skin.

She followed his arm, and his hand…which was pointing at his own boat just a few yards away.

Hattie bit down on her bottom lip, then nodded.

"Alright. Let's get you on your feet, then."

She struggled to get his body upright. All his strength had left him, and it was like pulling dead weight out of the water. He managed to grip the back of her neck, however, and after considerable effort the two of them limped through the ankle-high water toward Teague's boat.

Teague trembled in her arms. The pain must be near unbearable. With a tilt of her head, she offered, "If you got any whisky, it may help."

But his eyes weren't on Hattie.

The side of Teague's face illuminated in a soft red glow.

Hattie paused, cringing in terror.

She released one of her hands from around Teague's frame, and waved it in front of her face.

"Disappear, disappear..." she muttered, pinching light over the two of them with all her power.

And all was quiet, save for the lapping water at their ankles.

Hattie caught her breath. She opened her eyes and turned her head toward the shore. The creature stood at the water's edge, its eyes and fingers burning a cool red. Its face stared forward, directly at them, though it had lost the Greek mask of fury it had held just moments ago.

Hattie blinked at it, trying to hold as still as possible. The light pinch tugged hard at her already distressed heartbeat. There was no way she could hold this up for long.

The creature took a single step forward, its eyes lifting a little. It expression was almost curious. The water gurgled and bubbled around its bare feet...just ordinary human feet, by all reckoning. It reached out with its flickering fingertips, moving in slow motions along the bubble of illusion Hattie had assembled.

Hattie stared into its eyes, and for a fleeting second she saw something besides fire. There was depth to the empty orbits of its face. Impossible depth, reaching into some endless well of darkness. And within that darkness sat several points of light.

Stars, perhaps? Or something more brilliant. Something bright hidden in that inky shadow.

The creature stepped away, steam rising from its feet. It crouched down like a child playing in the mud and slipped its index finger into the mire, pulling its finger in lazy motions, just drawing in the mud.

When it seemed satisfied, it straightened up and turned back toward Hattie.

And looked straight at her.

Nausea bubbled up through her chest, and she released the illusion. There seemed to be no point. Whatever this thing was, it could see through her light pinch.

It balled a fist in front of its chest. Not a fist of anger. This was different, as if it were holding something in its hand, something that wasn't really there. The being raised that fist out to her in a pantomime of offering.

She stood stiff. What else was there to do?

The being unwound its fingers, then pulled its hand close to its chest. The creature ducked its head once in what could have been a nod, and then turned to march back to its shack.

The door swung shut on the opposite side of the building, and the red glow within faded to darkness. Water splashed along the coastline, and a light breeze rushed through the needles above. Then the surreal serenity was broken by a wet, hacking cough from Teague, followed by a weary groan.

Hattie renewed her grip on the man and tugged him forward toward the boat. Settling him along the deck just fore of the helm, she took a quick inventory of the vessel. Diesel engine. Pump ignition. She'd seen Raymond operate his own boat enough times, and he'd even let her pilot the thing in the open water. After a minute of acclimation, Hattie had the engine started. She reached over the side, shoving off from the land as hard as she could. As the craft eased away from the shore and rocked on the slight waves, she rushed back to the helm and throttled the boat away from Deltaville and into the Chesapeake.

Teague's scarred flesh swayed suddenly before toppling forward. Hattie sucked in a sharp breath, then eased the throttle back to an idle as she tried to steady him into a seated position.

"Sorry," he mumbled. "Apologize."

"Yes," Hattie urged as she crouched beside him. "I apologize. None of this was supposed to happen. It was just a little…"

"No. Me. I apologize. For selling you out. With the Feds."

His breath dissolved into a spasm of hacking, and she reached for his shoulder.

He didn't wince when she made contact. Not a good sign.

"We'll get you to a doctor, Teague. We'll get you some medicine."

He shook his head again. "Bimini."

"The what, now?"

"Take me…to Bimini."

"There's a doctor there? A hospital?"

Teague sucked in several breaths, ramping up enough air to respond. "It's an island. East of Newport News. There's a person there…Doc Freedman. They say he knows magic."

Hattie closed her jaw as her eyes bulged.

Teague continued, "Sounds crazy, but true. Heard from the Richmond boys, while ago."

"What are you yattering about?" she grumbled.

"He's a hoodoo man from Caribbean. He makes a potion that heals. They say it heals all wounds. All…"

His voice trailed off.

"Teague, you're losing your wits. Just lie down, and I'll get you straight on to Richmond. Must be a hospital there."

He swatted at her with one arm. "Won't make it to Richmond. Bimini. Find Doc Freedman. I'll die if…if not…"

Teague closed his eyes.

Hattie sucked in a breath and watched him for a moment. His breathing continued…shallow, but steady.

Bimini Island? Water magic? Hattie shook her head and returned to the helm to steer them south toward the James River.

What sort of nonsense was he spouting? He was hallucinating, surely. Hattie had never met another pincher in her entire life, though she'd naturally heard about them. They were all property of the mob. Such was the way in America. If her parents hadn't moved to the States, she'd have most likely been taken away by the Church. But here, where there were no kings and precious few bishops, the crime families were the ones who snapped up all free pinchers using them as tools in their business dealings. It was a life of servitude, of slavery. It was Hell.

But if Hattie could have lived this long without falling into the hands of the mob families, it proved that it wasn't impossible for there to be more free pinchers out and about. And just as the Bay provided endless inlets and tree-canopied rivers to hide the booze traffic, so too could they hide a water pincher.

She eased back on the throttle once again, and checked the compass mounted to the helm panel. Newport News was just southwest. And if this magical elixir could heal Teague's burns as life-threatening as they were…it might help her Da with his lungs.

She steered the helm southwest and pushed the throttle hard.

The boat sliced through the mild nighttime surf on its way toward Newport News. She knew the terrain fairly well. Each of the tiny islands scattering out along the mouth of the Bay offered solitude and privacy. It wouldn't be hard for a

Caribbean water pincher to set up shop and hide from the mob.

The boat sputtered a bit, and she slowed to an idle to check the sight glass for the fuel level.

"Well, you've cut it close with your diesel, Teague," she mumbled. "How'd you expect to get home in the first place?"

He didn't answer.

She turned to him. "Hope you have a fuel spot you don't mind waking up in the wee hours. Teague?" She nudged his arm.

He fell sideways, face landing against the deck with a slap. "Teague?"

She reached for his nostrils and felt no breath. Laying a hand on his chest, she found it still. No breathing. No heart-beat. Cupping a hand over her mouth, Hattie slid to a crouch, and sat on the deck alongside Teague's body. Tears welled in her eyes as the boat rocked on the slight waves of open water. Moonlight spilled over the eastern horizon and Hattie cried, sobbing into her hands. After who knows how long, she glanced up at the waning moon, wiping her tears away.

"Stupid," she muttered.

It *was* stupid, this mythical elixir. Even if Teague had heard about it from the boater scuttlebutt, it was just a hair-brained yarn. A big fish story. Hattie slapped her shoulder in frustration. She was smarter than this. There were no easy fixes. No simple miracles. Nothing ever came easy, and Teague had just learned that the hard way.

Standing up, Hattie gazed down at the corpse. There was nothing she could do for him anymore. The only thing to do now was to tend to her own business. Hers, Raymond's and Lizzie's.

She crouched down to grip the body by the arm, tugging it high along the hull. With a final twist, she shoved it overboard. Teague's corpse splashed into the water, floating along for a minute until it began to dip below the surface.

This boat didn't have enough fuel to make the trip all the way back to McComb's, so she turned it around and pointed it back at the inlet north of Deltaville where the trawler would be coming for her.

As she chugged past Deltaville from a distance, she spied the tiny clearing where so many lives had just been taken by that hellish creature. A tiny flicker of flames was still visible from the water, but it was already dying down. Probably the smoldering bodies of gangsters.

Whatever that thing was, whichever corner of Hell it crawled out of, it certainly despised being provoked. And yet, despite its blazing fury, she'd seen something else in its face as it peered directly through her magic.

Something almost innocent.

"And that, dearest friends, is all the power I have this evening," Vincent drawled in his languid faux-Arabic accent. "So, I must bid you all adieu."

He withdrew through the red curtains into his broom closet, shaking his head. French, again. What was it with the French, these days? He wondered as he pulled off his fez whether The Great Damir was Moroccan. Wiping the stage makeup off his face, Vincent waited for the customers to drop their honoraria and leave. Tonight he had two old ladies and a middle-aged man. They'd made it easy on him. The man had even written out a letter to his deceased wife. Vincent played that like a fiddle.

Once he'd pulled on his jacket and ventured back out into the spiritual space, he found a surprisingly meager take waiting for him. He grumbled as he stuffed the bills into his pocket, thinking that the soup kitchen would be disappointed. That letter practically sold itself. There was no arguing the fact, though. If people were strapped, then there wasn't much to squeeze from the stone.

Easy nights were short nights, and Vincent found he still

had plenty of energy. Rather than taking his usual route home, Vincent dropped his night's earnings at the soup kitchen then spun west toward the Old Moravia. There was no official business at this hour, that he was aware of. The lobby bar ought to be lively as hell on a Thursday night. Nothing better to spend his walking-around cash on than a couple spills of the good stuff from Canada.

The air packed a nice, balmy southern breeze. The walk to the hotel was comfortable enough for Vincent to whistle some Annette Hanshaw ditty he'd heard in one of the clubs the past week. He tipped his hat to passersby and they followed suit. By the time he'd reached the hotel, he was in a glorious mood.

A four-piece band was plucking out a rhythm in the corner of the hotel lobby nearest the lounge. A muted trumpet bleated out something slow and sultry. Vincent nodded to the music as he rounded the potted palm toward the long, carved mahogany bar top. He ordered two fingers of blended Saskatchewan and found a spot near the end of the bar to people-watch. Several young couples had turned out. Men in striped suits and cufflinks; women in beaded dresses and cloches. Tobacco smoke drifted upward to the story-and-a-half ceiling, gathering in a smooth pall overhead.

The whisky was smooth. Barrel aged. Up in Canada they bothered with taking their time, but in the States, where the only places one could find regular booze was the frontier or the Old Line State, the onus was more on speed than quality.

A figure stepped directly into Vincent's view.

"Heya there, Vinnie," Tony slurred with a sloppy, drink-fueled grin.

"It's Vincent," he corrected as he shook Tony's outstretched hand.

"You here to cause some rumble?"

"Nah, I'm peaches and cream tonight."

Tony snickered as if Vincent had told a devious joke. He swayed a little, then turned to lean against the bar.

"You got a birthday or something I don't know about?" Vincent asked. "Hittin' the cheer kinda flush, there."

"Naw. Just knocking the edge off."

Vincent stood in silence alongside Tony for a moment. Having a casual conversation with one of the Crew felt unnatural. No one paid him a second thought, unless it was to keep him at arm's length. If Tony hadn't been three elbows deep in his own gin, he'd probably have done the same.

The silence bothered Vincent, and he chose to pull the conversation forward.

"What's got your nerves up?"

"Ain't nothing. Just business."

"I know business."

Tony laughed loud enough for people nearby to look. "Hell, Vinnie. You know witchcraft. *I* know business."

"It's Vincent."

"It's just these jumped-up boat people causing trouble."

"What boat people?" Vincent asked.

"The ones what run our hooch out to the Carolinas and up the coast? You know."

"Hadn't thought much about it."

"Yeah, well, I have. Vito's got me in charge of keeping them in line and paid what he thinks is a reasonable fare. Problem is…what he thinks is reasonable ain't always what they think is reasonable."

Vincent nodded. "Them's the breaks, huh?"

"It's broke, alright. Had a nice thing going for a week or so, ever since these Dryfork Reubens tried to end-run us. Now we're missing a whole shipment, and I'm probably down to one boat now."

"Lost a shipment?" Vincent released a whistle. "You gonna be okay?"

"Depends on whether we keep things smooth with Richmond. If not…" Tony stared into space for a moment, then pounded his entire drink.

He slapped a hand onto Vincent's shoulder, which slipped off at a lazy angle, and turned to order another. Vincent shook his head and pulled his attention away from Tony. That was the biz. Great trust is placed, and great consequences are paid. Nothing was low stakes. Everything was life-or-death in this world he lived in.

A woman in a knee-length vermillion dress stepped into the lounge. A red velvet cloche sat atop her head, its tulip brim cocked just over her neatly lifted eyebrows, her bow mouth outlined in red.

Fern. Vincent leaned toward Tony, and said, "I'll see you later."

Tony released a non-committal mumble and busied himself with remaining upright.

Taking his glass, Vincent wove through the crowd around the series of settees and lounge chairs, ducking through the lazy green fronds of a palmetto pot. Fern was gripping a flute of bubbling white wine, staring out the front window at the street.

This was stupid. Dangerous. But what the heck. A guy should be able to talk to a gal without getting shot. Just in case, Vincent cast a glance toward the lobby. There was no sign of Cooper.

As he approached from behind, Fern twisted away, turning fully toward the window.

"Hiya, there," he offered, standing alongside her at the window.

She didn't respond, choosing to mumble something passingly polite.

He remained there in silence, before adding, "I wanted to thank you for what you done for me. Much obliged."

She tilted her face toward him, and her eyes widened. A brilliant smile swept across her face. "Oh, Lord! I didn't recognize you."

Vincent grinned, lifting his drink. "It's on account of I'm wearing clothes, I'm sure."

She laughed, the sound as elegant and beautiful as the rest of her. "Hello, Vincent."

He smiled. At least she got it right. "So, that's not usual for me, meeting ladies in my nightclothes. I'm usually more put together, I'll have you know."

She angled her head slightly to the side and gave him a charming smile. "Well, there was a good reason for that. You have a condition. Don't you?"

A *condition*? As if his ability to cast magic was on par with a persistent illness. Taking a breath, he let what he assumed was an innocent comment pass. "Sometimes the magic takes a lot out of me. Sometimes it makes me sick."

"Where…did you learn it?" she asked in a near-whisper, eyeing him with a mixture of awe and admiration.

"Learn it? Oh. No, I was born like this. All of us pinchers are."

"Pinchers? Is that what they call you?" she asked, her eyes warm on his face.

"It's a name that stuck. We pinch things, y'know? Like me? I pinch time."

"How?" she pressed.

"Don't rightly know. It comes to me like someone holding their breath. I just know that I mean to do it, and it happens. And I'd better start being more careful before it kills me."

She nodded. "It always hurts?"

"Every time. But not so bad, if I keep it cheap."

"Okay, well you'll have to explain that one to me."

He smiled and turned to face her, noting she was continuing to keep him partially in profile.

"It's like this. I decide to pinch time whenever it suits me. But it's not worldwide. Just where I am and where they are."

"They being…?"

"Whoever I need to mess with. Now, if I wanted that band over there to keep playing, but no one else would see it? I could do that. I'd pinch time, and everyone between me and the band would be frozen all sudden-like in their own bubble. But that's a hell of a distance, pardon my French. It's gonna cost me a lot more, as opposed to something like pinching a few feet around the two of us."

She dropped her head, then eyed him with a teasing smile. "You're suggesting you want to pinch me?"

He shot her a puzzled frown. "Well, I *could*. Or I could exclude you. You and me would be here, while everyone around us was stuck in place."

"Sounds complicated."

"Like I said, I just do it. And I know what I can get away with and what's going to cause me trouble."

Fern sipped her wine. "Then you are a rare man, indeed."

He frowned, unsure what that meant.

"You doin' okay?" he whispered.

"What do you mean?"

Vincent tried to lean in, but she stiffened, so he held his place. "I saw those marks on your arm, a week ago," he whispered.

She reflexively pulled her arm behind her.

"Look, if Cooper's hurting you, there's guys who'll take care of him."

"Like who?" Her voice was brittle.

"Like me," Vincent replied before he had a chance to think about the ramifications of what he was offering. Cooper was family. He wasn't. The price for sticking his nose in would be steep, but could he stand back and do nothing while that pig hurt a woman? He'd been complicit in the slaughter of so many. And that boy the other week… There had to be something he stood up for. Something or someone. Otherwise wasn't he just the monster they made him out to be?

"Don't." She looked away. "Everything's okay. Don't interfere. You'll only be stirring up trouble for yourself."

"It's not right. He shouldn't be treating you like that."

She set her wine down and turned for the lobby. "It was nice seeing you again, Vincent."

"Oh, wait. Don't go. I'm sorry for upsetting you."

She paused.

"It's bad luck to waste champagne," he added.

Fern sighed, then turned to face him. A bruise-purple half-circle hung beneath her right eye. Vincent sucked in a breath.

"I'm perfectly fine, Vincent," she stated with exaggerated clarity. "But thank you for your concern."

She took her flute, drained it, then handed it to him with a smile that wobbled a bit at the edges. Vincent gripped the stem of the flute dumbly, watching as she turned and made a quick exit.

A knot formed in his chest, and not from his powers. This was volcanic. Magma threatening to shoot up and out of his throat. What sort of untamed animal did that to a woman? He knew what sort…and he knew where the sonuvabitch did business.

Screw the ramifications.

Vincent set down both glasses and turned for the exit, abruptly altering his plans for the rest of the night. As he was about to leave Lefty stepped through the lobby doors, his wingtips clacking against the terrazzo floor. Vincent held up, taking several short breaths as Lefty approached.

"You weren't at home," Lefty grumbled.

"Having a drink," Vincent replied through gritted teeth.

Lefty's brow lifted. "What's your beef?"

"Nothing. Just…got a problem I have to tend to."

Lefty held up his arm, bracing it against Vincent's shoulder. "I saw Fern walk out just a few seconds ago. You need to ice your heels."

"You see her face?" Vincent spat.

"Listen, he's a cur-dog. Everyone knows this. And sure, someone's going to give him a what-for one of these days. Probably going to be Fern, but it can't be you. And anyway, right now you and me have business."

Vincent shook his head, staring at the doors. He released one more breath, then cleared his throat. "What business? It's late."

"I know, but this comes from Vito. There was some trouble down in Virginia."

"Yeah, I heard. Tony's on a toot back in the bar."

Lefty shook his head. "Don't half blame the palooka. He's on a riot seat."

"What's our business?"

"Took me all day on the phone with the Richmond boys, but we got an agreement. We gotta blouse down to some finger of mud by the name of Deltaville and meet one of the Upright Citizens' pinchers."

Vincent squinted. "One of their *pinchers*?"

"Yeah. What about it?"

He shrugged. Vincent had met a pincher from New York City, and one from Philadelphia. But those were rare moments in his solitary life. Any chance to share space with another of his kind was golden. This might be a good night after all.

* * *

THE DRIVE to Richmond was longer than Vincent had counted on. Before they'd hit the road, he had changed into something less urban, and Lefty had made a stop at the church for whatever it was he did there. The sun had filled the eastern sky with powder-blue by the time they'd pulled onto a miserable gravel dust road leading into a ribbon of pine trees.

Lefty eased the car up a tiny grade until the trees gave way to a clearing of dog-eared shacks. Vincent stepped out of the car, taking in the odors swilling around the clearing. Pine. Old fish guts. And something like burned bacon, but sweeter. And sicker.

And then his eyes caught the source of the odor. Several bodies lay beneath tarps, most of them in a row.

Lefty wound his way around the front of the car, pointing to a spot at the far end of the clearing. A man stood alone, his back to them.

Lefty nodded to Vincent. "That's the guy, I think."

The man raised a hand, angling it just an inch or so. The wind eased off the water with the motion, sweeping away the foul smells of the clearing.

Vincent smirked. "Yeah, that's our Jake."

They approached the man, who was decked out in a light gray suit and fedora. He kept his hand in the air and turned at the very last minute. His face was genial, if smug. He had light blond hair and eyebrows, with piercing blue eyes. His nose angled at just too perfect a shape to look natural. The man appeared as if he was chiseled from some hunk of marble by Michelangelo.

"Gentlemen," he purred. "Which one of you is Vincent Calendo?"

Vincent extended a hand. "That's me."

He shook Vincent's hand with an alarmingly firm grip.

"Elmer Capstein. It's a genuine pleasure." The man spoke with a white bread accent, no hint of color or heritage.

Lefty nodded. "You been here long?"

Capstein gestured at the campsite. "Only about an hour. What we're looking at is a massacre."

Vincent turned to take in the scene. At least a dozen bodies had been covered.

"You policed these bodies?" Lefty asked.

"I brought canvas, just in case. Almost didn't bring enough."

"What happened?" Vincent asked.

"That's what we're here to determine," Capstein answered. "We know this." He stepped forward to approach the road entrance. "We sent a party to pick up a delivery of six barrels from you people."

Lefty corrected him. "Four."

"My people say six."

Vincent muttered, "Maybe we're onto what went sideways?"

Capstein pointed to the nearest sheds as he continued. "I found wood all chewed up from bullets. Hell of a firefight."

Lefty said, "If your men got itchy over missing two barrels, things probably fell to shit."

"I'd accept that," Capstein said, "only for the fact that all these bodies were burned."

"Burned?" Vincent asked.

"Yes."

"Who would just burn a body and leave it lying here?"

Capstein smirked. "That's the question." He took a seat on the tailgate of an unblemished truck, slapping his hand against…something. A cloud of dust lifted from dried mud, slaking off to reveal barrels. "Another question being, who'd do this and leave four barrels of giggle water just sitting here all loaded nice and tight in a perfectly good truck?"

"These barrels came from West Virginia. I recognize the brand," Lefty said.

Vincent leaned in to brush away more of the mud, revealing a florid wood-burned DF-WV brand. "These came from that business with Tony and Coop?"

Lefty lifted a brow at Vincent, who decided to clam up. Capstein hopped back off the barrel, dusting off his trousers with a flick of a finger and a sudden gust of wind.

Vincent grinned at the motion. "So, you're an air pincher, huh?"

Capstein's smirk broadened into a genuine smile. "Born and bred. And you, sir, I hear are a time pincher. I find that impressive, believe you me."

They shook hands once again.

Lefty interrupted with a grumble. "These weren't *our* men. All our water traffic goes to freelance boat-leggers."

Capstein shrugged. "Then your men better say some prayers and give at church, because your boat-leggers are fried up nice and crisp."

"Feds?" Vincent asked.

"No," replied Capstein. "Feds may plug them all with lead, but this sort of thing is just…medieval."

"Any signs of car tracks?" Lefty eyed the gravel road.

"This truck was the only thing in and out. Doesn't discount a water assault, though."

Lefty shrugged his assent, then moved out to investigate the scene further. Capstein approached Vincent, hands in his pockets. Vincent gave him a nod, and the two watched as Lefty poked and prodded at the truck, the barrels, and the surrounding shacks.

At length, Vincent straightened up, then snapped his fingers.

"Lefty," he called from across the clearing, "what if this was the work of a pincher? Like, say a fire pincher?"

"No," Lefty said, "Not possible."

"Why not?" Vincent prodded.

Lefty answered, "Because there's no such thing."

Capstein added, "He's right. Pinchers come in all sorts of colors and flavors, but no fire pinchers."

"Oh." Vincent looked over to Lefty. "How did you know that?"

Lefty shook his head. "Think you're the first pincher I've met?"

Capstein took a step forward, his face easing into a calculating cast. "However…"

"What?" Vincent asked.

"Well, it's ridiculous. Odds are practically impossible. But, if we're talking about any given possibility…this could be the work of a Hell pincher."

Lefty cocked his head. "I never heard of no Hell pincher before."

"I suspect not."

Vincent made a winding motion with his open palm, and Capstein cleared his throat. "Hell pinchers. They're not like you and me. Not born with our powers. They're something different. They have access to dark, ancient secrets. Old secrets. Secrets that punch through the normal order of things."

"So…wizards?" Lefty asked.

"It's not a terrible term for it," Capstein answered. "They study dark arts. Methods of twisting nature and exerting their powers over the forces of Hell itself. Hence the moniker."

Vincent released a low whistle. "That's some head cheese!"

Capstein snapped his fingers. "In fact…" He trotted away without finishing his sentence.

Vincent and Lefty exchanged glances, then rushed after

Capstein as they took a turn down a slight hill toward the water's edge…

…and a burned-out shack with a tin roof.

"What?" Vincent prodded as they came to a halt in front of the shack.

Capstein led them on, off the gravel path, past the shack, and nearly to the water's edge.

"Peel your eyes on that." He pointed to the ground just above the tide line, lapping at the rocks and oyster shells tracing a white line along the coast.

Lefty crouched down, peering into the mud.

Vincent shook his head. "I don't see nothing."

"Then look harder," Capstein chided.

Lefty nodded. "Yeah…this make sense to you, Vincent?"

Vincent sighed, then crouched down beside Lefty. "It's mud."

Lefty pointed, his finger inches from the surface of the mud, and Vincent finally saw what it was that had Capstein in a lather.

A tiny circle had been traced into the mud, now dried and semi-firm. Three arcs circumscribed the circle, not quite touching each other.

"Someone had a tickle for art?" Vincent shrugged.

"So, this don't mean anything to you?" Lefty asked.

Vincent stood up. "Not a damn thing."

Capstein eyed Vincent, then nodded his assent.

Lefty shook his head. "You think this is all because of some sorta Hell pincher witchcraft?"

"It's possible. Worth looking up. It's more than we had, at any rate."

Lefty stood and dusted off the bottoms of his trousers. "So, we're talking about a rogue element. Some maniac with a head full of mischief, and this had nothing to do with either Richmond or Baltimore."

Capstein nodded.

Lefty continued, "It's damned unfortunate, and our sympathies go out to you and the families of your men up there. But, when I go back to Baltimore, I have to tell Capo Vito something concrete."

"And you don't want to spin a yarn about warlocks? I understand," Capstein said.

"I just need to know that the Upright Citizens aren't holding this against the Baltimore Crew. If we iron that daisy out flat, then I think we'll have sunny skies come tomorrow and the next day."

Capstein snickered. "I assure you, I'm confident that the Baltimore Crew is not capable of this sort of violence."

Lefty's face took a hard edge, but Vincent chuckled. The three men withdrew from the shack, but Vincent paused, spotting something odd. "What's that?" he asked, stepping toward the shack.

Capstein stiffened, then rushed to join him. "What is it? What'd I miss?"

Vincent paused at the side of the shack, running a finger along the outside of the planks. The finger came back covered in soot. But resting in the face of the wood, now cleared from who knows how much ash, was a deep rut.

"Don't know," Vincent muttered. "Sorta caught my eye."

"What?" Capstein urged.

Vincent gestured in an arc. "You don't see it?"

"No."

Vincent reached into his lapel to pull his handkerchief and began dusting off a wide swath of wood. Once he was done, and his handkerchief was pitch black, the wood revealed an ornate set of carvings. Two circles, one scribed around the other, with tiny glyphs dug into the wood at jagged angles.

Lefty released a low whistle. "That, right there, is infernal."

Capstein eyed the carving with suspicion, then leveled a glance at Vincent. "I've been here an hour and didn't see this."

Vincent shrugged. "I forgive you. Come on, let's take in the rest of this joint."

They circled the building, and when they were all the way around, Vincent had indicated one such carving on each of the four walls.

"It's like whoever built this shack," Vincent mumbled, "meant to keep something in."

"Why do you say that?" asked Capstein.

"Just…I don't know. They look like locks to me."

"Locks?"

"Locks."

Capstein shook his head. "The door's ajar. Not like anything's stuck inside." He stepped toward the door, and Lefty lurched forward.

"You sure you want to do that?" Lefty asked. "I mean, if whoever burned up your boys is still here…"

Capstein grinned. "Then they'd have burned us up by now, don't you think?"

He reached for the door. Vincent stood alongside him, peering through the crack of the opening at the darkness inside. Capstein eased the door open, which slid against crude hinges without much noise. Once the door was open, the three stared inside. The early morning rays still hung low over the eastern tree tops, and the scant light did little to illuminate the interior.

Vincent cleared his throat, then stepped inside the shack.

"Fellas?" he called from inside. "You should take a gander at this."

Capstein and Lefty joined him. The shack was surprisingly roomy on the inside. A neat cot rested along the far wall. A series of hooks on the wall carried a cold-weather coat, a rain slicker, and the third was bare.

"Cozy," Lefty muttered.

Vincent raised both hands, shooting his fingers at the walls. "This…this is something else."

As their eyes adjusted, the other two noticed another glyph carved into the inside of the wooden planks. Then another. And another. Hundreds. On all walls. Even the ceiling. No two were alike, and none bore a letter of any language they understood.

Capstein sucked in a breath, then whispered, "They weren't attacked from the water. This Hell pincher lives here. They just chose the wrong spot to do the drop off."

Vincent gazed at the array of occult carvings. They seemed ham-fisted and rough, like a child trying to carve his name into a tree with a pocket knife.

Lefty repeated, "This Hell pincher *lives* here?"

"Most likely," replied Capstein.

"Then, it's in our interests to leave before he returns. Yes?"

The three men exchanged glances, then made a quick exit, taking care to close the door behind them. Once they were on the opposite side of the clearing, and the morning sun had bathed their faces in warm light, Capstein swung his arm toward the truck, and the Volvo parked just beyond.

"Gentlemen," he declared. "Seeing that this was one enormous misunderstanding that nearly lead to some unpleasant business between our families, I suggest we capitalize on the opportunity and turn things around."

Lefty squinted. "How so?"

"Come to Richmond," Capstein answered. "Surely you haven't eaten yet. The Upright Citizens would be honored to host you for the day. Show you the city. Build bridges."

Vincent thought of the long drive down, and his back

began to ache preemptively. "Sounds aces," he said to Lefty. "I'm fit to eat a horse."

Lefty nodded. "We'd be rude to say no."

Capstein clapped his hands. "Excellent! You boys just follow me in. There's a gin joint off the river that serves meals all hours. Cook's name is Bertha, and she makes a poached egg and grits that'll give you religion!"

Lefty sneered at the comment but stepped into his car without another word. Vincent followed suit. As the auto roared to life, and Lefty steered them after Capstein's Volvo, Vincent turned in his seat to peer back down to the Hell Shack.

Those symbols. They were utterly alien to him. But they felt familiar...natural.

As if they were somehow a part of him.

CHAPTER 9

Hattie sat bolt upright in her bed, her nightgown soaked in sweat. Sucking in fast breaths, she willed away the image of Little Teague's scorched face. Two nights, now. Two nights of horrible dreams. His black-and-red crisped face, with the shocking whites of his eyes pleading for her to take him to the magic man on Bimini Island.

Two nights dreaming of that...whatever it was. That demon in the skin of a fisherman. Its eyes, those eternal depths, the rage and fury of a caged animal just yearning to be set free.

Hattie ran a hand over her forehead, checking that she didn't actually have a fever, but no, it was just night terrors haunting her. Getting out of bed, she peeled off her nightgown to mop herself off with a white linen napkin she'd lifted from a restaurant about a year ago. She hadn't heard from Lizzie, yet. Not since she'd spun the whole tale of Deltaville, and the massacre that ensued. Lizzie seemed to take the death of Teague and his men in stride, while utterly ignoring the more fascinating elements to the account. The woman didn't strike Hattie as the type to place faith in anything, much less tales of fire-spewing demons.

Since she wasn't sure if she'd have work that day, she hesitated near the foot of her bed. Her dress? Or her working clothes? Her mother called her for breakfast, and she made a snap decision. Dress.

Both her parents were sitting at the kitchen table, and Hattie blinked as her father turned to her with a smile.

"There's my girl!"

"Da? Not working last night?"

"Sixth day," he said, waving his hand over a bowl of oats set at her place. "I get to feel almost human…" He released a flurry of coughs, before nodding to her. "Almost."

Hattie took a seat to eat her oats. More water than grain, but it was better than nothing.

"And you? Are you working today?" her mother asked her.

"I don't think so. Not that I've heard, any rate."

Alton snickered. "Saints bless us…we're all free for a day!"

Hattie beamed at him. "Well, we can't waste it now, can we? What'll we do with our stolen time?"

Her mother crossed her arms and pouted at her bowl.

Hattie's smile faded. "Oh, Ma. You're…?"

"I work the second shift, thank you for noticing."

Alton waved his hand at her. "Now, Branna. Don't you go sulking at us."

Hattie put a hand on his arm. "Da."

He shook his head. "It's a fine thing she's working. We all do our part. And we all work hard and well. No one should feel guilty over a moment's peace, 'Attie."

Her mother sighed. "It's fine, Alton. The two of you should make the best of't. It's been too long since you've been under the same roof, and one or the other wasn't asleep."

Hattie nodded. "What, then? Waterside? The park?"

Her father winced. "Not sure I'm up for a long walk." He thought for a moment, then snapped his fingers. "Say…the Metropolitan's playing Little Annie Rooney. Have you seen't? Mary Pickford, you know."

Hattie shook her head, biting back a grin at her father's adoration for the spunky actress.

"There, then," he declared with a slap of his palm against the table. "We'll take in a picture show."

The two finished breakfast and lingered just long enough for Branna to insist that they get going. The weather was bright and sunny, and the warmer air suited Alton's lungs. They took a casual pace down to Light Street, being sure not to push his legs harder than his breathing could handle.

The matinee for Little Annie Rooney was nearly empty. The Metropolitan Theatre had turned the show back around in between new releases, but anyone who hadn't seen it the previous year was probably either at work or wasn't likely to see it at all. Hattie stepped up to the box office and fished in her clutch for coins when her father reached out to grab her arm.

"What're you doing?" Alton shook his head. "No daughter of mine is paying my way to see Mary Pickford!"

She jabbed him in the ribs but couldn't stop him from paying for their admission.

"You can't afford this sort of thing," she grumbled.

"I'm paid well enough to eat and see Mary Pickford. We may be poor, but poor people can have nice things, y'know. It's not just the fat cats up on Druid Hill."

"Still…"

"It's done. Now go hold the door for your Da."

As they settled into the dead center of the seats, and the screen flickered to life with its bold, bright flashes and shadows, Hattie entwined her arm around her father's, leaning into him the way she did when she was ten. He sat there, eyes glued to the picture. Her father had always been mesmerized by the cinema. She wondered if he wouldn't spend his life inside one of these kinos, if he had a million dollars and no reason to work.

They spent the next hour and a half together, all by themselves, in that dark, cool room. When it was over, Hattie helped her father to his feet, and they left, taking a stroll the long way up Charles Street. It was past noon, and Branna would have begun her shift at the mill by this point. So, there was no hurry in the world.

"You shoulda been a movie star, 'Attie." Alton leaned over and kissed the top of her head.

"I suppose so," she mused. "I could look like anyone, if I chose. As long as they kept the script short." She hopped forward a step or two, lifting a dramatic arm to her forehead, and affected a deep accent. "I could be...Greta Garbo."

Alton puckered his lips.

She shrugged. "Lillian Gish? I could make my face whatever sells tickets."

Hattie looked left and right and, satisfied no one was looking...she pulled a flat palm over her face to reveal the illusion of Lillian Gish.

Alton reached for her hand and batted it down. Hattie released her illusion, eyes to the ground. After a ferocious coughing fit, and a moment to catch his breath, Alton took Hattie by the hand.

"You shouldna do that in public!"

"Sorry, Da. I was only—"

"Damn it, girl. We've come this far. We can't have you doing this, not four blocks from those gangsters."

She blushed and kept her eyes glued to her shoes. After a long moment, Alton's wheezing subsided.

He squeezed her hand. "Besides. You're more of a Mary

Pickford than that Lillian Gish woman. You have her look without having to use your talents."

Hattie peered up at her father. "Nah, you're just biased."

"No," he urged. "She's a good Irish girl, like you."

"Da, she's from Canada."

"She's Irish," he insisted. "Fulla piss an' vinegar, just like my 'Attie. All you need is your own personal William Haines, now."

She snickered. "You found one of them at the market, did ya? Well, I won't turn away William Haines if he comes courting, but if I had my choice in the matter, I'd prefer Valentino."

He shook his head with a chuckle. "There she goes, pining away for Italian men. You'll drive me to drink, you know that?"

"Well, he'd be a fine Catholic. Wouldn't he?"

He draped her arm around his and pushed them forward. "You get on with it, then. Find yourself a Rudolph Valentino, and make me some fat, scrappy grandchildren."

She squeezed his arm. "I've got more than enough time for that sort of thing."

Even as she said it, a moroseness settled over her mind. Sure. She had time, but did her father? With this cough, she worried he wouldn't see Christmas, let alone any fat scrappy grandbabies. If there was anything that could clear his lungs, she'd burn down the gates of Heaven to find it. Any wizard's wand. Any magic elixir.

Bimini Island. Doc Freedman. A potion that heals any illness or injury.

But that was a myth…wasn't it? She shook her head clear of these thoughts, and tried to enjoy the walk, laughing over the opening scenes of the movie with her father. When they returned home, she found Lizzie's car parked in front of their apartment building.

Hattie pulled her arm free of her fathers, saying, "Da, go on up. I have some business."

Alton glared at the car, then at his daughter. Nodding, he made his way into the building alone while Lizzie stepped out of the car.

"Late in the day for work, isn't it?" Hattie asked.

"Get used to it," Lizzie replied with an eager smile. "I just had a visit from Tony. Didn't take long for the Crew to start panicking. They know we're their only business on the water, so they're loading us down with work before I have a chance to hike our rates."

"Why didn't you?"

"Because this is an opportunity," Lizzie said, pulling her by the arm out of the street. "We show the Crew that we're still more affordable than their own people, and we'll have work until we both retire."

"I suppose I should get my working clothes, then."

"Do that. I'll take you to Winnow's Slip. Raymond's already getting his boat fueled up."

"What's the job?"

"A courtesy scoop from the Carolinas. It'll be a water transfer. You're meeting a trawler with ten barrels of Jamaican rum."

Hattie wrinkled her nose. "Tribute to the Crew?"

Lizzie nodded. "Acknowledgment that they don't need to sell Vito their rum, but they do anyways to keep things nice and civil. And to keep him from flooding the back slopes with moonshine and driving down the prices."

Hattie nodded, pondering the notion that Lizzie was this eager to do business with the Carolinians after what had happened to Jake. But, it was business for the Crew and as much as she disliked dealing with the Carolinians, the mob would have their protective arm over the run. It should be easy. Safe. And ten barrels of Jamaican rum was some pricey cargo.

"How far do we have to travel?"

"Cape Charles. Right by the ocean."

Hattie groaned. "That's hours out. Another nighttime ride, then?"

"Like I said," Lizzie replied with a smirk. "Get used to this. We're working straight on to the weekend, according to Tony. Man's on the hot seat, and he's trying to stay a step ahead."

"Right. Give me a few minutes."

Hattie withdrew to her apartment. As she entered, she found her father with his tin cup and a bottle of something amber.

"Where'd you find that?" she asked, cocking an eyebrow at the contents.

"What? I bought it."

"From who?"

He scowled. "What business is it of yours? I'm a grown man, I am. And if I want a spot of whisky, by Mary I'll have it."

She rolled her eyes. "It's a waste. You should save that sort of coin for food."

"Bah." He poured his drink and took a quick sip.

"Besides, it's not strictly legal."

"Not according to our fine governor," Alton announced with a broad smile and a grandiose wave of his cup.

"You want to have the booze money coming in, Da. Not going out."

"Helps my cough." He took a quick sip.

Hard to argue with that. "Well, take it easy on the stuff, then. I have to go to work," she told him. "Tell Ma I won't be back until late."

Hattie ran upstairs, changed into her working clothes,

then paused by her father's chair to give him a kiss on the forehead on her way out. "Don't stay up for me. It might be morning before I get home, or later."

As she closed the door behind her, she could hear his coughing all the way down the stairs.

* * *

RAYMOND GAVE her a wave as she trotted up to the boat.

"Hey, girl. It's been a week of months."

"How are you, Raymond?"

"Tired. Can't get a wink of sleep."

"Little one still crying the colic?"

"Nadine says it ain't colic. Says he's just cranky and likes torturin' us."

She murmured in sympathy and hopped aboard. Raymond piloted them out into the water as the sun began to set, silent until they'd cleared the mouth of the river, rounded Kent Island and reached the wide Bay.

"So," Raymond barked over the chug of the engine, "Little Teague's gone?"

Hattie wrapped her arms around her chest, then nodded.

"Lizzie says I missed a hell of a show."

"She wouldn't know."

Raymond beckoned for her to join him by the helm. She held her position. This wasn't anything she wanted to talk about, but they'd be hours on this boat, coming and going. There would be no way to ignore it so she made her way aft and leaned against the engine housing as Raymond peered at her expectantly.

He said, "I hear he got burned up bad."

"Aye."

"What'd you do with his body?"

She shuddered and looked away. Finally, she said, "Dumped him overboard. Middle of the Bay."

He shook his head. "I hate to think about you being there all by your lonesome, like that. Wish I coulda helped."

"No, you don't. It was worse than all that. It was a horrible thing to see."

"I seen people get shot."

"You've never seen anything like this," she chided. "I don't think anyone has. It wasn't just the Richmond people spraying lead. There was someone…something…there. It did the burning. There was a sort of rage, about't. And fear. People were on fire and screaming. It was horrible."

Raymond nodded.

Hattie eyed him. "Don't suppose Lizzie told you about the demon, then?"

"Listen," he said with a sympathetic smile. "After what you seen, I'd see demons, too."

"Don't do that," she said. "I saw what I saw."

He lifted hands in surrender and busied himself with the helm.

She smacked his arm. "You brought it up, you bully."

"Brat."

They continued in silence down the center of the Bay, where eyes on the shore were less likely to pay much notice. The sun fell below the horizon, and stars popped into the darkening sky overhead. Hattie hummed one of the folk songs from the Old Country, which her mother used to sing when she cooked. As she did, the engine eased down to a dull chug. Turning, Hattie found Raymond grinning at her.

"Well, if you're gonna sing, sing so I can hear it."

She rolled her eyes. "I was humming. I wasn't singing."

"Why not?"

"I'm no good at't, is why."

He lifted a brow.

Hattie shook her head. "Spare your ears, Raymond. Let's get this boat moving."

He killed the throttle.

She turned toward him with hands on her hips. "Oh, now you're asking for't!"

"I am," he grinned. "I'm askin' for you to sing me a song."

"Are you, now? And what entitles you to a song, and not me? Why don't *you* sing, if you want traveling music so much?"

He released a thunder-laugh, and said, "That's fair." He cleared his throat, and as he hammered down the throttle to send the engine roaring back to life, he released a bass melody that rolled underneath the engine's noise.

"Gonna lay down my sleepy head, down by the riverside. Down by the riverside, down by the riverside..."

Hattie turned to watch the water pass by, her mouth drawn into a line of exasperation. She'd lived as a free pincher most of her life, but that freedom came with a heavy burden—a burden of constant vigilance. She had to watch for the gangs who'd scoop her up and press her into their service. She had to watch for short-dealing on the water from the rest of the freelancers trying to earn a penny more than she did.

"Gonna lay down my burden, down by the riverside..."

She had to make sure no one assumed they owned her, no one claimed a command over her actions. No one. Not even her best friend.

Her frown smoothed as Raymond sang. His voice was strong, but easy.

"Gonna lay down my sword and shield, down by the riverside..."

She hated to admit it, but the music made the time pass as if someone had pinched it.

An incoming boat approached, its lights low to the horizon. Raymond eased their boat toward the western shore and piped down. They sat in silence for several minutes as the boat passed. A single old man offered a polite wave as the vessels slipped past one another. Raymond kept an eye on it as it retreated behind them on its way to wherever. Satisfied that they'd earned no undue interest, Raymond bumped the throttle, but did not continue his song.

Hattie cleared her throat.

"When boyhood's fire was in my blood, I read of ancient freemen..." She turned to face Raymond, who finally heard her voice over the engine. *"For Greece and Rome who bravely stood, three hundred men and three men..."*

Raymond's smile opened into a laugh of joy.

Hattie marched toward him. *"And then I prayed I yet might see our fetters rent in twain, and Ireland, long a province be a nation once again!"*

She gestured at him with a kick of her toe against his leg.

"A nation once again, a nation once again! And Ireland, long a province, be a nation once again!"

She repeated the chorus for him, and he finally caught the tune. They sang together for a while, Hattie taking new verses, and Raymond propping up her lilting soprano with his basso profundo.

Once the song was done, Hattie laughed, then sighed.

Raymond gripped the helm as he leaned down to her. "Whoever said you weren't no good at singin' is a damn lying fool."

She shrugged. "Just not much point in singing."

"Why would you say something like that?"

"Because," she explained with a huff, "it's too dangerous. People notice you when you sing."

"Well, baby girl, you deserve some notice. And don't let anyone tell you otherwise."

She frowned. "I don't want't."

He eyed her sadly for a moment, then turned back to the tiller, the brief moment of joy slipping away into the silence of the night.

The moon was high overhead by the time they reached Cape Charles. A thirty-foot ocean trawler hung like a spangled shadow on the horizon. Raymond steered toward it, and it flashed a lamp in their direction. As they approached the trawler, a series of black letters across the bow spelled something in a language Hattie didn't recognize. An angular "S", an "O" with little feet on it.

"Can you read that?" she asked Raymond.

"Looks like Greek, maybe?"

Hattie nodded. There were several Greek ships that made routine runs up and down the Eastern seaboard.

A stout man with a long, black beard peered over the side of the trawler, waving them closer. Another younger, beardless man appeared near the bows, and tossed a dock line to Hattie. She caught the rope and lashed it to one of the bow horns, then followed the young man toward the stern, and repeated the process, tying the two vessels together.

The bearded man belted out commands in Greek to his crew, and shortly a ramp of sorts appeared, edging over the side of the trawler to angle down onto their deck. The ramp had a bow to it, running along its length. Hattie peered at the ramp, then to Raymond. He gave her a "don't worry" gesture before positioning himself at the end of the ramp. A rumble sounded from the trawler, and a barrel appeared at the top of the ramp. Two men sent it rolling down the ramp, cradled in its scoop to keep it running true. Raymond caught it, grunting softly as he eased the barrel to a halt. He rolled it on end to a spot fore of the engine housing, then returned in time to receive a second. The process continued wordlessly, efficient, peaceful. Hattie searched for a reason to involve herself, but these

Greeks had clearly developed a system that Raymond understood.

She'd ridden with Raymond for three years, now—two years under Jake, and one under Lizzie. She knew very little about Raymond's past or credentials, only that he'd worked hard to satisfy Jake's demands, and that the man and his wife had rewarded Raymond with a boat of his own. Hattie understood the magnitude of such a gesture. She was a poor Irish girl in Baltimore, saddled with the need to avoid notice of anyone of consequence. Raymond lived that reality as well. No matter how hard he would ever work, the odds were stacked against any a black man attempting to prosper. Owning a boat? No crippling debt? That was everything.

The courtesy scoop was received and stowed in short order, and Hattie untied the lines from the cleats of Raymond's boat. The bearded man waved as he called out a word in his language which sounded to Hattie, at least, like "good luck." The trawler disappeared behind them as each vessel turned in opposite directions. It could have been a total of a half hour to receive this shipment of rum. The efficiency was remarkable. Lizzie would have been pleased, Hattie mused, as they pointed north, and back home.

Taking a seat beside Raymond, she forced him aside just a few inches with a nudge of her elbow. "Lizzie says we'll be busy."

"Said the same to me."

"Think your little one will give you the free time we'll need?"

He shook his head. "Free time? Everything I do, every minute, it's for that little ball of fuss. I'll do whatever it takes to give him a better life than I had."

She rubbed Raymond's arm. "You're a fine Da, you know that?"

"We'll see, I s'pose."

Hattie tried out another of her mother's songs while Raymond loomed behind the helm, suddenly pensive. At length, he asked her to throw a tarp over the clutch of barrels they'd inherited, just in case they had a close call with a government boat. She complied, taking her time. Overnight runs were the worst. The peace on the water at night was welcome enough, but the boredom. Dear Jesus, the boredom.

She climbed atop the tarped barrels, spreading herself out to view the night sky. Maybe some sort of celestial messenger would descend and offer her a manner of divine revelation. But there was no such luck. There were only stars in the sky tonight, and none of them were particularly charming at the moment.

Sitting upright with a huff, she glared back at Raymond. The man could talk the ass off a horse, but suddenly he'd found silence when she needed a distraction. Her eyes lifted beyond the stern, toward the south end of the Bay. A series of lights caught her eye…another boat. Probably a fisher turning in for the night. She watched as it followed their wake in the distance, waiting to see when it turned off. As the minutes passed, she cast a glance to the west, and realized what they were passing.

Deltaville.

Hattie stiffened. Two points of red light peered at her from the coast. She felt its stare. No, this was her imagination. Those restless dreams, those images… That was simply the embers of a bonfire left behind by the day's fishermen. There was nothing watching her as they moved by. Surely.

They passed the point of Deltaville, and Hattie released several deep breaths as she cast an eye back to the south, to see if that fisherman had pulled away yet.

He had not.

Actually the boat had closed a little. Whatever they were driving, it had a heftier engine than their boat.

"Raymond?" she called out.

He grunted.

"You pushing us all out?"

He shook his head. "Maybe ten knots."

"Give us a little more, will you?"

"Why?"

"Just…please?"

He edged the throttle up, and the wind against the back of her head whipped a little faster.

Turning to sit cross-legged atop the rum barrels, she watched the boat with a squint and could have sworn the boat had matched their speed. Hattie sucked in a breath to ask Raymond for more speed, when the lights on the pursuing boat suddenly went dark.

Crap. Unfolding her legs, she stood up, balancing against the rushes and surges of the boat as it hit the surf. She was the second-tallest thing on the ship, only standing lower than the engine exhaust by four feet.

Raymond scowled at her. "What are you doing?"

She shook her head as she peered in the darkness. A silent, dark silhouette persisted in their wake—growing larger and larger. Hattie shimmied down the side of the rum barrels, landing with a thud on the deck as Raymond reached for the throttle.

She held up a hand. "Don't slow down!"

"What is in your head, girl?"

"We're being followed, is what."

He twisted around, releasing the helm as Hattie took it. Raymond grunted as he shook his head. "Don't see nothin'."

"Trust me. They're there. Been following us for a while."

"You see any flags? Faces?"

She shook her head.

"What…what do you think?"

Hattie searched her instincts. Was it just that ghost from

Deltaville haunting her? Were her nerves just keyed up? "Do you have that gun I asked you to bring? For snakes?"

Raymond squinted. "Yeah."

"Maybe polish it off, will you?"

They continued north, and it didn't take long to confirm that there was, in fact, a boat following them. And it was, in fact, faster than Raymond's boat could push at top throttle. Before long, they could hear the water splashing against the pursuer's hull.

Raymond lifted a seat beside Hattie, reaching into a compartment to pull a Colt .38 service revolver into view. He checked the chambers and stuffed it into his waist.

Hattie eyed the boat as they moved at top speed. "We're losing the footrace."

"Yeah."

"Time to think," she told him.

"I'm thinkin'."

"Think faster, will you?"

Raymond stretched up, eying the western coast, then pulled the helm hard. The boat listed to the left.

"Looking for an inlet?" she muttered.

"I think that's the Rappahannock," he replied. "A hundred places to hide up that river."

"Better move fast, before—"

The engine housing sparked next to Hattie's face, and a *PAP PAP* announced after the fact that someone had fired at them.

Raymond reached for her, jerking her to the deck as more bullets peppered the boat.

"The rum!" Hattie shouted.

"Hell with the rum!" Raymond bellowed.

They chugged west at a hard angle, and Raymond lifted his head between gun shots to ensure they weren't turning around to face the attackers. He guided the boat into the mouth of the Rappahannock River.

Hattie eyed the boat behind them. No lights.

"Raymond!" she shouted. "Kill the lights!"

He squinted at her, then nodded, reaching beneath the console to jerk a handful of switches.

With her hands crossed in front of her face, she pinched light, jerking her hands out to her side. It was the simplest light pinch, the first she'd learned when she was a child, the one she always turned to in a moment of need. Hide. Disappear.

The illusion tugged at her with intent. This wasn't cheap magic. She'd obfuscated the entire boat, complete with the engine noise and the wake it left behind. Hattie hadn't attempted this large an illusion in a long time. The immensity of it sliced through her midsection like a scimitar, but she gripped the top of the console, screwed her eyes shut, and bit down on her bottom lip. Keeping watch on the other boat wouldn't help anything. She just had to buckle down and pour as much of herself into this illusion as she could if they wanted to stay alive.

Raymond said nothing, and she hoped he'd dismissed her closed posture for fear of bullets. The bullets, as it turned out, had stopped.

The illusion was working, at least for now. She couldn't tell if the pursuing vessel had noted their course correction toward the west or not. Hopefully they would keep plowing forward up the Bay, leaving Hattie and Raymond behind. Either way, they were no longer firing their weapons. That was a victory for the moment.

The seconds pounded in her ears. How long would this have to last? Her stomach churned as it usually did, but this was a different sensation than she'd felt even at McComb's the past week. It was the distance, she figured. Too much distance for the illusion. Faking out the Feds to see and smell something that wasn't booze? That was sharp, potent magic. But this was all about radius. It was nighttime, and Raymond had killed the lights on the boat. All she had to do was to cloak a large vessel against a night-shrouded Chesapeake...and muffle the noise. Rather than "sharp and potent," this was "long and hard."

Her feet went numb.

She could taste blood in her mouth.

Wave-by-wave, the bubble of pinched light tore at her insides. Her brain throbbed with each heartbeat, and her fingers began to tremble.

She released a coughing fit and felt a fine spray against the backs of her hands. She opened her eyes for a second to find a dark spackle against her skin. Blood. This illusion was killing her.

As if seeing it made it real, a panic set into Hattie's chest. She sucked in breaths, and the cascade of fear and illness twisted and caught aflame. She hyperventilated, gasping and groaning. *Just a little long— Just a little longer.* But despite her determination, she felt the edges of the illusion began to shred as everything went dark.

* * *

A THICK HAND cradled her head as she stared up at the stars. She didn't even remember falling down.

Raymond peered at her. "Hattie? Hattie?"

She tried to respond, but before words could reach her throat, a dull gurgle thundered through her throat. She twisted to the side and managed to vomit onto the deck instead of onto her own shirt. The taste was vile...sharp and coppery. Hattie hacked and gagged until her stomach finally decided to offer relief. She spat several times to clear her mouth of the foul taste, realizing she'd vomited blood.

Hattie straightened up with Raymond's assistance, her head spinning. "Where…?"

"Up the river," he replied, pulling her clear of the sick. "Don't hear no one after us."

Her chest heaved to catch her breath. The illusion had long-since dissipated, leaving her alone with the wreckage of her insides to ponder whether she'd made enough difference.

Raymond peered down at her. "You okay?"

She cleared her throat several times, then just closed her eyes. "Are we safe, then?"

"Don't know. Like I said, they ain't followed us. I got us as far upstream as I could before you keeled over."

"Sorry."

He shook his head. "You just hold tight."

Raymond rested her head against a bundle of rope, then hopped up to the top of the cabin. He snatched something long and slender, which caught a gleam of starlight as he brandished it. And then he disappeared, feet landing onto wet ground. She heard hacking and chopping, and a rustling of leaves.

Hattie gripped the rope by her head to ride out another wave of nausea. Her stomach was already calming down. She must have blacked out for longer than she realized. As her fortitude leeched back into her tiny frame by inches, she pulled upright, then crawled for the side of the boat. Cupping her hand into the murky water below, she swished it in her mouth. It was muddy, filled with an earthy flavor that was an improvement over the bile taste by far. As she spat the water back into the river, she took long, sweet breaths of nighttime air. It was calming. Centering. Cold and oddly delicate.

When Raymond reappeared, he was hauling half a tree

behind his enormous arms. He jerked the limbs, full of new leaves and buds, over Hattie's head until he'd arranged it over the side of the boat. Then he lashed it to as many cleats as he could manage. He continued this exercise while Hattie regained enough strength to stand upright. By the time she felt human again, he'd camouflaged the boat with hewn branches of a white oak reaching over the waterside.

Hattie inspected the land alongside them. Raymond had moored them to the trunk of an enormous tree near the bow. The stern wandered, fishing in and out of the water without anchorage. It did nothing to offer any manner of reasonable cover, should their pursuers elect to venture up the river.

"Raymond?" she coughed.

He held out a hand. "Lie down, girl."

"We're swinging arse into the water."

"I know."

"Here." She reached for the side of the boat, then paused as her head swam.

Raymond jumped down alongside her, trying to ease her back to the bench seat at the helm, but she shrugged him off.

"Let me go. I'm fine."

"You're sick."

"And we're sitting ducks, out here. Aren't we?"

He frowned. "They ain't followed us. We're safe."

"And when the sun's up, you think those branches are going to fool anyone?"

He scowled. "If they're still here by sunrise, we both know we're dead."

She lifted her hands. "Let's survive tonight and we'll think on that come dawn."

He offered a hand, and with his help she got back to her feet. With tremendous effort, she swung a leg over the side of the boat, then the other, splashing down into ankle-deep mud. Lurching up the bank, she examined the tree. It was a magnificent thing, easily over a hundred years old. Hattie smeared some of the mud from her legs onto her cheek bones, sucked in the earthy aroma, and marched for the oak.

With careful effort, she reached for a branch, then pulled herself up with feet against the trunk. Then another. And another. The air filled her lungs with energy, and as she ascended the tree, she felt more herself. At last, she reached a point halfway up the tree where a long bough wound out over the water. She paused there, casting her glance toward the Bay. There was no sign of any vessel downriver but, with the moon now set, it would be difficult to spot a boat running dark from this viewpoint.

"See anything?" Raymond called.

"Nothing. But that don't mean all that much."

"Then come on down before you kill yourself."

She obliged, taking quick drops down the tree. On the ground, Hattie wrapped her arms around herself, refusing to set foot back onto the boat.

Raymond wandered toward the bow, resting his hand on the tarp-covered rum barrels. "Who'd you think those people were?" he mused.

"Carolinians?" she replied. "Last time we traded with them, Jake took lead in the back of his skull."

"Maybe they cut a deal with the Greeks, then sent their own to take back the rum? We take the blame, and they get to keep their booze."

Hattie shrugged. "The timing is hard to ignore. We just landed the monopoly on the Bay, and suddenly this happens?"

"You think it's the Solomons Island Boys?" he asked.

"None of them left," she replied. "One or two, maybe, but they're probably looking for farm work about now."

"Whoever just shot at us," Raymond said as he returned to the stern, "had a fast boat. That means they got money."

"Well, we can't stay here all night," she said. "Sun comes up and whoever they are, they'll spot us quick enough." She knew that she was far too taxed to toss up another illusion, a fact she couldn't exactly add to the conversation.

Raymond threw his hands into the air. "We're stuck, baby girl. If you got a plan, let's hear it."

She peered up the coast. "Is that a road?"

Raymond shook his head, then hopped up on top of the bench and squinted toward land. "Uh…maybe."

"How far upriver are we?"

"About twenty minutes."

She nodded. "If they haven't come by yet, then we're probably clear. But they might be waiting for us at the mouth of the river."

Raymond gestured with his outstretched hands. "So?"

"So, you get up on that road and find a telephone."

He cocked his head. "Are you crazy?"

"You find a phone, and you get a hold of Lizzie. She has people on the inside. Gangsters. They'll send guns down the river to make sure this much rum makes it back to Baltimore. The Crew isn't gonna want ten barrels of Jamaica's finest lost to pirates. They'll send muscle."

He spat into the river. "If I find someone with a phone who'll let me use it, I'll eat my pants."

"It has to be you," she urged. "I have to protect the boat."

"I'm the one with the gun. Remember? You're a cute white girl. When it comes to asking to borrow people's property, *I'm* not the one to send up the road."

She winced. He was right. This was Virginia.

"I'll be back before sunrise," she declared. "I promise."

The thick oak door cracked open for Capstein. A rugged brute with bushy eyebrows and long sleeves that barely contained overtaxed biceps stared at them all. Capstein nodded, and the door opened wide.

The interior of the basement speakeasy was dim, illuminated by only three gaslights arranged haphazardly along the stone walls. Beyond the rugged perimeter of the space, the rest of the lounge was as refined as one could imagine. Dark red velvet, smooth polished mahogany bar top, brass railing with a high sheen, and the finest liquor arranged in crystal decanters along a pyramid-shaped island behind the bar. The glasswork was noteworthy…like artwork.

Richmond had been a revelation for Vincent. He and Lefty had endured six hours of inane road tripping and glad-handing Virginian mobsters. They were all Anglo, and a shade predisposed against anyone outside of a certain complexion. Vincent knew better than to speak out of turn in such environments, and Lefty was there to remind him of this fact at every opportunity.

And when the sun had set, and they'd spent their entire

day in Richmond, Capstein had paid for a pleasant dinner of steak and potatoes before bringing them to the preeminent speakeasy in the city. The level of cloak-and-dagger jarred Vincent. In Baltimore, there was no need for secrecy. Maryland was still a "wet" state, despite Congress's declarations. However, Virginia had stood front and center in the quest to pass the Volstead Act. As such, the Upright Citizens had to behave as much like spies as entrepreneurs.

Vincent and Lefty stepped into the dank air of the basement speakeasy, tucked well below a tall four-story bank. Cigar smoke hung like a blanket of wispy white just above everyone's eyes. Those gathered there congregated together in tight clutches, whispering and conspiring as they sipped overwrought cocktails served in decorative glasses. *Those glasses*, Vincent pondered. They were remarkable—works of art in their own right. It seemed crude to simply pour moonshine or ferreted rum from the Caribbean into such finery.

He watched as the lean, whiskered fellow in suspenders and bow tie behind the mahogany bar flitted back and forth with an otherworldly confidence, secure in his position as the sorcerer of inebriation for this hidden, secret world. Baltimore, by contrast, was far more straightforward...and by virtue less sexy.

Capstein sauntered ahead of Vincent and Lefty, pulling a chair from the front of the bar with a grandiose wave toward bow-and-suspenders.

"Barley," he announced. "Three Satin Suzies for myself and our guests!"

Capstein had adopted the persona of a grand marshal since they'd arrived at the city. Every dog-eared street and alleyway was loaded with significance in his mind. The day was interminable, and Vincent had been glad to see the sun set as they wound their way to dinner. Lefty had taken it all in stride, acting as the mouthpiece for the Baltimore Crew.

Yet, it had been clear to Vincent that Capstein was eager for a private word with him.

They were both pinchers in the service of the mob. So many things to discuss, so many questions and answers. And none of that could occur in front of Vincent's "handler."

That *was* Lefty's job, after all…to keep Vincent in line. And to keep him loyal to the family.

The Upright Citizens were organized crime, just as they were, but these Virginians were not part of the family. They were, in fact, upstarts in the eyes of the New York *patria*, just local hoodlums who had lucked into securing a foothold in the Old Dominion State prior to the Volstead Act. As such, they controlled the manufacture and distribution on the Virginia side of the Appalachians, and all the moonshine that encompassed. Kings made of paupers, but still paupers at heart in the eyes of the family.

Vincent took a seat at the bar alongside Lefty, and Old Suspenders offered each of them a stemmed glass of some pink-toned liquid with an olive skewered by a toothpick.

He eyed Lefty as he reached for the drink.

Lefty sighed and they both took a sip together.

Whatever Old Suspenders had mixed in that glass…was delightful. Sweet. Boozy. Aromatic. Salty. All the conflicting flavors danced a tight polka across Vincent's tongue, at times offending him, at times seducing him. By the swallow, he was ready for another hit.

"The hell's in this?" he blurted.

Capstein released a gut-deep laugh, tossing his head back. "Trade secrets, my friend!"

Lefty took his sip, then set the glass onto the bar top without comment. Then he leaned back in his chair, looking about the interior of the speakeasy, clearly searching for something or someone. Capstein eyed him with a lift of his brow. "You lose your way?"

"Is there a phone in here?" Lefty replied. "I need to grab hold of my people, let them know what's stretching our clock."

Capstein nodded. "Not here, but there's a phone in the lobby of the Armstead Hotel, just four blocks up Broad Street." He snapped his fingers, and a young black boy popped out from behind a closed door. "Take Mr. Mancuso here to the Armstead. Make it snappy."

The boy nodded, bowed, then rushed for the door.

Lefty eyed the boy, then Capstein, and then straightened his posture with a measure of diplomat's comportment. Before he took his exit, he gave Vincent a steady glare. *Behave*, the glare instructed. Not that Vincent had any intentions beyond that, to be sure.

Once Lefty had exited, Vincent released two tons of weight from his shoulders, and pounded the rest of his... what the hell was this called? A Satin Susy?

Capstein took a seat beside Vincent, nodding to the door. "Hell of a handler you got there."

"Speaking of which...where's yours?" Vincent asked.

"Me? I don't need one."

"What are you, a true member in the Upright Citizens?"

Capstein smiled. "It's a comfort to have a purpose." He nodded to Vincent's drink. "Something less fussy?"

Vincent slid the glass forward. "Not used to blended drinks."

Capstein snapped his fingers, and Old Suspenders stepped to.

"Two fingers each...the Kentucky reserve."

Suspenders lingered a half-second longer than necessary, then retired to a closed door behind the bar. He re-emerged with a black-painted bottle, uncorking it to pour discreet measures each onto cubes of ice.

Capstein lifted his glass, and Vincent followed suit.

"To honest booze," he declared. "And straight dealing."

Vincent clicked glass and took a sip. It was transcendent, far better than his usual.

"You like that?" Capstein asked. "It's not easy getting the real article from Kentucky."

"I suppose not."

"It's a profound shame we can't produce this in the open. These brutes in Congress with their God and Brimstone. Horsefeathers!"

"Bushwa!" Vincent agreed. Those gathered nearby cheered in kind. Well...Richmond had proved to be more welcoming than Vincent had figured.

Capstein sucked back a strong pull of the amber liquid, then nodded to himself.

"Vincent?"

"Yes?"

"You're alone, up there. Correct? In Baltimore?"

Vincent eyed Capstein. "What's your meaning?"

"You're Vito's only pincher, right?"

"One and only."

Capstein nodded. "That must be hard on you."

Vincent leaned back in his seat, peering left and right. "What, you're not the Big Man down in Richmond, are you?"

Capstein released an uproarious laugh. "Oh...oh, no. No." Once the man calmed himself, he gestured toward the back wall. "I'm more fortunate than most, I assume. The Upright Citizens purchased me from down near Atlanta."

Vincent nodded thoughtfully.

Capstein continued, "I was their only pincher for a while, until we developed a recruitment scheme that pays off now and then without much layout. Last time, we got a real cherry." He clicked his tongue at Vincent, then gestured to the far end of the speakeasy to bellow, "Betty! Come on over here!"

From the shadows, a figure stirred. She gripped two

glasses in her hands and stepped with caution toward the two men. She was a blonde-haired beauty…nose short and straight. Brown eyes, tilted slightly toward the brow. Her lips were thin but sharp, curling upward at the corners into a charming hint of a smile.

"You need something, Elmer?" she murmured.

Capstein gestured to Vincent. "You'll be pleased to meet Vincent Calendo. He's the pincher from the Baltimore Crew."

Betty's eyes rose just a little, taking him in with a quick glance that he was sure missed nothing. Setting the glasses onto the bar, she offered a hand in a masculine assertion. "Pleased to make your acquaintance," she declared as Vincent shook her hand. She had a strong grip, indeed.

He eyed the glasses she'd left on the bar top. They were like wax figures wilting under a scorching summer sun. "Good evening," he mumbled. "Or…night. What is it?"

"Whatever you'd like." Her eyes wandered toward Capstein.

Vincent sensed a communication between the two and felt suddenly like a zebra amongst lions.

"He's just here for the day, Betty. Helping us with a little unpleasantness up by the Bay," Capstein told her.

She nodded, and with the last bob of her chin, lifted it just slow enough to seem engaging.

"Are you a pincher, too?" Vincent asked.

She smiled and walked around to Vincent's other side, putting him smack in the middle between her and Capstein. Then she reached across for one of the miserable glass figurines left on the bar top, pressing herself against his arm as she did. Holding it in one hand, she wove the fingers of her right hand just inches over the mass of glass. What had been an ill-formed clump stretched and squeaked underneath her ministrations. The glass pulled taught like hard candy, spiraling and weaving until it rested in a column atop a tulip base. The top of the glass beveled into a martini scoop.

She set the final product down on top of the bar beside Vincent's whisky. He recognized the attention to detail on each, and realized he'd been sipping from glassware wrought from this pincher's fingers.

"Well, what do you know about that?" he muttered.

"I have my talents," she murmured, standing so close he could feel the warmth of her body, smell the faint jasmine notes of her cologne.

"I see that," he replied, not sure if she'd meant the double entendre or not.

She looked up at him from under her eyelashes and reached for his arm. Her fingers trailed his bicep to his elbow, then drifted down to his leg.

Well. This was…uncomfortable? Seductive? Uncomfortably seductive? He peered at her, very aware that Capstein was on the other side of him, no doubt completely ignorant of Betty's wandering hands.

She returned a sizzling glare.

Vincent cleared his throat, and angled his stool away from her, sending her hand off his leg. He reached for his glass and drained it.

"Betty, here, is the product of our recruitment scheme," Capstein said in his loud barker's voice, clearly missing the exchange between Betty and Vincent.

Vincent straightened up, shooting a quick glance at the woman then gesturing for more whisky. "Yeah, you mentioned that."

Betty giggled, tilting her face toward the ceiling. The motion was oddly…artificial. When she lowered her chin, and met Vincent's eyes, the connection was as electric as it was desperate. There was a plea in her gaze, something frantic and distressed behind the seduction, something that stirred his protective instincts as well as other things.

He broke eye contact and shook his head. Where was that whisky? "I'm sorry…are the two of you…"

Capstein offered, "Married? Well, in a way, yes. Yes, we are."

Vincent lifted his hands. "I see."

The man released a polite laugh that seemed to Vincent at once to be both courteous and condescending. Then Capstein reached for Betty's arm and pulled her around to his side, giving it a squeeze as the bartender refilled Vincent's glass.

"Why don't you go upstairs for a bit?" Capstein told the woman. "I'll let you know if we have any…developments."

She nodded and snatched her artwork. With a meaningful glance over her shoulder at Vincent, she disappeared behind a doorway tucked behind a stone masonry wall near the end of the basement.

Vincent shifted away from Capstein. Holy hell, what was that all about? "She's a peach," he remarked, suddenly desperate to be back home.

"She is," he replied. "And she understands our peculiar pressures."

"Pressures?" Vincent asked.

"Surely, you understand our situation. We are pinchers. We are exceptional but sublimated human beings among the mundane mongrels who surround us every day. They assert themselves day in, day out, but *we* are the ones with unique power."

Vincent snickered. "Oh yes. And we are the ones with unique intestinal complaints every time we use our unique power."

Capstein scowled, smacking his fist against the bar top. "No. We are the ones who are destined for glory!"

Vincent blinked at him, searching for a response.

Shaking his head, Capstein blinked away the momentary fugue into furor. "I apologize. I simply mean that we are beings of power, who answer to beings of a lesser calling."

"I don't know much about that," Vincent responded. This discussion was going in a dangerous direction, one that might get a pincher killed if he wasn't careful.

"Who were your parents?" asked Capstein suddenly.

Vincent gripped his glass hard, disliking this topic even more. "Don't know."

"Your parents weren't pinchers?"

"Should they be?"

"Well, that's how it works. Pinchers beget pinchers." Capstein leaned in. "Unless you're one of the rare few who were born from common stock."

Vincent eyed Capstein with a vicious glare. "I'm no sort of farm animal," he snarled. "Nor are you. Or her," he added, nodding to the door Betty had disappeared through.

Capstein nodded. "No offense intended. But, you must understand. We are treated like livestock by our masters. No?"

Vincent blinked, hiding a wince.

"And so," Capstein continued, "we define our worth by the dictates of those who determine our destinies. Such is our lot in life. Such is our means toward significance." He took a sip of his drink, then set it down with a declarative pound. "Betty and I are trying for children. She's a skilled pincher, but *glass*? Her real value, what makes her priceless in my eyes, is her ability to give me children—children with our special aptitude."

"*Salute.*" Vincent nodded and lifted his glass, trying to ignore the man's crude assertions. No wonder the woman had been so desperately flirting with him if *this* was what she was stuck with.

"The family in Pittsburgh? They have two pinchers. Yes?"

"I couldn't tell you." Where was Lefty? It was definitely time to get out of here and back north.

"Two," Capstein acknowledged. "A man and a woman. They have a child, who will be a pincher when he grows old enough for his powers to manifest."

Vincent lingered over his glass.

Capstein continued, "Philadelphia?"

"I've met one. Two men."

"More's the pity. With a woman, they could increase the stock."

Vincent inhaled sharply and shook his head. "They're not interested in—"

"New York City?"

Vincent stiffened. It was an instinctive reaction from his time in the Crew. Invoking the mafia and their keystone city was never a moment to be taken lightly.

"Five," Vincent replied.

"Six," Capstein corrected. "They have a baby due next month, and another that should arrive this summer. This… this is how we rise, Vincent."

"We don't rise, Elmer," Vincent grumbled. "We obey. That's what we do."

"We obey," Capstein whispered, leaning into Vincent's ear, "until we have enough of us to speak in a unified voice. This is the point. It's a long game. This is why Betty and I are trying for another generation."

"Good for you, then." Where the hell was Lefty?

Capstein sucked in a breath to respond, then closed his mouth. Vincent eyed him.

"Any rate, the Upright Citizens are busy chasing their tails over the Piedmont moonshiners, you people up in Baltimore, and, of course," Capstein added with a sharp smirk, "all those poor bastards hunting down Doc Freedman."

Vincent straightened in his chair. "Doc Freedman?"

Capstein nodded indifferently.

Vincent prodded, "Who's Doc Freedman?" And why is everyone hunting the man down?

"Oh," Capstein answered with disinterest. "Some ghost haunting the Bay. Supposedly lives around the area. They say he's a witch doctor from the Caribbean." Capstein made a winding gesture with his finger by his temple. "Pinches water, if you can believe that."

"Why *wouldn't* I believe that?" Vincent countered.

"Well, it's because he's supposed to be some sort of miracle man."

"Aren't we all?"

Capstein released a patient sigh. "I don't believe in miracles. He's a water pincher, but he uses his powers to create some sort of elixir he calls the Water of Life. Magical moonshine. Cures all ills—sickness, injury, everything. Heh. I don't know...man's probably a fraud. A moonshiner with a strong sense of personal theater. But, people are looking for answers these days, and they'll grab onto anything." He took a sip of his whisky and stared into space wistfully.

Vincent followed suit.

Doc Freedman.

Water pincher.

Could that be simply a boat-legger yarn?

Capstein gave Vincent a sidelong glance, then set his glass onto the bar. "Doesn't matter. Listen. People like you and me need some frame of reference. We are unlike those we serve. Which is why I wanted to speak to you candidly...man to man. We are a distinct species, if you'll forgive the biology. The more power we exert as a distinct race of beings, the greater our bargaining power."

"Bargaining power? Against whom?"

"Who do you think?"

Vincent snickered. "Are you suggesting some sorta uprising?"

Capstein waved his hands in undue drama. "No, no! We simply need to think toward the future, and take it step by step. You," he spat. "You are the lone pincher among the Baltimore Crew. What does that tell you?"

Vincent shook his head in bafflement. "Not a lot."

"It tells you that Vito hasn't pursued his legacy. No one on the Eastern seaboard believes he will survive the coming years." Capstein ran a finger underneath his nose with a sniff. "Do you really think this is his moment?"

"I don't know what you mean."

Capstein slapped a hand against the bar top in a motion that reminded Vincent of his time pinch scam on the old ladies up in the city. Then lifting his head in a dramatic show, Capstein uttered words with practiced precision.

"The fate of our kind rests in our own hands, time pincher! Step one is to make sure you're aligned with the right people, strong families who are poised to survive what's coming." He leaned closer. "Have you ever given any thought about relocation?"

Vincent eyed him in disbelief, then turned to finish his whisky. "Can't say I have."

"Perhaps the time is ripe?"

"I can't leave the Crew."

"Why?"

Vincent opened his mouth to reply but couldn't find an answer that wouldn't have sounded infantile. He settled for, "It's just not the way it works."

"Three pinchers versus…what? If you were, just for the sake of argument, to move to Richmond. What would the Crew do, then? Come for you? With me and Betty, and yourself, all ready for them? The balance of power would be…" Capstein scoffed. "Laughable."

Vincent shook his head.

Capstein scowled at him. "You disagree?"

"I think you're full of pop and copper," he replied. "You and me are just accidents. Best to soak up what you got here —" he gestured to the bar, "—and just find some sorta happiness."

Capstein glared at him, then returned to his drink. "I figured you for a man of broader vision."

"Yeah, well, I'm a dimes-and-nickels kind of guy. You spin a yarn like this, and I start thinking that maybe you're gonna get your bosses in a lather sooner rather than later. I don't want to be around when that happens, so I'm okay. Thanks, though." Vincent lifted his glass.

Capstein eyeballed the glass, then Vincent…and lifted his glass to the toast.

"Fine, then," he said. "But you should know—no one prospers in this new world without an advantage."

"You think the *famiglia* don't got no advantage?"

Capstein held still. And Vincent smirked.

He had him. Whatever this air pincher from Richmond was stitching together for Vincent, he'd cut it short with a quick word.

Famiglia.

No one dared resist the power of a gang as large and organized as the Italian mafia. Such was the body of influence on the East Coast, emanating from New York City down to Baltimore and west to Chicago. Richmond, with its Upright Citizens could busy themselves with whatever scheme they liked. In the end? It was all family.

And Vincent was attached to *them.*

Lefty rushed into the speakeasy with a pasty expression. Sweat glistened on his brow. He took a second to peer left, then right. Finally, he spotted Vincent at the bar, and approached.

"Got a hold of Tony. We gotta head out to the waterside."

"What?"

"Waterside. The Chesapeake." Lefty reached for Vincent, pulling him clear of Capstein.

Vincent steadied himself, eyeing the other man with focus. "What's the story?"

"We got a situation. Freelancers for Tony got pinned down by the Rappahannock River, not a half hour from here. Word came down, we're supposed to escort them back home."

Vincent blinked, then squinted, then frowned. "What?"

Lefty sighed. "Some boat-leggers got their ass in a twist, and now we have to see the shipment through to Baltimore. That's from Vito."

Vincent stared at Lefty, who seemed unusually stressed about this situation. "Okay. You got the dime on these free-lancers?"

* * *

THE RIDE to Richmond hadn't seemed as long as the winding back-county roads they were taking toward this section of the Bay. Vincent scowled as the car hopped and jumped over the ragged, unkempt lanes winding through endless forest toward the swampy morass to the east.

Boat-leggers. This was their domain, this spindly, fish-gut stench through which they drove. And of all the places in the world, this was one of the very last he wanted to be in.

A car with several men followed behind them, along with Capstein. He'd pledged that the Upright Citizens would return Lefty's car to Baltimore. Vincent couldn't care less about the vehicle, but Lefty appeared indomitably invested in the disposition of his car—so much so that a full-breadth treaty was at stake between the Crew and the U.C. to ensure its protection.

Vincent dipped his head out the passenger side window, breathing in the balmy, humid air. "These boat-leggers," he declared, "they're for sure hunkered down on this river. Right?"

Lefty nodded. "That's what Tony says."

"Who's Tony been on the horn with?"

"One of the water side distributors," Lefty grunted. "Name of Lizzie Sadler."

"And why do we have to deal with this and not Tony?" Vincent grumbled as they rounded a turn alongside the water's edge.

"Because we're here, and no one else is." Lefty mulled over his own statement for a while, before continuing, "It's blind luck we were here, to begin with. Let's not get our oysters in a roast over it. These are simple people. We're here to break them clear of the river mouth and get them safe to Baltimore."

"Safe from whom?" Vincent prodded.

"I... I'm not one hundred percent solid on the whos and whats."

"Well, ain't *that* cherry?"

Lefty slowed the car as the road petered to a thin pad of mud and dust. Capstein pulled his car behind, parking it and stepping out to gaze across the inlet of the Rappahannock alongside Lefty and Vincent. Two other men climbed out and went to stand next to Lefty's car, waiting for the go-ahead to drive the Fiat back to Baltimore.

"Dark as shit," Capstein muttered.

Vincent nodded.

Lefty simply stepped forward, eyeballing the shadowed inlet with sharp eyes.

"You set?" Capstein asked, turning halfway to his own car.

Vincent nodded. "We're set. Thanks for your help."

"It's the least I could offer." He nodded to Vincent, then whispered, "You do what you need to do, and when you're free of prying eyes—" Capstein nodded toward Lefty, "—you give me a call."

Capstein left Vincent with a business card, then tipped his hat.

Trotting down toward the water's edge, Vincent stared over the length of water snaking toward the Bay. The moon was low to the horizon, near close to setting. They'd have no light to work with for about two hours before the sun rose. And when that happened…well, then they'd have a completely new concern to contend with, he supposed. Vincent squinted into the distance. A shape lingered near a muddy cove jutting out into the Rappahannock, a tall white oak tree curling its branches over the water. And beneath that oak sat a distinct shape. It seemed angular and familiar, but not quite what he had expected.

"See that?" Vincent asked.

"What?"

"That."

"Where?"

Vincent gestured with verve toward the white oak tree.

Lefty shook his head. "What are you babbling about, you gorilla?"

"Are we not looking for a boat with Vito's rum loaded up?" Vincent snapped. "Because I'm pretty sure that's a boat over by those trees, covered up with some branches."

Lefty eyed Vincent, then peered with intent toward the east. "You really see something?"

Vincent squinted again. "Yeah. That's a boat all right."

"You guys good? Can we get out of here?" Capstein asked.

Lefty sucked in a breath to respond, then held his response. Instead, he turned to Vincent.

Vincent simply smiled at Capstein. "Have a nice morning, Elmer! I think we're off the map, now."

Lefty tossed the keys to his car to him, then lifted a finger, pointing it at the car. The message was clear. That car doesn't make it intact to Baltimore, and it's war.

Capstein seemed comfortable with that arrangement. The two men waited until both cars pulled away, then continued onward along the shabby lane alongside a strip of mud that lanced out into the water, searching for the boat that Vincent had spotted. Lefty marched forward along the night-shadowed lane as Vincent followed. They continued for several minutes, the lights of both cars having long since vanished.

Vincent gripped Lefty after a while, jerking him to a halt. "Okay."

Lefty cocked a brow. "Okay?"

"Here."

"What?"

Vincent stepped toward the white oak, eyeing the boat. It was barely visible under all the tree limbs. As he walked closer he saw the dim outline of a large black man bent over the railing of the boat, tying off a mooring line. The other inhabitant, a woman of maybe twenty three or so, watched him from behind the lattice of tree branches with hard eyes.

He cleared his throat. "Good evening!"

The woman jerked backward at his address.

"You're Tin Lizzie's crew?" Vincent pressed, moving closer while Lefty remained behind, staring with a puzzled frown at some bushes about ten yards away.

The woman slipped soundlessly from the boat onto the shoreline. She was petite, a waif of sorts, light coppery-blonde hair cropped close to her ears, a farmer's shirt tucked loosely into pants.

She stood with hands on her hips and just stared.

Vincent nodded to her. "Hello?"

She peered at him with a face twisted in confusion. Vincent looked back to Lefty, whose eyes were alert over the water, focusing in a completely different direction on nothing.

"Lefty?" Vincent barked.

Lefty snapped his attention toward Vincent. "What?"

Vincent gestured to the woman standing thirty feet in front of him.

Lefty shook his head. "You see this boat, or what?"

Vincent curled a brow. "Are you serious, old man? I know it's dark as hell out here, but do you need glasses or something? Get over here. Closer, so you can see it."

The woman cleared her throat, and in the distance, he heard a profound thud, as if a million pounds of steel had been dropped thousands of miles away. Lefty walked forward to Vincent's side, sucked in a breath, then retreated several steps.

Vincent nodded to the woman. "I'm guessing you're our freelancers?"

She took a few steps forward, pulling the bangs from her face. She was…cute. Actually, she was *very* pretty, if one were predisposed to the wholesome, Mary Pickford type.

"Lizzie sent you, then?" she asked.

Vincent nodded. "By way of Vito Corbi. We're with the Baltimore Crew Who are you?"

At the name, the girl's eyes widened. She pulled her arms across her chest, shrinking inward as if she wanted to disappear. He took a step forward, and she retreated a half-step.

Vincent lifted a hand. "I'm not gonna hurt you. We're here to help."

The man haunting the boat hopped up, clearing the side of the vessel to land alongside the girl. He was a muscular man, wearing overalls and boots. His face was stolid, threatening.

Vincent peered up at him. "Heya there."

The man growled at him. "Start talkin'."

Vincent cast a glance to Lefty over his shoulder. "You wanna help here, or am I gonna get my head pounded into pulp?"

The other man composed himself, running his hand down his vest. And with a measure of poise Vincent had thought impossible, Lefty strode forward.

"You work for Tin Lizzie Sadler?" he asked.

The woman nodded. "Aye."

Lefty gestured toward the boat. "Are these barrels meant for Vito of the Baltimore Crew?"

She nodded.

Lefty gave Vincent a quick gesture, a flat palm moving toward the boat.

Vincent announced, "Then we're the cavalry. How do you do?"

CHAPTER 11

Hattie watched the two men as they boarded the boat and tried to control her panicked terror. Run. Hide. Disappear. She'd known Lizzie would call in the Crew, and that they'd send their gangsters, but she expected them to arrive via their own ship, clear the space where the river met the Bay and escort them home, not stroll up the lane and board their boat.

And that one…he'd seen right through her illusion. They were *right here*, next to her. If they'd realized what she was, then she was done. They'd drag her off, and her parents would never see her again. Everything she loved would be gone, and she'd be a slave to the mob.

Calm down. These gangsters were here to help them, not take her away. She needed to shove her fears deep down, and assess these men that were climbing aboard their boat.

The first one a middle-aged fellow with silver streaks by his temples and throughout his dark hair, seemed to have only one arm. He did most of the talking between the two, and Hattie figured him as the one in charge.

The second one, on the other hand…

He was young, a few years older than she was, and of moderate height. Dark eyes hung under inky brows, deep enough in their sockets to give him a brooding quality, but not so much that he seemed haggard. He had a somewhat hawkish nose, an angular jaw, and prominent cheekbones that would sharpen with age, but were now softened by the smooth oval of his lean face. If she'd seen him pass by on the street, he would have warranted a second furtive glance. He was handsome. He was *very* handsome.

And he was the one who'd seen through her illusion. She bit the inside of her cheek as she buried a surge of humiliation. It'd been several hours since she'd passed out from the last illusion. That had been a nasty pinch that had sucked the consciousness out of her, but she should have at least recovered enough to fade the boat into the leaves they'd decked it with. This was two illusions in one week that had failed. That demon in Deltaville...well, that was an extraordinary case, at least that's what she'd thought. But now, some hoodlum from Baltimore walked right up to the boat despite her light pinch.

He'd looked her square in the eye and almost seemed amused at how bad it was.

Hattie's frustration melted to exhaustion as Raymond pulled off the white oak branches and fired up the boat to edge them back onto the Rappahannock River. The moon had set. If that other boat was waiting for them at the mouth of the river, they wouldn't know until they nearly collided with it.

She eyed the younger man. "Begging your pardon."

He turned to her with a lift of his brow and a charming bow.

"Are you packing there, boy-o?" she asked.

He grinned, and the effect was totally disarming. "You got

a peculiar hang to your words. Where are you from? England or something?"

"Ireland, but late of Baltimore."

With a smug smile, he lifted his hands, indicating he was unarmed. "Don't need iron, miss."

Well, that was cocksure of him. What'd he plan to do, swim across to the other boat and beat half a dozen armed men down bare-handed, with bullets flying? His funeral. Unfortunately, it would probably be their funeral as well.

Hattie turned to the older man. "No offense, but I'm assuming you're not in any shape to hold a Tommy gun."

He pulled a revolver from his jacket, holding it low for her to inspect.

"I lost my right arm in the War," he muttered. "But I'm an adequate marksman. We have you covered, ma'am." He re-holstered his piece, then extended his hand to shake hers. "Lefty Mancuso. This here's Vincent Calendo. We're here to see you home safe."

She nodded to Vincent, then lifted a brow at the other man. "Lefty? You really let them call you that, then?"

He stuffed his hand into his pants pocket. "I was a southpaw before the War. I got worse things to feel sorry about."

Hattie nodded and turned from the man with a roll of her eyes.

"Don't mind him." The young Valentino double grinned. "He was born with a lemon in his mouth and never recovered."

Raymond shushed them as they approached open water. "Quiet, all of you," he grumbled. "Only got an hour of night left. Them buzzards will be waitin' for us."

Lefty stepped beside Hattie to address Raymond. "Who are they? Tony was light on the details."

"Don't know," Raymond replied. "We took these barrels

off an ocean trawler, and then half hour later, we had them shootin' at us. Came from the south. Thinkin' maybe they're the Carolinians doing a double-Dutch."

Lefty shook his head. "Horace Wellington's men wouldn't thumb their noses at Vito. Not like that."

Hattie sniffled. "They've done it before."

Lefty didn't reply. Vincent reached for the stack of tarp-covered rum barrels and stepped up, steadying himself a head-and-shoulders higher than the rest to peer at the water.

"Coast is clear," he declared. "They probably beat feet back to wherever they came from."

"I hope you're right. They had machine guns. Not just pistols," Raymond informed him.

Lefty scowled, then took a seat alongside Raymond. Hattie had nowhere else to be, and given the choice, she'd rather be on top of those barrels. So, she wandered closer to this Vincent fellow. He dropped down and offered her a hand to climb up.

"Thank you, courteously," she said as she scurried up the stack without his help. She glanced toward the Bay, eyes moving left and right. "They doused their lights before opening up on us. Won't be easy to spot if they don't want't."

"Then maybe it's best you come back down and take some cover?"

"Maybe it's best you mind your P's and Q's, Buster Brown," she snapped, resenting the implication that she was some delicate flower.

He lifted hands. "Didn't mean to ruffle your feathers, Miss."

"Hattie," she replied. "Hattie Malloy."

"Well, Miss Malloy, *you* called *us*. Keep that tucked in your bonnet, next time you feel like airing out grievances."

She sucked in a breath to release a tongue-lashing but elected against it. Because he was right. She *had* asked for their help. And if this new promise of business from the Baltimore Crew were to pan out in their favor, she'd have to do Lizzie the courtesy of not antagonizing the first gangsters they let onto the boat.

"Sorry," she grumbled in a grudging apology. "Don't mind me. I haven't slept, I've been shot at, and I'm not feeling particularly well at the moment."

He shot her a look filled with sympathy. "If you like, I can keep watch for you."

"It's fine. Wouldn't be able to sleep with trouble afoot, anyhow."

"I can understand that."

They remained silent for a while as the waves splashed up against the bow. Hattie turned back to watch Raymond, whose eyes were in constant motion toward the horizon, then back to the attractive young man slouching alongside the barrels below her.

"Calendo, huh?"

"Yeah?"

"Is that Italian, then?"

He smiled up at her. "By way of Brooklyn, and a few haunts between there and here."

"Were you born in the States?"

"Yes." His smile thinned. "Like I said. Brooklyn."

"I suppose that figures," she mused. "What with you being in the mafia and all."

"You'd be wrong."

"How's that?" She was genuinely curious, but the man seemed to take her question as some sort of attack.

He pulled his weight off the barrels, then turned toward the water. "Don't sweat it, Miss Malloy."

"I'm not sweating it, as a matter of fact. Just asking a question all courteous like."

When he turned back toward her, his face was filled with

mystery. "I'm not *famiglia*. I have other uses to the Crew. Uses which, with any luck at all, won't be needed before we let in."

She considered him for a moment. This man hadn't shown the first signs of fear or nerves, even though they were plowing directly back into harm's way. He acted as if he were bulletproof, which would be quite a thing to be in such times as these. Was he really as skilled as his confident attitude proclaimed, or was he just a fool?

Hopefully not the latter, for all their sakes.

Hattie pulled her head forward, then turned toward Raymond. "Stump coming," she called. "Starboard."

Raymond angled the boat toward the center of the river, eying the jagged hunk of wood protruding out of the water like the broken half of a bottle.

"Thanks, baby girl," he called.

"Why aren't you running with lights?" Lefty asked her.

"Our pursuers are running dark. And, so are we," Hattie explained.

Lefty nodded. "I see."

She caught a glimpse of Vincent as he turned back toward the bow. He almost seemed smug. Hattie had seen this sort of dynamic between men before. A grouchy pedant. A cocky upstart. Neither one with enough sense just to talk to each other. Rather, it would end up a battle of wills until one or the other got enough burr and blister to either go fisticuffs or end the relationship. It was exhausting to watch.

Men. She'd never understand them. Even her own Da sometimes. Although things weren't any easier between women in her experience.

The mouth of the river opened into the breadth of the Bay, and Raymond eased back on the throttle. Even at the slow speed, the engine pounded out enough noise to catch attention all the way to Virginia.

He steered the boat north, then hammered down to put as much distance behind them as possible. Both of the gangsters reached for a handhold, bobbing cartoonishly as the boat lurched forward. Hattie snickered. Vincent followed suit, wiping spray off his face with a grin. He was like a child in a candy store. It was appealing, boyishly charming, and conflicted oddly with his previous overconfident attitude.

"I think the water life suits you, Calendo!" she shouted from the top of the barrels.

"It's a swap from normal life, I'll tell you that for nothing."

She smiled at him. "Aye. That it is."

Her eyes lifted to look behind the boat, but as he went to continue the thought, she held out a hand for him to hush. A silhouette bounced up and down in the surf not far behind them. They'd been spotted.

Vincent followed her gaze behind them, stepping up onto the engine housing for a higher view before releasing it with a grunt of pain, pulling his hand away from the hot metal as Hattie fluttered her hands at Raymond.

Then Vincent withdrew toward the helm and spoke to Raymond. After a few seconds, the engine muffled as Raymond released the throttle.

Hattie shouted, "What're you doing? Push on!"

Vincent shook his head. "No. Kill the engine."

Hattie planted her hands atop the barrels and shimmied back down, marching up to both of them. "What're you going on about? They've more speed than we do. They'll overtake us."

Vincent nodded with patience. "Which is precisely why we should save our juice. Right?"

"What, you're going to deal with them single-handed?" With a grimace she turned to Lefty. "That...didn't sound the way I meant it."

Lefty stood up, then turned to eye the boat behind them.

They could hear its engine now, and the splash of surf against their hull. "Everyone get down," he stated with disinterest. "Heads down."

Raymond and Hattie exchanged glances.

Lefty pulled his pistol, keeping it at hip height. "I'm not asking."

Raymond stood stiff, but Hattie gave him a gentle wave.

"Come on, then," she groused. "The Baltimore Crew wants to have a little war here on the Chesapeake, then we'll let them."

Raymond waffled for a moment before stepping out from behind the helm, killing the engine outright. The enormous man lumbered down alongside Hattie as she tucked herself beneath the bench.

Lefty held his gun to his shoulder, nodded to Vincent. "You set?"

"Yeah," Vincent replied as he pulled off his jacket. "Had a big dinner."

"Ridiculous, wasn't it?" Lefty said.

"I think they were trying to impress us."

Raymond shot Hattie a quizzical glance as he tried to pull his frame as low as it could go. She simply shrugged at him while she did some quick calculation. Two gangsters with one pistol between them against a boatload of who knows how many with Tommy guns. It would be a massacre. They'd be dead in short order, and the rum would be gone along with them. Hattie couldn't hide the boat anymore, despite their killing the engine. Not having to cover up sound was one thing, but these people had their eyes on the boat now. That was worth sound and taste put together. Illusions worked best when there was little reason to doubt them.

Hattie gripped Raymond's forearm, giving him a reassuring nod. He wouldn't have known why, but she was confident in their own fates—confident that two people left alone, still, and quiet, with physical contact, could be hidden from these assailants without the illusion killing her. Assuming her magic worked at all anymore.

And then, to her surprise, Lefty pressed himself against the deck alongside Raymond.

Hattie glared at him. What the hell? He was leaving the other guy up there alone, weaponless, to face down a boat full of armed men?

Lefty simply nodded to her, then kept his eyes up at Vincent, who had casually unbuttoned his cuffs and was rolling up his sleeves. A lock of his jet-black hair drifted over his brow, fluttering in the Bay breeze as he stared calmly into the distance like some all-powerful Adonis facing his fate.

A notion settled inside Hattie's mind as the boat rocked beneath them. He was far too confident not to have a reason to be. And no man would jump directly into a firefight without *some* sort of weapon. But what *was* that weapon? Why would a man who said he wasn't even a member of the mob walk into a gun fight without...?

Her eyes widened.

And at the moment when she'd pieced together what Vincent was, the first shots rang out through the dying hours of night.

CHAPTER 12

Vincent steadied himself against the helm housing as the attackers sidled up alongside them. The darkness helped his case, as the dark figures swarming the opponent vessel jumped and stretched for a better view. This boat just went dead, and for all they knew, everyone had bailed and were swimming halfway toward shore by now.

But they weren't. They were huddled in a heap next to Lefty, watching Vincent as he waited for the distance to close between the two hulls.

They'd nearly made close enough it before one of the mooks on the other boat spotted him.

"There!" the man shouted.

Several guns lifted.

Shit. There was at least six feet between the boats. Vincent could make the jump, but he couldn't pinch a time bubble big enough for both boats and hold it for as long as he needed.

But then again, he didn't have to.

The first shots thumped through air, and Vincent lifted his hand…and snapped his fingers.

He pinched time over both boats. The load was enormous, but all he had to do was make it from one boat to the other then drop the pinch. He'd take it in small chunks and hope Lefty kept everyone on the other boat down and out of the way while he was doing his thing. It would be delicate work, but he could do it.

Vincent thrust his weight high over the side of the boat, slapping a shoe against the side rail as the thickened, muddy air globbed against his face. He counted five different plumes of muzzle flashes as he stretched his body out long enough to make the six-foot jump. Time bubbles were strange things. Running was near impossible in one of his time pinches, but gravity got light as the air got heavy, making jumps easy. He'd successfully done third-story leaps in a time bubble before that would've otherwise ended up with a Vincent-sized smear on the sidewalk below.

Vincent's shoes landed on the opponents' boat, and he side-stepped a hail of bullets, each creeping through the air in their powder-fired speed that managed to penetrate his time pinch. Landing was easy. Stopping? That was the trick.

He made it work for him, angling toward the one guy on the boat who wasn't firing a weapon, twisting his torso after one single hop on the railing of the boat, throwing a shoulder into his midsection.

And just as the time pinch began to tug at his guts, he released it.

A thunder of Tommy gun fire erupted all around him as gravity caught hold of his frame, sending him plowing into the poor bastard. The thug's head hit the side of a crate, and he released a sick cough as his neck went sideways.

With the sound and fury from the weapons, none of the gunmen had even noticed Vincent's sudden appearance. Only the helmsman remained unoccupied, and Vincent sized him up with a quick glance.

The helmsman took a good, long second to realize that Vincent didn't belong on the boat. And at the termination of that good, long second…Vincent snapped his fingers again.

Time congealed around him once more and he fought back a wave of nausea. Better make this fast. First order of business was the helmsman. He pushed through the mire of time and gripped the man by the shoulder. Planting his foot against the opposite side of the boat, he hip-threw the man overboard. The helmsman's figure hung in the stiffness of air, arcing in the velocity Vincent had given him. It was good enough for now.

The tug against Vincent's insides made the cost of this power known, and he gritted his teeth to engage each gunman in order. Snatch a gun, toss it into the air. Snatch a man, do the same. He plowed his way through the pre-dawn light, shoulder-checking a hoodlum while snatching the still-firing weapon to toss it into the drink. Three. Four. By number five, the toll the time pinch had exacted began to issue from Vincent's nose. He ignored the trickle of blood easing from his nostril as he gripped the final gunman by the collar and jerked his head toward the side of the boat.

That was uncharitable. He'd probably break his neck, or otherwise end up unconscious before dropping into the water. But this was war, not some gingham-and-daisies tea party. People brought weapons against Vito's boat. They were going to pay.

In a split-second, Vincent captured a notion. He reached into the time-stiffened air to grip the Tommy gun of his last victim. He pulled it to his shoulder, braced it tight, and then released his time pinch.

He heard two immediate splashes…probably one gun and one gunman. The rest were likely still in midair. There was a wet crack to his left. Yeah…broken neck. Poor bastard was dead, but at least he wouldn't drown.

The gun bucked up against Vincent's shoulder as he jerked back on the trigger, sending the last rounds in the drum through the bottom of the boat. Water gurgled up through the hull, and Vincent tossed the gun aside, pinching time once more across both boats.

He twisted on his heel as his gun lingered on its descent toward the deck. Several spouts of water lifted in midair like dark mushrooms rising through the wooden planks of the boat.

Vincent smiled as he returned to the freelancers' boat. This was easy. And what's more, the occupants of his boat wouldn't know what happened. To them, the entire caper would have lasted six whole seconds. Seven, maybe, counting his landing. Still though...they were face down in their own boat, their arms over their heads.

Or they were supposed to be.

As Vincent shoved off the attacker boat to make his midair glide those six feet back home, he spotted that pretty Irish girl.

Just standing there.

Watching him with wide eyes.

The man slid back onto the boat from midair, seeming comfortable in this strange, strangling moment. When his shoes clacked down onto the deck with wet thuds, almost as if underwater, he glanced back at the pursuers before stepping down.

And he spotted Hattie.

She'd taken several steps away from the others. They seemed paralyzed. Raymond wouldn't respond to her, no matter how hard she'd shaken his arm. Her lungs had gummed up with a sudden mire—like a humid day except her breaths were more labored. When she'd gotten to her feet, she'd found Vincent on the other boat, pulling guns out of their attackers' hands and sending them into the air, where they stuck like sticks in the mud.

Now he stood before her, a trickle of blood slipping from his nostril. He looked surprised, which was unusual for this man who had exuded absolute confidence until this very moment.

"What's happening?" she shouted. Her voice came out in

murky bleat. It would have been clearer if she'd dove into the Bay and screamed it underwater.

He lifted a finger to his throat and shook his head. Then he eased up alongside her, turning to place his foot in a specific spot on the side of the hull. He re-positioned once or twice before giving her a cocky grin and a wink.

And then he snapped his fingers. The air fell into its usual thinness. Hattie sucked in a long breath. Shouts and splashes sounded behind them.

Vincent ran a finger across the bottom of his nose to clear the blood, reaching into his pants for a handkerchief.

"Sorry," he told her calmly. "It's not much use trying to talk inside the bubble."

"Wh…what?"

Raymond and Lefty stirred at their feet. Vincent nudged Lefty's leg with his shoe, and the older man pulled himself upright.

Reaching out for Vincent's arm, Hattie jerked him closer. "The 'ell was all that?"

He smirked, then shrugged. "Probably something you should forget about."

"Not bloody likely."

Lefty separated the two as he leaned over to view the scene behind them. The offending boat was taking water, its stern already dipping underneath the surface of the Bay. Four men paddled their way toward the boat, and then recognizing its fate, toward the nearer coastline.

Two bodies bobbed in the waves.

Lefty nodded. "That's that, then." He gave Vincent a pat on his shoulder. "Good work."

Vincent beamed as he dipped his chin.

Hattie turned to Raymond, now standing upright and taking in the scene as well.

"What happened?" he bellowed. "They goin' under?"

Hattie nodded. "Looks that way."

"I heard gunshots," he said, peering at the rest with wide, wild eyes.

Vincent pocketed his handkerchief and unrolled his sleeves, meticulously buttoning each one at the cuff. "They got off a couple shots. The rum's intact, though. We can make easy time back for Baltimore, if you like. Be home by breakfast."

Raymond put the sudden shift in fortune behind him, perhaps not really believing it, and brought the engine back to life. As the boat sliced through the water, he continued staring forward.

Hattie eyed Vincent, who had picked up his jacket and donned it, smoothing the creases out before moving toward the bow. Once there, he seemed to intentionally place his face into the line of spray, wiping the moisture across his brow.

It was dangerous to be talking to this man. She should be on the opposite side of the boat from him, counting down the minutes until these two gangsters left, praying that neither of them figured out what she was. But he was a pincher. A *pincher*. Like her. Panic and fear collided with curiosity, compelling her to follow him and ply him with questions instead of ducking her head and keeping her mouth shut for the rest of the trip.

"You gonna talk now?" she demanded, moving to stand beside him.

"I don't know what to tell you that you'll believe," he replied, still staring forward. "So, what say we give the fine print a pass and skip straight to the part where we all get home and go our merry ways."

"I want to know what just happened," she insisted.

"What do *you* think happened?" he asked with a wicked smirk as he turned to face her.

"I think you did something to time."

His brow shot high. "You're quicker than most."

"You said you weren't mafia, yeah? Not a full member of the Baltimore Crew."

His smirk faded. "Your point?"

"It's because you're a pincher, isn't it? One of their magic men?"

Vincent squinted one eye at her. "You know more about this sort of thing than the average boat-legger."

"Maybe I'm not your average boat-legger, then?"

He snickered. "Well, alright. I'll tell you. I pinched a bubble of time around us. Froze time. Really, it was a couple different pinches. Gets kind of hairy trying to pull that much power over that much space for one long stretch of time."

She nodded, leaning forward a little, curiosity submerging the panic and fear.

He continued, "You felt the air thicken up. Right, like molasses? That always happens. Scared the guts outta me, first time I did it. You get used to it, though. You never really pass out from lack of breathing."

"How often do you do this sort of thing?" she asked, unnerved. He stopped time. He *stopped time*. It made what she did seem like a cheap parlor trick in comparison.

"Maybe once or twice a month. Depends on how brisk business gets."

"That's amazing. What you do is truly incredible," she told him with complete honesty.

Heaven help her, the man blushed. Vincent looked away, his cocky demeanor vanishing in a mess of boyish bashfulness. Then he nodded. "I try to be useful."

She stared at him a minute, the sudden change in him throwing her off balance. Curiosity faded, the fear and panic roaring to the forefront, and with them a spark of anger. He'd done this on purpose. He'd let her see what he could do *on purpose.* He was showing off, trying to impress her with his powerful magic and fake humility.

"Does this bashful boy routine work for you?" she drawled, furious that she'd let her guard down, let herself almost be duped, enamored even, by this show-off of a gangster. He was good-looking. He was powerful. He'd spun an enticing web around her, the cocky bastard. Lord help her, she'd nearly fallen for it. Nearly.

He cleared his throat. "What?"

"You've got it shined to a spit polish, I'll give you that. Completely fooled me for a hot second there," she snapped.

Vincent straightened a little, his face devoid of mirth. "I'm puttin' you off your feed, or something?"

"I think you're very proud of yourself, and you figure a simple girl like me out on the river'd probably swoon all over your magic self." She spat the sentence out, anger and hurt guiding her words instead of careful common sense.

"That's what you think, huh?" His voice was wooden and cold.

She folded her arms. "Yes, that's exactly what I think. I've got news for you, boy-o. I'm no Reuben on a boat. I've seen men like you before. Full of yourself, putting on the act so you'll look all disarming and humble. You want to know what I really see when I look at you?"

"Go ahead. Let me have it." He stepped in closer, his chest inches from hers, his face so close.

Hattie took a deep breath. "I see a gangster who's trying so hard to impress everyone that he doesn't realize no one really cares."

He blinked rapidly.

She cocked her jaw. "So, don't get any notions. I can see right through what you're spinnin' there."

A million conflicting emotions raced across the man's

face, then his expression tightened. Vincent stepped into her. She sucked in a breath.

He whispered, "You want to know what I thought the second I laid eyes on you?"

"What?"

"I thought…that you were a boy. Didn't even realize you were a woman until we were well underway. So, maybe you got me wrong."

She pursed her lips, something deep inside her chest aching.

He continued, "If I were trying to impress you, I'd pick something that didn't make you feel like you were suffocating. I don't know why you weren't affected. It wasn't on purpose. I probably just lost focus. Accidents happen. It wasn't intentional. And it sure wasn't meant to sweep a rude little hayseed like you off your feet."

Hattie snarled and leveled a venomous glare at Vincent. "Hayseed, is it?"

He curled a lip. "Hayseed. You look like a hobo that took up potato farming as a side gig."

She slapped him across the cheek. Hard. With all her might.

Lefty jerked his head in their direction, his arm inching toward his vest holster.

Raymond eyed them, as well.

Vincent lifted a hand to wave them off. "Don't mind us, gents."

Raymond called out to Hattie, "You okay?"

"Fine," she snarled.

Vincent added, "We're arguing the virtues of barrel-aged rum."

Lefty shook his head. "Idiot."

Hattie took advantage of the moment to withdraw back

toward the helm alongside Raymond. Vincent remained up front, silent for the rest of the trip.

Raymond nudged Hattie once Lefty had wandered off to join Vincent.

"What'd he say to you?" he muttered, his hands tightening on the tiler.

"Nothing."

"That's a damn lie," he said with a dry chuckle. "I see the way he's been looking at you."

"You're blind as a bat," she snapped. "He…he called me hayseed! Said I looked like a hobo!"

Said he'd thought she was a boy. Hattie winced as she remembered his words, the look on his face.

Raymond chuckled again, shaking his head. "And why d'ya care, baby girl?"

"It's rude," she sputtered.

"You're awful hot and bothered 'bout it." Raymond grinned. She sniffed. "Your point?"

"You goin' and slappin' a man when you never cared what nobody done thought 'bout you afore."

"I *don't* care," she insisted. "But he deserved it."

"Isn't it better if he stops looking at you? Gonna slap a man, he's gonna remember you, know?"

"There's no reason to be rude, is all I'm saying."

Raymond chuckled again. "There's no reason to get blood up, neither."

They continued up the Bay for a while, then Hattie said, "My blood's not up."

"Brat."

"Bully."

The sun rose to the east, spilling thin, pale daylight over the Bay from the Eastern Shore to the coast alongside Annapolis. Winnow's Slip appeared around the third bend as

Raymond piloted the craft beneath tree limbs. As they docked at the Slip, Hattie eyed Raymond's pistol sticking halfway out of the crew console.

She'd completely lost her cool on this "time pincher." And rightfully so. The man was an arrogant ass, as it seemed, but beyond that, she'd panicked. He was her first—the first pincher she'd ever met outside of herself. And the peculiar skill she wielded to pinch light suddenly became…secondary compared to his. What good was she, after all? Sure, he'd had his opportunity to impress her and he'd taken it. But, what could *she* truly do in comparison?

He seen straight through her illusions, to begin with. Was that the way it was with all pinchers? Were they all immune to one another? That couldn't be right. Her father had filled her brain with stories of magic wars between ancient orders, and even the crime families in the New World. Pinchers had been at war with one another in the name of their masters for centuries.

So, what then? Was he just better than her? Had he received more training? Maybe she'd just been tired. Maybe the illusion to hide the boat had been too soon after her last one to be completely effective. Like he'd said, accidents happen.

But he could *stop time*. It was frightening to think that someone held that much power, that this person was right there on the boat next to her. An entire ball of emotion had twisted in her chest as he'd spoken to her, and she'd lashed out in a provocative exchange of words. It felt poisonous to Hattie. She hadn't really wanted to pick a fight with the man. But once she had, he'd taken up the gauntlet and stuffed it right back down her throat.

And Raymond was right. She didn't want the attention. Especially since he worked for the crime families. This was her worst nightmare; the very thing her parents had worked so hard to protect her from. Had she betrayed herself somehow? Had he seen through her light pinch and figured out what she was? Once they were off the boat, did he plan on sticking her into a car and taking her at gunpoint to his mob boss? Hattie tried to steady her breathing and looked at the pistol beside the console.

Vincent hopped onto the land and gave Raymond a hand mooring the boat. Raymond pulled the tarp loose bit by bit, while Hattie reached down to grip the pistol. She tucked it against her body, pinching light with a very slight illusion. It was cheap magic…probably cheap enough to keep up for an hour without feeling the cost. This one wouldn't be like trying to hide an entire boat hours after she'd been passed out in a pool of her own blood.

As the gangsters stood indolently by the dock while Raymond jerked the tarp aside, Hattie kept the gun close to her side.

She shouted, "The two of you feel like lending a hand, or are you going to stand there gawking at honest labor like a couple o' tourists?"

Lefty lifted his hand. "I fear I'm not much good to you."

Vincent laughed.

She glared at him. "Don't be rude, you ass."

Vincent shook his head. "You think that's rude? You should see how *he* treats *me* on a Sunday."

"I don't care how he treats you on a Sunday. I only care about those ten barrels what're headed to your masters in the city."

Vincent winced at the word "masters." She grinned to herself, sensing the only weak spot she'd seen in this over-confident man since she'd met him.

Raymond and Vincent lugged the barrels ashore, storing them in one of the Winnow's warehouses. Once the cargo had been stored and Raymond had negotiated a lock from the dockmaster, the four of them stood facing one another.

Hattie kept the pistol in her hand, shrouding it in her light pinch as the gangsters nodded to them.

"So," Vincent declared, "our car's stuck down in Virginia. Would either of you have an auto to take us back into town?"

Hattie lifted her chin. *Don't panic. Don't panic. We'll leave. They'll wait for their car. They're not going to grab me and haul me off.* "Don't you have people who can ferry you about?"

Lefty shrugged. "We do, but it would save us considerable effort if we could simply hitch a ride. We would pay you, of course."

Raymond nodded instantly. "Where you fellas need to be?"

Hattie tapped the gun against her leg, reassuring herself, forcing the panic down.

Vincent eyed her, then his eyes drifted down to her hand. "You, uh…feeling like putting that piece to use, or what? Because if it's all the same, I'd rather walk than ride with a gun to my head."

Hattie's hands and feet tingled as her stomach dropped. Again? Her illusion had failed utterly. She was defenseless against this man. He could do anything to her. He could drag her off right now and she'd be powerless against him. Terror swamped her and she took a step back, turning to the side.

Lefty rammed his arm into Vincent's side, drawing an audible groan from the young man. "What're you gabbing about?"

He nodded at Hattie. "The iron. She's packing."

Hattie slipped the gun into her pocket while Vincent's attention was diverted. What to do now? Her illusions seemed to be useless against this man.

Lefty turned to face her, and she lifted both hands. "I think he's had enough of the water," she said, hitting back with the only weapon she had left. Vincent shot her a glare in response.

Lefty lifted a brow. "Shall we, then?"

Hattie drove the truck into the city, with Raymond shotgun. Her palms were sweaty on the steering wheel, barely staying on the road with the amount of times she'd looked into the rear view mirror to eye their passengers with barely hidden anxiety. The gangsters asked to be cut loose at the front of the Old Moravia Hotel and she felt herself begin to breathe a bit easier as they took their leave.

Hattie eyed Vincent as he stepped onto the street, adjusting his jacket. *Go away. Go away. By the time you come for me, I'll be long gone.* "You tell your lords and masters that their rum will be delivered by sundown," she told him, panic making her lash out once more. "You'll do that, won't you?"

Vincent stood stiff, jaw set, eyes hard.

Hattie turned to stare forward again, hammering the accelerator to steer the Runabout to her neighborhood. Why had she said that? Why hadn't she just let the man be and driven off into the distance? Why did she feel the need to verbally jab at him every chance she got? By the time she arrived home, she was close to hyperventilating. Pulling up to the curb, she set the brake and hopped out.

Raymond asked, "We're not going to Lizzie's?"

"You take the truck on in," she replied, her face tight and twitchy.

"You okay?"

"I'm...fine." She held the door for him as he switched seats. "I'll see you tomorrow," she lied.

Once the truck had slipped back down the street on its way to Locust Point, Hattie bolted through the front door of her red-brick apartment and bounded up the stairs.

She found both of her parents in the kitchen eating an early dinner.

"Ah!" Alton declared. "'Attie's finally home."

His beaming face melted into concern as Hattie stood in front of them, tears falling from her eyes.

"What's the matter?" he prodded.

Her mother stepped up to take her by her shoulders, guiding her into the room.

Hattie sniffled. "We have to leave. Tonight."

Branna eyed her in concern. "What happened?"

"A pincher…another one. He was there."

Her parents exchanged uneasy glances.

"Who, now?" her mother prodded, easing her into a chair. "Tell us what happened."

Hattie sucked in a few breaths to stave off hyperventilating. She'd been fighting to keep her calm as long as she could around the man, but now it was time to run. "One of the gangsters. From the Crew. He was their pincher…their slave. He was on my boat all night."

Alton stood and began to pace the room. "How?"

"The Crew sent him to help us out of a tight spot. We were pinned down halfway up the Rappahannock. The mob sent their pincher to do what he does. I…I think he knows."

"What happened? How does he know?" Alton asked while Branna got up and yanked a button box from the cabinet, behind the oats.

"I tried to pinch light around him. Twice. He wasn't fooled either time. Saw right through't. I think he knows I'm like him."

Branna set the button box on the table and flipped the lid open, her mouth tight. "How do you know that for sure? We have to know, Hattie. Have to know whether they'll be coming for us now or in a few days."

"Are you *sure* he knows?" Alton asked.

"If there's even a chance," Hattie gasped, "then we have to go. Tonight."

Her mother upended the box, coins and a few slips of paper falling onto the table. "Three. That's all we have. If we can wait until next Friday when I get paid, we'd have more."

Alton stopped his pacing and stood over the table, both parents staring down at the money. Hattie's heart suddenly sank. Three dollars. Plus, few coins that she had on her. It wasn't enough to start a new life somewhere else. They'd have to leave everything behind and take only what they could carry on foot. They'd have to sleep in fields or abandoned buildings, hoping to find jobs along the way to pay for a meal and occasional lodging. Her parents had sacrificed everything for her, and here they were about to do so again—at their age and with her father's poor health.

It would be the death of him. What right did she have to ask them to do this again for her? They'd done enough. Just then Alton nearly doubled over with a fit off coughing, making her decision all that much easier.

"I...I think we can wait until next payday," she said. "Maybe he doesn't know. Maybe I'm just panicking over nothing."

Her mother gave her a sharp look. "We're not risking your safety. We'll leave. It will all work out somehow. We've managed before."

"I promise if I have any notion that they're coming for me, I'll leave and you both can catch up to me later. Or maybe you can stay, and once things cool off, I can come back." Hattie got up and started to put the money back into the button box. "I just panicked. I don't know for certain he's onto me, so there's no sense in us running off like this."

"You go, 'Attie," her father told her. "Head west and cross the river into West Virginia. We'll meet up with you once your mother collects her pay." Alton went to sit back down, but as he did, another coughing fit wracked his body. He dropped into his seat and gasped for air between hacks.

His face turned dark red, and Branna wound around the table to rub his back. When the coughing fit finally subsided, she crouched down to the toe of the cabinet, pushed in one side to pivot the false panel out, and pulled out his bottle of blended Canadian whisky.

"I don't like you going on your own," Branna said as she poured Alton a finger, "but if your instincts say this man is going to come after you, then we want you to be safe."

Hattie stood in misery, watching as her father held his glass with trembling hands. He said nothing, balancing his efforts between sipping the whisky and struggling for breath.

How in the hell could she possibly leave them here? Without her income from Lizzie, they'd be homeless...and probably unemployed. Her father's health would never survive without her contributions. Besides, with the new spate of business Lizzie claimed they were facing, there might be a rare chance for them to save some back for a proper move. Somewhere with a roof. Somewhere away from the steel mill.

She reached for her father's shoulder. He lifted a hand and gripped her fingers. The whisky was taking hold, calming his lungs.

"I'm sorry," she whispered. "I got scared. I'll just lay low for a bit, and everything will be okay. I just panicked, that's all."

"Only...natural," he wheezed.

Hattie withdrew to her bedroom and shut the door. No, she couldn't leave. She'd probably overreacted. It was the very first time she'd ever met a real pincher besides herself. And with the guns and bullets and nearly getting shot, her nerves were raw. Yes, her illusions had failed, but he hadn't seemed to put two and two together. If he had, she was pretty sure he would have called her out on it right then and there. She was safe. She had to be. That pincher wasn't coming after her.

As she lay down on her bed, she winced. What a grouse she'd been to him! The things she'd said.... It was utterly uncalled for how she'd treated him. So impolite. Her mother would have been mortified. If she ever saw the man again, she'd have to dig deep for an apology.

If.

As she drifted to sleep, having been deprived of it for long hours, she thought of Bimini Island, and the magic elixir. The Water of Life. If only she had a dram of it, she could cure her father. He'd be better. They could save a little money. They could move as far away from these mobsters as possible. It was a fantasy, she was sure. But what a fantasy it was.

CHAPTER 14

Vincent stepped off the streetcar and onto Charles Street. The traffic was brisk, both pedestrian and vehicular. Bright and sunny Sunday afternoons meant everyone was out and about, particularly the churchgoers. Vincent stared up at St. Eustace, wondering how much longer Lefty would be. He hadn't attended Mass in a tree's age, personally, and wasn't sure how it really went anymore. When he'd been sold to the mob at the age of two, he spent most of his childhood in the care of priests as he learned how to read and write. Their peculiar approach to his spiritual education was somewhat more ascetic than he figured was the average person's. Prayers three times a day. Confession. Studies. And very little time for anything else.

Someone laid on his horn two blocks up the road, and a pair of older ladies hopped off the street and onto the sidewalk. The driver jerked the car to a halt alongside a shabby row house. When he stepped out of the car to give the old women a bit more what for than was called for, Vincent held a breath.

Cooper.

The squat man bustled to the alley between buildings and disappeared. What had Tony said? Cooper ran one of Vito's gambling parlors in a basement near St. Eustace. Vincent thought once more about Fern's bruises. Someone needed to teach this man a lesson. And here was his opportunity. There would no doubt be some retaliation on Cooper's part, but would the man really risk making himself look weak by going to Vito and whining that Vincent had threatened him? The Capo didn't appreciate men who couldn't take care of their own business, but Cooper was family, where Vincent was not.

No, he'd probably be more likely to stab Vincent in the back some night. And that prospect seemed a whole lot less unpleasant than the thought of facing Vito's anger. Either way…

Might as well go out knowing he'd done something good for once in his damned life.

Vincent checked the church. Doors still closed. He turned up the block and wove between cars near the intersection to cross the street. The thin alley revealed a single basement stoop, covered in a green-painted tin awning. A flight of brick steps led beneath the street level to a thick wood door below. Clacking down the steps, Vincent rapped on the door. A panel swung open, revealing bulging eyes and bushy eyebrows.

"Yeah?" the doorman shouted.

Vincent removed his fedora and lifted his face to the daylight.

"You know who I am?" he said with cold detachment.

The eyes bulged even wider before the panel slid shut. A bolt threw open, and the door opened. The doorman eased to the side, ushering Vincent into the smoke-filled cave of a space. Three tables ran alongside one another, each illuminated with a hurricane lamp. Cards sprayed across each table, side-by-side. Coins and cash sat in messy stacks. Men in suits and worker's jackets sat with their cards clutched to their chest, or chin, or even resting neatly on the tabletops.

The doorman grumbled, "Sorry, I…uh…I check everyone."

Vincent waved him off. "Don't sweat it, big boy."

He eased into the room, blinking at the cigar smoke.

A young man—a boy, really—stood in sleeves and a vest behind a makeshift bar top. He lifted two corked bottles. One was amber, the other was clear.

"Drink, sir? Dollar each."

Vincent grinned, reached into his pocket, and dropped a quarter onto the bar top.

"What say we skip the drink and I tip you, anyways?"

He beamed and snatched the coin. "Thank you, sir!"

Vincent nodded to a narrow hallway acting like a choke-point between the front room and an even darker back room. "Those the big spenders?"

"Ah, I believe so, sir."

Vincent stepped toward the hall. A drowsy, unshaven fellow sat in a chair nearby, balancing on its back legs. As Vincent approached, his eyes popped open, and he dropped his chair onto all fours to stand up.

"Keep your shirt on, fella," Vincent said.

The man replied with a stiff arm directly into Vincent's shoulder, checking him back a step. He rattled off three quick sentences in Italian. Vincent had never actually learned the language—just a few choice phrases from his dealings with the family.

The doorman rushed around the poker tables, nearly bowling one of the steelworkers off his chair. He jerked the bearded man aside and whispered into his ear. Vincent picked up the word *"stregone,"* and the bearded man leapt backward, eyes wide and dark.

Vincent nodded to the doorman again, stepping into the hallway.

He checked the door nearest him...a broom closet of sorts. Another door revealed a sort of storeroom with wood-plank shelves bearing boxes and bins of this and that.

When Vincent reached the back room, he had to squint to make sense of the sight. Two wall-mounted gas sconces flickered through a haze of tobacco fumes so thick it looked like a London fog. A long table reached through the length of the space. About six people gathered around, three women and three men. A tuxedoed fellow with eastern features presided over the table, reaching to gather dice as one of the women shot them.

Vincent shook his head. He hadn't figured Cooper was well-connected enough to mount a craps table in this miserable crawlspace, but there it was.

Speaking of which, he spotted Cooper guzzling some hooch alongside a dark-haired, Slavic-looking gent and an older man. Cooper nodded profusely as the old guy droned on about some arrangement he'd made with "John D. Rockerfeller himself, by God."

The Slavic man patted Cooper on the shoulder and went to place a bet. At length, the old man's interest drew toward the table and a scandalously clad young lady who seemed young enough to be his daughter, but whose posture toward the man seemed anything but daughterly.

In a space of a few seconds, Cooper was alone, and no one had eyes on Vincent.

Wiping his fingers along his jacket, Vincent snapped time to a halt. The bubble was tight, efficient. He reached for Cooper's lapels, snatching them both with one hand and jerking him along the warped floor boards as Vincent made his way to the store room. Vincent pulled the door open, shoved Cooper inside, then joined him in the darkness. He reached into his jacket for a box of matches he'd palmed from the Old Moravia bar, then snapped his fingers again to release the time pinch.

Cooper's breathing returned, then halted again. It returned with a grunt, then another.

"What?" he blubbered.

Vincent struck a match.

Cooper jerked back with a hiss, striking his head against one of the wooden shelves. His eyes were wild and panicked. The man released a string of vulgarities suitable for only the saltiest of sailors. Once his eyes had registered the scene before him, and he'd taken a second or two to figure out where he was, Cooper's face adopted a red cast.

"What in hell're you doing here?"

Vincent held the match vertically alongside his own face and said nothing.

Cooper caught his breath.

"You…you scared the shit outta me. Freak. What's this all about?"

Vincent replied, "You're going to leave Fern, Coop."

"What? What're you—?"

"You think you're a big man because you hit women? Make you feel strong?"

Cooper's eyes narrowed, and his mouth set hard. "What're you butting into my business for? What I do with my dames is none of yours."

"She's bringing your calling cards into the hotel. Sportin' a nice shiner for all of us to see. You think we're just going to let this happen?"

Cooper grinned and jammed a finger into Vincent's chest. "You ain't family, freak. You get no say in nothin'."

The match burned low, and he released it to fall to the floor. The flame extinguished on its way down.

Vincent spoke into the darkness. "If you lay another hand on Fern, either kindly or unkindly, I'll find you again."

He heard a rustling in the darkness. On instinct, he struck another match to find Cooper pointing a pistol at his face.

Vincent grinned.

He pinched time…he didn't even snap his fingers.

From Cooper's point of view, it would have been instantaneous. One second he was holding a gun to Vincent. The other…he was holding a match, and Vincent was the one holding the gun.

Vincent asked, "Is this yours? Remember. You'll never see me coming. It'll happen in the space between seconds. Maybe you'll blink, and you'll end up facedown in the harbor. Maybe you'll find yourself falling off a six-story building. Maybe I'll take my time and get real creative."

Cooper's face blanched, and a fine bead of sweat popped up across his brow.

Nodding, Vincent uncocked the pistol. "You're cutting her loose. Today. And you'll never hit another woman again. Are we crystal clear?"

Cooper nodded dumbly.

From Cooper's angle, he was suddenly standing back with the big rollers. His pistol sat heavy in his holster. The craps table erupted with a lucky roll. And Vincent…was gone.

The Slavic man turned to Cooper, then lifted a brow.

Cooper followed his stare. He was still holding a lit match.

* * *

VINCENT HOPPED up the street toward St. Eustace, a sappy grin on his face. As a child the priests had driven into his skull that Vincent was never to use his powers for self-advancement. Only in the service of the family.

This wasn't precisely self-advancement, but it sure felt good. It felt more than good.

The doors to the church were open, and a few people were stepping down the stone stairs to the street. He found Lefty leaning against a light post with a newspaper double-folded in his hand.

Lefty lifted his eyes and scowled. "Where've you been?"

"On a walk. It's a cherry day. Thought some fresh air'd do me some good."

Lefty nodded, then took a sniff next to Vincent's lapels.

"Uh, huh. You smell fresh, alright."

Vincent sighed. "So, I had a drink."

"I don't care," Lefty said. "Come on. I'm hungry."

They walked up the street toward Alfie's. The restaurant was open only a handful of hours each week, and Lefty made sure to carve himself at least one of those hours each Sunday.

As they were seated at a corner table, Lefty smirked at Vincent. "You oughta come to Mass with me next Sunday."

"Thanks but I'll pass on that."

"Ain't you a Catholic no more?"

"Only when it counts."

Lefty shook his head with a weary grin. "Someone like you oughta put more thought into his immortal soul."

Vincent shrugged. "I didn't have an army of Huns firing machine guns at my sorry hide to give me religion."

"Don't forget the land mines and the mustard gas."

They ordered iced teas and sat in silence for a while. Lefty eyed Vincent hard.

Vincent squinted. "What now?"

"I was just wondering what your angle was with redheads?"

"Don't have no angle I'm aware of."

Lefty smirked.

Vincent sucked in a breath, then released it in a sigh. "You mean that river rat?"

"I saw the two of you chewin' fat up the front of the boat. Pretty girl, but didn't think she was your type, ya know?"

"She's not," he snapped back, appalled. "And that fat was more like shoe leather. She's a shrew."

"What can you do? She's a redhead. They got tempers and they don't hold back tellin' you what they think."

Vincent reached for the glass of tea and took a long pull, gathering his thoughts. "I don't know what crawled up that little hellcat's drawers, but she had it out for me from minute one. I'm trying to put that behind me. Besides. She's Tony's problem."

Lefty nodded thoughtfully. "Problem, for sure. Vito's spittin' nails over this Deltaville nonsense."

"How'd he take it?" Vincent asked.

"I gave it to him, well…let's say less straight, more in a wide curve. Kept it business. Didn't mention the weird symbols and the Hell pincher mumbo jumbo."

"Probably a good decision."

"You ain't telling me twice!"

Their meal arrived and all thoughts of sharp-tongued red-haired women and Hell pinchers took a back seat to the food as Vincent tucked into his breakfast.

CHAPTER 15

It was a sunny Sunday afternoon. Springtime in the city was always welcome, particularly after a bitter winter. Hattie watched passersby from her bedroom window. They strolled up and down the street in their dresses and jackets, taking in the bright blue sky and the fresh air. She reached out and placed a hand onto the pane of glass, wondering when she'd feel safe enough to join them.

"Oh, for the love of Mary," her mother called from the doorway, "just go outside."

"I don't know who's watching," Hattie muttered.

"It's been four days. I think if something was going to happen, it'd happened by now."

In the four days since Hattie had met Vincent and had nearly uprooted her entire life to run away, she'd stayed holed up in her house. Lizzie stopped by that Thursday, urging her to get out onto the water to fill some of the orders from the Crew, but Hattie simply told her it wasn't safe.

That was three paydays she'd foregone in the name of safety. Much more of this, and they'd have real problems making rent.

"Go to church, at least," Branna urged. "You're sick to your soul. It'll do you good."

Hattie grinned. Church. Well, that was an idea.

She knocked the dust and wrinkles off her dress and shimmied into it. On her way out the door, she gave her mother a kiss on the cheek. "Tell Da I'll try to bring home some meat."

"With what money?" she asked.

"I'll find some. Strangle something myself, if I have to."

The sunlight was glorious. Bright yellow and bold, not the dry-sifted white light of wintertime. It warmed her arms as she stepped out onto the street, turning south for what she told her mother was church.

Church, as it turned out, was actually a speakeasy tucked into the side of an old retail shop down on Orleans. It was called the Fontainebleau, and though its owner, Leon, insisted on referring to it as a speakeasy, it was open to the public and unmolested by the police. On Sundays, Leon kept a fellow on the piano most of the day. It was a fine place for Hattie to hide out and still feel like she belonged to the human race.

Hattie stepped through the white-painted French doors of the Fontainebleau and slid behind the tables in the center of the space to a spot at the far end of the bar…her spot. There were about ten people haunting the place, each with a glass of something clear. Gin, probably. That was a Sunday drink.

A dark-skinned fellow in a bowler hat sat at the rickety upright along the far wall, tickling the keys to some Chicago style jazz. It was languid and calm—not dancing music. This was drinking music.

A lean black man stepped through a pair of drapes concealing the back room. He smiled to Hattie as she settled onto a stool nearest the wall.

"Hattie!" Leon called with reserved volume as he approached behind the bar. He'd learned that she didn't want anyone calling her name out in public and was an excellent guard of discretion.

"Leon," she replied as he reached over the bar and gave her a peck on the cheek.

"It's been too long, ya?" he said in his Caribbean drawl. "Where ya been hidin'?"

"On the water," she replied. "Making an honest living. Much like yourself."

He chuckled. "I won't water my gin, if you won't pass no slugs."

She smirked. The first time she visited the Fontainebleau, she'd ordered a second drink without enough money to pay for it. She managed to pinch light over a wood slug. It fooled him at the time, but when she'd left he put it together. To his credit, he didn't kick her out the next time she stopped by. Hattie wasn't sure why that was. Still, he never skipped an opportunity to bring it up, and she never actually apologized for it.

"Speakin' of," he said with a lean and a leer. "Ya got any real money today?"

She fished a nickel out of her clutch and slapped it onto the bar top.

Leon lifted it to inspect against the light from one of the windows.

Hattie chuckled. "It's real money, Leon."

"I know, I know. I'm just bein' cautious." He pocketed the nickel and winked at her. "What's ya poison today?"

"Got any white lightning?"

His eyes bugged. "Dat's a six-foot drink for a five-foot woman."

She scowled. "Is that a challenge, little man? I'll take you round for round!"

"Nah. I don't drink da stuff. I only flog it!"

"Then less lip, more hooch. Aye?"

He hummed a tune to himself as he poured a tiny portion of moonshine into a tulip glass, sliding it over to Hattie.

She raised the glass. "Putting some pearls on this pig?"

"Eh, I am a believer in beauty. All things are beautiful to those who—"

"More of your navel gazing, then?"

He laughed. "It's a free service."

She took a sip of the hooch. It was fumey, strong, jagged. She winced and sucked in a cooling breath.

Leon smirked at her. "You're da one person in all God's Green Earth who sips that."

"Cost me a nickel, didn't it? I'm going to enjoy it."

"Enjoy," he said. "What's with da rotgut? Workin' dat hard?"

She sighed. "Yes and no. It's just been a complicated week, is all."

He nodded and left her alone.

Hattie cupped the tulip glass, watching the people as they came and went. No one seemed to notice her. If any young man cast a glance in her direction, she pinched the light around her face just enough to discourage them. That had almost become instinct for Hattie when she was in public. She didn't want to talk to anyone. She just wanted to be.

Hours passed, and she'd barely touched the moonshine in her glass. Leon had offered her replacements several times, but she wasn't really interested. Liquor was something she liked to have in her hands, but not to drink. It was like having some sort of power, an option to do something... whether or not you did it.

As for actually drinking the sauce, she wasn't sure what her reservations were. Perhaps it was fear? Fear of losing control? Fear of being discovered?

An orange haze of sunset plowed through the windows, and the crowd had swapped out a third time. All new faces, many of them dressed up a bit nicer for the evening.

Leon had left her alone for quite some time, as if she'd finally faded into the wall. But as a few young gentlemen took seats at the bar beside her, the bartender gave her a questioning glance.

The young man sitting beside Hattie cast a quick peek at her glass, then to her. She popped up the illusion of an older, unattractive woman, but he didn't seem dissuaded.

"Evening," he chimed. "Drinking alone?"

She said nothing.

"What're you having?" he prodded.

Leon approached. "My friends…what'll ya have?"

Hattie appreciated the deflection. It was an opportunity to leave discreetly. But even as she pivoted to leave, the notion of going home fell heavy onto her shoulders, pressing her back down onto the stool. Home had been prison, lately.

Instead of giving an order, the young man gestured to Hattie's glass. "This gin?"

Leon leaned in. "I think maybe this young lady's having a private moment. So, what can I get ya?"

"Young?" He turned to face her with a smirk…quicker than she could restore the illusion over her face.

His eyebrows lifted. "Huh."

Leon tensed.

Hattie sucked in a breath, then replied, "It's white lightning, boy-o. Think you're game?"

His face erupted into a joyful smile. "Absolutely."

Leon cocked his head at Hattie, but she tapped her fingers on the bar top, smoothing out his confusion. He turned to pour both of the young men a single finger of the moonshine.

Hattie's neighbor turned to face her fully. "Cheers."

She lifted the tulip.

He pounded the hooch, shaking his head with a wince. And then he watched her.

Hattie put the glass to her lips, then upended the entire contents into her mouth and down her throat.

The burn was intense and immediate.

Hattie pinched light over her face as she stuck out her tongue and made all sorts of repulsed expressions. But to the man watching her, she'd simply quaffed the moonshine and offered a steady, challenging lift of her brow. It was a tricky illusion to maintain, distracted as she was with the fumes choking her from inside her own gullet. But she managed it.

He shook his head and laughed. "You're alright."

The man turned back toward Leon, ordered a gin fizz, and tipped his hat to Hattie.

And that was that. No more conversation. No pressing. No flirtation. He'd just had a fine moment with a stranger and now he was back to chatting up his friend. Hattie smiled. The weight on her shoulders eased. It shouldn't have been such the revelation that not every individual in the city was out for her blood. Maybe she didn't have to hide all the time. Maybe sometimes she could be one of them after all—a regular, normal person.

The moonshine hit her stomach, spreading like a brush fire through her chest and arms. The smile on her face remained.

The poor old fellow on the piano called it quits, easing off the bench with arthritic care, nursing his fingers as he reached for his cane.

The men beside Hattie turned to watch.

Her neighbor muttered, "Aw, nuts. Music's gone off to die of old age."

Leon nodded. "Kirb's been at it all day. Can't say I blame him."

The young man said, "You should get some dame in here. Real songbird, y'know? That'll pack them in."

Leon shot a glance at Hattie.

She'd spent one or two Sundays at the Fontainebleau when there was no one around singing a few tunes to an empty room. She'd even convinced Old Kirby to bang out something from the Old Country. He only knew one or two Irish songs, so it was rare.

Hattie sighed, and leaned back on her stool to stretch. Her brain fuzzed a bit, sending a quick jolt of blithe joy into her body.

"Well," she announced, "I don't know if I qualify as a songbird, but I'm dame enough."

Her neighbor peered over his shoulder at her. "You can sing?"

Hattie nodded to Leon. "You play, don't you?"

Leon nodded.

"Know anything from my homeland?"

"Which land dat be?" Leon asked.

"I'll take that as a no."

He lifted his chin. "If ya so eager, I could stagger my way through something modern. Ya ever listen to a radio?"

"If I could afford a radio, I wouldn't be drinking moonshine, would I?"

Leon shot her a sharp smirk, then tossed his apron onto the bar top. "Right, then."

He wound his way out onto the floor and took a seat at the piano.

Hattie sat rigid on her stool. How…how did this happen?

Leon gave her a beckoning gesture with his finger, and the two young men at the bar beside her began to applaud.

Several others joined in.

Hattie felt a blush spread across her cheeks. The iron-vice dread that usually clamped down onto her lungs softened. It may have been the moonshine, but instead of fleeing she found herself slipping off the bar stool and inching her way toward the piano. Leon took a couple passes before he managed the pickup to "Everybody Loves My Baby."

Eyes fell onto Hattie.

She cleared her throat, turned to face the piano rather than the audience, and sang.

Afterward, she ran home. Bolted up the stairs. Sprinted past her parents who looked on in surprise. After Hattie had shut the bedroom door behind her, she lingered by the window, staring out at the night sky at the rising moon, and laughed. It was time to rejoin the world. If she could find the courage to stand up before a bunch of strangers and sing, then she could certainly handle running booze on the waterfront for the mob. Besides, what were the chances that she'd ever see those two gangsters again?

CHAPTER 16

*A*knock on the door jarred Vincent from a midday nap.

He leapt from his sofa, turning to the door. Lefty tended to knock with one rap, then two, then one more. It was just some stupid thing he did, but Vincent had come to recognize it.

This was different…just four heavy pounds, not from the knuckles, but from the meat of a fist.

Vincent scanned his apartment, considering his options. He owned no guns, and every piece of iron he'd liberated during his duties to the Crew, he'd discarded with precious little emotion. His typical go-to was to pinch time and turn his opponents' weapons against them.

Another pound.

Vincent crept toward the door and eased it open against the chain, keeping his body mostly behind the wall. He found two besuited fellows in the hall. They were unarmed and looked a bit familiar.

"Can I help you gents?" Vincent asked through the crack in the door.

"We're here to collect you," one of the men replied.

"Collect me for what?"

"The Capo."

"Vito?" he blurted. "What's the angle?"

"We're just here to collect you."

Vincent squinted. "Where are we going? Where's Lefty?"

"Havre de Grace," the man responded with an air of gravity. "I think Mancuso's already there."

Vincent's stomach dropped. Panic tore through him.

Havre de Grace. That was Vito's private estate. No one was called to Vito's home unless there was something so serious that it couldn't wait for him to come into the city. That always meant bad news. Had Cooper decided he didn't mind looking weak in order to rat Vincent out, or was there something else he'd done wrong? Vincent quickly ran through the last few days, the trip to Deltaville, the conversation with Capstein, the boat trip with the rum. When it seemed like just breathing was enough to cause offense, anything could be the reason for this summons.

Knowing better than to keep the Capo waiting a second longer than was necessary, Vincent pulled a jacket and hat off the chair next to the door and joined his unfamiliar escort downstairs.

The drive out to the hillsides northeast of the city took longer than Vincent had imagined it would. Maybe that was because he'd spent the entire trip questioning whether he was about to die. They'd already summoned Lefty. That was another bad sign. Lefty was Vincent's handler, and escorting him back and forth was Lefty's specific job, not these two goons. If Vito wanted Lefty there without Vincent, it was to discuss Vincent.

Cooper. It had to have been Cooper. Or maybe someone had lied and told Vito that he'd been receptive to Capstein's overtures and was planning on running off to join the

Upright Citizens. One could possibly be an offense punishable by death. The other definitely was.

The sun had bowed toward the west, sending warm light of the Golden Hour across fields of stakes and vines running in rows across the gentle hillsides. An imposing villa stood at the end of a stone-paved lane, built in the style of Italian architecture, nestled at the fore of the vineyard surrounding.

The driver parked the car, and the two men escorted Vincent away from the villa and up a gravel-dusted lane into the rows of vines. This didn't feel right. The hill swept up behind them as they progressed, blocking the view from the estate. Who the hell would be out here? Vincent considered his options for the first time. He could, in all truth, pinch time and make a run for it. None of this was strictly compulsory.

Or…was it? If he ran, where would he go? What would be his purpose? What would Vito do to Lefty?

Vincent knew he had at least one option. Capstein had made insinuations, but Vincent had dismissed them at the time. Richmond already had two pinchers. Adding a third would put them higher than Philadelphia in terms of the balance of power. Sure, Vito could conceivably launch all-out war on Richmond, but he would have to rely on other *famiglia* to shore up his efforts.

All this musing sent Vincent into a swell of anxiety. Pinch and run? Join the Upright Citizens? Or just face his fate as he'd been trained his whole life to do?

The anxiety ebbed as they turned a corner around a knoll, and a plaza of flagstone slipped into view. A lumber arbor covered half the plaza, vines trained up and along the posts and beams. A single wood table stood at the center of the stones with two folding chairs pulled haphazardly away.

Vincent sucked in a breath as he spotted Lefty standing to the side of the plaza, his arm folded in front of him. Beside

Lefty stood Fern, clad in a bright yellow dress and gloves. Her hair belled out from beneath a white cloche, covering the bruised side of her face.

Well, at least now he knew for sure what offense he was here to account for.

Lefty gave Vincent a long glare before nodding to the center of the plaza, where Vito stood holding a glass of red fluid to the light of the sunset. A mousy young man lingered at his elbow, holding two glass carafes.

Vito swirled the wine and sniffed it.

"Last year's cabernet franc," the mousy man said.

Vito wrinkled his nose.

The man added, "The phenolic notes are still…problematic."

Vito tossed the wine out of the glass to the side of the stones, then presented it to the mouse, who poured a bit from one of his carafes.

As Vito took a sniff, then a tiny sip, from the second choice, he nodded. "This is the Meritage?"

"I feel we should continue with the blends."

"Agreed," Vito said, handing the man his glass.

The mouse man bowed and withdrew, disappearing down the gravel path.

Vito shook his head and gestured to Vincent without really looking at him. "Come."

Vincent complied.

Taking a seat at the table, Vito spread his hands flat against the wood. "I cannot grow proper grapes in this state. Winters are too long. Too wet. Ah…to plant fields of Nebbiolo. But I must settle for these Bordeaux cultivars. It depresses me." He finally looked up to Vincent. "Sit."

Vincent took the second chair, pulling it across to the opposite side of the table from Vito.

The old man ran a hand along his broad face. "I hear

things, Vincenzo." He popped Vincent's name with Italian flare. "Troubling things."

"What do you hear?" he asked flatly.

"That you have eyes on someone who is not yours. Someone who belongs to one of our family."

Vincent peered over his shoulder at Fern, then sighed. "Only rumors."

Vito's eyes narrowed, and his mouth drew into the slightest of scowls. "You choose your words carefully. While I respect that, I need to hear more."

"Apologies, Capo. Who accuses me of this?"

"Not two hours ago, I received a visit from Luigi Capucci." Vito snarled. "He calls himself Cooper, now. I had words with him regarding that."

Vincent lifted a hand. "We had a disagreement, Capo. That's all."

"Is it?" He gestured for Fern, who stepped across the stones toward them, her hands trembling by her side. "He tells me that you threatened his life. Held a gun to his face. Told him to leave this girl, because you wanted her. Do you deny these things?"

Vincent peered up at Fern. She stared straight forward, making eye contact with no one, her face ghostly pale.

"I deny that I expressed an interest in Fern to Cooper."

"Then you know her name?"

Vincent shifted in his seat. "I do. She helped me recover from our encounter with the Dryfork family."

Vito peered up at Fern, then back to Vincent with a grunt.

Vincent added, "I noticed she had bruises. Like she'd been grabbed. Then I saw…" He gestured to her face with a lift of his finger. "Someone socked it to her, and she looked like she needed help."

Vito pushed away from the table and stood before Fern.

"My dear," he cooed. "May I see your face?"

Fern reached up with a shaky hand to pull aside the locks of hair covering her eye. She sported bold eye shadow, and lots of foundation. The bruise under her eye was almost, but not quite, covered up, yellow-green now instead of deep purple, and beside it on her cheekbone was a fresh set.

Vito nodded. "*Grazie.*"

Vincent stared down at the table, the anger he felt at Cooper resuming its fire in his chest. Had Cooper gone back to Fern after their "talk" and done this to her? Had nothing he'd done had any impact whatsoever?

Vito paced around the back of Vincent's chair. "But you do not deny you attacked Luigi?"

"He's hitting women, Capo. Someone needed to get involved."

"And who do you think should make that decision. Hmm? You? Or me?"

Vincent nodded. "You."

"Correct." Vito turned back to Fern. "My dear...does Luigi mistreat you?"

She cleared her throat. "Sir?"

"Does he hit you?" Vito clarified.

She stood stiff. Vincent could hear her breaths as she struggled through the moment. Finally, she answered in barely more than a whisper, "No, sir. He treats me fine. He's never hit me. I fell. I told Vincent I fell...that I was okay."

Wonderful. He'd put his neck on the line, and not only was Cooper still hitting her, but she'd just hung him out to dry. Why had he even bothered to get involved?

Vito blinked at the woman, then smiled. "Thank you. You may go." He snapped his fingers, and one of Vincent's escorts stepped forward.

Vincent continued to watch Fern. She didn't look at him. She simply turned and left.

Placing his hands on his wide hips, Vito marched back and

forth along the stones. "We take oaths, Vincenzo. Every member of this family takes an oath. We do not kill one another. We do not covet another's woman. It is *proibito*." He stopped at the other chair and took a seat with a huff. "But you? You are not family. You have not taken the oaths. You are a tool. A weapon."

Vincent recrossed his legs and pulled his hands tight into his lap, watching the other man carefully for any sign of what was to come.

Vito shook his head. "Do you know how the other branches of the family see me? Philadelphia has two *stregore*. Pittsburgh? Three. New York? Eight. And these are prized stock. All second generation, and they've had offspring."

Vincent cringed to hear Vito speak of pinchers in the same manner Kentucky blue bloods spoke of Thoroughbreds. Was this all he really was to them? His whole life in service to the family, and he was no more than a racehorse and potential stud?

The Capo released a long breath. "Even the Upright Citizens have two. And what do I have? One. Just you."

Vincent wilted.

"Just you, Vincenzo," he repeated, leaning forward. "And here I have you using your witchcraft against my own. You have taken no oaths, as you are not permitted. Nevertheless, I absolutely cannot have you raising your hand against *famiglia*. Do you understand me?"

Vincent nodded. "Yes, Capo."

Vito asked, "Are you in love with this girl?"

"No, Capo. I just don't like it when a man treats women with disrespect." He added as he ventured a glance up at Vito, "It makes us all cheap."

Vito looked over to Lefty, then back to Vincent. "This…is Old World thinking." He pointed at Vincent with the words, then stood up again. "Luigi is a pig. It is well known. One day, he will push too hard, and someone will push back. Probably this girl…who knows? But it can't be you, Vincenzo. It can't be you."

"I understand."

"As for the rest of it, I doubt you even think on it."

Vincent cocked a brow. "Sir?"

"Our situation, you and me. My only *stregore*. How tight a grip I must maintain, and how little help I get from you. How it makes me look."

He sucked in a breath, realizing where Vito was going with this. Quickly he thought through the conversation with Capstein. "If I may…I was just thinking about it as I walked here."

Vito wandered to the edge of the flagstones, watching the sun dip below the far rows of vines. "Is that so?"

Vincent stood up but remained by the table. "There is something you should know." He checked on Lefty.

Lefty squinted, and then nodded.

Vito turned to Vincent. "Yes?"

"When we were in Virginia, we were entertained by the Richmond pinchers. A fellow by the name of Elmer Capstein."

"I am familiar with the name."

"You should know…he made overtures."

Vito grinned. "Overtures?"

"Yes. To *me*."

Vito's grin receded, and he marched toward Vincent. "What did he offer you?"

"A place in Richmond," Vincent replied. "He's got the Crew figured as weak, like you said. Distracted by the West Virginia moonshiners trying to cut you out. Distracted by these pirates on the Bay. Distracted by the dust kicked up in New York between Salvatore and Masseria."

Vito's eyes widened. "You do think of such things. Well, then? What did you tell him?"

"I told him to take a walk."

Vito smiled. "Then, you are happy here?"

"Here's where I belong, Capo. I got no delusions otherwise."

"Then," Vito declared, "you have a new task, my *stregore*. And your task is this—find me more."

"More?"

"I do what I can to keep these *idioti* in the hills from outgrowing us. And the Bay...well, this is a conversation for Antonio. But I need more like you." He grunted, reaching for Vincent's shoulders to give them a quick shake. "And this is your primary task from now until you succeed. No more errands. No more security. You find me another *stregore*. For us."

Vincent sucked in a ragged breath, then replied, "I will."

"Go, now."

He released Vincent's shoulders.

Vincent turned to approach Lefty.

Vito called, "Alonzo...stay a moment."

Vincent halted in front of Lefty, waiting for the man's nod before proceeding. The remaining escort accompanied Vincent back down the gravel path toward the villa. The sky began to darken overhead, and a young boy emerged to light the gas lamps along the drive. There was no sign of Fern, but Lefty's car was still there. Seemed he'd driven in. Vincent was so full of cascading dread when he'd arrived, the car had slipped his notice.

Now, instead of dread, Vincent's thoughts spiraled around his new task. He'd known for years that Vito wanted more pinchers. That was obvious, but Vincent assumed he'd buy one from New York, or trade for one. Or perhaps that he had people already on the lookout. But now that lookout was Vincent.

Before long, he heard crunching along the gravel path and turned to find Lefty pointing to his car.

"Get in," he grumbled.

Vincent nodded and slipped into the passenger seat of Lefty's car.

The wheels spun in the gravel before the car lurched into a tight turn back down the drive.

"So," Vincent mumbled. "What a day, huh?"

Lefty's jaw set hard. "Don't talk to me."

"Listen, I'm sorry I got you into hot water."

"I told you," Lefty said, struggling to form articulate words as he focused on the dark lane, "to leave that girl alone. Didn't I tell you that?"

"You did."

"And I turn my back for a hot second, and you go strong-arming Cooper in his own establishment? It's like you're trying to give me a condition."

"I said I'm sorry," Vincent said. "What did Vito say to you?"

"We're going back to Cooper's, is what."

Vincent frowned. "What for?"

"An apology."

THE NIGHTTIME CROWD in Cooper's basement gambling parlor was a bit more raucous than the Sunday morning crowd. It was shoulder-to-shoulder in that hole, and the air was double-thick with cigar smoke. Lefty shoved his way through the gathering with Vincent following in his wake.

At one point, a boisterous poker player stood up with a shout of victory, slapping his chair against Vincent.

The sudden motion sent Vincent into someone lingering by the bar. He reached out to steady himself, his fingers landing onto the bare arms of a woman in a yellow dress.

Fern.

He jerked his hands away as he looked into her eyes.

She stood stiff, then lifted a hand to check the swoop of hair that covered her bruises.

"Sorry," he muttered.

She took in a breath to answer but reconsidered. With wide eyes and a quick shake of her head, she turned away.

An arm reached in front of Vincent, tapping Fern on her shoulder.

Lefty nodded to her as she whipped back around. "You're with us."

"What?" she squeaked.

"You're coming with us. We have business with Cooper."

She paled. "No. I…I can't."

"You don't have a choice, ma'am," Lefty urged. "Unless you want another invitation to Vito's vineyard."

She blanched further, then she nodded and followed Lefty with Vincent taking the rear. It seemed she was meant to witness this public humiliation Vito had sentenced Vincent with.

They wove through the tiny hallway leading to the back room. The crowd wasn't as flush as the front room, but it was still nearly impossible to see the craps table from where they stood.

Lefty snapped his fingers several times over the heads of the crowd, and failing to capture Cooper's attention, he lifted his hand to his lips and released a loud whistle. The gamblers fell silent, turning to face them.

Cooper wove from behind the table, his face flushed and sour.

"What's he doing here?" Cooper hissed.

Lefty lifted a calm hand. "We're here on behalf of the Capo. Can we get the room?"

Cooper stared at Lefty, then released a sudden laugh that sprayed Lefty's face with spittle.

"You jerking my rope with this?" Cooper blurted. "Where do you think these people are gonna go?"

"Then we do this outside," Lefty replied.

Cooper shook his head. "I ain't got time for this." He turned back toward the table.

Lefty laid his hand onto Cooper's shoulder. "You want to call Vito now, and tell him you're too busy for an apology?"

Cooper's brow lifted. "An apology?"

"Yes," Lefty replied. "That a problem?"

Cooper turned to smirk at Vincent. "No beef. I'm just surprised Vito let him off so easy. Is he back on his chain? Gonna behave himself?"

Vincent stuffed his hands into his pockets before balling them into fists.

Lefty shrugged. "He's not here to hurt you, Cooper. He had a long talk with the Capo, and now we're here."

Cooper snickered, then turned to the room. "Alright, everyone! Give us the room! Just be a couple minutes. Have a drink on the house."

The gamblers murmured and grumbled, gathering their things and filing one-by-one back through the hallway into the overstuffed front room. The last few came to a halt just outside the hallway, as there was literally no room left to go.

Lefty ushered Fern and Vincent closer to the craps table.

Cooper stepped up to Fern, his eyes narrowed. "What, you're here for this, too?"

Lefty nodded. "At Vito's request."

Vincent took a step forward and cleared his throat as Lefty gestured for him.

"Okay, so..." Vincent said. "I'm supposed to—"

"What are you doing?" Lefty asked.

Vincent's eyes shifted over to Lefty. "I'm...apologizing. What do you think?"

Lefty shook his head. "No, no. We're here for an apology, but not from you."

"Huh?"

Cooper shook his head. "What, now?"

Lefty reached into his jacket and pulled his revolver. With a quick, matter-of-fact motion, he aimed the piece at Cooper's foot and pulled the trigger.

Screams spilled from the hallway and front room as the shot continued to ring in everyone's ears. Soon, a thundering noise of people pressing into one another to make a quick exit shuddered the entire building.

The sounds from the front room subsided enough for Cooper's screams of pain to meet their ears as he slid to the ground, gripping his foot in his hands.

Cooper drew in rapid breaths, then blustered, "What the fuck?"

Lefty crouched over Cooper. "Now. About that apology."

The man's cheeks puffed in and out as he tried to breathe through the pain.

Lefty eased the gun to his kneecap.

In a spate of syllables, Cooper shouted, "Okay, I'm sorry. I'm sorry." He lifted a bloodied hand to Vincent. "Sorry I dimed you out to Vito. I was stupid."

Lefty lifted the pistol, then brought it in a quick swipe against Cooper's temple sending him sprawling across the floor.

"No," Lefty snapped, "not to him." He cocked his head toward Fern. "Apologize to her."

Cooper clamped his eyes shut, rocking back and forth as he bled onto the floor. "Sorry, sorry..."

"Sorry for what?" Lefty prodded with a whimsical lift of his ear.

"Sorry I hit you."

Lefty straightened up, then peered over to Fern. "Do you accept his apology?"

Fern watched the scene as it unfolded, her face finally regaining its color, her eyes wide. "No. I do not."

Lefty sighed. "Oh well. Them's the breaks. I'm sorry, ma'am, but Capo Vito only required that he apologize. He's done that. What you do with that apology, I leave to you."

She nodded.

"You should probably leave, now," Lefty stated.

Fern took a deep breath, then nodded again. As she turned toward the hallway, she paused in front of Vincent.

He braced himself.

Her eyes moved to the floor, then to his hat, and then finally she looked him in the eye. "Thanks for…your help."

He grinned and watched her leave. Lefty stepped over top Cooper, whose face was white. "I have a message from the Capo. He says if you continue to behave like a rabid dog, he'll put you down like one. *Capisci?*"

Cooper nodded.

Lefty added, "And he says to stop calling yourself Cooper."

Vincent and Lefty made their way back out of the basement gambling hall, a much easier task now that it had mostly cleared out. Once they were back on street level, Lefty holstered his pistol.

"You did that on purpose," Vincent said, "didn't you? Keeping me in the cold like that."

"You deserved it."

"I suppose so."

Lefty nodded to the car, and they made their way up the block. "Now what?"

"Now we find Tony."

Lefty squinted at Vincent. "What's your beef with Tony?"

"Nothing," Vincent answered. "I just need to find those boat runners."

"What, the ones from the other day?"

"Yeah." They climbed into the car. "I'm supposed to find another pincher for Vito. And I think I know where to find one."

"Where's that?"

Vincent replied as they pulled onto the street, "Somewhere on the water."

CHAPTER 17

Despite the previous day's abundant sunlight and fair temperatures, Monday had turned into a cloudy, brisk mess. Winds whipped off the river, filling the city with a late spring chill. Hattie pulled the collar of her working shirt up over her neck to stave off the breeze as she marched up to the Locust Point warehouse. The main doors were open, and Hattie simply stepped inside.

Lizzie stood beside a skid of bottle crates, a notepad in her hand. She glanced up at Hattie with a start.

"Oh, lord," she blurted. "You have cat's feet."

Hattie shrugged. "I don't get anywhere making a fuss, do I?"

"You just missed the excitement," Lizzie said, tucking her pad under her arm. "Two trucks just left for Winnow's Slip."

"Barrels?"

"More of these." Lizzie nudged one of the crates with the toe of her boot. "The Crew's sent us wine, this time. Hell, I almost feel respectable."

"Do you need me, then?" Hattie asked.

"I always need you. Better hustle on to the Slip, though. Raymond's getting used to quick runs."

Hattie nodded. "So, it's been quiet on the water? No more incidents?"

"None so far."

"I suppose I'm a jinx."

Lizzie turned for her office. "Tick tock, jinxie."

Hattie headed for the waterfront, parking the truck beneath a tree at the Slip, then jogging along the pier toward Raymond's boat. Four men lugged crate after crate of wine bottles onto the boat. More specifically, two men did all the lifting while the other pair watched. She smirked and shook her head. They must've been higher on the mob food chain.

One of them turned as she approached, and she stopped dead.

His tipped his hat with a smile, his dark eyes sparkling with amusement. "Good morning."

It was the pincher...Vincent. Right, that was his name. Last time they'd spoken, she'd given him a good tongue-lashing and she felt embarrassed about that. Moment they were alone, she really did owe him an apology. Although she was hoping there wouldn't be any moments alone with this man.

"Good morning," she replied.

Vincent's older companion, the one with only one arm, offered her a quick, silent nod.

"Well, fancy meeting the both of you again," she said with a genial grin.

"I hope that's copacetic," Vincent replied. "Don't mean to cause you any undue grief."

"Nah," she gave him a wink. "Having a strapping young man on the boat is something a girl could get used to." She brushed past the pair and walked on.

Raymond emerged from the boat house, his face

exploding into a smile as he set eyes on her. "Hattie! Where you been?"

"Drinking and singing for the public," she announced, spreading her arms wide and doing a quick spin around.

He chuckled. "You're a filthy damn liar."

"You're a bully."

Raymond nodded at the boat and whispered, "You seen we got company?"

"What are they," she whispered back, "security?"

"Somethin' like that. They say this stuff came from their boss's own property, and that we should be good and careful with it."

She rolled her eyes. "When we're not getting shot at, we're smooth as babies' arses."

"Between you and me," Raymond added, "I think the whole bunch of 'em on edge. Actin' jumpy. Especially that one." He nodded at Vincent, who was hopping clear of the two workers.

Hattie smirked. "He's got good reason to be jumpy."

Once the crates were loaded, and the extra men had left, Raymond piloted them out onto the river. Daytime boating was less serene than night runs, but easier for them to blend in. Several fishing boats and recreational craft were out on the Bay, and they were just one more among them. The Feds tended to get more active down by Virginia, at any rate, so the ride was something she could simply sit back and enjoy.

Unless, of course, there was another pincher on board.

Hattie kept her distance from Vincent as best she could. To his credit, he made it easy, keeping company with his companion more than anything. They pulled up toward the Elk River on a rare northbound run. Raymond's boat could navigate a good distance up the river, but that put them square into the hands of Prohibition. Treasury men liked to stake out the mouth of the river time-to-time, watching for boat-leggers like them. Lizzie was good at keeping the right eyes and ears greased up with kickbacks, and as such kept a fair sense of when the Feds were sniffing around. And ever since she'd started seeing that mafia man, Tony, that intelligence had only improved.

A slope-hulled skiff sat about a mile into the river, a rust-colored stripe painted up its sides. That was their client. An old man and a boy not older than twelve reached for the side of the boat, then the boy climbed aboard and hauled the wine crates over the edge into the old man's shaky hands. Hattie wasn't sure if this was a grandfather-grandson freelance operation, or if the Philadelphia people were running shy of proper laborers.

Once they were back underway and headed into the Chesapeake, Hattie turned from the bow to find Vincent standing directly behind her. She gasped, then frowned at him. "Don't go sneaking up on women, you daft bastard."

He held up his hands. "Sorry, Miss. I'm told I have a quiet step. Cat's feet."

"Aye," she replied, shaking off her temper. "I get that, too."

He took a final step forward to join her at the railing. She swallowed a few times and sucked in a deep breath. "Been wanting to offer you an apology for what I said last time. It was right unkind of me. You weren't deserving that sort of thing at all and I regret it."

He was silent for a minute. Uncertain of his reaction, she took a peek up at him from under her bangs and saw him regarding her with a quizzical expression. "Said some things I regret as well," he told her.

"Well then, all's good between us?"

He gave her a short nod, that odd look still on his face. "All's good."

Hattie turned to look back over the railing, very aware

that he remained beside her. Fighting a twinge of panic, she asked, "Did you need anything?"

He shifted his weight, bending to lean on the railing with his forearms. "I was wondering how long you've been working out here on the Bay."

"Long enough." She wondered what he was getting at.

"Then you know your way in and out of most of these rivers?"

She cocked her head, glancing over at him. "More than a couple, any rate. You have a look about you."

"I do? What kind of look?"

"Like you're trying to butter me up before you sell me a bridge."

He chuckled, the expression on his face alarmingly endearing. "Reading my mind?" he quipped. "You oughta put in for a position with my boss."

"Your boss likes mind readers, then?"

"Well, he's taken a particular shine to magic, so he'll take what he can get."

Hattie held her tongue for a moment. Either this man was baiting her into discussing magic on purpose and was a natural at making it seem casual, or he was terrible at small talk.

"Is that you?" she asked. "Magic man? Mind reader?"

He offered a tight-lipped smile. "A little of both, maybe."

"I suppose you can you read my mind?" she nudged, unable to help herself from continuing the conversation.

"If I've learned anything this week," he confessed with a sheepish grin, "it's that I have no idea what's going on inside a woman's head. So, I better stop trying."

Hattie could tell there was a story behind that comment, as he stared off into the distance for a moment, seemingly forgetting that she was there—which she found highly irritating. Honestly it didn't matter whether he could read minds or not, the man could *stop time*, for cryin' out loud.

"Whatever it was you did," she said, her voice soft, warm, and full of honesty, "with time the other night...I've got to say that was right impressive."

Vincent cleared his throat and slid his fingers along his forehead to slip a few loose bangs back underneath his hat. *Good Lord*, she thought, *he's blushing again.*

"It's what I do," he confessed with that humble tone she'd once thought was affected. Maybe it wasn't. Maybe this was who he really was under all the cockiness.

"How do you do't?" she pressed.

"People ask me that question more than you realize," he said. "I never figured out a good answer."

She turned away and waved a hand. "Well, it's none of my business, anyhow. Don't mind me. I stick my nose where it doesn't belong. As far as vices go, it's not so bad."

He released a single snicker. "Okay, okay. So, it's like a reflex. Like when someone throws a rock at your head, and you duck without thinking about it?"

"People throw rocks at your head on a regular basis, do they?" she teased. It was a heady feeling conversing like this with him. What had happened to the girl who hid in the corner of a jazz club, who used illusions so people wouldn't notice her? Singing in front of strangers, playfully conversing with a man who could end her freedom in a second if he knew what she was. When had she become so bold?

Vincent waved off her comment. "Only, you decide that you're going to duck outta the way long before they even throw the rock. It's that moment when everything feels like the world's stopping moving—everyone except you. And you do what you need to do. They call us pinchers. It's a stupid word, but it works for what people like me do. We twist things. Grab them. Manipulate and control them. For me, I pinch time."

She nodded. "But there's others like you that pinch other things?"

He choked back a laugh and looked away.

Hattie snorted. "You're blushing, aren't you? Saints preserve me, I've embarrassed the man!"

"I'm not embarrassed."

She reached for his jacket and gave it a playful tug. "What, talking about pinching things doesn't make you feel uncomfortable? Pinching people's bits…"

He stepped away from her with a chuckle. "Hey, you're crowdin' me."

"Alright, I'll stop. I just had you figured for a lady's man."

"Oh, hell," he barked. "That…that is *not* what I am."

Hattie put a hand to her face. "Ohh, I see. You like the fellas?"

"No!" he sputtered. "I just… I don't have a lotta time for dames, is all. I…I work a lot."

She decided to cut him off the hook. "Aye. I understand that."

"So, by that, I'm assuming there's no Mister, uh…"

Hattie jabbed him in the ribs. "Mister what?"

Vincent winced. "Confession? I've forgotten your name."

"Oh, well," she groused with extra drama. "Vincent. I suppose, Vincent, that I'll forgive you for that, Vincent."

"Alright, alright."

"It's Hattie. Hattie Malloy."

Even as she said it, she regretted it. What was she doing? The last thing she wanted was to make herself more memorable to this man, and here she was nearly flirting with him. This pincher was in the employ of the mob. He was a one-way ticket to a life of servitude, and she'd just reminded him what her name was. She could've said anything and he would have never known the difference.

But then again, he'd probably forget her name by tonight. An arrogant guy like this, bragging over his powers as a time pincher, wouldn't remember her name now any more than he had the last time they'd met. But, was he really *bragging*? Now that she thought it through, it seemed more like all he was doing was making conversation.

And trying to sell her a bridge.

"So, Vincent the Time Pincher," she said. "Why do you want my credentials? Do I know the rivers and back bays? Aye. What's it to you?"

"I'm looking for someone," he replied. "Someone who lives out here."

"Is this a special someone?"

"You could say that," he answered. "And if you and your pilot back there were so inclined, I could make it worth your time to help me sniff him out."

Hattie squinted at Vincent with a half-smirk. "Is this some sort of side business?"

"Business is business, Hattie Malloy. And I have an extra century note for the both of you, if you're willing to lend me a day or two."

She withdrew a step.

"A hundred?" she whispered.

"That's right. I'm motivated. And I need discretion. I know from experience that comes at a premium."

She wrinkled her nose. "What're your plans for this man? Once you find him?"

He crossed his arms. "That's outside the scope of my proposal."

"So, this is officially a proposition?"

"I've stated my offer," Vincent replied. "Two days. You, me." He nodded to the rear. "Your pilot, and my friend. Give me two days and as much of your navigational knowledge as you can offer, and you'll come out one hundred dollars richer." He added with a whisper, "I don't care how you split that with your driver. If at all."

Hattie cast a quick glance back to Raymond, who was watching them with amusement. As if she'd ever stiff him his share. Looking out over the Bay, she searched the surface of the water for a downside to this arrangement. The obvious downside was spending more time with a dangerous man like Vincent. The less obvious downside would be the fate of whatever poor bastard was in this man's sights.

In truth, that was the poor bastard's problem, not Hattie's.

"I suppose that's simple enough," she declared.

Vincent offered a hand.

She reached out and shook it with a firm grip. "You have a boat, Mister…"

He lifted a brow.

Hattie bit down on her lip.

"What, you forgot my last name? You did, didn't you?" He laughed.

She bore down on his hand, and he winced.

"It's Calendo," he offered, pulling his hand away and giving it a quick shake.

"One hundred dollars. Up front, Mr. Calendo."

He shook his head. "You're hanging one on. I'm not ponying up a C-note while we're out here, all alone where you can dump two bodies nice and casual."

"Like you did to those gunmen the other night?"

He grinned. "Right."

"Fine. After. But you'll keep your hands where I can see them. And no monkey business pinching time and taking a look where you're not welcome." She reached for her collar and tented her shirt away from her chest.

"Hey," he grumbled. "That's not the sort of person I am, so you can just apologize now."

"What, I've offended you?"

He scowled. "Yes!"

"Good to know." She let him seethe for a moment before asking, "So, do you have a name or a location? Somewhere to start?"

"I have a name."

She gestured for him to offer it.

Vincent turned and asked, "Have you ever heard of someone by the name of Doc Freedman?"

Hattie stared at Vincent, solid as stone.

He added, "He's supposed to be some mystic from the West Indies. Makes a magical elixir everyone just sorta whispers about. He's supposed to live on an island somewhere in the Bay, probably down by… Are you okay?"

She blinked. "Hmm?"

"You look a little green around the gills."

Hattie cleared her throat. "Doc Freedman, you said?"

"Right. You've heard that name before?"

As Hattie's stomach continued to plummet toward the center of the earth, she responded, "Never. But, we can give it a go."

CHAPTER 18

"What's the word?" Lefty asked as Vincent returned to the bench seat behind the boat pilot.

"We have a boat," Vincent answered.

"How much?"

"Think we can part with a C-note?"

Lefty groaned. "You're shit at haggling."

"Do we have it, or not? Because I get the feeling that girl up there will pull a knife on us and dump our bodies in the Bay if we welsh."

Lefty sighed. "I have it. What's our first stop?"

Vincent nodded at Hattie, who remained at the bow. "Mouth of the Chester River. Just across the Bay from Annapolis. She says there's a hobo colony there who like to keep their ears open. Might could get some leather outta them."

"What's this mystery man you're looking for?"

Vincent leaned back, pulling off his hat to run his hands through his hair. "Capstein gave me the skinny on this fella.

Supposed to be a water pincher, lives by himself 'round the Bay somewhere."

"Why hasn't Capstein scooped him up for the Richmond boys?" Lefty asked.

"I got the feeling he doesn't fully believe he exists. Has him chalked up as a yarn the local fishers spun up."

"And you're sure enough that he's not some tall tale that you're throwing down a C-note on it?"

Vincent shrugged and replaced his hat. "It's a start."

"Not much of a start."

"I don't know, Lefty. I just got a feeling. Like there's a pincher on the Bay. I feel it. Ever since Deltaville I felt it."

Lefty shook his head. "Whatever that was that happened there, it wasn't one of you."

"You're gonna have to tell me what all you know about pinchers, sometime."

"Don't hold your breath."

Vincent scowled at him. "Like, knowing there's no such animal as a fire pincher. Stuff like that, like you're some kind of expert."

Lefty turned to Vincent and smiled. The expression on his face put a chill through Vincent's guts. "You'll live with the suspense."

"You know what a horse's ass you are?"

* * *

THEY RODE in silence until a strip of land came into view that had snaked its way into the Bay, separating the Chesapeake from the mouth of the Chester River. It was more swamp than dry land. The boat driver eased the craft alongside a straight patch of muddy coast, brushing aside cattails as they swung around to present the side of the boat to the land.

Vincent adjusted his hat and stepped up to the railing, offering a hand to Hattie.

The girl eyed him with a smirk, then hopped up to the side of the boat and leaped out, landing firmly on solid ground. She beckoned for him to join her.

Vincent rounded a leg over the side of the railing and stepped off. Both shoes sunk into thick, dark mud. He pulled one foot out of the mire, but the second stuck a little more than he'd expected, sending him staggering forward, flailing to catch his balance. Hattie snickered and reached out to grab his arm, steadying Vincent enough for him to gaze morosely at his Italian leather wingtips. Lefty landed beside Vincent with a hefty thump.

Vincent eyed Lefty over his shoulder. "Just another beachhead for you, huh?"

Without reply, Lefty tossed an elbow into Vincent's side, sending him sprawling onto a thicket of reeds.

Once Raymond had tied the boat to an enormous felled tree trunk bleached white from years in the sunlight, the group formed a line and ventured inland. Hattie led the way, angling them along the shoreline once the ground was solid enough. Before long, he could smell a campfire and over-boiled coffee as well as hear a tortured refrain from a mouth organ.

Hattie held up a hand for them to hold position, then ventured farther into a copse of trees. She traced her fingers along one of the thick white oak trunks, a freshly-carved symbol beneath her fingertips. Then she turned back to the group with a satisfied nod.

"What was that?" Vincent asked, nodding at the symbol.

"Survival language," she replied. "It's how hoboes get the word out."

"So, what did that mean?"

She smiled. "It means this is a good place to camp. Listen,

I want all of you to stay here while I work it out. I know some of these men. They don't take to strangers, so it's best if you—"

Vincent lifted a hand. "That's fine. We're looking for Doc Freedman. See if they've heard of anyone passing through by that moniker."

She nodded. "I'll be quick. Make yourselves at home. I hear it's a good place to camp." With a wink and a smirk, she turned to Raymond.

"You okay going up there by yo'self?" he grunted.

"I'll be fine. These fellas never give me any grief."

He shrugged, and Hattie turned to march on up a path. Lefty searched around the area, then whistled for Vincent. The two stepped down toward the water's edge, and a flat of surf-polished stones.

"Gimme a hand with this," Lefty urged.

Vincent grabbed the other end of a driftwood log to help the man carry it to the center of the space. They continued gathering smaller bits of wood, and Raymond took up the cause by arranging the kindling into a tiny pyre. Lefty loomed over the stack of wood and reached into his pants pocket to produce a shiny metal square.

"What's that?" Vincent asked.

"Old flip lighter. Won it off some RAF jackass outside of Reims." He lit a clutch of marsh grass and settled it beneath the wood. Soon they had their own campfire and Lefty took a seat alongside Vincent atop the log, pocketing the lighter.

Vincent lifted his chin to Raymond. "How long've you been working with Hattie?"

"Hmm. Better part of three years, now," Raymond answered.

Vincent asked, "She your sister, or something? The resemblance is uncanny."

Raymond smiled, then laughed. The sound was like a freight train horn.

Vincent prodded, "No, seriously. Looks like you do the driving. Most of the lifting. What is it she does for your outfit?"

Raymond thought the question over for a moment. "I suppose she keeps me outta trouble."

Lefty remarked, "She's not very good at that."

Another laugh from Raymond. "You want her job? Naw, she's got a brain on her for sure. She reads the Bay like a book. Maybe she's got waterman blood in her."

"Doesn't hurt that she has a white face," Lefty added.

Raymond nodded. "That does help, especially when we head south."

Vincent said, "Well, for what it's worth we got no beef with Negroes."

Raymond shook his head with a beleaguered grin. "I guess I'll be happy about that."

Lefty fished for his lighter as the flames threatened to die down. "God damned wet lumber." As he fumbled with his pocket, a rosary fell into the grass.

Raymond scooped it up for Lefty, admiring it in the sunlight. "You a Godly man?"

Lefty took it with a lift of his brow. "I like to think there's something more to this life than eating and sleeping."

"And dyin'," Raymond added.

"Are you a man of faith?" Lefty asked.

Raymond nodded. "Every Sunday, anyways. The Good Lord blessed me with a baby boy just a couple weeks ago, so I'm prayin' double-time."

Vincent smiled. "Hey, congratulations."

Raymond nodded then shrugged. "Not a Catholic, though."

"Ah," Lefty said with a smirk. "I knew there'd be a catch."

The large man hunkered down onto the stones across the fire from Lefty. "A catch, huh? So, you think your God's bigger?"

"No," Lefty replied. "I wouldn't say bigger. The Church, maybe…"

Raymond grinned. "Then tell me—do you believe in original sin?"

Vincent huffed and stood up. "Oh, Jesus. I'm gonna let you two eggheads talk this out on your own."

Lefty extended an accusing hand at Vincent as he leaned toward Raymond. "You'll have to excuse my partner. He's both a heathen and a Philistine."

"Yeah, whatever," Vincent groused, heading down a path by the hobo symbol.

A ways down he caught a glimpse of the hobo village, peering through the tree trunks, shanties ringing a campfire. There was no sign of Hattie, or any hoboes. Still, it was their nature to be mysterious. Vincent walked back to the tree with the carved symbols, touching the carving as if to divine its meaning. His thoughts slid back to Deltaville, and the glyphs painted onto the burned-out fisher's shack. Whereas this hobo language appeared utilitarian, crudely drawn and clearly indicating something as a pictogram, those Deltaville scribblings were more like art.

More like religion.

Vincent looked over his shoulder at the other two, who were already so deep into conversation that Lefty was gesturing with his one arm. He rarely did that. In fact, Lefty wasn't much of a talker, in general. That boat driver really stepped in it when he brought up religion. Good, Vincent mused. That would get it out of Lefty's system for a bit.

Vincent wandered into the woods just a little, peeking at the village now and then.

At last, a set of footsteps rustled nearby. He turned in its direction to find Hattie stepping from behind a fat trunk.

Vincent shook his head. "Isn't the village over—"

She turned behind her with a confused twist of her brow. "It's there."

He looked behind her, finding nothing but trees.

"You must've got turned around," she added, patting his arm. "Easy to do in the woods."

Vincent hopped up alongside her as she wound her way down toward the others. "Any word from the hoboes?"

"Yes. They said an oyster boat came through the other day. One of the men on the boat either knew Doc Freedman or was Doc Freedman. Seems my source was a bit…" She made a bottle gesture with her thumb and finger, tipping it into the air over her face.

"Got a name of that boat?" Vincent asked.

"The *Bianco Fiore*."

He repeated the words, then asked, "Going south?"

"That's the word." She stepped down onto the rock flat, hands on her hips. "Well, you boys do any fishing while I was gone? Catch us some dinner, or what?"

"Actually," Raymond declared, "we was discussin' the doctrine of the Immaculate Conception."

Hattie blinked rapidly.

Lefty shrugged. "It's a work in progress."

She stepped around toward Raymond. "You still have that bottle of grappa stowed under your bench?"

Raymond nodded cautiously. "A couple. Why?"

"Payment for information rendered," she answered with a thumb thrust in the direction of the hobo village.

Raymond sighed, then hauled his frame to his feet. "Well, alright then. But I'm gonna steal me back a couple bottles from those Baltimore Crew people."

Lefty squinted.

Raymond added, "That last bit was a joke. But you know what else I keep on the boat? Fishin' line." He nodded at Lefty. "What do you say, old man? Any good with a fishin' pole?"

Lefty waved his one arm in the air. "Not unless you have a harpoon."

Hattie pulled at Raymond's arm. "Come on, we're losing daylight."

Vincent moved to follow, but Hattie lifted a flat palm at him. "Stay here, boy-o. Or go catch a deer in case Raymond's no better with a line than your friend."

The two trotted back down the path toward the boat.

Vincent lingered in the woods, turning back toward where he'd seen the hobo village, and then to the point closer to the shore from which Hattie had emerged. He could spot the tiny campfire near the makeshift shelters, but she'd come from the water. Were there two hobo villages? Or maybe these folk made a habit of meeting people away from where their shacks stood.

With a squint, he ventured deeper into the woods along the path Hattie had taken. The trees thinned quickly, and a sliver of the Bay came into view. It was a muddy patch of bog, and nothing else. A few seagulls eyed him from a floating log, bobbing in the late afternoon sunlight.

Then Vincent turned inland and climbed through the brush, stepping over as much foliage as he could to keep his shoes from further ruin. Despite Hattie's warning, Vincent resolved to approach the hobo village. Her caution in treating with these vagrants made sense enough, but his instincts needled at his brain. Something wasn't quite right, though he couldn't put a finger on it.

A trodden dirt path emerged from the brush, swinging back to where they'd moored the boat. The other end of the path terminated at the village. So, whatever Hattie was doing out by the waterside had nothing to do with the hoboes. Either that, or she'd circled around to misdirect Vincent. Which meant she'd lied to him. It was a piss poor lie, too. He could see the shanty town from the far end of where they'd camped. As he turned to take the path into the hobo village, he wondered why she was so protective of these people. Simple *esprit de corps*? Was she beholden to them in some way he wasn't aware of? Anything was possible.

The mouth organ started up again, its notes sour and trembling. Vincent winced at the noise as he rounded the first of the shacks to find three old men hunkered around the fire. They were covered in filth, hair falling in strings from the sides of dog-eared hats. They froze as Vincent came to a halt behind them, rheumy eyes watching him, waiting for him to make a move.

"Gents," Vincent offered with a wave.

The man with the mouth organ pulled it from his lips.

"Don't mind me. I'm just passing through," Vincent added with a cough.

One of the vagrants, a silver-haired fellow with ferocious stubble, eyed his shoes. Then, with a grunt, he turned to the others. "He's with Harry."

The others nodded. The mouth organ resumed.

Vincent ventured forward a step. The hoboes ignored him.

"I'm traveling with a friend," he asked. "A short woman with red hair. You fellows seen anyone come through here the past hour?"

Silver-hair replied, "Just Harry."

"Well, I don't know a Harry."

The hobo with the mouth organ dropped it to his lap. "You lookin' for Doc Freedman?"

Vincent nodded.

The musical hobo said, "Well he ain't here."

"No, I suppose he isn't. Word I hear is he's on some boat called the *Bianco Fiore*."

The musician nodded. "That's what we told Harry."

Vincent cocked his head and approached another step. "Listen, I'm not with anyone named Harry. Just my associate, Lefty, you wouldn't miss him, and my boat driver. Goes by Raymond." Vincent searched their indifferent faces for reaction. "And my short friend, goes by the name of Malloy. Hattie Malloy…"

The man's eyes lifted slowly to the trees overhanging.

Vincent asked, "Do you mean Hattie?"

"No," Silver-hair grumbled. "Harry. Ain't been no girl in this camp since I been here."

"Well," Vincent offered, "she's got a masculine way about her. Wears pants. Keeps her hair over her eyes. Maybe you'd mistake her."

The third hobo stood up, his mouth drawn into a smirk. "Look, pal. Harry's a friend of ours. He gets us the little luxuries we feel we deserve, and we pay him in scuttlebutt. That's the skinny."

Vincent shook his head. "So, you know this…man?"

"Friend of ours," he replied.

"And you just gave this Harry some info about Doc Freedman."

Silver-hair snickered. "And we're drinking tonight. What's it to you?"

"Harry's paying you in hooch?"

"You can't have any," the musician groused.

Vincent nodded. "Thank you, gentlemen. Sorry to intrude." He backed away several steps, then turned for the path.

Harry. Hattie.

These hoboes thought *she* was a *he*. And in spite of what

he'd snapped at her when they were coming back with the rum, Hattie was *clearly* not a man. No pants and shirt hid that fact. He could see from twenty yards away that she was a woman, but these men looking at her close up saw otherwise.

"Well, what do you know about that," he mumbled as he trotted back to the gravel flat.

Raymond had a line in the water already, wading halfway to his knees into the drink. Lefty stood as Vincent approached.

Vincent looked around. "Where's the woman?"

Lefty shrugged. "Taking her booze back to the hoboes."

"I just came from the hoboes," Vincent said. "Which way did she go?"

Lefty nodded back up the path.

Vincent shook his head. "She must've wound her way back around the shoreline again."

Lefty squinted at Vincent. "What's the angle?"

Vincent cocked his head for Lefty to join him, easing away from Raymond. He whispered, "Listen, remember when we first found these two characters? Last week, after our day trip to Richmond?"

Lefty nodded.

Vincent continued, "You remember when I spotted their boat, but you didn't?"

"What about it?"

"What did you see?" Vincent asked. "Exactly. When you finally saw the boat."

"I mean…they'd tied some branches to the side of the hull as camouflage, and up the engine house. Didn't look that impressive once you got up close, but seemed to do a good enough job in the dark from a distance."

"But *when* did you see it?"

Lefty shrugged. "You pointed it out, and when I got closer

up beside you, I saw it. Like when you spot a snake in the grass under your feet at the last minute."

Vincent nodded.

Lefty urged, "What's going on?"

"And when we landed back at their pier," Vincent continued. "The wharf, whatever. That woman—Malloy—she was pawing some iron when we got off the boat. I had a moment, wondering if she was about to plug us in the back of the head, but you didn't look like it was any concern. So, I let it go."

"What iron?" Lefty grumbled.

"Looked like a service revolver or something. Nothing big. But it was there, in her hand before she shoved it in her pocket. You're telling me you didn't see no gun…ever?"

Lefty shook his head with an impatient squint.

Vincent nodded. "I got a theory. But it don't make a lotta sense." Maybe he was wrong. Maybe Lefty's eyesight was going. Maybe that camouflage hid the boat well enough in the dark. Maybe she'd pocketed the revolver before Lefty noticed it.

Or maybe that prickling in the back of his mind was right.

"You gonna share this theory of yours, or do I have to guess?"

Footsteps approached, quick and hustled. Vincent lifted a hand to suspend the conversation and took a step away as Hattie trotted into view. She puffed several breaths, then said, "I was looking for you. Wandering off, are you?"

Vincent gestured for Lefty to follow. "Come on."

He eyed Hattie, who joined them as he led them both back to the path. "So, you delivered your booze already?"

She nodded.

He turned to Lefty. "Which way does that path go?"

Lefty sighed. "What?"

"The hoboes. She just came from their little shanty town, right? So, which way did she come from?"

Lefty pointed toward the shoreline.

Hattie said, "They're skittish. If you barge in on them, you'll probably just scare them into their holes."

Vincent eyed the faint glimmer of the village campfire through the trees, and then turned back toward the bog closer to the shore. "Those guys?" he pointed.

She nodded again, her brow wrinkling.

Vincent brushed off his jacket. "Alright, then they're happy?"

Lefty asked, "You gonna come out with it, what?"

"Yeah," Vincent blurted, turning back for the gravel flat. "I don't think this Doc Freedman is on the boat. But whoever *is* on the boat has probably heard of him. Cashing in on this fellow's name to do business."

Lefty followed Vincent back toward their own fire. "What makes you say that?"

"Because this Doc Freedman is supposed to be a pincher." He turned to Hattie, who watched him with a guarded frown. "Like me. Only, he's just living out here on his own. A free pincher, as it were."

Hattie asked, "He's a pincher, then?"

"Yeah," Vincent replied. "A water pincher, to hang a name on it."

She stepped down onto the stones. "You said he was a mystic."

"Well, I wasn't lying, was I?"

"What's your interest in free pinchers, then?" she asked.

"Well, you see, people with my sort of talent are highly prized among the family. There's opportunities for this man in the city—opportunities to use his powers for something more than whatever he's doing out here."

She curled her lip. "Isn't that little more than servitude?"

"You can call it what you want. I don't feel like no servant. I got a job. A real purpose. I belong to something that matters."

She sneered. "And here I thought you were looking for his magical elixir." She stepped past him, calling to Raymond. "You catch anything, yet?"

Raymond glanced at her from the water. "Just drownin' worms, so far. Might need to dig up some more."

She replied, "I'll do it."

As she brushed past Vincent again on her way to dry land, he lifted a chin at Lefty.

"Why don't you toss some more wood onto the fire before we lose it?"

Lefty shot him a beleaguered scowl before reaching down to grab a length of driftwood. As he dropped it onto the fire, sending a sharp crackle into the air, Vincent snapped his fingers.

Time pinched tight in a bubble to the left and in front of Vincent. The sparks hung twinkling in the air just over Lefty's face. Raymond stood in the water, his line suspended over his head mid-cast. This was a little test, just to see if his theory proved correct.

Vincent watched cross-armed as Hattie continued to rummage in the dirt for a few seconds. She lifted her head slowly, breathing the thick air, looking at Lefty, the fire, and then at Raymond. Then with a wary expression, she stood and walked toward Vincent. As she neared him, she sucked in a deep breath, her eyes wide.

He said, "This is a small bubble. Just holding the others so we can have a word."

"We can talk this time? So you're freezing time, but you're not inside it, not like you did before?" Her jaw dropped.

"Yes." This pinch wasn't particularly cheap, with him on the outside of it, but the distance wasn't too large—just big enough for Lefty and Raymond. Hopefully they'd have enough time for this conversation before he passed out.

Hattie looked around, gaining her bearings. "This is a bizarre thing to do, you know that?"

Vincent angled his head as he watched her. "You don't get it, do you? I was the *only one* out of the area of effect. Not Lefty, not your friend in the water back there, and not you. All of you should be frozen in time together. *All* of you."

She shrugged. "Everyone makes mistakes."

"Not like this," he said, uncrossing his arms. "For some reason, my pinches don't work on you. This happened back on your boat. It's happening again. Once, maybe, I could say it's a fluke. But twice? With me making absolutely sure you were on the inside this time? No."

"Then I guess that makes me special," she muttered.

"It makes us both special," he replied, gritting his teeth against a sudden twinge in his stomach. "Because it seems that not only are you immune to my powers, I'm immune to yours."

The blood drained from her face. "What're you talking about?"

"I'm talking about you being a pincher like me. Not sure exactly what it is you're supposed to be doing, but other people see things around you. Or don't see things. What is it, mind control or something?"

She took a step away.

"Maybe you shouldn't run off like that," Vincent called. "I mean, where do you think you're gonna go, anyway?"

She balled her fists as Vincent strode toward her. Reaching down for a stick, Hattie brandished it near her shoulder like a club. "You stay right there!"

He extended his hands in surrender. "I'm not gonna hurt you."

They stared at one another for a long moment.

Finally, she lowered the stick. "It's not mind control. I...I pinch light."

"Huh. What do you know about that."

"I can make people see things. I can make light bend around things. Change the way things look."

Vincent nodded with a grin. "That's why those hoboes thought you were a man?"

"You spoke with them?"

"Where'd you think I really was? Yeah, I talked to them. They're not as skittish as you said they'd be." He pointed for the shoreline. "And what's with making everyone think they were down the shore?"

She tapped her stick against her boot. "Didn't want you sniffing around them."

"Because I'd find out they thought you were Harry?"

"Something like that."

Vincent shook his head. "How come you two are keeping this a secret? You're running booze for the Crew already."

Hattie snarled. "Because I won't be anyone's slave, is why! I work for myself. Not your gang."

"Hey, easy. I think you got the wrong idea about how pinchers live in the real world."

She waved her stick at the Bay. "*This* is the real world, not your birdcage in the city. I want no part of that!"

"Listen, you could make some real cabbage working for Vito," he urged. "Get yourself some proper clothes. Eat in nice restaurants. Pinching light? Do you have any idea how useful a skill that would be for us?"

"Aye...I do," she grumbled. "Which is why it's a secret. And it's my secret." She pointed at Raymond. "He doesn't know."

"That a fact?" Vincent mused. "I guess it's easy to pull the wool over someone's eyes if you can do what you do."

"It *was* easy. Until you came along." She shook her head. "I know what you want with Doc Freedman. You want to recruit him, whatever you call it. But if he truly exists out there somewhere, I need him. I won't help you. You can keep your hundred dollars. We're done."

Vincent smirked. "You need him? Or his magic potion?"

"One comes with the other, doesn't it?"

"So, what? You're going to steal it from him?"

She jabbed her stick at him. "I'm not like you. I don't just take. I'll trade for it."

"Trade? With what?"

"I have money."

"Not much," Vincent said. "You'd have more if you worked for us proper-like. Enough to *buy* this elixir, if you need it so bad. Though you look healthy enough."

"It's not for me, you thick gobshite. It's for…" She swallowed her words, her face turning red.

"It's for someone you know? Someone close to you?" Vincent asked, not really liking the direction his thoughts were taking on this.

She glared at him with venom. "You'll have to drop this time pinch eventually, else it'll eat through your insides."

He chuckled. "Ah. Good to hear it's not just me, then. Well, I'll tell you something, Hattie Malloy. This little time pinch is cheaper than most. It small, contained, just big enough for the other two. Which means I can keep this up for a while before I get the twist."

"So, I'm a hostage now?"

"I want to talk this out," he urged. "Like adults."

"Then talk."

"Alright, here's the skinny. I have to find a pincher for Vito Corbi. That's my task. My purpose. Capo Vito is a fair man, but his patience won't last forever. The sooner I find a free pincher to join up with the Crew, the happier Vito will be. Which will pay off for yours truly. Now, you don't have to be that pincher. Right? I just need any pincher. It could be this Freedman."

She sniffed. "Your point?"

He paced a few steps. "I realize all this changes things. But you still have the knowledge I need. Knowledge of the Bay and its backwaters. I think you're the best person to help me find Freedman. And if we can work together with our powers, more's the better."

"You want me to help you enslave another pincher? You can't be serious."

"It's not slavery!" he shouted before calming himself. "It's *meaning.*"

"Tell me something, Vincent Calendo. If you didn't want to find another pincher for your masters, could you say no?"

He pursed his lips.

She sneered. "You don't have a choice, do you?"

"You have to understand—"

"I don't think *you* understand. You're trapped in this errand. And you want to trap someone else along with you. Forget it."

Vincent crossed his arms, stared at the ground, then set his jaw as he looked up at her. "No."

"No?"

"No," he repeated.

Hattie wagged her head. "What do you mean, 'no'? It's decided. I won't help you. You can keep me in this bubble of time only so long. I'll wait it out. And then I'm gone." She added with a squint, "And maybe my illusions don't work on you, but they do work on your friend, there. I can make him see anything I like. Horrible things. Maybe even see you pointing a gun at him. He may have to defend himself."

Vincent stared at the rocks.

Hattie concluded, "So don't think this time pinch will

stop me. Eventually, I'll get myself away from you, and you'll never see me again."

Vincent replied, "Maybe so. But I know who you work for. Lizzie Sadler, right? Over by Locust Point? She does business exclusively with the Crew. That's because all she does is run booze down the Bay. And that doesn't happen without our knowing about it. If the Crew were to decide she was a liability, what do you think would happen?"

Hattie stared daggers through Vincent.

He continued with a nod to Raymond. "What would happen to him? He's got a little boy now, right? You don't think he needs his job now more than ever?"

"Are you threatening my friends?"

Vincent pointed at Lefty. "You threatened mine. I suppose this is how pinchers negotiate."

Hattie fumbled over words for a moment.

Vincent felt a stab of guilt. This wasn't the way he'd wanted this conversation to go. There had to be a way to turn it around, backpedal from all the threats.

"I didn't want to start a fight," he said. "I'm offering you something: A life of means in the city, working for the Crew, or a hundred dollars and my fondest wishes if you help me find Doc Freedman. You come out ahead both ways. Only way you lose is if you shine me off."

Hattie hissed, "That's it?"

"That's it."

She tossed her stick toward the fire. It stuck in midair. As he watched her, Vincent felt a spasm in his stomach. It was a tiny cramp, nothing enormous, but the time pinch was definitely making itself known. This conversation would have to end sooner rather than later. Vincent reached for the stick and set it onto the ground at a specific angle. "It was here."

"If I help you find this water pincher, you'll leave Lizzie and Raymond be?" Hattie asked, her voice choked.

"On my word."

"Your word means little to me," she snapped.

"Then I swear by Calvin goddamn Coolidge."

"You kiss your mother with that mouth?" Hattie rolled her eyes.

His face hardened. "Funny."

She sighed, then extended a hand. "Right, then. We have a new arrangement."

Vincent peered at her hand, then took it cautiously. She might still try something, but at least she didn't have a weapon anymore.

Hattie gave his hand one tug, then whipped her fingers in the air. "Fine. Now pull this down."

Vincent said, "You'll need to go back where you were."

"What?"

He pointed at the spot near the dirt where she'd been rooting for worms. "You were over there."

"So?"

"So," he replied, "it's jarring to be one place, then another when the pinch comes down. Trust me. I've done this my whole life. You learn how to keep track of who was where and such."

Hattie shook her head, then turned back for the grass.

Vincent urged, "A little further, and crouch back down."

She complied with a huff.

Satisfied that Hattie was positioned more or less where she wouldn't call attention, he returned to his spot and snapped his fingers.

The fire snapped and crackled as the log settled in the flames.

Vincent turned to Lefty. "Thanks."

Hattie went back to digging for worms, while Vincent watched her carefully. He wasn't sure how this was going to play out. He was absolutely certain that she trusted him even less than before, but at least he knew what she was, now.

A free pincher.

She was *right there*. This whole search for Doc Freedman could end right now, and he'd have what Vito wanted. He'd return a hero.

But it didn't feel right. Besides, she was a spitfire and hell-bent on rubbing Vincent raw. Having her in the Crew would be an unceasing headache, no matter how useful her skills would be. She'd never accept it. She wasn't raised in the service of the mob. No, this girl had lived an entire life outside of the family—out here, on the Bay.

Hattie stood up and turned toward the water. She lifted her hand and shouted to Raymond, "Got four big ones."

Vincent examined her face. It was well-practiced, blithe and smiling. But there was an edge to her eyes.

No, she wouldn't do. And to make sure she remained out of Vincent's hair, he'd have to keep her secret from Lefty. He regretted grilling Lefty so thoroughly before. The man was sharp as a whip, and he was probably already putting together what Vincent had deduced.

With any luck, Doc Freedman would be more open to negotiation. Although he should probably polish his sales pitch a bit more between here and there...wherever there would be.

CHAPTER 19

The two gangsters stood forward of the engine house, while Hattie haunted the bench behind Raymond. She balled up as much rage as she could manage without exploding into tiny pieces, silently fuming while Raymond piloted the boat south. The sun was setting, and soon the evening hours would capture the Bay. That meant boats that were out for legitimate business would dock, and the passengers would either go home, or would hunker down for a night of booze, gambling, or perhaps even reading. The timing was right for their purposes, but Hattie didn't care a lick about whether it was sunrise or sunset.

She'd been found out by the Crew's pincher. And when it came down to it, he'd let her know that she was in his grasp, regardless of whether she chose to join or not. Help him enslave another free pincher, or doom all of her friends in the world to financial ruin…and possibly a late-night visit from a man with a gun. No way out. No clear course. She had to play his game, or he'd end her world.

That sort of power was obscene.

Raymond shot her a look, then nodded to her. "You okay, over there?"

"I'm starving to death, is what I am," she deflected. "If you'd caught at least one fish, maybe I wouldn't waste away."

"Can it," he grumbled. "Tide's high. Fish won't bite when they got a tide over their heads."

She bit down on her lip, still on a slow simmer.

Raymond asked, "What's next?"

"Kent Island," she replied. "Long Narrows Wharf."

"Oyster boats don't let in at Narrows."

"This isn't an oyster boat," she replied. "It's a trawler."

Raymond cocked a brow, then leaned in. "Why'd you tell these clowns it was an oyster boat, then?"

"Because," she whispered, "I don't trust them."

"We're getting paid, right?"

"Yes," she said. "Fifty-fifty, like we discussed."

"So, why are you givin' them the business?"

Hattie held a hand to her forehead. "Things are just… we're still negotiating."

Raymond's eyebrows shot up. "Well, as long as I get my fifty bucks, I'm gonna go where you tell me to go. You can get twisted up about it all you like."

She smiled. Oh, to have his simple take on the situation. All he needed to do was drive the boat. He didn't have anyone's livelihoods hanging on his shoulders.

Kent Island wasn't far from the Chester, and they'd made it to Long Narrows Wharf before the last of the sunlight had faded into a dark cobalt overhead. The wharf sported several piers with nice, solid moorings. Raymond and Hattie made quick work securing the boat, and before long all four passengers were standing on solid ground. Or rather…solid planks.

"Alright," Hattie announced to the group. "I know the

wharf better than any of you. So, I'm going to look for this *Bianco Fiore*."

Raymond hopped to her side. "What she meant to say was…we know the wharf better than the two of you. So, *we're* going to go look for this boat."

Vincent grinned. "Hey, that's peachy with me."

Hattie did not return his grin. Instead, she pointed at a squat two-story clapboard building at the end of the piers. "Boats are coming in. They usually serve soup or something they call soup about this time. Go see what they have on."

Vincent nodded as he glanced to Lefty. "Hope it's not minestrone. That's all Shakes knows how to make."

Lefty sneered his agreement. "No one said Shakes was a gourmet."

The two stepped up the planks toward the inn, Vincent adding, "But his gnocchi, though. With that walnut sauce?"

"Yeah," Lefty muttered. "Yeah, not bad."

Raymond crouched down to Hattie and whispered, "Who do you suppose Shakes is?"

"Doesn't matter. Come on," she grunted, leading him along the lines of fishing trawlers.

"What's got you in a stink?" Raymond asked.

"Nothing…it's just…"

"Come on. You been chewin' your own face off ever since that hobo camp. What gives?"

Hattie stopped, crossing her arms. A wave of frustration washed over her, threatening to jerk tears from her eyes. Flee. Run. Hide. Disappear. It's all she'd ever known to do, and right now the urge to run for it was almost more than she could stand.

"I'm not so sure we can trust this lot," she muttered, lifting her chin to the mobsters.

"Well, yeah. I know that. But, a payday's a payday."

She turned back toward the water, casting a glance at the Bay. "We're about even with Winnow's Slip, aren't we?"

Raymond nodded.

"If we took off right now, while they're inside the inn, they'll be here until they get another boat. Maybe they could hire one of the fishers…not sure."

Raymond frowned. "Now, what are you talkin' about?"

She reached for his arms, gripping them as tears welled beneath her irises. "How fast could we make it? Straight on to Winnow's. We could find Lizzie. You could get your family." She made some mental calculations. "It'd take a half hour just to get into the city. By then, do you think these two could—"

He brushed her arms aside and thrust a finger into her face. "Hey, now! You calm your ass down!"

She blinked and shook the tears away.

Raymond said, "You're talkin' crazy, girl. Packin' up my… what? We got two days with these mobsters, just cartin' them around. And we get paid big. All off the books."

Hattie whispered, "It could be dangerous."

"More dangerous than gettin' shot at over a couple barrels of rum? What's gotten into you? This is easy money."

"The money isn't worth it, Raymond. The young one, there? He has…powers. I've seen it."

He blinked at her, then straightened up. "The what, now?"

"He's what they call a pincher," she explained. "It's like a wizard, or a warlock."

Raymond's eyes widened, and he bent over to whisper, "Oh…he's a devil worshipper?"

"Not like that. He has real powers. He can stop time. Do things while the clock's frozen."

"You seen him do this?"

She nodded. "I got stuck in one of his pinches. He… threatened me."

Raymond's expression of alarm eased into one of anger. "Oh, yeah?"

"Aye. Threatened me. Threatened you. Even Lizzie."

He closed his mouth, sucking in breaths through his nostrils causing them to flare. "Oh, no he didn't."

"The hundred isn't worth it, Raymond," she pleaded. "I know how much you need that money, but this whole arrangement is going to cost us more than we gain."

He shook his head, clamping his eyes shut as he held a hand up to his head. "This don't make no sense, though. He's been nice to us. Both of them have been. Why would he just up and get the itch like that?"

She swallowed hard. More than anything in the world, she wanted to tell Raymond why Vincent had threatened her. Why the person he was looking for could never be found. Why she was the real danger to Raymond and his family. But that would only increase the chances that he would say the wrong thing. Do the wrong thing. Take a swing, maybe even pull a gun.

And even if they ditched these two right here, they would still know where they lived. The entire enterprise Jake Sadler had built, and Lizzie had continued in his name, would come crashing down.

She wasn't being smart about this. That realization swept through her brain, and she took several breaths.

Raymond gestured for her to say something. "Well?"

She whispered, "I… I'm just being stupid."

"What? You're tellin' me this white man can do magic, and he's got his thumb on us. And now you're saying you're bein' stupid?" He shook his head. "You're a lot of things, but stupid ain't one of them."

Hattie ran her hands over her face. "I was wrong. I'm… tired. Maybe I've gone barmy, I can't say. Maybe there was something in that drink those hoboes gave me."

Raymond jerked his head back. "Wait, you took a swig of hobo rotgut?"

She latched onto the moment. "Aye. Foul skite, it was. I got dizzy, almost walked into the water. Maybe there was something more potent in that booze?"

Raymond released a long breath, then bent over, holding himself up at his knees. He released a long chuckle. "Oh, Lord!"

"I know, I know," Hattie said.

"Girl, I…" He laughed, then caught his breath. "You had me goin'. I…warlock? Oh, Lord Jesus!"

Hattie pinched as fiery a smirk onto her face as her abilities could allow. "You're getting gullible in your old age."

Raymond lifted his brows, then shook off another fit of laughter. When he calmed down, he reached out and play-choked Hattie before chucking her shoulder. "I'll get you for that one."

"Well, wait for it," she added. "I was about to tell you I was a pincher, too. And that I always was but could never tell you because the mob would swoop in and take me prisoner."

Another spate of laughter, and a plea for her to stop.

She turned away and released the light pinch over her face. In truth, she was terrified.

"Right," Raymond gasped. "You're a witch. That would explain so, so much actually."

She snapped her fingers. "Come on. We have easy money to make, and we're not going to earn it farting around."

They walked up and down each pier, Hattie squinting in the dying daylight at the names painted along the backs of each boat. Raymond stepped past her, taking one side while she surveyed the other. One pier…two piers…no *Bianco Fiore*.

As they made their way back toward the dock and the

third and final pier, Raymond said, "Maybe it ain't here? Coulda gone on south to Poplar or Tilghman."

Hattie shook her head. The hoboes had painted a colorful picture for her. A boatload of young men picking their way along the Bay, looking to trade tobacco for booze. They dropped the name Doc Freedman once, and the hoboes recognized it. The name was something of a tall tale on the Bay…the hoodoo man with the potion that can cure anything. It sounded like hokum, and she was inclined to agree. Only…she knew there were such things as pinchers. And now that she'd crossed paths with a man from the city who was certain he was real, it made her wonder.

What if Doc Freedman *was* real, after all?

What if that magic elixir was real?

Hattie had no illusions that this *Bianco Fiore* would be at Kent Island. This was her way of dragging out the search. And it was plausible. The longer they spent combing the waterways, the longer it would take to stumble across some real information about Doc Freedman, and his location.

Which Hattie already knew.

"Could be," she answered. "But we can't very well go skipping the largest wharf this side of the Bay, and not check it out. Can we?"

Hattie continued a couple steps, and Raymond didn't answer.

She turned to Raymond.

"Eh, boy-o?"

He stood stiff, lifting a hand to the third pier.

Hattie followed his finger to a dull-white fishing trawler. The words *"Bianco Fiore"* were painted across its transom.

"Well, what d'ya know about that?" she whispered.

This was the last thing she wanted to see. Her best-case scenario would be that these poor saps had chugged on south during the night, never to be seen again. But, here they were. Sitting right on this pier.

Raymond nudged her arm. "So, should we get the goons?"

"No," she answered. "We can do the heavy lifting, I think."

The two rounded the dock toward the third pier, approaching with slow steps.

Hattie cupped her hands around her mouth, and shouted, "Ahoy?"

Raymond followed suit, bellowing, "Hey, anyone aboard?"

They listened to silence for a long moment before turning to face one another.

Hattie said, "Maybe they're in the inn?"

Raymond nodded. "Wouldn't that figure?"

As they turned back to the dock, a gunshot rang out. A tall post near Hattie's face erupted into splinters. They both simply stood, stricken, for the next second.

A second shot fired. Raymond pawed at his ear, ducking reflexively. Their nerves caught up with the situation, and Raymond reached for Hattie to pull her to the deck.

She tried to focus on their whereabouts...the quality of light, the motion of the boat and the men on board lifting guns at them. Her instincts rammed together. What would she pinch? Disappear? Would that even work?

A shirtless young man hopped up onto the railing of the boat and eyed them with a sick leer. He lifted his revolver, pulled the hammer back with his thumb, then pulled the trigger.

Hattie flinched. When she opened her eyes, she found the tiny slug of lead hanging in the air several inches from her face. It spun slowly, almost imperceptibly, as it crept forward...hair's breadth by hair's breadth. The air was thick, and she had to tug on her lungs to inhale. She peered up at the gunman. The muzzle flash spread across the end of the pistol like a bright orange blossom. Then Hattie pulled her head to the side, watching as the bullet eased forward in its straight-line trajectory.

Strange echoing breaths sounded in her ears...but the breaths weren't hers.

She turned to her left to find Vincent pushing through the frozen air toward the two of them. His motions were odd, jerky. One foot pounded down against the pier, pushing hard like a piston to propel him forward. He was a man running underwater.

His face was flushed, and a stream of red had emerged from his nostril.

Hattie shouted, "Vincent?" but the word came out a garbled mess.

He coughed and pitched forward, releasing a red mist as his face landed against the pier. With flailing arms, he scrambled back to his feet.

She reached for Raymond, still frozen in his protective posture trying to cover the space where Hattie had been. With effort, she rose to her feet.

Vincent, as if a reflection of her motion, dropped to his knees several yards away. His face was clammy, and a stream of blood erupted from his nose. As she took in the distance between the third pier and the dockside inn, she realized he'd extended his power way, way too far.

Which meant this wouldn't last long.

Hattie spun on her heel to face the leering gunman. With the same piston-footed motions, she swam her way through the frozen time until she reached the boat. With a gentle hop, her body rose through the air, if slowly. The speed of everything was diminished, but her weight seemed somehow suspended.

Hattie reached for the man's gun, her fingers slicing through the muzzle flash with a quick sizzle. A prickle of pain rushed through her fingertips, but she bit down on her tongue to power through it. Her feet landed on the railing, continuing over with an unnatural momentum until she'd slipped into the gunman's midsection. The air rushed into her lungs in spurts. The muffled sounds washed in and out.

The time bubble was collapsing.

She wrenched the revolver from the man's grip, hoisting it high over her head. The time bubble popped as she swept it down against the side of his head. Air thinned, and sound resumed its normal timbre, offering a satisfyingly wet THUNK as the gun hammered against the man's temple.

Voices shouted all around her. Metal clacked. Rifle bolts chambered.

Hattie lifted her eyes to find three men lifting weapons at her.

No time to think, now.

She clamped her eyes shut, then whispered, "Guns down."

All of the gunmen sucked in heavy breaths, jerking their faces up toward the pier. In the space between her illusion and real life, the added dimension of sound echoed through her ears, and the ears of the gunmen.

What they heard were authoritative voices shouting, "Guns down! Hands in the air!" What they saw was a dozen Treasury Men surrounding the boat.

One of the riflemen dropped his weapon immediately.

The other two retreated a few steps.

The illusion tugged at her guts hard. Just like Vincent, she was over-extending herself. It was a wide radius for a light pinch, and she was adding noise to the package.

Rather than wait to see how the illusion played out, she reached for the dropped rifle, gripping it by the barrel. With a quick slash, she swung the stock against the first thug's knees.

He released a howl of pain, tumbling to the side as his leg released a sickening crack.

Hattie hoisted the gun, jabbing the butt against his face twice, each making contact before he managed to lift his hands to defend himself. His finger slipped around the edge of the stock, pulling it to the side in a firm grip.

She pulled back on it with a gentle tug, then released it.

The rifle whipped back in his grasp, smacking him one more time in the face, just as she rounded on him to ram her heel into his crotch.

With another yelp of pain, the man doubled over into a ball.

Hattie nodded to him with a smirk, then lifted her gaze to find the third gunman.

He had his rifle trained directly at Hattie.

A shot fired.

The man jerked backward, spinning into the wall of the cabin before slumping to the deck, leaving a red smear behind him.

Hattie turned toward the pier to find Lefty holding a smoking pistol in his hand.

He gave Hattie a nod. "You okay?"

She nodded several times. "I'm intact."

Lefty threw his pistol hand over the railing, pulling himself aboard with a loud groan. He scooped up the weapon, training the pistol in front of him as he stalked the rest of the ship.

Jumping back over the side of the boat, Hattie nearly collided with Raymond. His eyes were wild with panic.

"G…girl? You okay?"

"I'm fine," she urged.

Raymond kept pawing at his ear.

She reached for his arm, easing it down to find his fingers bloodied.

"Are you hurt?" she asked, peering up at his ear. A slow

trickle of blood slipped from a neat gash near the top of his ear. "Oh…looks like you took a graze, there."

He fumbled his fingers around the wound, wincing as they finally made contact with his flesh.

Hattie slapped his shoulder. "You've got more luck than sense!"

"Why were they shootin' at us?" he blurted. "We ain't done nothin'!"

She shrugged, then caught a glimpse of Vincent lying in a heap several yards away. Slipping around Raymond, she trotted toward the pincher, reaching down to roll him onto his back. He'd vomited, leaving a puddle of blood and sick on the pier. His face was stark white, except for the blood smearing his upper lip.

"Lefty!" she shouted.

The man peeked over the side of the boat, then holstered his gun as Raymond offered a hand back onto the planks. Lefty jogged forward to join her.

"Is he…?" she whispered.

Lefty laid two fingers along his throat, then shook his head. "He's alive." He got to his feet and motioned for Raymond. "Hey…driver."

"Name's Raymond," Raymond chided.

"Yeah, okay. Raymond. Give your friend here a hand, will you? Carry him to the inn. Get him sitting upright. It helps."

Raymond squinted at Hattie. She stared up at Raymond, unsure what to do. Was this her opportunity? If this man died here on the wharf, she'd be free. They'd all be free.

And yet, he'd nearly killed himself to save her from a bullet.

Save her, sure. Saved for the mob, so they could collect her later. Still though, he'd saved her life. Fair was fair.

Hattie looked up at Lefty. "Where are you going?"

The man's face adopted a grim resolution. "We left two of

them alive. One of them's conscious, more or less. I have questions."

She nodded. "Fine."

Hattie pulled one of Vincent's arms as Raymond took the other. They draped him around their necks at an awkward angle by virtue of the difference in their heights, and hauled him back up the pier. As they took the last corner, Hattie checked on the *Bianco Fiore*. Lefty's head disappeared into the cabin. She wasn't sure what this man's particular skills were, when it came to "questions," but he was capable enough with a pistol for only having one arm. She resolved not to underestimate Lefty Mancuso. Ever.

The innkeeper balked as they lugged Vincent into the front shop.

"Hey, now…what's all this?" he blubbered.

Hattie left Vincent with Raymond, then confronted the innkeeper. "He took a spill, is all. Hit his head on the pier. He'll be right as rain. We just need to get some water inside him."

The innkeeper squinted at her, then nodded. "Malloy, isn't it?"

"Aye."

"Yeah, okay. Sure. Got some clean water in the back."

Raymond slipped Vincent onto a wood banquette near one of the bay windows overlooking the dock, propping him up against the window casement. Vincent's eyes opened and closed, fluttering in addled confusion.

The innkeeper brought a pewter mug of water. Hattie eased it to Vincent's lips, but it was useless. So, she gave him some time to recover. Finally, with a chest-shaking cough, Vincent pulled in deep breaths.

"Wh…what…" he gurgled.

Hattie tried again with the water. This time, he took to it, taking small, short sips.

"Thank you," he whispered, opening his eyes. "Ah. Yeah. Thanks."

She set the mug onto the table nearby, and said, "I suppose it was the least I could do."

A meager smile crept onto his lips. "Are they dead?"

"One of them," she whispered, easing a finger onto Vincent's mouth as she checked whether the innkeeper was within earshot. "Let's not talk about that sort of thing in mixed company, though."

Vincent glanced toward the shop front, then chuckled. "Oh. Thought we were on your boat."

Raymond made an offended noise, then reached for the mug to take a long swallow.

Hattie slapped his hand. "That's Vincent's water."

"Well, he weren't drinkin' it," Raymond groused.

Vincent collected himself enough to sit upright, pulling a handkerchief from his pocket to clean his face.

"You gonna make it?" Raymond asked.

"Believe it or not," Vincent replied, "I've had worse. I'm, uh…gonna see if they have a washroom."

As he disappeared through a door at the far end of the dining room, Raymond hopped up to see what food was available, ordering two bowls of she-crab soup. When he tried to put it on Vincent's "bill," the innkeeper simply shook his head so Hattie paid out of her pocket. As Raymond took a seat, she gazed through the windows at the darkened docks outside. What was Lefty doing on that boat?

Vincent reemerged from the washroom, his hair wet and slicked back over his head. He set his hat on the table, and Raymond reached for the second bowl of soup to pull it away.

"That's Hattie's," he grumbled.

Vincent shrugged. "Not hungry."

"You should eat something. All of that had to suck the wind out of you," Hattie scolded.

He stepped over to join her at the window. "Is Lefty out there?"

She nodded.

"How many were there?" he asked.

"Three that we saw. There's two left."

"You took one out?" he asked.

She chuckled. "Your friend did. But I appreciate you giving me the credit."

"I should go see what he's up to."

"I wouldn't," Hattie said. "I think he's plying them for information. If you take my meaning."

"I do," Vincent said. "And he might need help." He took a step for the door, then reached for the wall to steady himself.

"Sure you shouldn't just sit for a while?" Hattie eyed him with concern. "Get some food in you?"

Vincent gathered himself, then returned to the table to grab his hat. "We don't know who these people are or why they fired on you. If it has anything to do with Doc Freedman, then I should be there."

"Then I'm coming with you," she stated.

Raymond lifted his brow, staring at the two bowls of soup in panic.

Hattie lifted a hand to him. "Stay here. Eat your soup."

He mumbled with a mouthful of soup and crackers, "I ain't leavin' you alone with these people."

Vincent lifted a brow. "I'm no threat to either of you. Especially right now."

Hattie released a dry laugh, then told Raymond, "I'm fine. We'll be back shortly."

She and Vincent stepped into the night, easing their way along the piers. An occasional oil lamp hung on a post alongside one of the moored boats offered scant illumination as they made their way to pier three. When they reached the *Bianco Fiore*, they found Lefty looming inside its cabin, a silhouette within a halo of flickering orange light.

Hattie jumped aboard, offering a hand to Vincent as he pulled himself carefully over the rail. Lefty turned to face them and Hattie held a breath as she spotted a blade in his hand, dripping with blood.

"What've you done?" she whispered.

Lefty's face was stony. He blinked at the question, and with a tiny shake seemed to return from whatever nightmare he had fallen into. "Asking questions."

Vincent stepped around Hattie to inspect the scene behind Lefty. He winced at what he saw, and Hattie was grateful to be outside the cabin.

"I recognize this one," Vincent muttered. "From the other night."

"What other night?" Hattie asked.

"The night we met. This mook and this one." Vincent added pointing to the thug Lefty had shot. "They were on the boat I scuttled."

Lefty nodded, crouching next to a dead man to wipe the blood off his hand. "They're from Richmond."

"Richmond?" Hattie spat. "These are the Citizens?"

"Not exactly," Lefty replied. "They hang back behind you boat-leggers, like tigers in tall grass." He nodded for the dock. "Where's your driver?"

"At the inn," Hattie said. "Why?"

"Because these idiots weren't after your rum. Or your whisky. Or your boat." Lefty stepped out of the cabin to take in a deep breath. "They're after your friend."

"Why him?" she pressed.

Lefty answered, "His complexion."

Hattie lifted a hand over her mouth, then balled that hand into a fist. "They're a lynching party?"

"In so many words, yes. *Bianco Fiore* isn't just the name of the boat. It's the name of their group. These people take issue with coloreds on the water and have decided to do something about it. From what I could get out of them, there are more of their number. Enough to be a real problem for any waterman on the Bay."

Hattie turned toward the cabin, spying the red smear on the inside wall. "Then I'm glad you asked your questions the way you did." She glanced at Vincent, who made eye contact, then nodded thoughtfully.

Lefty ventured off for the inn, while Vincent policed the bodies. Hattie left the other pincher to the work, standing on the pier as he bundled the three corpses. It seemed Lefty's interrogation skills had proven fatal for the two survivors. After about fifteen minutes, and three splashes in the water, Vincent emerged from the cabin with the oil lamp in one hand, and Lefty's jacket draped over the other.

Hattie reached for Vincent's hand, but he managed to hop off the boat without too much embarrassment.

"You're on the mend," she said as they started back for the inn.

"I told you I've had worse. Got laid up bad a week or so ago. Never really get used to it."

She nodded. "If only you had some magic potion to patch you up again."

Vincent harrumphed. "Hadn't thought of it like that. Imagine being able to take a drop or two of some tonic, and you keep extending your powers? That's money, is what that is."

They walked in silence for several steps before Vincent said, "When I was out of it, you had a chance to do me in."

"Hmm?"

"Coulda put a blade between my ribs, dumped me in the

water. Covered it up with one of your illusions. No one would know. Your secret would be safe."

She nodded. "I suppose so."

"Why didn't you?" he asked.

"Not *everyone* on this dock is a cold-blooded killer."

Vincent sniffled. "Death comes with this job, Hattie Malloy. Cost of doing business."

"You asked a question. I answered."

"Fair enough."

Hattie stopped, grabbing his arm. "These Fiore people… they're monsters. You know that?"

"Agreed."

"Just another group looking over my shoulder. I'm used to it by now, but lately it just feels like the sky's closing in on my head. You're the only one I can call out for it, so if I do that, you'll understand?"

He nodded.

Hattie added, "I didn't want to find that boat. I wanted to spend two days hauling your sorry hide around, then dropping you off and taking your money. But knowing what you know about me… I feel like you'll never leave me be, not as long as you have masters to serve."

Vincent didn't respond.

"So," she declared, "this can't ever end, can it? Not until you get your pincher."

"That's why I'm looking for this Freedman character. Did those hoboes actually point you at this boat? Or was that all bushwa?"

She nodded. "They did. Probably on the hunt for him, since he's creole."

"Maybe Lefty got something about Freedman out of them before…"

Hattie gripped his arm. "I need something from you, Vincent Calendo. I need you to listen."

He turned to face her fully. "I'm listening."

"I don't know you," she stated. "And I don't trust you. But I feel I do understand you. We are unique, and that means something." She stepped closer. "I need this water pincher as much as you do. More to the point, I need that elixir."

"For the magic sickness?" he asked.

"It's not for me," she said. "It's for my da. Now, I'm telling you this because I want to change our arrangement. My da is sick, and this elixir may be the only thing that can save him. He's sacrificed too much for me already. It's time I gave back. So, I'll help you find this Doc Freedman—more than just two days. I'll even help you recruit him. In exchange, I want access. I want access to his elixirs. And I want your masters to stay the hell away from me and my family."

Vincent took a step away from Hattie. His face roiled with emotions. Anger. Confusion. Accusation.

What had she said? This should've seemed like a peace gesture.

He sputtered over words for a moment, all dignity leeching out of his posture. Finally, he managed, "You *know* your father?"

Hattie nodded. "Of course."

Vincent scowled and turned away.

She said, "He's a good man. He deserves a longer life. A better life."

Vincent lifted his hand for her to hush.

Hattie ran her last few words over and over, trying to figure out what had hit a raw nerve.

Vincent asked, his back still turned, "Your mother, too? You know her as well?"

"Yes. They've given everything to keep me free."

Vincent shuffle-stepped in a slow circle to face her. His face was leaden.

"My parents sold me to the mob when I was two years old," he said in a quiet, clear tone.

She winced but held her tongue.

He continued, "The family has been my life. Not *my* family, but *the* family. If you're all torn up over your father's health, then perhaps you do understand me." He lifted his eyes to her. "The family is in trouble. We're surrounded by sharks and rats, all trying to eat away at everything we've built. You want to give back? So do I."

She ventured a step forward. "Then we are agreed? I help you, you help me?"

He stared at her hand, then turned away. "It's dark."

Hattie stood as Vincent stormed up the pier, the oil lamp swinging in his hand with his long strides. With a sigh, she followed him up to the inn.

CHAPTER 20

Vincent stared out the window of the room Lefty had rented from the innkeeper. There was barely enough space to walk between the wall and the bunk-style beds, much less gain any privacy. It didn't matter, really. Lefty fell asleep quickly and stayed that way the entire night.

Vincent, on the other hand, was out of luck. The conversation he'd had with Hattie that night had upended all his thoughts, dragging him awake. Memories of his years under close guard by the priests at his parochial school flooded his brain along. The attic space he'd called home for twelve years. The time upstate where he'd been "trained" to serve the family. The grimy grotto apartment he'd slept in for another four years before the Crew put him on his official stipend. The day he'd gotten his own place with a kitchen and a real living room.

The whole time it was only ever Vincent.

Lefty stirred in bed, shuffling off the scratchy wool blanket they'd found in a footlocker near the beds—only one blanket in a room rented for two.

After a loud yawn, a few coughs and a snort, the man peered up at Vincent. "How long you been awake?"

"Not sure," Vincent replied.

"You gonna be dead on your feet today, or what?"

"Don't get antsy. I'm steady."

Lefty got out of bed to stretch his one arm up to the ceiling. Vincent watched the fishermen on the dock below. Several had emerged from their boats and had filed along the warped boards toward the inn for breakfast.

"Hey, Lefty," Vincent said. "You know anything about my parents?"

"Your parents?" Lefty repeated with annoyance. "What's got your parents in your noodle?"

"Just wondering about them. Whether they made out good with the money the mob paid for me."

Lefty chuckled. Then he frowned. "Vincent, this ain't nothing to get your head wrapped around. They're out there somewhere, living their own lives. Or, maybe not. You know? They might be long gone."

Vincent nodded. "Wasn't sure if you knew their story, or what."

Lefty approached Vincent and put a hand on his shoulder. "You was born in, what? '99? Got real work with the Crew just about six years ago. Right?" Lefty stared up at the ceiling. "I came home around 1919. Met you the next summer, when Vito put me in charge of you. So, no. I was only around for about a year before they put you to work."

"Yeah, I guess it's a dumb question. Huh?"

"Not so dumb," Lefty said, stepping away. "Wondering about your heritage is perfectly normal. It's just that your heritage don't figure into your life the way it does for the rest of us. That's just the way it works for people like you."

Vincent winced. People like him. There was another

"person like him" somewhere downstairs, and *she* still had a family.

Lefty added, "I suppose it don't seem fair to you."

"No one asked my opinion."

"Yeah. Well, if they got paid, then they got paid top dollar."

Vincent turned to Lefty. "And what if they *didn't* get paid?"

Lefty squinted. "Then, I suppose you shouldn't worry about them. Look, Vincent. You got real value to the family. Never forget that."

"Value? Like some race horse?"

"More like a weapon."

Vincent shook his head. "Well, this weapon's getting tired of giving away credit for what he does."

Lefty shook his head. "That's what you want? Credit?"

"Maybe a damn 'thank you' every now and then wouldn't kill anyone."

"If you're waiting for Vito Corbi to call you up in front of the Crew and shine your knob in front of everyone, you're gonna die frustrated. He's too worried about his own sad story to give anyone else the time of day. He's got the other families breathing down his neck. No one thinks he's up to the challenge here. Now there's bootleggers in West By God giving him the works. Tony's letting the Bay business slip through his fingers. And sure, he's got just the one pincher to speak of. You think booting us out here to sniff out another pincher is busy work? You think it don't matter to him?"

Vincent said, "I know it matters. I'm just not sure that *I* matter."

Lefty thought it over for a moment, then simply turned for the door. "I gotta wash up."

Vincent looked back out the window, releasing a long breath.

Pausing with the hall door half-open, Lefty said, "If you feel like you need credit, then you'll get it from me."

"Thanks."

"If it feels like you got a raw deal, consider maybe it's not because Vito hates you. Maybe he's afraid of you," Lefty added.

"Afraid? You're yanking my chain."

"Well, a man's got two options when he's faced with someone of rare quality. Either he puts him on a pedestal and lets him shine brighter than anyone else. Or, he puts a lead weight around his neck and keeps him grounded. Either way, it's not about being fair."

Vincent nodded, and Lefty exited for the washroom.

Rare quality. He smirked.

After the morning's ministrations, Vincent haunted the front dock while the rest took their breakfast. He hadn't made a face-to-face with Hattie just yet and was taking his time to frame a response. He wasn't particularly interested in apologizing for storming off the previous evening. In fact, the woman's entire attitude about him and his upbringing still rankled his guts. But, that didn't mean he should act the fool. In fact, it meant he should have risen above. And he hadn't.

Footsteps approached.

Vincent turned, but instead of finding Hattie approaching, he saw Lefty, shaven and changed back into his clothes.

"You got your head outta your ass?" Lefty asked as he stepped alongside Vincent on the pier.

"Tell me something," Vincent said without acknowledging the question. "Those sheet-wearing Reubens pony up any useful information while you gave 'em the works?"

Lefty nodded. "Doc Freedman, whoever this joker is, apparently hangs his shingle someplace called Bimini Island."

"Bimini Island," Vincent repeated. "Ring any bells for you?"

Lefty shook his head.

"Yes," a voice called from behind them.

Vincent turned to find Hattie and Raymond standing behind them, packed for pounding.

Vincent nodded at Lefty. "Give us some space, huh?"

Lefty gestured at Raymond, and the two retired for the boat. Hattie stood stiff-armed, watching Vincent with hooded eyes.

Vincent asked, "So, you know where that is?"

She replied, "I might."

"Feel like cutting me in?"

Hattie held up a hand. "First, we need to cinch up our conversation."

He nodded. "Yeah, I've been thinking on that. Look. The way I walked out—"

"Forget it," she grumbled.

"Wish I could, but I was coarse and rude, and you deserved better than that."

Her face twisted into a question mark. "Beg your pardon?"

"Shouldn't a walked off the way I did," he explained. "You hit a nerve, and I recognize that. If you can see past that, then maybe I can see past you having…being what you are. For the time being."

"The time being?" she prodded.

Vincent smirked. "Well, we have a water pincher with some potent horse liniment you need to deliver to your father first. Or did I read you sideways?"

The faintest of smiles flickered in the corner of her lips. She whispered, "Aye. We do."

"So. Bimini Island. You got the bead on that little slice of Heaven?"

Hattie walked past Vincent toward the boat. "I think so, at any rate. Had a moment not long ago with one of my competition. He fed me a line about this Doc Freedman and Bimini Island. Gave me a rough direction. And whether it was God above or sheer, dumb luck, I might've stumbled over the damn place on my own without knowing where I was."

Vincent trotted up to join her. "Think you can roll those holy dice one more time?"

"I'll give it a go, but you have to know this was the middle of the night, and my information came from a place of..." She winced. "Desperation."

Vincent grimaced. "The poor bastard. Where is he now?"

Hattie looked over the water, then shrugged. "Either at the bottom of the Bay or floating on top of't."

They set off south along the Chesapeake, bound for a point that existed in the recesses of Hattie's memories. The journey should take only a few hours, and there was copious light left in the day. Lefty lingered by the driver, involved in another deep-seated and arguably sterile religious conversation. Vincent kept to himself amidships, lingering by the railing as the spray of the water misted his outstretched hand. That boat-legger woman was correct about one thing. Life out on the water felt simpler. Cleansing. Though Vincent was certain it was little more than a passing sensation. No real sort of life could be led out here. There was nothing on this boat but rote errand-running. Hours whiled away amidst this vast, murky expanse of water. Where were the clubs? Where was the music? It was good for the moment, but ultimately, he needed more. More lights. More sound. He needed...consequence.

Vincent caught Hattie watching him from time to time and put it out of his mind. More than ever, he was convinced that it would be impossible to share a city with a woman like this, let alone work with her. She was smart, and he had no doubt she had skills, but he'd never met anyone so stubborn, so independent and plain-spoken before. The woman was downright disruptive. She'd upset the structure of his life in short order and leave him standing in the middle of the wreckage. No, having her as Vito's second pincher would be a disaster—for him *and* the family. Hopefully this Doc Freedman would be a better fit.

The border between Maryland and Virginia approached, and Raymond pointed out the mouth of the Potomac River as they passed. Both Vincent and Hattie advanced toward the bow, eyes on the western shoreline as they watched the scenery go by.

"Lose something?" she jibed as he eventually took a step away.

"No. Just wondering about…wondering where we were. Exactly."

"Past the Wicomico, just north of the Rappahannock and Deltaville," she said.

He nodded. "Ever been there? Deltaville, I mean."

"Once. You?"

"Yeah, just the one time."

Hattie peered at Vincent with a wrinkled brow. "What brought a man like you out to a thin bar of mud and pine trees?"

"Lots of dead people," he replied. "There's a fishing camp there. Boat-leggers like you tend to use it to store—"

"I know what it's used for."

Vincent sighed. "Not sure that place is…right. You know?"

Hattie looked over the water at the advancing jut of land slicing into the Bay. "I do, at that." She turned and whistled at Raymond. "Eh, boy-o! Let's let in."

Vincent asked, "Is this where you found Bimini Island?"

"No," she said. "I just want to take a look."

"At what?"

"That fishing camp."

Vincent winced. "You sure that's a good idea? Maybe there's some of your river-running competition out there? Maybe the Richmond boys?"

She grinned and thrust a finger into his shoulder. "You scared, Vincent Calendo?"

"Nah. Just more interested in water pinchers than Hell…" He didn't finish the comment. That was too much information.

Her eyes narrowed. "Than Hell?"

Vincent glanced back at the helm, and the others waiting for some sort of consensus from the bow. He turned to Hattie, and muttered, "Did you see a shack? Old piece of work, nearly burned out?"

She nodded. "I know what you're talking about."

"Word from the Richmond people is there's something called a Hell pincher holed up in that old heap."

"Hell pincher? What in the name of Jesus Henry are you on about?"

Vincent eased closer. "I met the pincher from the Upright Citizens. Guy by the name of Capstein."

"Never heard of him."

"Probably a good thing," Vincent said. "He's a bit of a windbag and a true believer, if you take my meaning. Anyways, he and Lefty and me gave that shack a once-over. Found lots of weird symbols carved into the wood. Capstein says it's probably someone who studied forbidden text, or some horse crackers like that. Called him a Hell pincher."

Hattie asked, "It's one of us?"

"Nah. Not like us. Not born to it. More like a goon what got delusions of grandeur and sold his soul for the real deal."

Her face soured. "I don't think that's right."

"Yeah? Why's that?"

"Because," she said, "I saw him."

Vincent took a moment. "You *saw* him?"

"Aye. Him. It. Some sort of thing, any rate."

"What happened?" As she didn't answer, Vincent prodded, "Were you there? That night, when everyone got burned alive out in the mud?"

Hattie turned away, crossing her arms.

Vincent pursued. "You were, weren't you? I maybe missed you by a day, tops."

"Good for you."

"You're telling me you laid eyes on this Hell pincher what did that to those men?"

She nodded. "It wasn't some goon with book learning. Whatever it was…wasn't human."

Vincent checked the others again. Both Lefty and Raymond were watching them with gathered annoyance. "I think we should drive on. Go find Freedman. I mean, this is interesting and all, but—"

"Don't you want to see it?" she asked. "See if it's still there?"

Vincent couldn't answer. He didn't want to see it. Well, more to the point, he wanted to find Freedman first. But sure, there was something to that mystery on Deltaville that felt oddly compelling.

"Where's this Bimini Island, anyways?" he asked.

"Supposed to be right at the mouth of the ocean," Hattie said. "East of Newport News, but I think it was farther north than that. After my encounter with whatever lives in that shack I tried to get a man to this water pincher. Trying to find the elixir. Maybe save his life."

Vincent whispered, "What happened?"

"He didn't make it. By the time I made headway, he was gone, so I dumped him into the Bay."

"Then what makes you think you found Bimini?"

She shook her head. "Maybe I didn't. But...something tells me I did. I'd looked down the east side of the Bay, but when I was heading back north and about to turn home, I saw a campfire on a tiny bar. Nothing more than a patch of trees and some shoreline. But, it felt close. *He* felt close." She shivered, then rubbed her hands over her arms. "Thought maybe I'd gone Bedlam."

"This is all about some gut feeling, then?" he asked.

"Which is one reason why I want to stop at Deltaville. That's where I set out. Better chances to retrace my path."

Vincent took a long breath, then nodded. "Okay. Let's grease this monkey."

Hattie joined Raymond at the helm, and after a short conversation she'd convinced him to turn toward Deltaville.

The boat eased along the muddy bank near the burned-out shack. Vincent stood beside Lefty as Hattie hopped out into the surf to wade her way onto land, tying a mooring rope to a downed pine.

Lefty said, "Back here, again?"

"Our lady-legger thinks she ran across Bimini Island. Started from here, so we're letting her run through the paces."

"Do you really think you'll find a pincher on this island?" Lefty asked.

"I think it's my best shot. My only shot."

"We're in the Upright Citizen's territory, Vincent. We get thumbed sniffing around this joint uninvited, they could kick up one hell of a fuss."

"I know that," Vincent grumbled. "But they got two pinchers already. We gotta work this angle."

"Fine."

Lefty jumped out of the boat and joined Hattie on the shore. Vincent followed suit. The three of them approached the charcoaled shack and Vincent spotted the length of wood he'd cleared with his hand to reveal the glyphs carved along the outside of the shanty.

Hattie muttered, "There."

She pointed to a patch of mud just past the high tide mark.

Vincent nodded. "Yeah, I saw that."

The image of three arcs surrounding a circle remained barely visible in the mud, having been washed by lapping waves here and there.

"What's it mean, do you think?" he asked Hattie.

"Three lines around a center," she said. "Could mean anything."

Vincent said, "So, what you're saying is you don't know."

"Yes," she snapped. "I don't know."

"Fine. All I was asking."

Lefty shook his head and turned back toward the boat. "So, we're here. Now what?"

A sound captured Vincent's attention. Crunching. Steps. Footsteps. He glanced toward the main clutch of buildings up the path.

And held his breath. Hattie stepped up alongside him, shaking her head.

A man was approaching. An old man with a gray beard and grizzled, weather-worn features. He wore rubbers and a wide-brimmed fisher's hat.

Vincent whispered, "You see him, too?"

She reached for his arm, gripping it tight.

Vincent asked, "Is…is that him?"

Hattie nodded once.

The old man continued down the path, eyes narrow slit with the barest slivers of shocking pale blue irises peering from between his heavy lids.

Lefty hustled to join the two of them, arriving just as the fisherman reached the shack.

The old man gazed at the three in silence.

Hattie cleared her throat. "Hello?"

The old fisherman didn't respond.

Vincent gave it a shot. "Do you live here?"

Again, no response.

He shrugged at Hattie.

Lefty tipped his hat. "Well, sir, don't let us detain you. Come on, friends and countrymen. We have business."

The fisherman cocked his head at Lefty. A rumble filled the old man's chest. That rumble swelled in intensity until Vincent felt it through the soles of his shoes. What was happening?

Hattie pulled Vincent away a couple steps as the fisherman pivoted to face Lefty.

Vincent whispered, "Uh...Lefty? I think you shined him off."

Lefty didn't respond. His jaw was set, as were his shoulders. There was no way an elderly fisherman could scare off a man like Lefty Mancuso. Unless, of course, his eyes began to scorch with what looked like the flames from an under-trimmed candle.

Lefty scooted away.

Hattie held out her hands. "We don't mean you harm. We're just passing through."

The fisherman glanced back at Hattie, and the flames that had erupted from his eye sockets subsided, leaving the icy-blue orbs they'd seen before.

"Okay, old-timer?" Vincent nudged. "We're leaving."

The fisherman turned on his heel, grabbed the door to the shack, and entered slamming the door behind him.

Lefty muttered, "Cheerful bastard."

The three hustled back for the boat.

Raymond lifted a chin at the shack. "What was that all about?"

"Nothing," Vincent replied.

Hattie pulled the mooring line off the tree trunk, then splashed through the surf to climb aboard. "All right, that was a bad idea. I'll admit it."

Lefty shook his head as he sat on the bench behind Raymond. "What was that thing, exactly?"

Vincent answered, "Hell pincher."

"No," Hattie countered. "That was no wizard, or warlock, or what have you."

"You've met a lotta warlocks?" Vincent asked.

"I'm saying that creature isn't human. It's trying to look human. Maybe it's even wearing a human like a suit. But…I could feel something beyond our understanding. Something deep. Infernal."

Vincent nearly returned a flippant jibe but thought better of it. Instead, he asked, "So, you're saying that was what? Some sort of devil?"

"Or demon," she whispered.

Lefty crossed himself.

Raymond snickered. "Demons, huh? Well, that just figures with you people."

Hattie turned back toward the Bay. "East by southeast, Raymond. Give me ten knots."

Vincent leaned against the engine housing as the boat chugged to life, swinging an arc through the Piankatank to turn back into the Bay.

Those eyes. Flames.

Was that really a demon? And if so, why didn't it burn the three of them alive like it did the others? One mystery at a time. He'd have ample opportunity to contemplate that old weathered fisher-demon after he found Doc Freedman.

If he found Doc Freedman.

CHAPTER 21

Hattie peered at the eastern shoreline peeking into view over the waves of the Bay. Nothing but water and the long, even line of the Delmarva Peninsula.

"Anything?" Raymond muttered.

She shook her head. This was harder than she thought it would be. Last time she'd made this trip, her body was filled with panic, fear, and awe from the encounter with the Deltaville demon. Nothing seemed real that night, as Little Teague died slowly on the deck of his own boat. Had she even seen an island at all? Or was it a fevered illusion?

Raymond grunted and turned for the sight glass protruding from the engine house. He gave it a couple taps.

Hattie asked, "What's wrong?"

"Nothin's wrong, baby girl," he said. "We're runnin' about three gallons."

"Will that get us back to Winnow's?" she asked.

"Barely."

She crossed her arms. "Why didn't you fuel at Kent Island?"

"Didn't know we were set to comb every inch of Bay

between there and Newport News, is why." He shook his head. "If we keep at this, we're gonna need to make a stop."

Hattie turned to check on Vincent and Lefty standing by the bow, then said, "They won't like it."

"Think they're gonna like floatin' dead in the water? 'Cause that's the option."

"Right. I know." She half-climbed the engine house and peered over the side of the boat. "There's the James. Hell, our closest friendly fuel stop will be up near Richmond, won't it?"

"Okay," Raymond said with a shrug.

She jabbed a thumb at the gangsters. "They're going to love this."

Hattie hopped down and called the two from the front to join them. They stood casually, watching as she chose her words.

"We have to let in up the James to refuel."

Vincent shrugged.

Lefty, on the other hand, scowled. "No good."

"Sorry," she said. "No choice. We hadn't figured on quite so much dilly-dallying, so we didn't fuel at Kent."

Lefty shook his head. "We're a stone's throw from Richmond, as it is. Being on the water, the locals won't take us quite so seriously. But if we shore up and buy fuel?" He tsked. "That's asking for endless trouble."

Hattie snickered. "Endless trouble is precisely how I'd describe the two of you."

Vincent grinned in response.

"We're on unsteady terms with the boys down Richmond way," Lefty told her. "Before we met the two of you, Vincent and I managed to build some bridges. I just feel as if putting in directly underneath their noses is the same as dousing that bridge with gasoline and striking a match."

Vincent held up a hand. "Well, wait. All we're doing is

buying fuel. It's not like we're hauling casks up underneath their noses."

Lefty sneered. "It would be better if we were. At least we'd have a reason to be in their territory. But with nothing to show for it, we look like we're snooping around, scaring up trouble."

Hattie sighed. "Listen, boys. Either we fuel here, or we turn back now and fuel up on Kent. That loses us a whole day if we do, and Lizzie's got business lined up with you hoodlums. We can't be out here chasing our tails all week, you know."

Lefty tilted his head back. "Well, all things considered, that's the better option. Listen, we're in no hurry out here. If we have to turn back—"

Vincent interrupted, "Then we fuel here."

Lefty dropped his head, took in a cleansing breath, then turned toward Vincent. "What?"

"Like she said," Vincent replied. "We're out here on their boat, presuming on their goddamned hospitality. We're not really gonna turn them around and waste their time on account of fluttering nerves. It's not like we're doing business out here."

Lefty squinted. "Aren't we?"

Vincent didn't respond.

Raymond cleared his throat. "It ain't like we're rollin' up into the middle of the city, folks. We got a boy halfway down the James who runs a pier with a couple pumps. He knows what side the bread is buttered. He won't kick up a fuss."

Lefty sniffed, and wound up for a response, but Vincent cut him off. "Good enough for us. Right, Lefty?"

Lefty eyed Vincent with increasing displeasure, then finally nodded. "Your call."

They angled into the mouth of the James River, chugging inland a while before a series of rickety piers slipped into view. Raymond eased the boat alongside one of the piers, then he and Hattie moored them to the pilings. A clutch of young men hovered around a pair of low-slung, sleek boats. They were varnished wood, cut into long, feminine angles. These were not working boats. These were pleasure craft.

Raymond reached for the railing to hop off, when Hattie took another glance at the crew. They were very young, mostly in their twenties. They were all white. And they were all staring at Raymond.

"Eh, boy-o," she mumbled to Raymond. "Maybe let me kitty up this time?"

He blinked at her.

She added, "Safer that way."

Raymond's face twisted in confusion, expecting Hattie to explain. The thugs they'd dealt with on the *Bianco Fiore*—more accurately *from* the *Bianco Fiore*—lingered in her mind. She hadn't filled Raymond in on the particulars of that group's ambitions, nor had she wanted to, but this close to Richmond, she knew they were borrowing trouble sending Raymond to do the talking.

She said, "Just lay low, alright? Things gone and went complicated for us. I need you to trust me."

"I trust you," he replied.

"Good. Now, give me some money."

Hattie hopped up onto the pier, and as she turned to approach the grease-haired proprietor of the slip, a thud pounded onto the boards behind her. She turned to find Vincent at her heels.

"I can manage," she grumbled.

"I suppose you can. But I'm on strict orders to keep you from getting into trouble."

"Strict orders?" she repeated with a smirk. "From whom, if you don't mind me asking?"

Vincent rolled his eyes, then turned to nod at Lefty.

Hattie reached for his arm. "That old man's got you on a short leash. You know that?"

"He'd probably say I have him on a shorter leash, but he ain't here to defend himself. So, yeah."

Hattie curled her arm around Vincent's and steered him forward toward the pump house. Having Vincent alongside her would only help their chances of fueling quick and heading out without too much notice. Young women in working clothes only gathered attention this far south. A well-heeled fellow with a scrappy young companion could be written off as eccentric. No fuss.

They negotiated for fuel with what Hattie felt was far too much effort. The local gangsters must have put the screws to the simple businessmen on the water these days. She wondered if that wouldn't soon be the fate of their tidy enterprise closer to Baltimore.

Vincent stood on the edge of the pier, head held high, hands in his pockets. He betrayed not the first sense of danger of the situation. He just loomed there confident that no trouble could befall him. It was bizarre. But then again, the man was a pincher, like her.

Well…not like her. He had the good faith and backing of an entire crime syndicate that traced its roots all the way back to New York City. How wonderful it must be to fear nothing.

As the fueling progressed, a clutch of young men wove their way around the piers toward their boat. Vincent picked up on the movement and gave Hattie a quick, reassuring nod. Hattie weighed her options. She could pinch light around her figure to present as male. That was her immediate plan when facing cocksure lads with attitudes. But she wasn't the problem.

Raymond was the problem.

She spied Raymond, busying himself with the rubber

hose winding from the pumphouse to the fuel tank of the boat. There were no options there. Even if she pinched light to make Raymond disappear, or otherwise present as something more fitting for these sharks circling her crew, it would cost more magic than she could afford.

With any luck, Vincent would redirect these boys, and no one would get hurt.

Vincent tipped his hat as one of their number stepped forward. "Afternoon, gents."

The young man glared at him with a toothy leer, then turned to the others. "Oh, Lord Jesus. Looks like we got us one of those up-north wops, boys. Nothin' funnier to me than a wop in a suit."

A round of snickering from behind the man brought his leer into a smile.

Vincent shrugged, gesturing at the man's wrinkled but clean shirt. "There's something to be said about good, honest working clothes. Can I help you fellows?"

The smile faded from the young buck's face. "Yeah. You can." He nodded at the boat, and Raymond who was watching stiff-armed. "You can take that darkie and go back up where you came from."

Hattie balled a fist, then felt a hand on her shoulder. She glanced back to find Lefty giving her a firm nod. He stepped behind her and reached into his coat, and the pistol holstered within.

Vincent said, "We'll be gone as soon as we're topped off."

Two of the thugs from the rear of the clutch stepped away, turning for the pump house. The rhythmic thumping of the fuel hose running beneath the wooden planks fell silent.

"Ain't no fuel for animals here," the young man grumbled. "Even ones in fancy-ass suits."

Vincent took a step forward, and the entire crew braced, some drawing knives from their belts. "You sure about that?"

Vincent lifted his hand into the space between the two of them, fingers poised to snap.

Hattie braced herself. She knew what was in store...a time pinch. The anxiety bled out of her as she pictured the schemes available to them. By Vincent's casual tone, he was likely to play with them a little before dumping them all into the water.

Before he could snap his fingers, a sudden gust of wind pounded into the young buck. His hair tossed into a cloud all around his face, and he teetered on unsteady feet on the edge of the pier. As he craned his arms in circles to keep his balance, another short, sharp breeze sent him flailing into the water.

Vincent stared at his fingers, then took a step backward. He peered at Hattie with a lift of his brow.

She shook her head.

A voice called from the pump house, "You boys better run along, now."

The gang turned toward a man in a tidy off-white suit standing by the pumps, inspecting his nails. Mumbles spread through their number, and they quickly dispersed, returning to a low-slung speedboat at the far end of the wharf. The young buck treaded water, scowling at Vincent before swimming off to join the others. They pulled him aboard, and their craft eased out onto the water. As it angled away, Hattie spotted the words *Bianco Fiore* written across its transom.

The man in the suit threw a lever to restart the pump, then turned to pay a quivering man hiding inside the pump house before approaching Vincent. Lefty stepped around Hattie, his pistol remaining in its holster.

Vincent laughed. "Elmer Capstein. We meet again!"

Capstein nodded. "Sorry about those." He gestured at the receding boat. "I can't abide rudeness."

Vincent said, "Glad you came around. I was about to make an ass of myself. What are the odds of running into you?"

Lefty underscored, "Yeah. What are the odds?"

Capstein returned a tight smile. "We have a shipment of hash coming in from Dominica. I'm here to broom away any unwanted notice before nightfall. I was certainly not expecting to find anyone from the Baltimore Crew here."

Lefty said, "Nor were we expecting to be here. Emergency stop for fuel. We'll get outta your hair in two shakes."

Capstein glanced past the two at Hattie, then at Raymond. "I see. Bold move bringing a colored crewman this far south."

Raymond popped his head up. "What, now?"

Capstein lifted a hand. "No offense intended. But, you should know, conditions have grown unfavorable for coloreds in the south end of the Chesapeake."

Vincent grumbled, "These Bianco Fiore goons?"

With a sigh, Capstein said, "They're growing in numbers every week. Making it difficult to do business with the Caribbeans, but they're not centralized. No head to cut off. It's a conundrum."

"And," Vincent added, "it seems they've got a beef with us *paisans*." He nodded to Lefty. "Which is kinda ironic, considering they're calling themselves Bianco Fiore."

"I think it's their notion of being clever," Capstein said. "It's an enormous mess. If the Feds could've come up with a better scheme to shut down boat-legging on the Bay, I can't imagine what it would have been. But this is all grassroots. Best we can do is double our guard and keep our eyes open."

Lefty said, "Perhaps it's worth a little cooperation between our people and yours?"

Capstein glanced from Lefty to Vincent, his gaze holding steady as Vincent squirmed. "Perhaps." Capstein cleared his throat and turned away. "I took care of your fuel. Again, my apologies for such inhospitality."

"Thank you," Vincent called as Capstein disappeared around the corner of the wharf.

Hattie reached for Vincent, pulling him close. "Who was that, then?"

"That," he replied, "was Elmer Capstein. He's one of the Upright Citizens' pinchers."

"Is that what the wind was all about?"

Vincent nodded. "He's an air pincher." He leaned in to whisper, "Best to stay clear of him. He's a stand-up guy, best as I know. But, he's on the hunt just like Vito."

She nodded thoughtfully, releasing his arm.

They finished fueling and turned the boat back toward the Bay. Raymond piloted in silence beside Hattie while the others conferred in privacy.

"You okay?" she asked Raymond.

His mouth curled into a tight frown, and he took a few breaths. "What's all this nonsense? Blanco Fury?"

"Bianco Fiore," she corrected. "Remember that night we holed up under the tree before this lot came to bail us out?" She wagged a finger at Vincent and Lefty.

"Like I'm gonna forget that."

"Well, those were the Bianco Fiore."

Raymond's face soured. "Well who the hell are they? Thought it was some gangster business."

"I'm afraid not, Raymond. They weren't after the booze or the money."

He muttered, "They was after me?"

Hattie nodded.

Raymond shook his head with a sardonic chuckle. "Well, that's just fine...ain't it?"

"Sounds like a bunch of hoodlums out to make life difficult for your people."

"Hell, Hattie. It ain't never been easy for us."

"No," she agreed, "but it's getting more dangerous with these gunmen hunting down anyone of a certain complexion. I don't know what's emboldened them, but you've already been singled out."

He tightened his grip on the helm. "Well, they ain't stoppin' me, if that's what you're askin'."

"I'm not asking that at all. However," she added with a sigh, "this running about looking for Bimini Island? It's putting you at risk, and I won't have't."

"Where you expect me to go?" he grumbled.

Hattie peered over the water, gaining her bearings. "How far is Maudite's? You can hole up there until we get this business concluded."

Raymond sighed. "Hattie, no. I ain't leavin' you with these criminals."

She leaned in close. "I can handle myself, Raymond. It's you we have to protect, now."

He grimaced at her.

Hattie said, "Look. I don't trust them, alright? But I do trust that they don't cause trouble without a reason. And we haven't given them any reasons. That's more than I can say for these Fiore lunatics."

"Shit," he spat. "Yeah, Maudite's just across the Bay and a bit north."

Hattie made her way to the bow and informed the others of the new plan. Lefty seemed especially enthusiastic, casting a concerned glance back toward Raymond. Vincent wasn't thrilled at the prospect of doubling back, no matter how short a throw it was. Hattie explained that they were basically at the mouth of the Bay, and that they'd managed to overshoot Bimini Island anyway. Turning north was inevitable, at this point.

The sun began to set as the boat rounded the mud flat landmark leading to Maudite's. The golden glow spread across the water, bathing the marsh grass and sporadic trees on the shore with its warm hues.

Vincent stretched and frowned. "This gin joint got a kitchen?" he asked. "I'm starving over here."

"Didn't you eat anything this morning?" Hattie chided.

"I did not," he stated. "Nor have we had a lunch."

Raymond chuckled. "That's life on the water, big man."

Vincent smirked. "Well, I'm more of a solid land and regular meals sorta guy."

Lefty lifted his hand. "Quiet. All of you."

Hattie swallowed back her pithy retort and followed Lefty's glance.

A plume of dark smoke rose from the marsh to the north.

Hattie whispered, "That's…"

Raymond hammered down the throttle, and they all swayed to catch their balance. Hattie climbed the engine house to gain a better line of sight. Within minutes, orange and red flames rose into view, flickering in and out of the remains of Maudite's.

Raymond nearly grounded the boat, easing it into a broadside against the marsh grass before leaping ashore. Hattie killed the engine and looked for a spot to moor the boat, finding nothing suitable. With a shrug, she dropped the mooring line and jumped ashore to follow Raymond. He'd made it almost halfway to the blaze before she caught up with him.

Raymond stopped at a safe distance, shaking his head at the scene. The flimsy roof collapsed into the rubble, sending a spray of sparks into the darkening sky.

Vincent trotted up alongside Hattie. "Any survivors?"

She peered into the fire and sucked in a breath, spotting two charred bodies beneath the fallen timbers before she could look away.

Raymond paced, then released an anguished shout.

Setting her jaw, Hattie stared out at the water, the grass flickering from the flames behind her. "Was this the Bianco Fiore, do you think?"

"What makes you think that?" Vincent asked.

"This was a place for…" She couldn't find the words.

"I see," Vincent said. "Then it probably was those sons of bitches."

Raymond wheezed, "Why? Why would…?"

Hattie wove her arms around Raymond's midsection to give him a squeeze. Being shot at was one thing. It was short, direct. It was war. But this? There was a savagery to burning people alive inside a building. It was an act of terror. A message.

Lefty approached and Hattie shook her head, warning him of the scene. The man's eyes were in constant motion, watching the fields of grass and the scattering of trees surrounding the area.

Unwinding herself from Raymond, Hattie took a cautious step toward him. "What is it?"

Lefty lifted a finger to shush her.

Vincent joined Lefty in his vigil. "You see that, too?"

Hattie asked, "See what?"

Something whizzed past Hattie's ear just as a distant pop sounded from the trees.

Raymond grunted.

More shots.

Lefty reached for his pistol to return fire as Vincent pulled Hattie down into the marsh grass.

A heavy thud beside them knocked a breeze across Hattie's face. She turned to find Raymond gripping his stomach. He coughed and moaned as his face drew into a mask of agony.

"Raymond!" she screamed as she crawled toward him.

The man cried out in pain as she reached for him.

Lefty dropped to a knee on the other side of Raymond, tossing his pistol to Vincent. "Here!"

Vincent caught the gun and fired two more shots toward the trees.

Lefty leaned down, trying to pry Raymond's hand away from his wound. "Help me."

Hattie rested a hand on Raymond's forehead. "Let us see!"

Raymond's eyes clamped shut, his teeth bared in a silent wheeze of pain. Lefty managed to pull the man's finger high enough to inspect the wound.

He nodded to Hattie. "Roll him toward you."

Vincent fired another shot, then dropped to the grass. "Empty. Got a reload?"

Hattie reached over Raymond and pulled hard on his hip to angle him off the ground.

As Lefty reached beneath him, he shook his head. "On the boat." Lefty fished around for a few seconds, then nodded for Hattie to ease Raymond back down. "Exit wound. Went through. If it didn't clip anything important, he could survive."

Hattie asked, "Can we get him to the boat?"

Vincent peered up above the grass and was answered with a single gunshot. "They're closing in. I think they know we're outta bullets."

Hattie snarled. "Can we get him to the boat?"

"Won't do much good." Lefty shook his head. "Closest decent hospital's in Richmond, but I don't think we'll have any luck getting someone to help him there."

"By the time we get him to Baltimore, he'll bleed out. No choice but to take him to Richmond," Vincent told him.

"Then he'll die here, or he'll die in Richmond." Lefty shrugged.

Hattie reached over and slapped his face. "Don't you say that. Don't you ever say that. He will *not* die!"

Lefty kept his face turned, staring into the grass as Hattie drew heavy breaths.

She gasped. "Do you understand? He will *not* die. Not while I'm alive to do something about it."

Vincent peeked over the grass again. "Six of them that I can see. Maybe more in the trees, but it's too dark to tell. Coming right for us. They know where we are."

Hattie covered her ears and shut her eyes, rocking herself as she tried to think. Raymond coughed, groaning some more as she knelt beside him. Vincent placed a hand on her shoulder. With a quick, explosive motion she slapped it away.

"Hey," he shouted. "Listen to me! How sure are you about this Doc Freedman?"

She scowled. "What?"

"This elixir. This Aqua Vitae?"

Hattie's scowl eased. "I don't..."

"If he's real," Vincent pressed, "and if he's out there, he may be your friend's only chance."

Hattie whimpered. She knew very little about this Doc Freedman. All she knew was that Little Teague had enough faith to run for Bimini Island when he was dying. Did Hattie have the same faith?

"How bad is he?" she asked Lefty.

"I'm not a battlefield medic. I was infantry. But I've seen men last a full day in the field after taking one in the gut. It depends on if he's bleeding."

Vincent grumbled, "We'll all end up bleeding, if we don't do something about these backwater bastards."

Hattie balled fists, then reached for Raymond's arm to give it a squeeze. "Hey."

He opened his eyes just a little.

She smiled at him. "You hear that? You got a battlefield medic here with you."

Lefty mumbled, "Actually, I said I wasn't—"

Hattie continued, "He's going to take care of you, and we'll get you to a doctor. One way or another." She turned to Vincent. "You and I will deal with these idiots."

"You got a plan?" he asked.

"Just get ready."

Hattie waved her hands in an X over her face. "Disappear."

Light pinched over her face, curving all the way around her so that she became invisible to anyone besides Vincent. She stood up in the grass to survey the field.

Six gunmen approached, rifles lifted. They looked like hunting rifles...not the machine guns the gangsters preferred. Hattie took a step forward, testing her illusion. It seemed to hold, as none of them reacted.

The illusion was cheaper than she'd figured. Night was falling, and the entire field was shrouded in shadow, dancing with the blaze beyond them. Nothing was easy to spot, here. Which would make a more ambitious illusion equally as economical.

Hattie reached out to claw the air in front of her. "Soldiers!"

Light popped in several points around the field as she willed illusions into being. About three dozen soldiers in helmets, all carrying machine guns—all of them colored folk. Her illusions opened fire on the gang of riflemen, sending them sprawling into the grass themselves.

Hattie turned to Vincent and nodded. "Go get 'em."

Vincent snapped his fingers, and the sound of gunfire from her illusions folded into a muddy mumble of thuds. The flames rising from Maudite's curled into lazy sweeps until they froze in place, glowing red sculpture of blazing ice.

Vincent shoved his way through the marsh grass, the stiff brown stalks remaining parted as he plowed forward. He reached the first gunman and snatched his rifle. As he took aim at the man frozen in time, he paused. With a curl of his finger, he beckoned Hattie forward.

Hattie shoved her way through the stiff air and marsh grass to stand beside Vincent. Peering down into the grass, she saw the same young buck who had threatened them at the James River wharf.

Hattie mouthed the words, "That wee bastard!" but her voice couldn't press through the bubble of frozen time.

Vincent twisted the rifle in his hands and offered it to Hattie.

She gripped the stock and hoisted it to her shoulder, aiming the barrel at the back of the young buck's head. Her hands trembled. This could have been the very person who'd shot Raymond. Even if it wasn't this man, he would have if given the chance. They all would. These weren't men. They were animals—rabid animals that needed to be put down.

Hattie eased the barrel closer to his skull. The gun bobbed and swiveled as her hands quaked. She bit down on her lip, eased her finger onto the trigger.

And let out a silent scream as she lowered the rifle. Her fingers released the weapon, which hung midair. Vincent scooped the rifle from its frozen spot and watched Hattie as she lifted her hands to cover her face.

She should have! These monsters deserved it! So, why couldn't she pull the trigger? As she wept, her lungs burned, heaving against the stiff air. Hattie pulled her hands away, giving her cheeks a quick wipe to clear away the tears.

Vincent tapped her arm, bobbing his head at her to ask if she was okay. She nodded in response. The time pincher turned to consider the young buck, still hunkered in the middle of the marsh grass, then looked back at her, motioning for her to turn around.

He didn't want her to watch. Her stomach lurched as she saw him press the barrel against the man's head and pull the trigger. Cringing, she shut her eyes. Vincent was a gangster. This is what he did—it was what all of them did. They were on mob business, and an act of violence against them was an act of war in the eyes of the Baltimore Crew. Such a thing could not go unpunished. He'd let most of them go the first time, when the men had accosted their boat on the rum run, but clearly it was time for a stronger message. Don't mess with the Crew. It was a message Hattie got loud and clear as she peeked over at Vincent. He was making his way around the scattering of gunmen, delivering what would be a killing bullet to each of them before tossing their weapons aside, pausing once to grip his stomach.

They'd shot Raymond. They would have killed all of them given the chance. It shouldn't have bothered her, but it did. This was what her life would be like if the Crew pressed her into service. This was what she would become.

Once the last of the gunmen had been dealt with, Vincent snapped his fingers once more. Time returned, and Hattie's mirage soldiers flickered into darkness. Six shots cracked out from the field around them as the Bianco Fiore thugs lurched to the ground, dead. Vincent coughed and spat into the grass with a moan.

Hattie dragged in a deep breath, trying to forget what she'd just seen. "Now what?"

"Now," he replied, "we find a water pincher."

CHAPTER 22

"You're getting this man to Richmond," Vincent whispered to Lefty.

Lefty checked Raymond's pulse, then shot a quizzical glance up at Vincent. "You're serious. I can tell when you're serious."

"He's not gonna make it to Baltimore," Vincent urged. "I know we got people, but the boat ride will kill him. You get him to Richmond. Hattie and I have to find this Freedman mook."

Hattie gripped Vincent's elbow as she eased around to crouch beside Raymond. The man had fallen unconscious at some point during the firefight. Lefty had determined that the bleeding had been patched as well as he could manage with the clothes on their backs. Most of Vincent's jacket had been broken down for field dressing, and Lefty's shirt had been sacrificed for the cause already. The through-and-through gunshot hadn't produced what Lefty referred to as "bad signs." Still, he needed medical attention fast.

Stroking the side of Raymond's sweat-pelted face, Hattie stared up at the men with desperation. It twisted something inside Vincent to see her worried like this. If Raymond didn't make it…

"If this son of a bitch really exists, and if he has some magic potion that can deal with this, then we'll find him," he told the other man. "And we'll bring it back. In the meantime, you have to get him to real doctors."

Lefty shook his head and drew a breath for a retort, but Vincent lifted a hand.

"I know it'll be work. And that's why I'm asking you to do it. You can talk to those backward pieces of work. I'll just get in their faces. We can't gamble everything on Doc Freedman. If we get that elixir, we'll find you, and we'll solve the problem. But if we don't?"

Lefty nodded. "I get it, I get it."

"Do you know how to operate the boat?" Hattie asked him.

Lefty peered at the craft over the grass. "How hard can it be?"

She sighed, then reached to Vincent for a hand as she got to her feet. "Come on, old-timer. We've a quick bit of learning to work through before I trust you on the water alone."

Vincent remained with Raymond as the two rushed back to the boat. He gripped the man's hand in his own fist, searching for something in him that was still awake and aware. Raymond's fingers slowly clamped down onto Vincent's.

Peering down at Raymond, Vincent's heart leapt several beats as Raymond opened his eyes. "You…get her…to that island."

Vincent lifted a finger to his mouth to urge Raymond to silence, but the stubborn bastard gripped his hand tighter.

"You…keep her…" The man sucked in several breaths and closed his eyes for a few seconds before saying, "Free."

"I will," Vincent immediately replied, gripping Raymond's fist with both hands.

"Good." He opened his eyes with a slight smirk. "'Cause I'll bust your jaw if you give 'er any grief." Raymond jerked Vincent's arm with enough force to drop his face inches away from the other man's. "I know…what you are. I know what she is." He coughed, then added, "No one…puts a collar…on Hattie Malloy. You heard me?"

Vincent eased away, then grinned. "That's the plan, my friend."

Raymond nodded before his eyes fluttered closed, and his fist relinquished all its strength to drop against the mud.

Lifting Raymond by his shoulders, Vincent hauled him back to the shoreline just as Lefty fired up the boat engine. Then he and Hattie hoisted the injured man over the railing, settling him comfortably along the deck beneath the helm.

Vincent wiped his hands off on his trousers and caught his breath as Lefty made mental notes while he touched the helm and the throttle.

"You set?" he asked the other man.

Lefty shook his head. "Better if I had this one driving." He nodded at Hattie.

"The question is can you manage this boat to Richmond?"

Hattie shouted, "He's as good as I'd be, ya daft twit! Let him shove off. We have to find that other boat."

Vincent exchanged glances with Lefty. This was, as far as the family was concerned, a minor matter. The only real problem if this boat driver perished on his way to dry land was that the Crew would be less one boat-legger. With any luck they could replace him by the weekend and be back in business without so much as a hitch. But Hattie and Raymond had become more than just a couple of freelancers to Vincent. They'd all shared a day or two of life-or-death in the pursuit of a phantom, and thus this meant much, much more to him than just Crew business.

Vincent steeled his nerve, then told the other man, "Get moving! Get him to a doctor."

"Easier said than done," Lefty replied. "What am I supposed to do when they turn us away?"

"Capstein will probably be there. He always is. But in case he isn't...just do what you do. Throw your weight around."

Lefty sighed. "That works in Baltimore. Not in enemy territory."

Vincent waved him on. "Make it work, then. In case we don't pan out."

Lefty raised his hand in the air. "Yeah, fine. Whatever. You'll catch up with me, in case this tall tale spins itself into something real?"

Vincent nodded. "That boat of theirs looked light and quick. We'll probably beat you back to Richmond."

Hattie crossed her arms. "Assuming we find it."

"Oh, I know where it is," Lefty chimed.

Both Vincent and Hattie shot him a look.

Lefty explained, "While you three were thundering through the grass for that burning building..." He hopped atop the bench behind the helm and nodded to the north. "I bothered to read the land."

Vincent followed Lefty's gaze up the shoreline, and a tiny metal hull bobbing along the side of a felled tree.

Lefty spat into the water over the side of the boat, then said, "Best get moving. I'm hauling ass to Richmond if this man wants to see his son again."

Vincent's chest tightened with a flash of panic, and he nodded. "Go."

Lefty reached across his body to edge down the throttle, then reached quickly for the helm. The boat churned its way into the Chesapeake, and was soon out of sight.

Hattie rushed along the shoreline for the speedboat, and Vincent sprinted to catch up. They reached the small craft, took a quick inventory—no weapons aboard—checked the fuel, then set out. Hattie took the helm while Vincent sat behind her.

"Any ideas?" he shouted over the motor.

"I'm coming at it from a completely different angle," she replied. "I'm groping in the dark."

"Doesn't sound like much."

She nodded. "I know, but it's all I've got. Last time I saw the island, it was like it knew I needed it. I'm hoping for the same luck."

Hattie sliced the boat toward the middle of the Bay, weaving in long angles to view more of the horizon. Before long, a shadow appeared in the distance, long and inky.

Vincent stood up. "Is that land?"

"Aye," she muttered.

"Could it be…"

"I believe that's Tangier Island. Which means we're too far north, already." She kicked the deck. "It's like hunting for Avalon."

Vincent shook his head, unsure what she was referring to, then turned back to the south. "And you'd never heard of Bimini Island before that competitor of yours mentioned it?"

"Some of the smaller bars don't have proper names, so people just call them what they will. It's not uncommon."

She steered to the right, easing the boat a full turn to head south again.

Vincent blinked as a something caught his eye. The speedboat wove a neat half-circle as Vincent turned against it, cupping his hand over his eyes.

"Hey, hang on," he shouted.

Hattie eased up on the throttle. "What is it?"

"Do you see that?" He pointed due east to a point of light in the distance.

She shook her head.

Vincent crouched a little, and the light disappeared. When he straightened his legs, it popped back into view.

"Here," he said, holding out a hand. "Climb up."

Hattie eyed him dubiously, then took his hand and planted a boot onto the side of the hull. As she lifted herself, her eyes widened. "I…see it."

"Maybe you weren't crazy, after all?" he offered as she dropped back down.

"Little Teague's boat sat higher in the water," she said, rubbing her forehead. "I hadn't realized."

Vincent squinted into the distance. "Looks like a campfire. Must be something on the ground covering it from a certain angle."

Hattie turned the boat back around, taking guidance from Vincent. As they approached a long, narrow bar just east of Tangier the campfire became visible, its flames lighting the smoke lifting into the night. The fire was housed in a neat circle of bricks with an empty spit swung clear of the flames. Beyond the fire pit stood a lone structure, a well-maintained shack. Near the far end of the shack was a post-and-beam pavilion covering what looked like a still.

Vincent muttered, "I think we found our potion maker."

"Think he's here?" Hattie asked.

"Well, someone started that fire."

Slowing the boat, Hattie drove it gently onto the beach. The sloping hull rushed along the sand until the boat stuck. Hattie killed the engine and hopped out along with Vincent. Together, they pulled the boat farther against the sand to situate it, then splashed through the ankle-high surf onto the muddy sand.

"Should we just walk up?" Hattie asked. "He might have a

gun, or worse. Not sure what a water pincher would do to defend himself, and I've no interest in finding out."

"Good point." Vincent stepped up the berm of sand and cupped his hands around his mouth to shout, "Hello?"

There was no response.

He tried again.

Hattie joined in. "Doc Freedman? We need your help!"

Vincent shrugged and approached the campfire, his eyes on the shack.

Hattie crouched down near the fire pit. "Footprints. Someone's here."

"Maybe he's shy?"

"I'd be."

"We mean you no harm. We have a friend who's injured. Badly." Vincent peered over to Hattie, whose face twitched with impatience. "We're like you. Pinchers, or whatever you call yourself. I understand if you're short on trust, but it's important that we speak to you. A man's life depends on it."

Hattie stood up and wound around the fire pit, mumbling, "We can't wait."

Vincent said, "Be careful."

As she took several steps toward the shack, the door cracked open. Hattie froze. "Doc Freedman?" she asked in a half-whisper.

The door swung slowly on its hinges. The interior was completely dark. Vincent stepped up alongside Hattie, ready to duck for cover if a rifle appeared.

A voice called from inside the shack, "Well, well. Found yourself a pincher, huh?"

Vincent blinked. That voice... A figure emerged from the shack, and Vincent's stomach twisted.

Capstein.

"What are *you* doing here?" Vincent muttered.

Capstein grinned. "My job." He removed his hat and ran a

hand through his blond hair. "Please understand, it's nothing personal."

Hattie took a step backward and the man nodded to her. "Ma'am. You'll want to stay where you are."

Vincent narrowed his eyes. "What is this, Capstein?"

"So, you said 'we're pinchers' out there by the fire." The man ignored the question and eyed Hattie. "Where did you find this pretty little thing? Took my words to heart, I see."

Vincent watched the air pincher warily. He and Hattie were in his territory. He'd need to tread cautiously. And there was only one reason he could think of for Capstein to be here—the man had decided to take the rumors seriously and scoop up a third pincher for the Upright Citizens.

"What have you done with Doc Freedman?" Vincent asked him. "Have you hauled him back to Richmond already? If you have, perhaps you've got some of his elixir we can purchase?"

Capstein laughed. "Oh, Vincent. You are not nearly as clever as I'd thought. In truth, there is no Doc Freedman. Or Bimini Island. It's all a myth."

"What?" Hattie gasped.

"Boat-leggers and watermen are a chatty group," Capstein explained. "You drop one rumor into that pond, and the ripples spread all the way from Newport News to Dover. Keep dropping the same rumor into different ears, and the myth becomes common knowledge. It's proven useful in scaring up free pinchers."

Suddenly it all made sense. "Is this how you found Betty?" Vincent asked.

"It is, in fact. I've been at this for a while. Sometimes I lose them here on this beach when they get punchy. It's a terrible waste of resources, but at least it keeps free pinchers from going to the Italian mob."

"So, this was all a lie?" Vincent groaned.

"Yes, but a very useful lie." Capstein nodded at Hattie. "So, my dear. What is it that you can do?"

She lifted her chin and glared at Capstein in silence.

"Come, come," the man urged as he stepped out onto the beach. "We should treat one another as equals. Despite what you may think, the Upright Citizens would be a far better home for you than the Baltimore Crew. We value our pinchers. We give them purpose. You could thrive among our numbers, not simply survive."

Hattie shook her head with wild, incredulous eyes. "You're trying to recruit me?"

Capstein lifted a calming hand. "I am. I can offer you more. Both of you."

Vincent thrust a finger at Capstein. "How's anyone supposed to believe you, after this…" he waved his hands around, "…stupid lie?"

"It is a lie, yes," Capstein replied. "But far from stupid. It is equal parts ruse and test of will. It takes knowledge and cunning to root out the truth from the threads I've sewn throughout every waterman village on the Bay. To make it this far demonstrates aptitude that we require among our numbers."

"And yet you've only managed to nab one," Vincent commented. "I suppose this test of yours is washing out every free pincher you've ensnared."

Capstein laughed. "Free? No pincher is ever truly free."

"I am," Hattie snapped. "And I intend to stay that way."

Capstein's eyes shifted back and forth between Vincent and Hattie. "Have you not snatched this one up? I thought she was yours."

"I don't belong to him, or anyone," Hattie shot back.

"Yes, she does belong to me," Vincent blurted out. "I've already claimed her for Baltimore."

Hattie took a step away from him, eyeing him uncertainly.

"Tsk, tsk. And here you are trying to recruit Doc Freedman as well. Greedy much, Vincent?"

"We'd mainly come for the elixir, although if Freedman had been amenable, I was prepared to pitch him an offer." Vincent shot Hattie a warning glance. "But this one...she's already claimed. She's mine."

"The lady seems to think otherwise." Capstein waved a dismissive hand. "All this doesn't matter. It is not too late for both of you. Imagine it, Vincent," he said stepping forward, "you've seen what we have to offer. We've discussed this. Legacy!"

Hattie scowled at Vincent. "Discussed?"

He shook his head. "All I heard was a man asking me to exchange one master for another. Treating us like brood mares. It was sickening."

Capstein winced. "That...that is hurtful."

"So sorry."

"You still don't understand, Vincent. There are no masters. *We* are the masters. We decide."

Hattie watched him warily. "The Upright Citizens is a mob like any other. And they own you, just like any other."

"That is where you're mistaken," Capstein said with a wag of his finger. "Sure, there are two-bit rumrunners and hash den proprietors in the organization, and perhaps they feel as if they are the ones who make the decisions. But they have come to rely on my power—perhaps too much. They have given me all I need, and I have taken every inch and more. Betty and I are the *real* Upright Citizens. And you two could join us." He turned to Vincent. "I know you have no real love for Vito Corbi. You were born into servitude. I'm offering you your first taste of what your quarrelsome friend calls freedom."

Vincent felt Hattie's eyes on him. "That is not my idea of freedom. Thanks, but no thanks. If there is no Doc Freedman and no elixir, then we'll be taking our leave now."

"I'm afraid I can't allow that." Capstein brushed the dust from his sleeve. "You should know that I have several men in the grass all around us. They're good shots—better than the ones I left at Maudite's."

"That was you?" Hattie's eyes widened.

"By association, I suppose," Capstein replied. "In any event, I'd prefer we speak with civility."

"You sent goons to gun us down, and now you want to speak civilly?" Hattie snarled.

Vincent reached out to grab her arm, giving it a quick squeeze as he sent her another warning glance. "This isn't wise, Capstein. You don't want to mess with Vito and the Crew. Just let us go, and we'll keep the peace between our two families."

Capstein laughed. "You must be joking. They'll never know what happened to you, never find your bodies. But there's no need for this. Join us. Between the four of us, we'll rule the east coast from the Carolinas to the Jersey Shore."

Vincent kept a firm hold on Hattie's arm and dragged her a step backward, raising his hand.

"You can pinch time if you like," Capstein warned, "but you'll never hear the bullet coming. And knowing what I know from the Baltimore Crew I've chatted up these past years, there's a limit to how long you can hold your power. You'll never find all of my men."

"I know where *you* are," Vincent said. "That'll be a good start."

Capstein laughed. "Yes. You could kill me. And then you'll die, as well. As will your friend who is in such dire need of a magic elixir. Tell me, it wasn't Mancuso, was it?"

"No. It was *my* friend," Hattie spat.

"The colored fellow? Ah. Well, I suppose that figures. These Bianco Fiore boys aren't the most reliable resource, but they *are* predictable."

"Two against one," Vincent informed him. "You've no idea what her powers are, and I'm far stronger than you think. Could be we're both willing to take the chance, knowing at the least we could kill you and maybe half your men out there."

Capstein shook his head, a bewildered expression on his face. "But why? I've delivered you an offer with incredible opportunity. Don't risk your lives when you can align your-self with those who will win the eventual conflict between our groups. It's an easy choice."

"This isn't a choice," Hattie retorted. "It's a demand. How can anyone call this a choice when the only other option is to be murdered on a beach?"

"And what choice would you have given Freedman?" Capstein lifted an eyebrow.

Hattie shook her head, then glanced at Vincent who scowled back.

"Well, we wouldn't have threatened to kill him," she muttered.

"Bushwa!" Capstein snorted. "Your well-heeled compan-ion, here, is more a murderer than I am. He is beholden to monsters. He's under a mandate to gather pinchers at any cost. Am I wrong?" he asked Vincent.

Vincent replied, "Your silvered words would sound a helluva lot more convincing if you hadn't unleashed boat-loads of gun-toting gorillas after us."

Capstein rolled his eyes. "Dear God, man. Can't you see we're at war?"

"What?" Vincent grunted, preparing himself for the right moment to take action. "War between the Citizens and the Crew?"

"No, no. Pinchers and the seats of power! We've languished for centuries beneath the heel of one king or another. Sultans of the Levant. Kings of Europe. And now the lords of crime in the New World, but it's all the same. We are captured, or we are culled. And if we are very lucky, we are born into servitude."

Hattie said, "You're doing the same thing. Aren't you? Capturing or killing?"

"Yes, but it is in the service of our kind! Imagine what we could do, Vincent. Me and Betty. You and this one? We could raise entire generations together. We could bury Vito once and for all, then challenge Philadelphia. By the time we reach New York, we'll have pinchers flooding to join us in Richmond. We could begin an entire new kingdom—"

Vincent snapped his fingers and time froze.

Gesturing to Hattie to capture her attention, he pointed to the boat. Or pointed to where the boat should have been. He shot Hattie a questioning glance, but she only shrugged. Vincent lunged against the frozen air, feet slipping in the beach sand. Walking through a time bubble was hard enough, but the sand made it extra strenuous.

When they'd reached the water's edge, he spotted the speedboat floating in the distance. A pair of footprints remained pressed into the wet sand, running in and out of a patch of grass nearby. Vincent pointed to the tracks and beckoned for Hattie to follow. They marched through the sand, the exertion already wearing on Vincent's guts. Within a six-foot-tall tuft of dried grass blades, they found a short man with a hunting rifle still trained to the spot where they had been standing in front of Capstein.

Vincent nodded to Hattie with intent, then pulled the rifle from the man's surprisingly firm grip. He spun the weapon around and swung it against the head of the sniper. As Vincent reached for his stomach, staving off a wave of prickly nausea, Hattie tapped his arm. She pointed at Capstein, then made a gesture with the rifle.

Vincent squinted at her, then offered her the rifle. She refused it and he'd done enough killing for the day. All he wanted to do was to escape.

Hattie tapped him again, making a snapping gesture with her fingers. As Vincent shook his head, she snapped again, pointed to herself, then waved a hand in front of her own eyes.

Vincent nodded. He released the time bubble, and as Hattie made a brisk gesture with her hands, he could hear Capstein finishing his monologue.

"…a kingdom meant for us!"

The gunman slumped forward into the grass with a grunt.

Hattie turned to Vincent and rolled her eyes. "You were right. He *is* an intolerable windbag. Saint's above, I thought he was gonna *never* stop with the blah blah blah. Just kill me already. Put me outta my misery before I die o' boredom."

Vincent made a panicked shushing gesture with his finger, but she waved him off.

"It's alright. I'm hiding our voices, as well. What should we do now?"

His jaw dropped. "You can *do* that? I thought you were a light pincher?"

She shrugged. "If I pay the cost, I can fool any of the senses. What should we do?"

"You can fool any of the senses?" Vincent shook his head. "*Any?* So someone could drink down a whole bottle of poison, thinking it was raspberry ripple, and wouldn't be the wiser until he was dead?"

"Why is it always about killing with you gangsters?" she countered with a huff. "Yes, taste, although that one's pricey 'cause I gotta also throw touch, smell, and sight into the mix or it doesn't quite work."

Capstein called out, "There's no way off this island."

"Wait, *touch*? So if you conjure up a tommy gun, and someone goes to grab it—"

"Vincent! Questions after we get off this island, if ya please."

They turned to find Capstein walking a tidy circle where they had stood, scanning the immediate area.

"So, he can't hear us?" Vincent urged.

"Not as long as I can hold out."

"How long is that?"

She frowned. "About as long as you could hold a bubble the size of this island. Which isn't long."

"The boat's a good fifty yards out, by the look of it," he grumbled. "I can swim that, but I don't think we can do it without catching notice."

Hattie jerked with an idea. "Hey, when you freeze time, things get solid. Right? Can we just, you know, walk on water?"

Vincent sighed. "'Fraid not. I've tried it before, and nearly drowned. Water gets strange inside a time bubble."

Capstein shouted, "I'll assume you've found at least one of my men. I won't tell you how many more there are. But, truly…we should have a conversation as adults."

Hattie rolled her eyes. "This bag of gas is driving me to drink."

Vincent lifted the rifle. "Sure you don't want to shoot him?"

Hattie snickered, then reached out to grab Vincent's arm as her head spun. The tightness of the illusion clamped down onto her brain.

"Your power?" Vincent asked.

"We need a plan. Sharpish."

Vincent offered, "I can pinch time again. Maybe we can find another gunman."

"We can't find them all."

"Then we hide," he said. "Make them come to us."

Hattie looked around. There was very little on this island apart from tall marsh grass and the shack. "Down."

They hit their knees, crawling a few yards away from the sniper's position. Hattie lifted a finger to her lips, and as her eyelids fluttered, Vincent could feel an electric prickle against his arms.

She released a long breath and dropped her head. They couldn't keep using their powers like this. The strain was too great.

Capstein remained by the shack, hands on his hips. "That's how it'll be, huh? Fine. I wanted to do this amicably. And to be sure, I wanted you both alive."

Hattie leaned close to Vincent, whispering with the barest of volume, "What's his power, again?"

"Air," he whispered back.

Even as he said it, a light breeze kicked off the Bay, pushing the grass at an angle.

Vincent spied Capstein between blades of bent grass. He was picking up something from the ground. It looked like a length of firewood.

The breeze grew to a wind, and the marsh grass had nearly bent flat all around them. Vincent and Hattie pressed hard against the muck beneath, but the air became near a gale force.

Vincent's hat flipped off his head. He reached to grab it but was too late. As it rushed into the sky, Vincent returned his gaze to a patch of grass that wasn't quite as bent over as the rest. A man lay prone, his rifle tracking backward from the hat's path, and directly at them.

Vincent shoved Hattie to the side as a gunshot rang out.

He thought she'd punched him in the arm for shoving her, but as he shrugged her off, the ache of the strike turned into a searing heat.

He'd been hit.

Vincent pinched time once again, not even bothering with snapping. He shoved against the ground, gripping his wound as he got to his feet.

Hattie joined him, eyes wide, then pointed to the rifleman who'd just shot Vincent in the arm.

He shook his head, knowing he couldn't hold the pinch long enough to take these guys out one at a time.

Hattie tilted her head eyeing him with a perplexed frown, then her eyes traced down his shoulder to the blood staining his shirt and seeping between his fingers. The pain was shredding his control, distracting him. Soon he'd be no help to her. Soon he'd be no help to anyone.

Hattie made a panicked sound, then threw her hands into the air, looking around then pointing toward the shack.

They shoved against the wind-flattened grass toward the shack. As they approached Capstein, Vincent realized he'd left the rifle in the grass. Hattie tugged on his arm as his guts began to twist, but he remained standing in front of the casual figure of Capstein, considering his length of firewood.

Vincent reached for the firewood, snatching it from Capstein's hands. He sucked in a lungful of thick air, then swung the log as hard as he could against Capstein's head.

The tiny log rushed against Capstein's head...and shattered. The log simply disintegrated into tiny splinters, chipping away against an invisible capsule spread around Capstein's body. The flecks of wood and sawdust spun away from Capstein in a simple arc, swerving over their heads and remaining in frozen space.

Vincent shook his head in confusion.

The pain in his arm swelled, as did the nausea. Spittle

filled his mouth as a retch threatened to erupt from his throat. The arc of splinters began to move, easing in tiny tumbles, then rushing higher…faster…

Time was returning. And Vincent had no more power to stop it. Capstein slowly blinked, his icy-blue eyes shifting to him as time eased back into its own proper tempo.

With a smirk, Capstein said, "Hello, Vincent."

The capsule of rapidly circulating air, only a hair's width before when it had shredded the log, now swelled into an enormous surge, leeching away from Capstein to hammer into Vincent's chest with the force of a hurricane.

Vincent tumbled into the doorway, the world canting as the side of his head struck the door jamb.

Capstein thrust a hand toward a spot beyond the doorway, and as a hacking, sobbing noise filled the air, Vincent realized it was Hattie. He tried to clamber to his feet, but his dizziness sent him sideways into the ground. Half his body fell outside the shack's door, and he rolled over to find Hattie reaching for her throat, her face drawn, her mouth wide open gasping for air.

Capstein lifted his hand in a sort of claw, stepping toward Hattie. "This could have been so much simpler. Alas."

Vincent's vision blurred, and Hattie went double.

Capstein turned to face him, a trickle of blood flowing from his nostril. "You don't see it, yet. But don't worry." Darkness leeched into Vincent's vision as his head throbbed. "You shall."

*H*attie opened her eyes and tried to lift her arms to wipe the moisture from her face, discovering that her wrists had been bound with some scratchy jute behind her back. Wriggling against the rope did no good. She stared up at the sky, a deep charcoal of overcast clouds against the ink of night. No moon. No reflections from the city. Nothing but darkness.

The hull beneath her back slapped against waves. She was on a boat, and it was moving fast. Blinking away more of the spray from the water as it plumed over the side of the tiny craft she found Capstein looming over her.

"We're nearly to shore," he cooed. "Rest."

Hattie tried to speak, but her throat was raw and dry. No words came.

Pulling a handkerchief from his jacket, Capstein dabbed away some dried blood from underneath his nose. His powers over air had sucked the breath from Hattie's lungs, and had thrown Vincent into the building. That was the last thing she remembered. The man had demonstrated his power, but as with all pinchers that power seemed to come at a price.

Hattie craned her neck to look about the boat, spotting Vincent nearby, tightly bound with ropes around his arms and legs, and unconscious. Capstein had taken precautions against Vincent's awakening. If he'd had any power left after his gunshot wound and having his head rammed into a length of pine, no amount of time pinching could undo those knots.

They were captured—well and truly prisoners of the Upright Citizens. How did this happen? Hattie sighed as she ruminated on their fate. This was her doing. She'd learned of the Bimini lie from Little Teague. The poor bastard had probably believed it—so much so he begged her to take him to Doc Freedman with his last breath. How many others had met such fates in pursuit of a fiction, she wondered? And how many lives were now in jeopardy because of her foolish belief in such a bald-faced fairy tale?

Raymond's?

Vincent's?

Her own?

The boat pounded against waves, traveling faster than the simple chug of the engine indicated. Another pelting of Bay spray explained their unusual speed. Capstein was using his wind pinching to shove the boat along the surface of the Bay. Good. Expending that much more power meant he'd run out eventually.

Hattie took stock of her own reserves. It wasn't an exact science, to be sure. She knew that having the life literally choked out of her hadn't done her any favors. Top that off with a double-sense illusion just before, and she wasn't sure how long she could maintain one of her light pinches. And so, she rested in the boat as her captor continued to expend his power. *Wait,* she urged herself. *Just wait. You're getting stronger, and he's getting weaker.*

The wind subsided after a while, and the boat slowed with a jerk. Capstein and two of his attendants jumped from the vessel, splashing into shallow surf to drag the boat ashore. The sand scratched along the underside of the hull beneath Hattie's head.

As she wrestled against her bonds, she noticed Vincent's eyes fluttering open. He released a long moan, and she shook her head. There was only one opportunity left to get them out of this. One. Hopefully he'd understand.

"A fine predicament you've gotten us into," she snapped at him.

A cough was his only response. His eyes lolled about, searching for up versus down. The injury to his head was likely to be worse than it had seemed, which meant she couldn't rely on Vincent to help save them from this situation.

And yet…

She shuffled up to her backside to sit upright with a solid push. After a bit of work, she found her back against the side of the boat, and she was staring down at Vincent.

She repeated with added volume, "You've really put a foot in it, haven't you?"

Voices called outside the boat, and footsteps approached. Good.

"You hear me over there, boy-o?" she shouted, giving Vincent a kick and thanking the Heavens that Capstein hadn't thought to tie *her* feet. He'd underestimated her. And as far as she knew, he still had no idea what her powers were. "You. Shake off those cobwebs and listen."

Capstein appeared near the front of the boat, watching with mirth.

Hattie continued, "All I wanted was some way to cure my

father. But could I hope for that? No. You had to come strutting along, telling me what's what and who's who. And *now* where are we? Tied up on a boat. You daft little skite-eater."

Capstein lifted a hand. "Please, miss. You can hardly blame—"

"Oh, don't you start," Hattie said with a shrill crack. "You think you've got me figured. Well, I'll give you a what for. I was born free. My parents kept me free. And I'll roast in the circles of Hell they reserve for people who talk on trains before I give you the time of day. So, go on. Off with you. I'm staying right here."

Hattie focused as she swung her legs over the side of the boat.

Capstein chuckled, sauntering forward to lean against the rail with a smirk. "I'm perfectly aware of the absurdity of the situation."

Focus. No sound as her feet hit the surf. With any luck he'd launch into one of those endless monologues. She could be halfway to Richmond before he paused to take a breath.

He continued, "And you still see us as slave-drivers. That will change, once you meet Betty. She was once where you are now."

Focus. He's still watching you on the boat. Step slow. Step quiet.

Vincent groaned, "Huh… Hatt…"

No. Focus. Forget the man. Keep walking. The trees are only a few yards away.

Capstein laughed. "So, you're finally awake. I do hope this encounter has demonstrated two vital lessons. The first… you cannot outthink me. The second…"

His voice faded as Hattie hustled for the cover of the forest ahead. The illusion tugged at her head, spinning her brain while simultaneously clamping it in an iron maiden vise.

Distance. Sound and sight. Too much power required. The cost was too great.

A trickle of blood seeped from her nostril. Out of sheer force of economy, Hattie released the pinch over sound, her footsteps now audible as she rushed up the beach toward the trees.

A gunman appeared from the canopy ahead, his rifle half-lifted, his head craning back and forth to zero in on the sound.

Hattie gritted her teeth, balancing her weight as she ran with hands tied behind her back. With a leap and a flourish of her knees, she swept the gunman's chin with her foot. They both landed in the sand, kicking up a cloud as he moaned in pain.

The illusion snapped into oblivion as her body slammed against the ground. That was it. All she had.

Heads swept toward land as the illusion disintegrated. Hattie had only seconds before they'd see her. She scrambled to her knees, brushing through the sand on her way to the tree line. Voices barked behind her, shouting alarm and confusion. She lunged into a squat and got to her feet, bobbling her way into an awkward sprint.

Sand gave way to grass, which gave way to pine needles. The jute scratched the skin of her wrists raw as she ran. Uneven terrain caused her to stagger, balance more difficult thanks to her bonds. But she kept running—running hard, sucking in breaths as she penetrated the pine forest.

Once her lungs felt as if they were set ablaze and she couldn't heave in enough air, she paused to lean against the shaggy bark of one of the trees. Her throat sobbed as she drew in air, bending at the waist, then straightening up again. She choked on spit and coughed. Too much noise! Hattie clamped her mouth shut as she coughed. Her lips sputtered, and ultimately, she surrendered to the reflex.

Once she'd caught her breath and the coughing had cleared, she took a moment to listen.

The pine needles overhead rustled in a tiny nighttime breeze.

Something took off from a branch nearby, probably an owl.

The distant sound of waves lapping against the shore.

Footsteps.

She held her breath, pressing hard against the tree trunk. The footsteps paused, then continued. Whoever it was had heard her coughing, but now that she was silent the pursuer had begun to wander.

She remained frozen, keeping mental track of her pursuer. The footsteps paused again, silent for a long while before resuming.

They were approaching.

Hattie reached deep into her well of energy. It was thin. Hardly anything left. But there was no way she could outrun anyone with her hands tied behind her back. If there was a drop of power left, she had to use it now.

She split herself in two, one illusion to sprint to her left, and her physical self to run to the right. Hattie gave the illusion self just a second lead, then bolted. No reserves for sound. No reserves to hide herself. She had to trust the illusion would catch her pursuer's attention first.

As she rushed over the brown needle-covered forest floor, she listened for footsteps. Even as she heard the man grunt and rush after the mirage, the threads tying her to the illusion snapped. She was empty. The illusion only lasted a few seconds, but hopefully it was enough to buy her a little bit of a lead.

A husky voice shouted, "Hey!"

Hattie pounded her legs as hard as they could run.

A gunshot sounded behind her, and she ducked on reflex.

The motion sent her stumbling, and before she could regain her footing she rammed her shoulder into a skinny pine trunk.

With a shout she pitched forward into a roll, landing onto some gravel. She'd tumbled into some manner of clearing. No cover. No chance.

Her pursuer stepped out of the forest, a rifle trained on her. As she scuffled her feet against the gravel to inch away, he worked the lever and grunted, "Hold still, girl."

She complied, gasping for air as she held herself up on her elbows.

The gunman lifted a hand to his mouth and released a long, loud whistle.

"Now, just you sit tight," he said.

Before long voices sounded from the surrounding woods. One by one, gunmen emerged from the pines, each training a weapon on Hattie. At last, Capstein himself stepped into the clearing, shoving Vincent in front of him at a forced march. Capstein's typically smug expression had worn thin, and he glared at Hattie with menace.

Vincent dropped to his knees as Capstein released the rope around his arms and chest. The time pincher's face was pale, a film of sweat covering his brow. The wound on his arm had soaked his sleeve, and he didn't look like he could walk much farther.

Capstein stepped toward Hattie, pausing at a safe distance. "You done?"

She scowled at him, her shoulders stiff.

He shook his head. "She pull any tricks?"

The pursuer nodded. "Thought I saw her take off one direction, but then it was all poof. Vanished. Caught her scurrying off this way."

Capstein said, "She's probably out of power. But just in case, tie up her ankles."

The pursuer lowered his rifle and searched his company for cord. Lacking any proper rope, he removed his belt and crouched by Hattie's feet, looping the belt around her ankles and cinching it tight.

Capstein surveyed the clearing. "How far off the main road are we?"

One of his company replied, "Only a mile or so."

"I don't feel like hauling these two back through the forest," Capstein grumbled. He reached into his jacket to pull a tiny gun from his belt. He tossed it to one of his people. "Send up a flare. The truck should see it from the main road."

His man caught the signal pistol and lifted it over his head.

"No. Get some height," Capstein snapped. He gestured toward the end of the clearing. "Climb on top of that old busted cart."

His man nodded and hustled off.

Hattie sat up once the belt had been tightened and her captor had stepped away. She scuffled along the gravel beside Vincent. "Are you still alive, then?" she whispered.

He nodded.

"Are you going to make it?"

He shook his head.

Hattie sighed. "Perhaps neither of us are that lucky."

She peered around the clearing, spotting the cluster of ramshackle shanties surrounding them. Hattie had ducked into nearly every hobo camp and fishing village on the Bay, and there came a point where they all looked the same to her.

"What I said back there," she whispered. "That was for show. I hope you know that."

Vincent sucked in a husky breath, then mumbled, "Does it matter?"

"Yes. It matters a lot." Hattie squinted at the buildings nearby. They were altogether too familiar. She turned her head to watch the man with the signal pistol as he climbed the old busted cart Capstein had sent him to.

Busted cart, just like the one at… Hattie yelped. Capstein turned toward her.

With wide eyes, she shouted, "Capstein! No! Wait!"

A loud pop sounded. A tiny spray of sparks launched into the air, then with a hiss a ball of red flame flickered overhead, bathing them all in murky light.

The ground rumbled.

Capstein peered about the circle of buildings, and the tiny lane of gravel that led to the waterfront…and the burned-out shack below. A bright plume of flame sizzled overhead, arcing from the bottom of the waterfront to the man holding the signal pistol. The cart erupted into flame. The hapless crony of Capstein's leaped off the cart, shrieking as his entire body was consumed in fire.

Capstein crouched lower to the ground. "Shit!"

Vincent opened his eyes, confounded by the sudden brightness. Hattie gave him a nudge with her foot. "We have to get out of here!"

"Where are we?" he muttered, eyes widening as another fireball flew overhead to strike down Hattie's pursuer.

She winced from the blast of heat and the screams of the man being burned alive. "Deltaville!"

Vincent sat upright in a panic. "Bushwa!"

"It's a fact. That creature—"

"I know about the creature," he said. "We saw it, remember?"

A hand landed on Vincent's shoulder, jerking him away from Hattie. Capstein snarled as he shouted, "How did you manage this?"

Vincent's eyes rolled as his head jerked backward. "I didn't do shit, Capstein."

Hattie reached deep in her chest for some power. Even

the tiniest drop. But there was none. Instead, she called out, "Leave him alone, Capstein!"

He released Vincent, sending him rolling onto his back. "This was you?"

"No! I ran and ended up here. It's a mystery to me."

Capstein balled a fist, winding it up to give Hattie a shot to the chin. Another flash of fire erupted behind him. This time it wasn't a central explosion, but a wall of flames cutting off the fishing village from the gravel road leading back to the mainland. The burning wall arced in a slow, graceful slither around the entire village, sending flames up the pine branches all around.

The two ends of the circle conjoined at the bottom of the hill, where a solitary figure loomed in silhouette. It stepped forward, bright points of light shining where its eyes should have been.

"What's that?" Capstein shouted.

"A demon," Hattie replied.

Capstein lifted his balled fist in the air. "Kill it!"

The two remaining henchmen lifted their weapons and fired at the demon. Their shots might have found their target, but it was impossible to tell from the creature's approach. It simply marched forward. Step by step. Eyes shining with fury. The gunmen emptied their weapons, then stood dumbly with their rifles hanging low.

Capstein shook his head. "Useless idiots."

With a lift of his hand, the wall of fire canted toward the ground. Wind circled around the site, shoving the fire lower and lower. The ground shook again, and this time Hattie could hear the voice of the demon over the infernal thunder. It roared—not in pain, but in anger. In outrage.

Cracks opened up in the gravel as the tremors intensified. Gravel poured into the crevices. Loud crashes of shearing rocks echoed beneath them. Hattie's feet slipped over one of the faults. She yanked them away as superheated air geysered out of the ground.

One of the gunmen screamed in pain as he stood astride one of the cracks, his trousers catching fire as he tried to leap away. He ran down the hill past the demon, sprinting for the waterfront. But when he reached the wall of flames, the demon flexed his arms and the fire curtain erupted into a ten-foot hedge of instantaneous death. Capstein lowered his hand, and the rushing wind subsided. He glanced down at Hattie and Vincent, blood spilling from his nose.

Approaching with grave deliberation, the demon flicked its wrist and fired a tiny sphere of heat into the chest of the final gunman, sending his flaming corpse into the fire curtain. It paused as it reached the trio of pinchers, its eyes tracing slow, dancing flames like candles, its mouth drawn into a sullen slit as it pointed at Hattie.

They were trapped, surrounded by a wall of flames and faced with an angry being that neither bullets nor magic seemed to stop. Hattie held her breath as the demon pointed at her, waiting for the killing blow. It never came. Instead, the being reached for her, palm open. Hattie released her breath and peered up at the creature. It was no longer a living avatar of rage. Rather, it seemed captivated by her.

With a slow, cautious motion, Hattie lifted herself to her knees. The demon waved a tiny circle with its fingers. A sharp, intense heat sizzled her wrists, and she hissed at the pain. The rope that had held her wrists behind her back went slack. Jerking against the smoldering rope she shook it off and pulled her arms in front of her to inspect the damage, but there was only a tiny red mark, and black smudges where the jute had scorched close to her skin.

Hattie looked up at the demon then untied the belt binding her ankles, before turning toward Vincent.

Capstein stepped in front of her. "Oh, no you don't."

The demon's eyes brightened, and it released another earth-shattering roar. Capstein eased away from the others, keeping his hands in front of him, his eyes darting around the wall of fire that contained them.

Hattie scooted over to work at Vincent's bonds. When he was loose, she stood and pulled him to his feet. He planted a foot against the ground and met her halfway as she tugged on his arm. With a few deep breaths, he nodded.

"I feel…better."

Hattie closed her eyes for a second, feeling a rush of calm ease into her chest. "Me, too."

The demon strode around them, sizing them up with its flaming orbs before coming to a halt between them. They stood, a synod of three, staring at one another. Waving her hand in front of her face, Hattie felt the light pinch effortlessly. She released the illusion with a blink of surprise. "I feel like I've slept for a week."

Vincent nodded, rubbing his arm. "This is unbelievable." He prodded at the hole in his jacket, poking himself with his own finger. "It's healed."

"What?" Hattie gasped.

Vincent turned to the demon. "Did you do this?"

The creature gestured at the ground. The gravel popped and hissed as a thin line of flames etched a symbol onto the ground. Three arcs surrounding a circle.

"Enough of this!" Capstein's voice shouted. "I don't know what Hellish bargain you've struck with this beast, but it's clear there's no room for you in my Kingdom!"

He circled his hands by his side, then thrust them toward the demon. A tight blast of air beamed into its chest, sending it sailing several yards.

When it landed, it hopped back onto its feet with inhuman agility. The demon flung its wrist at Capstein, hurling another burst of fire. However, when it reached

Capstein, it boiled away against the capsule of air that had destroyed Vincent's bludgeon a few hours ago. Capstein released the capsule with an exhale of fog from his nostrils.

Capstein lifted a hand at Vincent. "Die, already."

Vincent reached for his throat, mouth agape as the wind sucked out of his lungs. He fell to the ground, spasming as he suffocated…and as Hattie concentrated.

A finger tapped Capstein on the shoulder and he turned to find Vincent smirking at him.

Hattie released the illusion of her suffocating companion just as Vincent hammered Capstein with a right cross.

The air pincher tumbled to the ground, his face bloodied not from the punch, but from the powers he'd already expended. "Impossible," he growled.

Vincent lifted his fingers to snap them and freeze time, but before he could a sudden shockwave smacked them in the face. Hattie struggled to her feet against a breeze that kicked against her legs. She lifted a hand as dust and smoke flew into her face. Once she'd blinked away the smoke, she squinted past the demon's shoulder to find Capstein hovering in midair.

"Look!" she shouted, pointing at the air pincher.

A column of air rushed into the site, pulling the fire curtain in with it. Flames licked the backs of their legs, and they hopped closer to the center of the village. Capstein clenched both fists at his hips. His suit flapped in the hurricane force winds that were propelling him into the air. He peered down at them with intense scorn, the bottom of his face covered with the blood that was pouring from his nose and mouth.

The demon bellowed and launched a fireball at Capstein, but when the flames hit the column of air they rushed into several tendrils of light before extinguishing. It tried once more, with the same effect. Capstein's escape was also protecting him.

Vincent clapped his hands, and the air went stiff. The flames bowing into the center of the circle billowed like drapes in the breeze before locking into place, dimming slightly. Hattie walked a half-circle, mesmerized by the beauty of the frozen tableau.

The demon reached for Capstein, and the sudden motion made both Hattie and Vincent jump. It seemed this creature was also immune to Vincent's time pinch.

Waving at the demon to capture its attention, Hattie gestured for it to try the flames again. It lifted a hand, but the fire did not come. As with the curtain around them, its powers of flame were impotent inside the time bubble.

They couldn't reach Capstein without Vincent releasing the time pinch, but if he released it, the man would surely escape. It seemed there was nothing they could do at this point but let him go.

The demon strode over to Vincent, who eased away a half step. The creature pressed a flat hand against his chest, shoving him just a little. It seemed to be trying to communicate, but its meaning was lost on Hattie. What did it want? For him to release the bubble?

Vincent lifted his fingers to snap them, but the demon covered his hand with its own. It thumped Vincent's chest, then its own, then turned to point at Hattie.

Suddenly it dawned on Hattie. It wasn't the demon that had healed them. It wasn't the demon that had returned their powers to full strength. It was something about the three of them together—something connected them. Together, they were stronger.

A circle, surrounded by three arcs. A triad.

As if he also understood, Vincent closed his eyes and spread out his fingers. The flames frozen in toward the center of the circle began to move again. The curls and billows slipped in a creeping motion, oddly unnatural against the otherworldly nature of Vincent's time bubbles.

Hattie pulled in a slow breath. The air was thinning. Sound returned as the flames continued to flicker and sway with slow grace. The noise of the crackling flames was peculiar. She called to Vincent, but her own voice came out wrong. All sounds swelled and tapered in a bizarre fashion that made her skin crawl. Peering up at Capstein, she watched as the man looked up into the sky…and began to creep back toward the ground.

Her eyes went wide. Vincent wasn't just freezing time. He was reversing it!

Capstein's feet inched closer and closer to the ground. Finally, he was within reach. The demon snatched Capstein by the ankle.

Vincent snapped his fingers.

With a thunderous roar, the demon swung Capstein by the foot, sailing him in an arc over its head until his body smashed against the ground.

Capstein released a sick, crunching gurgle as his body pounded against the gravel. Spitting out a tooth and a gob of blood, Capstein wheezed, "What…was that?"

Vincent crouched down to answer, "Real power, you jumped-up piece of work." The time pincher got back to his feet and gestured toward the fire curtain. "You know, I'm sure Vito would love to hear your side of this whole tale. But with things being what they are, and Baltimore being a good bit away, I think I'll just let this demon have you."

A flash of bright light exploded. Capstein screeched. His body sizzled and charred in a matter of seconds as they watched. The fire curtain surrounding them dropped into a ring of tiny embers, the rocks super-heated nearly to the point of melting.

Vincent pulled Hattie away from the smoldering body of Elmer Capstein and nodded toward the demon. "We're connected. Somehow. I don't know how, but that much seems pretty damned obvious to me."

The demon lifted fists and snarled. Hattie gripped Vincent's shoulder and turned him around to see what the demon had seen…a truck approaching. Its bed was filled with men. Men with guns. Capstein's pickup crew.

The ground trembled as the demon mustered more strength, but Hattie turned to halt the creature.

"I've got this," she declared as she turned to approach the truck. No sense in having the creature burn half the shore down, when a simple illusion would do the trick.

The gunmen had already jumped clear of the bed and had their weapons trained on her.

One of them shouted, "The hell's going on?"

Hattie's fingers formed claws at her sides.

And she whispered, "Nightmare."

All the men froze in place. One of them released a low, husky shout as he dropped his rifle. Two more turned and fled. The men inside the truck cab shrieked, flailing their arms at the worst torments their own minds could conjure.

Vincent joined Hattie, shaking his head. "What are they seeing?"

Hattie turned to Vincent, and he hopped back. Her eyes sizzled with an eerie green glow. She blinked it away and uncurled her fingers.

The truck spun its tires as the driver attempted to escape the terrors flooding his mind. After a three-point turn, the truck careened off the gravel lane and smashed into a pine tree, ejecting one of the passengers through the windscreen.

Hattie sucked in a lusty breath, then shook out her fingers. "I feel like I haven't used my power at all."

"Me, neither. What just happened, do you think?"

"I do believe our new friend, here, has something to do with't." Hattie turned to the demon…to find it gone.

The flames still consuming Capstein's corpse died abruptly and the only light remaining in the village was the glow of embers from the ring surrounding them. Vincent pointed to the burned-out shack by the waterfront as its door eased shut with a delicate clap.

Vincent whispered, "Show's over, I guess."

"Should we try to talk to it?"

He shook his head. "I don't think it says much. And I don't know why it helped us but right now, I feel lucky to be alive at all—and I don't feel like pressing my luck."

"Fair enough," she conceded. "We can make sense of it all some other day." She frowned. "We should get to Richmond."

Vincent nodded at the wreck near the road. "Well, that truck's in no condition to drive. I suppose it's a long walk for us?"

Hattie tapped his nose with a flick of her finger and a sassy grin. "As it so happens, boy-o, I know where we can find a boat."

CHAPTER 24

The early morning sunshine flowed through the second-story window of a white clapboard house just outside Richmond. Vincent buttoned up the white shirt he'd liberated from the owner's chest of drawers, examining his face in the mirror above the bureau. Both he and Hattie had washed up and borrowed clothes from the upstairs bedrooms. It was the third house they'd tried to enter with the aid of Hattie's illusion magic, but the first which had an unlocked door. The residents weren't home, and as luck had it the gentleman of the house was roughly Vincent's build.

He slicked back his hair and stepped out of the bedroom to find Hattie waiting for him near the stairs. She'd pilfered a tidy blue-and-white dress with a matching cloche. Locks of her red-blonde hair slipped from beneath the hat to curl forward in the hollows under her cheekbones. She had her bangs pushed to the side under the hat and as she looked up at him, he could see her clear gray eyes, her wide generous mouth, that determined pointed chin, the dusting of freckles that danced across her upturned nose. He'd never set eyes on her outside of those muddy trousers and her feminine appeal had eluded him until this point.

She was very pretty—fresh-faced, with a gamine beauty that tugged on something deep inside him. She *did* look very much a Mary Pickford-type, if a man was partial to that sort of dame. Vincent never thought he was, but with her standing here in front of him, that open, honest look on her face, as if she were seeing right through the time pincher, through the gangster to the man underneath, he wondered...

He cleared his throat and pushed the thoughts away. "Got yourself squared, I see."

She eyed him shoes to brow. "Hmm. You'll do."

Vincent gestured for her to precede him down the stairs, and the two made a discreet exit of the building, their filthy and tattered clothing from the night before folded and tucked beneath Vincent's arm. He tossed them into a trash bin on Broad Street and they stepped into the various stores to inquire after doctors. After a bit of investigation, they found that there was a man on the north end of the city who treated charity cases. And with about an hour's walk, they arrived at a sprawling farmhouse with a wrap-around porch...and a familiar figure loitering beneath the eaves.

Lefty called, "Hope you had a better night than I did."

"Fat chance of that," Vincent replied as the other man trotted up the main walk.

Lefty nodded to Hattie, then asked, "I'll assume this magic man was a bust?"

"A bust and change," Vincent grumbled. "I'll tell you all about it later." Hattie eyed him hard, but he gave her a reassuring glance.

"Where's Raymond?" she asked.

Lefty cocked his head at the front door. "Inside. The old man inside patched him up. He only got to sleep a couple hours ago."

"I'm going to see him." Hattie brushed past Lefty and into the house, leaving the two behind.

Lefty peered at Vincent with fatigue. "You're shy a pincher?"

"Yeah."

"Them's the breaks."

Vincent glanced down the lane. "You remember where Capstein's speakeasy was?"

"More or less. Why?"

"There's a pincher left in this city who I might have better luck with."

Lefty shook his head with a snicker. "You're going to try and poach Capstein's woman out from underneath him?"

With a sly smirk, he replied, "Might not be as hard as you'd think. I'll be right back."

Vincent stepped inside to find a silver-haired fellow with spectacles reading a paper. He motioned toward the side room and continued reading. Entering the room Vincent found a pair of beds, one of which barely contained Raymond's enormous slumbering frame. Hattie stood beside the bed, gripping Raymond's hand in two of hers.

"How is he?" he asked.

She shrugged.

"Listen, we never got a chance to discuss things since last night."

Hattie squinted and lifted her chin just a little. "Aye. Suppose it's time for a conversation."

"So, about our deal…"

Her shoulders stiffened and she shook her head. "You didn't get your pincher, and I didn't get a magic potion. Looks like we're both empty-handed—unless you intend on hauling *me* in as your catch, that is."

No. He'd keep her secret, and hopefully, if no one else found out, she'd be able to keep her freedom.

Vincent met her gaze squarely. "I want you to know, I have no intention of diming you out to Vito and the Crew. Your secret's safe with me."

Her eyes softened. "That a fact?"

Vincent grinned. "Hell, moment I met you, I was convinced I didn't want your contentious self anywhere near me, or anywhere near Baltimore for that matter, but now I'm not so sure. Whatever that hocus pocus was last night with…" He checked over his shoulder, then whispered, "…you-know-who. That *meant* something. We're connected, you and I."

Hattie slowly nodded. "Which means…?"

Vincent continued, "Which means we'll probably need to put up with each other more than either of us would like. Here's my deal. You keep doing what you do. Work with Tony and your boss and keep the boat-legging business nice and brisk. And you keep living free as you like."

"That's *your* deal?" She shifted her weight, biting her lip as she eyed him. "So, what's mine then?"

"I want to meet every now and then. Compare notes, catch up. From what Capstein said these demons, or whatever that thing was, were probably conjured up by a Hell pincher."

"Never heard of a Hell pincher before," Hattie scoffed. "Sure he wasn't just full of it?"

"You have to admit, Capstein was far more connected than either of us. I intend to find one of these Hell pinchers, and maybe get to the bottom of this circus. I work on that, and you'll meet me regular-like?"

She stared at him, uncertainty in her eyes.

"This is bigger than just booze and boats," Vincent urged. "If there's a secret truth behind what that thing in Deltaville is, and what we are? I want that truth. And I think you do, too."

He extended a hand.

Hattie sighed, then shook it. "Deal. Every other Sunday?"

"I can do that. Where?"

"Ever heard of a club downtown called the Fontainebleau?"

Vincent nodded. "Sure. Jazz joint, right?"

"I'll see you in two weeks."

As Vincent released her hand and stepped away, he nodded at Raymond. "Oh, by the way, you don't have to keep your friend here in the cold. He knows what you are."

Her eyes shot wide. "What?"

Vincent smiled, and turned to leave.

* * *

AN HOUR LATER, Lefty and Vincent had walked all the way back into the middle of Richmond. Vehicles putted along the lane, swerving around a clutch of dogs being walked by a young man who wasn't up to the challenge. They wound around a law office and descended a series of steps to the speakeasy Capstein had brought them to the day they'd met him. Vincent rapped on the door, and a slot slid open as a pair of bushy eyebrows stared at them.

"Yeah, so what do you want?" the doorman grumbled.

"Is Betty working?" Vincent asked.

"Who wants to know?"

"Name's Vincent Calendo. I'm a friend of Elmer's."

Bushy eyebrows remained unmoved.

Vincent asked, "Could you just ask Betty if she remembers me?"

The slot rammed shut, and Vincent waited.

Lefty asked, "What're you gonna tell her? About Capstein?"

"The truth."

"Sure that's the call you wanna make?"

"She's been lied to enough. If we have any hope of talking her into moving to the Crew, then we have to be the opposite of what Capstein…"

Vincent clammed up as the door inched open. The doorman nodded to Vincent. "Okay, you can come in. But only you."

Vincent turned to Lefty with a sigh. "Maybe you can get us a couple tickets back to Baltimore?"

Lefty nodded. "Suits me. I'm ready to leave."

As Lefty trod back up the steps, Vincent ducked into the dim light of the speakeasy. Betty stood behind the end of the bar, her long blonde hair done back in a simple braid, rustic and unrefined. It made him wonder what sort of background she'd had before Capstein ensnared her on Bimini Island.

"Well, there he is again," Betty cooed. "I was hoping you would be back, although I hardly expected it would be so soon."

"Me either," he said as he took a stool.

She lifted an Old Fashioned glass. "Whisky?" With a smirk and twist of her fingers along the rim, the vessel creaked and lengthened into a skinny pilsner glass. "Or a beer?"

Vincent smiled. "Neat trick. Liked your sculptures better, though."

She shrugged. "Gotta be useful, right?"

His smile faded. "So, listen. I want to talk to you about Capstein."

Something sparked in the woman's eyes, a sort of predatory hunger that made Vincent feel he was on shaky and unfamiliar ground. She leaned over the bar, rolling the pilsner glass between her fingers. "I'd rather talk about us."

Vincent tried not to let his eyes drift down the hang of

her blouse, which had billowed quite on purpose. She lifted a finger and traced it down the back of his hand.

"I could leave him," she whispered. "Join you in Baltimore. Elmer would never know. You and me. I'd be of great service to your boss." Betty glanced up at him from under her eyelashes. "And to you as well."

This…this was not how he'd expected the conversation to go. He hadn't even laid out his proposition, and she was already agreeing to work for Vito. But as for the other…. Why did he feel like he was being manipulated? Stalked by some vicious big cat?

Maybe he needed to step back a pace before telling Lefty to get this pincher a ticket to Baltimore as well.

"Tell me, something." He slid his hand away from her. "Are you and Capstein truly in charge of the Upright Citizens?"

Her face pulled into a twist of shock before she released a long belt of laughter. "Oh…huh. What's he been telling you?"

"Grand schemes."

She rolled her eyes. "Sounds like him."

"So, the Citizens have the two of you under their thumbs just like everyone else?"

Betty squinted at Vincent, then straightened up. "We're treated fairly. They need us, value us. It's been a mutually beneficial partnership. I'd rather be with you, though. I'm sure things are better in Baltimore. You and I—"

"Can you come and go as you please?" he interrupted.

A cautious expression settled on her face. "Elmer does what he wants. Try stopping him. The man has his ideas, and the rest of us need to fall in line with them, or else."

Vincent tapped the bar top. "What about you? Are you happy here?"

Again, there was that predatory gleam in her eyes, there one second and gone the next. "No, I'm not happy here." Her hand reached for his. "But then you came into the bar, I saw how happy I could really be if I just had the strength to leave him, if I just had a powerful man, a powerful family, to shield me and keep me safe."

He'd always been a sucker for a lady in need of a hero, but this made him uncomfortable. It sounded like a load of bushwa, but he couldn't rule out that she might have been abused and was desperate to get away by any means. She *had* been kidnapped and forced to serve the Upright Citizens, after all.

Either way, he had to give her a choice. He had to let her know it wasn't about escaping Capstein anymore, but choosing which family to align herself with.

"You should want to be where you are. Whether that's here, with the Baltimore Crew, or free and on your own."

Her laugh was bitter as she twisted the glass in her hand. "Free? I used to think that was all I needed, but when free means running from city to city, trying to hide your powers, not sure where your next meal is gonna come from…well, that ain't exactly free now, is it?"

"He told me how the two of you met," Vincent said. "Capstein told me how he captured you."

Betty stopped working at the glass and stared at him.

He continued, "On the island. His test…the mousetrap with a fake water pincher instead of cheese."

"It's true. Capstein captured me. I was his hostage until I gave in and did as he wished. You see why I want to leave? Why I need to leave and get away from him at last?"

He needed a better motivation than her leaving Capstein. More than this strange damsel-in-distress seduction of hers that seemed so forced.

"He's dead," Vincent stated. "Capstein is dead."

Her eyes stared blankly, before the words caught up with her. They widened, and she took a half step away, worrying away at the glass beneath the bar as it creaked and squeaked under her ministrations. "How?" she whispered.

"He played with fire."

"Did…*you*…?" A tiny frown creased her forehead as she eyed him uncertainly.

"He had me shot and beaten and hogtied. I wasn't in a position to save myself, much less hurt him. And God help him, he tried his best to talk me into joining this Kingdom."

A calculating look scuttled across her face. "Was it quick?"

Vincent nodded. "Quicker than he deserved."

This time the calculating look settled in to stay. "He's gone." Her eyes appraised Vincent. "Gone. And now I'm the only pincher here."

Vincent hesitated, wondering if he was making the right decision. "I would like you to join the Baltimore Crew, Betty. I want to make you an offer."

The squeaking of the glass ceased and a disturbing smile lifted the corners of her mouth. "Me, too."

Her motions were alarmingly fast, and she was so close. Her arm lifted over the counter and thrust at Vincent's throat with such speed that he could barely pinch time before the blade of glass she'd wrought beneath the bar would have pierced the skin near his jugular.

Vincent eased his head away from the weapon. It was a work of art, really. Faceted glass refracted the tortured beams of sunlight slipping through the windows along the tops of the walls, sending rainbows spraying across her arm. Its blade possessed a single, deadly-sharp edge, recurved in the fashion of an Arabic dagger.

He glanced up at her frozen face. It was cold, hard, manipulative. Her lips were pulled back to reveal a toothy snarl. This was a face bent on murder. Not just murder…self-advancement.

Why hadn't he seen it before? She had been desperate to

flee Capstein, but not because she wanted to escape an abusive situation. The air pincher had been stronger than she was. She could never assert her place in Richmond with his thumb firmly placed on her head. She'd read Vincent as some weak Rueben to easily seduce then claw her way to the top in Baltimore. But with Capstein dead, there was no need to flee north.

And if she had managed to kill him, Baltimore's only pincher, how much better it would have been for her. Capstein had wanted to rule the eastern seaboard, and clearly Betty did as well, but what the air pincher hoped to accomplish through kidnapping and recruitment, Betty was comfortable doing through murder.

Vincent nodded to himself as he slipped off the stool. There was clearly no recruiting her, and he had no stomach for harming the woman, though it would've been easy to do her in right now. He'd witnessed far too much death in the past two days. It would be better to return to Baltimore empty-handed, leaving her in power here, than shed one more drop of blood. So, he pushed in the stool and turned to make his exit, maintaining the time bubble until he was out of the speakeasy and out of sight. She would be left with her pinched glass dagger and sole responsibility for the Upright Citizens.

It wasn't Vincent's problem.

The Fontainebleau had a thin crowd for a Sunday. The weather was dreadful. Late spring rains had come to turn the streets into tracks of mud and grime. Hats and hair were doomed, as were fancy dresses and shoes. Hattie sat on a bar stool waiting for Leon to pop out of the back, and considering the dress she'd stolen from that house in Richmond. It was her second dress. It wasn't a hand-me-down. It wasn't inherited from her mother. It might have been stolen, but now it was simply hers, and happily it was short enough not to suffer from the muddy streets.

The door opened, and Vincent stepped inside. He pulled off his fedora to shake off the raindrops. This was more his look, Hattie considered. A proper suit, tailored to make him look taller than he really was, to give him that aura of fashion and prestige. He was in his element here in the city, that cocky expression firmly back on his face, confidence in his swagger. He gave Hattie a nod and she caught a glimpse of the Vincent she'd gotten to know on the boat. There was a sort of intimacy that stretched between them, something that only two people who had shared a profound experience could claim. Then with a grin and a spin of his fedora, he approached.

"Hello again," he said as he sat beside her and plopped his hat on the bar.

"Top of the mornin'. Are you drinking?"

He shook his head. "Too early for me. I've got a show tonight, and I have to keep the old well filled until then." He tapped his chest.

"A show?" Hattie asked. "What, you're in showbiz? Theater?"

"It's like theater, but nothing so grand."

"Well, then," she declared, gripping her glass of what was mostly melted ice at this point. "I'll drink for the both of us."

Vincent eased in to lower his voice. "I've poked around, like I said I would. Looking for information on this Hell—"

A voice boomed from behind the bar. "Well, I be painted red! Another customer!" Leon smiled at Vincent, his broad Creole accent draping itself around their shoulders. Vincent nodded in reply.

Leon gave Hattie a wink. "So, ya gonna introduce me to this drink of water, or will I have to pry his name out on my own?"

Hattie lifted a hand. "Vincent Calendo, this is Leon."

Vincent shook the man's hand. "Hiya."

Leon jerked a thumb at Vincent. "This handsome fellow buyin' ya drinks?"

Hattie sniffed. "I'll buy my own drinks, thank you."

Vincent eyed Leon with thinning patience, and Leon seemed to pick up on it. "Tell what. I got something special for ya both. Be back in a shake."

Once Leon had stepped out of earshot, Hattie nudged Vincent in the side. "I think he likes you."

"He'd be the one mook in this city who does."

"What about your friend, Lefty?"

"He's not my friend. He's my handler," Vincent scoffed.

"Ah, well. You make joining the Crew sound so appealing."

"It's not like that," he urged with a hint of recovery. "We have a good relationship. Not that it's *that* sort of relationship."

"That's not really what I thought, but you *are* adorable when you're all flustered and uncomfortable," she teased.

Vincent scowled at her. "Hell pincher."

"Aye, what about him?"

"Nothing to say it's a him or a her," Vincent chided. "But word is there's a pincher in Philadelphia who might could fill in some blanks. Had a run in with a demon once and did some book-thumping of his own. I'm planning a trip once I can talk the Capo into it."

Hattie squinted. "How did your lords and masters take the news of your failure?"

He shrugged. "It's not a failure yet. There's still pinchers out there. And I've learned a valuable lesson from Capstein. No one wants a strong-arm, when a reasoned argument would do."

"Reasoned argument?" A laugh burst out of her. "Is that what you think you have? You better truffle around for a better plan, boy-o."

The door opened again, and Vincent turned on reflex as a lean brunette entered. She brushed her hands over her arms to dry them as best she could.

Hattie shook her head. "Shite weather, today."

Vincent didn't respond. Instead, he eased off the stool, standing stiff as he stared at this woman. She peered around the room, and once she locked eyes with Vincent, her entire posture blossomed. She approached with quick steps, and Hattie wondered for a hot second whether she was about to throw her arms around the man.

She did not. Instead, she stopped directly in front of him, gripping her clutch in both hands.

Vincent muttered, "Fern?"

The woman whispered, "Lefty told me you'd be here."

"What's the matter?"

She shook her head. "Nothing's the matter. I just... I wanted to talk."

They gave each other one of those long wordless stares that belonged in the cinema. Hattie rolled her eyes, fighting back the urge to gag. After a few seconds, Vincent turned to her.

"Do you mind if I..."

Well. At least he'd remembered she was still there. "No problem. I'm assuming we're done with this conversation anyhow."

Leon appeared behind Vincent with two glasses of champagne. He set them down onto the bar behind Vincent with a gracious nod. "Here ya go. It's on da house, my friends."

Vincent took both glasses by the stems and made as if he were about to walk off with them.

"Eh! Boy-o! Where're you going with my bubbly there?" She snatched one from his hand, biting back a laugh at his flustered expression. It was so much fun riling this guy up. And he *was* adorable when she managed to knock that confident expression from his face.

"Oh. I just...I mean..." He stared at the one glass in his hand, then at Fern, then back down at the glass.

"Give it to her, why don't 'cha," she chided. "Hurry it up, before I take that one off your hands as well."

He shot her a wry grin, for a moment returning to the Vincent she knew. Then he turned with a sappy expression to hand the glass to Fern before escorting the other woman to a table on the opposite end of the room.

Hattie watched as they walked, an irrational tightness

balling up in her chest. The way he looked at this woman bothered her. He was acting like a schoolboy, and it wasn't a behavior she found particularly appealing.

Hattie turned back to face the bar with a scowl.

Leon snickered.

"Shut it!" she hissed.

"Won't last. Don't worry your head on't."

"I'm not," she snarled.

Leon approached, hands up in surrender. "Okay. I'm not sayin' nothin' more."

"Good."

"I'm glad ya came in today, Hattie, even if pretty-boy Valentino over dere is making moon-eyes at some other girl."

"Thought you weren't sayin' no more?"

He chuckled. "Glad ya here, Hattie. Missed ya mighty."

She cocked her head and took a sip of the champagne. "Well, get used to it. I'll be here every other Sunday."

Leon's smile disappeared. "I'm afraid ya won't."

She blinked. "What, now?"

"I'm sellin' da place, is what."

Hattie's eyes shot wide. "Leon! Why? What's happened?"

"Oh," he sighed as he leaned over the bar, "dis city done got too dangerous for a man like me to make a comfortable livin'."

"Why, because you're Creole?" she asked.

He shook his head.

She whispered, "Because you prefer men?"

Leon snickered. "Oh, no. It's an easy town to make *dat* sort of living. Trust me."

"Then what's got you running off?"

He reached into his pocket to produce a tiny glass vial. "I hear ya had a caper on da Bay a couple weeks back."

She nodded. "It was a disaster. But I learned a thing or

two." She peered over her shoulder at Vincent. "Maybe made a friend or two."

Leon nodded. "Raymond came in yesterday."

"I didn't know he ever drove to the city."

"He does, time to time. Not often, but when he does he asks about ya." Leon added with a whisper, "He tells me ya were hunting for Bimini Island."

"No such place. It's a myth," Hattie scoffed.

"I know," Leon replied. "I coulda told ya that, if ya'd asked."

"I was in a rush."

"It was the land of *Beimini* that the Fountain of Youth was supposed to reside. Least dat's what the locals told a certain Spaniard hell-bent on findin' it."

Hattie shook her head. "What? No, it was just some stupid scam run by a crook down in Richmond."

"Right," Leon chimed. "Lookin' for Doc Freedman. I know all about dat. Doc Freedman, and his magic elixir."

Leon set the vial onto the bar top.

Hattie stared at it.

Leon gave her a wink.

"What's that?" she whispered.

"I call it Aqua Vitae, because I'm all refined-like."

Hattie straightened on her stool, her eyes screwing into a question. "Leon, what is this?"

He flattened his hand and gestured for her to keep her volume low. In a jarring moment, his accent faded into perfect locution, spiced with the barest hint of Latin inflection. "*Beimini* is a myth. But Doc Freedman? He's very real. That crook in Richmond didn't spin that name out of whole cloth, you know. Baltimore is technically on the Bay, so the story plays out."

"You?" she gasped.

Leon nodded to the vial. "That's enough to last you a

good year, if you're not greedy. It'll keep back the ravages of time, as well as the ravages of bullets, blades, or whatever else you insist on hurling yourself into."

She reached with trembling fingers to take the vial. "And…lung complaints?"

He nodded. "Whatever feels like putting a man into the grave. It's powerful magic, so don't waste it."

She gripped the vial tight to her chest, sucking in several panicked breaths. Her father. The elixir. So many unanswered questions.

"Leon, I…"

"Don't ache your head over it," he assured her. "With a man like that looking for pinchers…" he nodded at Vincent "…I think it's time I put some distance between myself and the sea."

"Where will you go?"

"With this Prohibition on, a man havin' my talents could do well closer to the action. Maybe I'll go to Chicago."

Hattie chuckled. "You're kidding!"

"Oh, I kept myself hidden in plain sight here. I figure I can do the same in Capone's backyard. I've always enjoyed a challenge."

"Who are you…really?"

Leon smiled. "People think of Spaniards of lore, and they assume they're white as Anglos. I've lived a long time, Hattie. And I've seen the same currents wash over and over again. These same forces that assert over men. I was one of them, to be honest. But I learned a thing or two." He peered up at Hattie with a haunted smile. "I'll not see that again, if I can help it."

"The Fountain of Youth," she whispered. "That was always a scam?"

He snickered. "Obviously."

She reached over the bar to hug Leon. "Thank you."

He whispered, "Just don't let that time pincher put chains on you. That's all I ask."

Leon stepped away, gave her a gracious bow, then disappeared through the door to his storeroom.

Hattie stuck the vial into her camisole bra, drained her glass of champagne, and stood up, her head spinning.

She marched for the door, pausing with her hand on the knob to check on Vincent. He was absorbed in conversation with the beautiful woman who seemed to have a lot to say to him, but some instinct played out between the pair of them and Vincent lifted his eyes for a quick second.

Hattie gave him a quick wave.

He smiled and waved in return.

With a tug on the door, she stepped out into the squall. Her shoes splashed in the puddles, squishing in the mud of the street as the rain beat down onto her head. Her bangs flattened with the water, plastered to the side of her face. Pulling off her cloche, she lifted her face to the clouds and smiled.

Slapping the hat back onto her head and kicking a puddle into an arcing splash with a laugh, Hattie Malloy rushed home to her father, a tiny bottle of magic nestled against her thundering heart.

***

Read on with Bum's Rush, White Lightning Book 2!

DEBRA DUNBAR
J.P. SLOAN
BUM'S RUSH
WHITE LIGHTNING SERIES BOOK TWO

ACKNOWLEDGMENTS

A huge thanks to our copyeditors Kimberly Cannon and Jennifer Cosham whose eagle eyes catch all the typos and keep Debra's comma problem in line, and to Damonza for cover design.

We're grateful for Sarra Cannon's early read-through of the series. Her her input was so valuable and we definitely owe her a nice bottle of wine.

Special thanks to all our readers who have individually followed us to Hel and back, and enthusiastically cheered us on during our first collaborative project. May there be many more ahead!

Debra and J.P

ABOUT THE AUTHORS

Debra lives in a little house in the woods of Maryland with her sons and two slobbery bloodhounds. On a good day, she jogs and horseback rides, hopefully managing to keep the horse between herself and the ground. Her only known super power is 'Identify Roadkill'.

A Louisiana native, J.P. relocated to the vineyards and cow pastures of Central Maryland after Hurricane Katrina, where he lives with his wife and son. During the day he commutes to the city of Baltimore, a setting which inspires much of his writing.

For more information:
www.debradunbar.com/white-lightning or
J.P. Sloan's Author page
Debra Dunbar's Author page

ALSO BY DEBRA DUNBAR

The Templar Series
Dead Rising
Last Breath
Bare Bones
Famine's Feast

* * *

The Imp Series
A Demon Bound
Satan's Sword
Elven Blood
Devil's Paw
Imp Forsaken
Angel of Chaos
Kingdom of Lies
Exodus
Queen of the Damned
The Morning Star

* * *

Half-breed Series (Imp World)
Demons of Desire
Sins of the Flesh
Cornucopia

Unholy Pleasures

City of Lust

* * *

Other Imp World Novels

No Man's Land

Stolen Souls

Three Wishes

Northern Lights

Far From Center

Penance

* * *

Northern Wolves Series (Imp World)

Juneau to Kenai

Rogue

Winter Fae

Bad Seed

ALSO BY J.P. SLOAN

<u>The Dark Choir Series</u>
The Curse Merchant
The Curse Servant
The Curse Mandate
The Dark Interest
<u>Other Novels</u>
Yea Though I Walk

www.ingramcontent.com/pod-product-compliance
Lightning Source LLC
Chambersburg PA
CBHW032208180726
48284CB00001B/244